HITTING THE JACKPOT

TOM ALAN

BLOODHOUND
— BOOKS —

To Jill – who buys the tickets.

PROLOGUE

WIN THE LOTTERY? The jackpot? He's waited years for this moment. Eight or nine to be imprecise, he can't remember exactly. He's prayed for it twice a week. Although let's be honest, they're not the sort of prayers usually heard in church: *I was praying for him to score; I was praying for them to leave* – that sort of 'prayer'. Fervently meant, at times with almost fundamentalist intensity, but hardly real prayers in any meaningful sense of the word, coming, as they do, from an on-the-fence agnostic. Or is it atheist? He's always mixing them up. What will surprise him most of all, when it happens, won't be the feelings of jubilation, freedom and opportunity he's expecting, that anyone would expect. No, what will shock him will be how quickly, and how bitterly, he'll come to regret it...

PART 1

WINNING

1

THE WIN

JACK RIPS the cap off his Spanish beer and takes a sip. He checks his watch and doofs on the TV. This is his twice-weekly ritual. Next, open the pizza box. Now he's ready. Ready for another slim chance, fourteen million to one, apparently, for a little bit of luck to change his life completely, utterly, absolutely. He doesn't know it, not yet, but for him, and him alone, in the words of Rod Stewart – 'Tonight's the Night'.

'Num-ber sev-ennnn...'

'The King!'

Jack lifts a quadrant of pizza in salute. He always tells them to cut it into four; he hates the weedy little eighths that droop onto your chin before you can get them into your mouth. He once sent a Hawaiian back cos they'd sliced it into eight. Substitute cook didn't read the bloody chit. It's pepperoni tonight, one of his favourites. He's got nine. Nine favourites. Tonight's pepperoni is a double: for the regular reason that he loves pepperoni, and a double favourite because tonight it's free. *Perky Pizza,* one of London's best pizzerias, around the corner on Cricklewood Broadway, does this loyalty card thingy: buy eight in a calendar month and the eighth is free. He once had three freebies in a month. Two of those were pepperoni. He hesitates...

'*Num-ber twen-ty-twoooo...*'

'Happy birthday *me!* You beauty!'

Lucky he's ordered thick crust, which withstands the suspense admirably; he takes an enormous bite. That's another thing about eighths: you can't get a really good mouthful without your tonsils gagging on the weedy little tip – if it hasn't already attached itself to your chin. He chews contentedly. Seven and twenty-two, good start. He feels a mild tingle of anticipation...

'*Num-ber tennnn...*'

He nearly chokes as an involuntary intake of breath pulls the massive lump of semi-masticated dough deep into his windpipe. He's barely able to breathe, and wonders momentarily how long it takes to choke to death. Will it all be over before he hears the end of the draw? Or will he go to his doom knowing that he was – at least briefly – a millionaire...? He finally manages to cough the doughball back up, before flushing it away with a massive slug of San Miguel, which works with all the efficiency of half a bottle of Mr Muscle.

'Wazza! My man. *Get* in there! Three outta three,' he finally has enough wind to splutter, as he feels the doughball touch down somewhere slightly more comfortable. He goes for a sideways bite, but his mind's not really on it. He got three numbers once before, really thought he'd won thousands – thirty quid was all it was worth. He snorts at the memory. The pizza hovers as he waits...

'*Num-ber thir-ty-niiiine...*'

'Yes! 39 Maple Road...'

Four! He's got *four*. What the hell is *that* worth? This is serious. Four! Stay calm, stay calm, it might be a thousand or so. Who knows? Bloody hell. But four is good. Better than three, that's for sure. A small disc of pepperoni slides from the hovering slice and lands on his crotch. *Jeezus! Best bloody cream chinos, what the–*

'Num-ber twen-ty-foooour.'

The sliver of pepperoni sausage that's messing his best (bloody) cream chinos departs from his mind as quickly as a puddle of poodle piddle from a tarmacked road on a hot summer's day. Twenty-four? Rich's birthday. He's – got – five. That's thousands. Could it be a million? He has no idea. All he needs now is April. All he needs is his own birth month. April. Oh shit! Come in number four. Come in number four. Come in...

'Num-ber fooouuur!'

He stares at the television. The six balls line up next to each other in the order he scores them out on the little card every week in the Banerjees' corner shop: 4, 7, 10, 22, 24, 39. There they are, *his* numbers, on the television. He knows this sequence of numbers almost as well as he knows his own name, he's been doing the lottery that long. Four: April, his birth month. Seven: Eric Cantona, king of Old Trafford. Ten: Wayne Rooney, top United goalscorer. Twenty-two: his own birthday. Twenty-four: Rich's birthday. Thirty-nine: Maple Road, the house he was born in. His numbers. He knows them backwards, forwards, in Spanish (although his pronunciation is a bit shit...). He's hit the bloody jackpot.

He snatches his phone, fumbles for the app, fingers like warm jelly, then stares at the screen...

'One winner? Two point three *million* quid. Jesus Christ.' His skin feels like it's shrinking; he imagines himself shaking off his old skin and emerging – a millionaire! Then he thinks about every other house in the country, well, except for the few who've won thirty quid, or a few thou, he thinks of all the rest, all the unlucky suckers, ripping up their tickets, tossing them in the bin, grumbling again that it'll never be them. But, this week, it's him. He's got the one winning ticket.

He stares around the room, wondering what he should do. He feels like he should be screaming, or dancing, but he knows he'll feel ridiculous screaming in an empty room, and he's never been much of a dancer. He realises something he should've realised before – you shouldn't check your lottery tickets alone; you should always have a gang of mates around, ready to slap you on the back, pop open a bottle of (cheap) bubbly...

So, he continues sitting, tries to take in what he knows is undoubtedly true. His life has changed. Everything that's happened before happened to a different person. Everything that happens from here on in will happen to someone else. A new Jack. Jack the millionaire.

Ding, dong, the witch is dead...

Oh God! It's Cindy. Bloody Cindy. She must've been watching. Course she was bloody watching. Panic rises like post-binge-drink vomit. He stares at his phone until it goes to answerphone. He has to hide the ticket.

His ticket? Where's his bloody ticket? The pizza box slides unnoticed onto the floor, a steaming quadrant flipping over and adhering to the threadbare carpet as Jack hauls himself to his feet from the giant red sponge that masquerades as a sofa. He rifles his jacket on the back of the door. He scans the flat; hunts through the bills and takeaway flyers that litter the small dining table, which he doesn't use for dining anymore, not since... Nothing. Christ! Has he left it in the car? Where are his car keys? Back to his jacket. He hurricanes the table again. Nothing.

A sheen of perspiration sucks his sweatshirt to his skin. He stumbles back to the sofa and slumps onto it, a sharp object stabbing him in the left buttock. He delves between the cushions into the flotsam of old bus tickets and cold chip fragments and pulls out – his car keys! He runs for the door, stops with his hand on the handle, prays another of his pseudo prayers, returns, lifts the cushion… Hallelujah! Halle-bloody-lujah! There it is. His wallet. And inside his wallet…? His ticket! Scrunched between a couple of tenners. He slumps back onto the sofa.

His phone starts again. *Ding, dong…* She knows he's never without it. Knows he never lets it run out of juice. Then it stops. Oh no! She'll come round. Course she will.

He jumps up, pulls a book out of the centre of his bookshelf, and slides the precious ticket in between the pages. He takes a couple of deep breaths. Switch the channel. He hunts the doofer. Where the bloody hell is – it's on the floor next to his beer.

He hits Beeb One: *Still Open All Hours*, no chance. Beeb Two: *Antiques*, as if! Four: *News*, yeah, really! Five: some documentary, looks like a battle re-enactment. Sky One: *Simpsons*. Again? Beeb Four: what's that? No idea. Sod it. Put a film on. He scans his DVDs. Bond. Yeah, Bond. Let's have… *Thunderball!* No! Christ, no. Let's have… *Live and Let Die!*

He rattles it out of the case and slots it into the player. *Come on, come on… there we go, and let's get a scene in the middle… Great!* He swigs his beer and rescues his pizza from the clutches of the carpet. It needs a bit of TLC to get the hairs out of the cheese. He sits in a daze for a few minutes, munching and sipping, unable to concentrate on how his life is going to change. The doorbell shocks him back to the present. He takes a deep breath as he heads to open it – still a pauper…

2

THE LIE

'Oн, hi Cind. Sorry, on the bog, left my phone by the telly. Was about to call...' Jack holds the edge of his front door in one hand, his mobile in the other.

She stares at Jack like he's stolen her car – that sleek black Golf she wasted twenty grand on last year, it still needles him.

'What are you talking about, Jack? You were watching?'

He suppresses his post-breakup distaste for her HRTs (that's high-rising terminals – Jack's a linguist, not a doctor). What he once thought a cute 'Aussie' trait now irritates him every time she goes up the scales. There's a cheese-grater-on-knuckles quality to the pain that seems all the worse for suffering it less often.

'Watching what?'

She sways backwards slightly, like a new coronavirus is in town and he looks peaky.

'The draw, you pillock. The lottery?' She points at the television, which is showing Roger Moore looking about as menacing as Dora the Explorer.

'Ah, no, I stopped doing that. Waste of money. Why?'

'You stopped – doing – the – *lott-er-y*...?' It's her overexaggerated, pompous *I'm pretending I'm a character in an episode of F-R-I-E-N-D-S* voice, which he used to just about tolerate but now loathes.

'Yeah.' He shrugs. 'Why?'

Now it's the goggle-eyes, the gaping mouth, the open-palmed pose she's probably copied from some Sandra Bullock straight-to-meme.

'Hello? Your numbers came up.' For a failed wannabee actress, she's utterly crap.

'Don't be daft,' he says dismissively, like he *really* doesn't believe her. Like he *knows* she's talking bollocks. He turns back into the flat. She follows, closes the door.

'I'm *telling* you; your numbers came up: your birth month, Eric, Wayne, your birthday, Rich's birthday, 39 Maple Road. Crikey! You didn't buy a *ticket?*'

Jack does his best impression of someone slowly going into shock – but resisting manfully. How much should he egg this? Should he cry? Beat his fists against the wall? Smash the TV set? Better not. Not yet. He knows denial is the first stage of grief, decides to do a bit more of that. He's not sure what the other stages are, so a long denial it is...

'You're taking the piss. What's this? April Fool?' But he laces it with more than a hint of trepidation, not too much. *Dawning realisation* is good. If either of them were ever likely to succeed at acting – it was him.

'Look, you *drongo. Look!*' She whips her fancy phone out and punches the screen with her thumbs, all the while muttering *drongo, dipstick* and *dill*. All the Australianisms for *idiot* seem to start with a D, he notices. 'See?'

She holds her phone in front of his face, tonight's winning balls displayed across the screen: his birth month, Eric the King, Wayne Rooney, his birthday, Rich's birthday, 39 Maple Road. He has to force himself *not* to dance for joy.

'You stupid dill!'

Jack stares at the numbers, his numbers, not *her* numbers, *his* bloody numbers! He remembers when they got married, when was that? A year or so ago? She tried to get him to swap Rooney for her birthday. Where would *that* have got them now, eh? Not that he can say that. No, best not. He lets his mouth drop open in a sort of *shocked* manner: like he thinks it probably would if an alien started chewing its way out of her stomach.

'You're joking...' He says this in what he considers to be a plaintive whine, like she's told him his cat's got run over (not that he has a cat). He's running out of acting skills, as well as stages of grief, decides he'll check his own phone like he still doesn't believe her. A final cry of denial. She watches him with an amateurish roll of her eyes. His phone shows the same six numbers: April, Eric, Wazza, his birthday, Rich's birthday, Maple Road.

He can feel her staring at him, but he can't bring himself to look at her, can't trust himself to carry on the deceit. He stares at his phone and tries not to show any emotion except shock; that must be one of the stages. And a bit of disappointment. Quite a lot of disappointment, maybe even a touch of sadness. Anger, even? No, no anger. A little bit of anger, with himself maybe?

'Oh Jack, I'm sorry.' She goes to put her hand on his shoulder – but stops herself before he sees her make the move.

Yeah, I bet you are! he thinks – *thinks*, not *says* – in a suitably disappointed, sad and a little bit of an angry manner. *You're sorry because you thought you were going to collect half my winnings just before our divorce comes through. Sorry, Cind. That ain't happening...*

3

THE TRUTH

CINDY DOOFS HER CAR OPEN – sleek black Vee Dub Golf, it still bugs him, so obvious – then doofs it shut again. Up at Jack's window, she sees the light from the TV flickering. What a loser, but struth, is she better off without him! The breakup had been rough, but it'd been a long time coming. She sees his shadow moving across the ceiling, wonders if she should've stayed longer. What if he – *does* something…? It must be a hell of a shock for him. The length of time he's been doing the lottery… But no, Jack wouldn't do anything like that. Funnily enough, the shadow almost looks like he's dancing. But then, Jack? Dance? Sooner see a kangaroo on skis in the outback.

Across the street, the lights from the corner shop flood the pavement, like a version of Van Gogh's *Café Terrace at Night* from his Cricklewood period, complete with a battered newspaper stand and a couple of dollops of dog shit. Before she moved out, she'd been quite friendly with the Banerjees – well, she'd been a polite customer, and they'd been attentive shopkeepers – should she pop in to say *hello*? It must be what now, four months? Five? Why not?

———

'Cindy! Oh, come quickly, Ananya, it's Cindy!' Mr Banerjee moves (he's way too old for *hopping*) from foot to foot like an excited seven-year-old who's caught sight of the ice-cream van, but he resists the initial instinct to come out from behind the counter. He claps his hands, a cartoon prisoner who's discovered that his cell door is open but doesn't dare step through it. Mr Banerjee's wife is not so reticent.

Ananya Banerjee bustles out from the back, hands flapping, hips threatening the unsteady stacks of chewing gum and football stickers. Cindy steps forward, her gap year in Barcelona has given her a Latin tic of bestowing kisses on people she barely knows, or has only just met, but she pauses – as does Ananya, as if she's suddenly realised that she's an Indian shopkeeper who's spent years trying to learn how to behave with traditional British reserve. The moment is lost, and they stand looking each other up and down, like they're inspecting fridges in an electrical shop.

'We thought you might be unwell,' Ananya blurts, and Cindy immediately translates *unwell* into *pregnant,* as she sees Ananya eyeing her obviously empty icebox with a look of disappointment.

They would never have asked Jack, would they? *Haven't seen Cindy for a while...* No, of course they wouldn't, desperate as they are not to offend or appear nosey. And Jack would never have said anything, course he wouldn't, desperate as he is at small talk and idle gossip. They'd gone into the shop, obviously 'together', many times, especially if they'd been for one of their long walks, when they were endlessly trying to *sort things out...* Their usual picks were a bottle of wine (always her choice) and some nachos and dips (always his) – but the feast often remained untouched on the dining table as they first bickered, and then fought, over which film to watch: Cindy claiming it was Hugh or Colin's turn to star, Jack insisting it surely had to be Scarlett's go...

'No, no, I'm fine.' Cindy smiles, clasping her hands across her stomach involuntarily. 'It's just that Jack and I...' She leaves the sentence unfinished, grimaces, shrugs, raises her eyebrows, a clear indication to anyone with an ounce of social nous that (*wince, another shrug*) Jack and her... You *know*... But Ananya widens her eyes in a look that obviously says she's waiting for the punchline. 'We're not *together* anymore...'

Ananya's eyes widen further, from *what?* to *WHAT!?* Her hands tense, her mouth opens with an audible gasp. Mr Banerjee deflates visibly behind the crisps.

'Oh, what *terrible* news,' Ananya mutters, shaking her head as she would if Cindy had told her that one of them – well, Jack, obviously – had recently died.

'I'm living on the other side of town now, which is why you haven't seen so much of me.' She smiles apologetically, shrugs apologetically, looks around the shop in the hope that they've redecorated, but it's obvious they haven't.

The Banerjees' twins suddenly scamper noisily out from behind the counter, hiding in the folds of Ananya's vermilion sari, and peeking out with curious brown eyes. They're like a pair of kittens, exploring the world. Everything Cindy wears, or does, or says, captivates them. If she ever came in wearing one of her 'exercise' ensembles, the girls would follow her around the store, poking their heads out from behind the fridges to point and gawp, eyes popping with rapt inquisitiveness.

Cindy treats them to a Disney wave and curtsey combination, followed by the smile she could never contain in their presence, and they giggle and wrench feverishly at the silk, exposing the smooth folds of Ananya's belly.

'At least you didn't have children,' Ananya says, almost to

herself, pulling the twins closer into the layers of the material, and her belly, as if afraid Cindy might not be as trustworthy as she'd once assumed.

Cindy nods. *Thank god for that*, she thinks, sardonically. The thought of sorting out such an additional mess with Jack makes her shudder. A *mini*-Jack – or Jackie? *WT...?*

'So, I thought I'd pop in, say hello,' she says, now remembering that they never really had *conversations*. 'And a bottle of wine...' she adds quickly, grabbing the nearest bottle, the twins following her every move like she's an exotic dancer on a brightly lit stage.

'We still see Jack,' Mr Banerjee snaps suddenly, as if the lengthening silence has severed a trap that had been holding his tongue in place. 'Every Wednesday and Saturday for his San Miguels and lottery ticket, without fail...'

'Really...?' Cindy says, just managing to stop the bottle slipping from her grasp. *'Really...?'*

4

THE LESSON

JACK'S HEADACHE IS EPIC. Just the *thought* of lifting his head off the pillow makes it worse. He doesn't have many headaches; he's not a big boozer so he rarely suffers hangovers. This is a pulsating sort of headache: there's a background level of agony that feels like his brain has swollen to four times its usual size and is threatening the joints between the bones of his cranium.

Then comes the pulse – when his aching head hosts a medium-sized nuclear explosion, complete with shock wave and sirens. He realises the sirens are in the street outside when the next pulse comes with another nuclear explosion but no sirens. He has no idea why he has such a headache. He can't remember a thing about last night. He doesn't know what day it is. He barely knows his name.

He sits up as slowly as he can and realises he's not even in bed. He's on the sofa; his TV is on, showing some daytime-TV nonsense. What time is it? He looks at his watch, it's five to ten. He moves his head and feels something pulling at his beard. A pat of vomit covers the front of his sweatshirt and his best cream chinos, small rivulets of solidified vomit connecting his beard to the pat like an unusually colourful frozen waterfall. What the–?

The pizza box sparks one of his synapses to reconnect with reality. Then he spots his empty San Miguel bottle. Then he sees another! And *another!!* What – the...? Jack's unbreakable rule is *one* bottle when he's got work the next morning. The doorbell rings like a cue in a play. A *farce*, obviously. That'll be Puerto-Rican María and Iker the Catalan, he thinks automatically – realising immediately that in less than five seconds he'll have to get up, clean himself up, put on a fresh shirt and trousers, hide the vomit-strewn stuff, open all the windows, tidy the flat (a bit), let them in, then teach an English lesson. This is gonna hurt...

'Sorry, sorry! Sorry to keep you. I was late getting up and had to tidy a few things away...' He swings the door open with as much of a flourish as he can muster and ushers them in.

'Why you say *keep you*? Ees phrasal verb? Why so many phrasal verbs in English...?' María, as usual, is at him like a four-year-old whose only word is *Why?* She's the keenest student he's ever taught. His lesson plans, never more than vague ideas he cobbles together in his mind in the moments before any class arrives, are rarely necessary when Puerto-Rican María is present, now that he knows how she operates.

She usually starts every lesson with a list of questions she has on the topic of the last class she attended. Or things she's heard on TV that she hasn't been able to find in any of her dictionaries, assorted textbooks, or myriad internet sites and blogs and chatrooms that she follows avidly. Then there are her 'spur-of-the-moment questions', like today, usually provoked by something Jack's said without realising that he's throwing her a linguistic hand grenade.

Just pop it on the table once kept them busy for twenty minutes or so, although she was quick to pick that one up. Soon she was popping out for some milk, popping down to see her friend, or popping around the corner. It was clear he was creating a monster – there she goes, popping all over the world. Then there was the time he asked her to *give him a bell*, the look on her face provoking a laughing fit he took most of the rest of the lesson to recover from.

There was also the day he was daft enough to tell her the traffic was *chock-a-block*. On a good day, one where he hasn't been awake for only ninety seconds and spent half of that time spring-cleaning the flat and redressing himself, it usually takes him a good few minutes backtracking what he's said to find the offending phrase that she hasn't understood. Today, he can't remember saying anything at all.

'Wha'...?' he says, breaking the rule he teaches all his students, to always say *pardon* instead of *Wha'...?*

'You say you keep me. What eet mean, *keep me?* I no unnerstan...?'

Jack wracks his brain, or maybe he racks it, he's never sure. It can't add any more pain to the tsunami of agony already coursing through his head, carrying fallen trees and mid-sized cars with it.

'I said I'd *keep* you?' he asks, trying to buy time as he sweeps fast-food flyers, junk mail and a large pizza box off the table.

'Yes, you say you sorry you keep me. What eet mean?'

Jack scratches his head, rubs his fingers through his beard, encounters a couple of stray pieces of pepperoni, or vomit, or vomited pepperoni, which he flicks floorwards. '*Keep* you? Oh, yeah, I got it. Sorry to *keep* you, yeah, it's a phrasal verb, I think, sort of a truncated one; you should say keep you *waiting*. Sorry to keep you *waiting*. It means to *make* you wait.'

'Ees make or keep?'

'Wha'...?'

'Ees *make* you waiting, or *keep* you wait?'

His brain's not prepared for a degree-level linguistics question asked in pidgin English.

'Best to say keep you waiting – although you can say make you wait...'

'Ees deefeecult.'

'We can practise – if we ever get to sit down...?' He indicates the table, which is now free from debris – unlike his head.

María sits and scribbles in her notebook, tongue edging out between her pristine teeth and blood-red lipstick, a look of intense concentration you'd hope to see on the face of your favourite brain surgeon. She shakes her coat off onto the back of the chair, eyes still locked on her notes.

'I have the go?' she asks, looking up, her face filled with childlike enthusiasm, breaking his heart for the thousandth time.

'Yes, have a go,' he encourages, knowing there isn't a teacher in the world who'd refuse her. Probably not a police officer either, even if she asked to *have the go* at strangling the King, for example, or kicking one of the guards.

'Okay,' she says to herself, rubbing her hands together as if she's at the foot of the Eiger and is about to set off up. These little theatrical tics captivate Jack; it's like watching a consummate performer: Ronnie Corbett in his armchair; John Cleese in the dining room; Dawn French *anywhere*. Except he knows there's not a shred of 'performance' about María's 'performance', this is just María; Puerto-Rican María, the woman he loves with all his heart and most of his spleen. The woman he can't confess it to.

She always rubs her hands when it's her 'turn', hands being as important for speech to most native-Spanish speakers as lips, tongue, teeth, vocal cords and lungs are to everybody else. When she really lets rip, it's wise to socially distance at least a couple of metres, lest you end up with an inadvertent slap around the face, or a poke in the eye – the shape of her blood-red fingernails threatening a fate almost as bad as a drunken juggle with samurai swords.

She reminds him of one of those sign-language interpreters you see in a little box on the TV, except María always seems to be translating for a particularly fast and animated speaker, who's describing a lively punch-up outside a boozer at throwing-out time. Her skills in the 'hand signals' department certainly make Boris Johnson's efforts to 'perk up' his non-verbal signalling look like the half-hearted efforts of a particularly arthritic toad. Jack, being a linguist, was amused to hear that Johnson's arm-waving antics (while talking bollocks) had spawned a new verb: to testiculate.

'I am in shower. I am washering my hairs,' she begins, hands rinsing her long brown hair(s). Jack adjusts his position and bites his tongue. 'I hear doorbell!' The doorbell mime comes complete with hand to ear and raised eyebrows; Iker looks towards the door in bemusement. The fact that her intonation is Manuel-to-a-tee doesn't help. Jack has long ago realised what incredible preparation for the role Andrew Sachs must have done. 'I rubber myself weeth towel and then I-I- ...' She mimes the next movement and begs him with her eyes. His heart does things no human heart was ever meant to do.

'Wrap,' Jack offers, transfixed, like he's watching Laurence Olivier playing the Prince of Denmark, or Meryl Streep as Thatcher, or Kylie singing 'Can't Get You Out of My Head' dressed in half a bed sheet.

'Yes! Ees eet! I wrapper me weeth towel, and I go door, and I open door, and I say...' She readjusts herself in her seat: a Puerto-Rican Martin Luther King about to have a dream: 'I say, I sorry I keeped you! Ees good?'

Jack nods. 'Very good,' he says, unable, despite all his training, to burst her bubble of unrestrained joy – and afraid his voice will crack if he says any more.

'And – how – are – you – today – Iker?' he says, dragging his eyes away from María's stunning smile and petite shiver of raw pleasure.

Iker leans forward at the sound of his name. He blinks frantically, then does what he always does whenever Jack addresses him directly – he turns to María and whispers, '*Qué dice?*' What's he saying?

María's English isn't great, what she lacks in grammar and knowledge of irregular (and some regular) verbs, she makes up for with kitten-like curiosity and the concentration of a sniper. She knows Jack doesn't want her to help Iker too much, knows it won't help Iker in the long run. But what can she do? If she doesn't help him in *español,* Jack will have to try to help him in *inglés* – and they both know where that will lead. The same place it always leads: Jack using more and more words that Iker doesn't recognise.

'*Qué tal? Cómo siempre,*' she whispers. How are you? As always.

'Ah! I good,' Iker replies, with a sigh of relief appropriate for a first-time Channel swimmer scrunching up the Calais beach.

Jack wonders the same thing at the start of every lesson: is it fair to take his money? He has, in the past, suggested to Iker that he take up something that he might find slightly easier than English – astrophysics, maybe? Or a trapeze gig at the Cirque du Soleil? The first time he suggested it, Iker simply hadn't understood what Jack was trying to say – a hippo and a giraffe could've had as coherent a conversation.

Jack had been teaching Iker one-to-one for a few months when María called him on the recommendation of a friend of hers, looking for a fifteen-pound class. One-to-one classes were twenty quid; a class for a pair was fifteen quid each. Jack made the fateful mistake he's regretted ever since, of suggesting to Iker that he might like to save a fiver a week by sharing with this

María person, who was nagging him over the phone on a daily basis.

Explaining the idea was beyond the power of any language known to man – or Iker – so Jack, again, made another fateful decision he's regretted ever since. He presented Iker with a *fait accompli*. No, he didn't attempt to explain what that meant, he simply told María to come along the next Thursday morning to meet Iker, and see if between the three of them, Jack could finally make linguistic contact with Iker's brain.

And that's when fate intervened, and Jack fell in love with María the first time he opened the door to her. Her smile almost sent him across the room and out through the brickwork onto the street. She apologised like a cracked record for pestering him, *so sorree, so sorree,* bowing like a geisha, touching his arm, and smiling a smile that film directors and professional photographers spend lifetimes searching for. Jack decided on the spot that he would teach her for free, pay her to come, but the linguistic fates were already working evilly against him.

Puerto-Rican María – being Puerto Rican – spoke excellent Spanish, which Iker, a Catalan, would speak grudgingly, if he had to. In a flurry of machine-gun español and extravagant hand-flapping, María apparently explained to Iker that she'd like to share the class with him and save him a fiver-a-week to boot (whatever *that* is in Spanish). Here she was, clearly intelligent, stunningly pretty, speaking Spanish so melodiously that Jack was almost crying, *begging* Iker to let her join his weekly class.

Iker had shrugged his acquiescence like he *really* couldn't give a shit.

And over the subsequent weeks, Jack suffered the agony of María's infectious enthusiasm, her utterly innocent flirting, the Latin *swing* to her walk, and her jogging wardrobe, which made the best efforts of Nike's summer advertising campaign look like a 1950s Edinburgh Woollen Mill catalogue.

Jack's heart raced every week as the lesson neared; he'd plan more than he'd ever planned before: she only had to suggest that she needed to practise *indefinite pronouns* and he'd scrape the barrel of the internet to find out what they were and set something up.

He fell for her big time. He spent hours daydreaming about her; he lost plots in books and on TV as his mind eloped with María to Puerto Rico, or southern Spain, or Dollis Hill, where she lived. He let her borrow his books, he even lent her money – she *always* paid it back.

But he would never have betrayed Cindy. That wasn't Jack's way at all. And he thought María knew that. He'd mentioned Cindy countless times in their conversational practice: *my wife and I this, my wife and I that, Cindy would love those trainers...* He almost wondered if María's flirting and touchy-feeliness was all the freer and more affectionate because she *knew* Jack was taken, unavailable; she was too innocently nice, and caring, and Catholic, to ever *dream* of breaking up a marriage. It was *never* going to happen.

And then, the last thing he expected to happen, happened. The last thing he'd have *wanted* to happen, if he'd ever been able to foresee it happening, happened. He replays the moment in his mind more frequently than he does Solskjær against Bayern; Eric against Liverpool; Springsteen, The Boss, – even at the Etihad.

Jack's toes curl when he remembers that dreadful morning; his fists clench as he replays the memory of the door handle turning, the door opening, the look on her face, oh the look on her face...

...as María walked into his flat, holding Iker's hand.

He could have accepted it, he really could. María: sweet

and pretty, delicate and funny, effervescent, completely his kind of woman, hooked up with Iker: a hairy, untidy, lazy, hulk of a guy who has as much conversation as the statue of Ronaldo. Jack could have accepted it all, given them his blessing – if Cindy hadn't announced, the following week, that she wanted a divorce.

5

THE SHOP

IT'S ONLY as Jack's showering, after the lesson, that he remembers the lottery. Or thinks he does... He stands, water pounding onto his face, trying to piece together the fragments of memory that are slowly appearing in his mind. Is it memory? Did he dream it? He's no more than fifty-fifty.

It's the reverse of his usual problem. Jack's a vivid dreamer: he's forever running for a lesson he's late for, usually dragging something like a piano around toffee-coated streets, for no obvious reason – he doesn't play the piano, he doesn't like toffee. Or sometimes he's being chased by people who want to sign up for lessons he doesn't want to give. Jack turning down paying customers is one of those outlandishly unlikely things that only happen in dreams. Once, this was Cindy – the obvious question to ask: why would Cindy be pestering him for *English* lessons, didn't occur to him as he hightailed it through the Land of Nod. She might be Australian, but suggesting she needed English lessons would really make her spit her dummy.

His most common recurring dream is María telling him she's pregnant with his child; the disappointing fact that he never dreams any of the obvious preliminary shenanigans to this event is something which makes him wonder if a trip to a therapist might be in order...

Whatever the dream, he usually wakes in a sweat, wrestling with damp sheets, and trying to convince himself that it was all a bad dream. Now, he stands in the shower, trying to convince himself that it *wasn't* a dream.

What finally convinces him that it's actually happened (even before he looks at the lottery website) is his sick-drenched sweatshirt, oh, and the six – *six!* – empty San Miguel bottles that had been scattered around the living room. Why would he have wasted himself on *six* bottles of brew on a Wednesday night, unless he *had* won the bloody lottery? Answer him that! He can't. So he has. Christ!

He wonders where the jubilation is. He's won the lottery, the jackpot, but the only feeling he has is a tremendous sense of foreboding, instead of celebration. There's a stifling sense of dread, closing in on him. He can't work out why... Then another fragment of memory returns in a ghostly apparition, making him gasp involuntarily. Cindy came round!

Yes, she did. He remembers it pretty clearly. Jesus! What did he tell her? Nothing, he's sure. He was stone-cold sober at that point; she came round practically straight away, but he wouldn't have told her. He's *certain* of that – in a blurry sort of way.

Then he does what he always does at moments of tension: he panics, and his mind switches to an involuntary, high-speed, tunnel-vision mode, where the only thing that drives him is an urge to find a resolution to the problem – and fast! He dries himself just enough to convince most unobservant people that he *hasn't* just stepped out of the shower, then pulls on a tracksuit and trainers.

Gotta get the money! It's the only thought in his mind. Get the money. Hide it. If he leaves it where it is, he's not in control.

Cindy might find a way of identifying that he's won. They had one of those lottery accounts for a while when they were together, but he forgot the password and went back to pen and paper – what if she can trace him through that? The lottery people might phone, call at the door when she was visiting, he can't remember whether they put a phone number in the profile, or whose. His mind races down fourteen million rabbit holes of permutations. Gotta get the money. He'll go to the shop. That's where he bought the ticket. He'll need a bag. Will one be enough? How big is two point three million pounds? He's no idea...

How – much – does – one – million – pounds – weigh...

He decides to go for a mil and double the answer, as there's not likely to be an answer to the two point three question. And there's the answer. Actually, there are over forty million answers, but the first one tells him all he needs to know. A million quid in twenties will weigh about fifty kilos. So, two point three mil will weigh a hundred kilos, and a bit. Shit! That's a lot. Rich's eighty-odd kilos and he can lift him at a stretch. Maybe he can ask for fifties? Brilliant!

How – much – does – one – million – pounds – weigh – in – fifty – pound – notes...

Bingo! Twenty-four point two kilos. So double that and a bit of loose change – fifty kilos. Fifty-five, maybe. Christ, Cind was fifty-five and he could lift her, no bother. Job done. Fifties! He reads on, notices that a million quid in fifties will have a volume of thirty-five litres, so that'll be seventy-ish litres all together. He has little idea why the volume of money would be measured in litres, surely that's for liquid?

Then he remembers that his big rucksack is fifty litres, which never made sense, unless you were planning on filling it with orange juice. That'll take the bulk of it. And he's got a little day bag that must hold ten or fifteen litres. Couple of carriers just in case. He's done. He hunts his rucksacks off the top of the cupboard, grabs his wallet, and heads for the door...

———

Banerjees has been there since Jack first moved in, and a lot longer before that. Jack's sure he's never seen it closed. If he's ever up early for a run, admittedly a rare occurrence, Banerjees is open. If they're – if they ever *were* – back late from the cinema or something, Banerjees was open.

He pushes the door, the bell tinkles, and he slides in, until his rucksack snags on the paper rack that guards the entrance and knocks a couple of copies of *The Sun* out onto the floor. He picks them up and slots them back, giving a cheery little wave to Mrs Banerjee, who acknowledges him with a sympathetic smile. She knows he won't have any chat.

It's mostly a mini-supermarket, food and drink, but in the labyrinth of aisles and nooks you can find pretty much anything you might want this side of a coffin – not that he's ever had the need to ask... There's a little electrical corner with plugs and fuses, light bulbs, small kettles, torches, mini-fans. There's a stationery section (always surrounded by schoolkids at home time) stuffed full of envelopes, a kaleidoscopic collection of pens and pencils, diaries, notebooks, rubber bands, mini-staplers.

Near the counter is a small selection of medicines, paracetamol, condoms, plasters. There's a kitchen corner where you can find cutlery, plates and dishes, table mats with pictures of the Taj Mahal on them, glasses – speaking of glasses, they've also got a little stand of *reading* glasses.

Jack remembers, with a smile, the time he came in looking for a lightbulb. He couldn't find the one he wanted, so he asked Mr Banerjee. Mr Banerjee ransacked the shelf with the dedication of a sniffer dog attacking the baggage carousel, presumably in case someone had hung it up on the wrong hook. He then called through to Mrs Banerjee to join the investigation. Jack tried to tell them that it was no big deal – but he was wrong. It was a big deal.

Mr Banerjee disappeared back through the doorway behind the counter, and moments later he reappeared holding the lightbulb Jack needed. He wrapped it up in a paper bag. Jack noticed two grumpy little faces appearing over the counter as he paid, but he thought nothing of it – until he got home and found that the bulb was warm. What warmed his heart was the fact that no charge for a lightbulb appeared on his receipt.

He hovers around the birthday cards, reading some of the funny ones, pretending he needs one. The fact is, he doesn't, but the old biddy from down the road is in the drinks fridge – metaphorically speaking – and he doesn't want her appearing at the counter while he's scooping bundles of fifties into his rucksack. Might give her a nasty turn.

She seems to be comparing bottles, he can't be sure whether she's looking at prices, ingredients, or calorific values. He doesn't care; he just wishes she'd get a move on. Finally, she drops a two-litre bottle of Fanta into her basket and waddles down the cereal and biscuits aisle. *Oh, hurry up!* He wonders if he can just zip in front of her and get it done, but she's on her way back, monster box of economy Cornflakes in her basket. To Jack's relief, she heads for the counter and Mrs Banerjee helps her drop her things into her wheelie trolley. *Blimey*, thinks Jack, *a couple of them would've been ideal for my loot!*

She pays and collects her change but continues a conversation about a young couple down the road, next-door-but-one to her, who have a new baby. *Rabbit, rabbit, rabbit. Jesus!* She winds it up, says goodbye, and lugs her trolley towards the door. Jack slips his wallet out of his pocket and opens it one-handed as he moves towards the counter, readying his rucksack and feeling like Bond, preparing to rappel out of a helicopter and take on a gang of thugs in a gunfight. He hears the doorbell ring again, checks to see it's the old bid going out, but to his horror, sees two kids coming in. He veers left towards electricals giving Mrs Banerjee a bit of a surprise as she was clearly on the point of greeting him.

He hides behind some coils of wire, while the children bicker about whether they can afford half-a-dozen Bear Buddies *and* a couple of Fruity Frogs, or would they be better off with six Happy Cherries and a dozen jellybeans? Jack, meanwhile, discovers how uninteresting the packaging of wire is. He sighs quietly as he hears Mrs Banerjee do the children's calculations like she's a particularly kind-hearted maths teacher.

Then one of the children suggests a Twix. *Mother of God!* If they got a Twix, how many Fruity Frogs could they afford? What about a Twix and some Terrific Fucking Turtles instead? The children don't ask for Terrific Fucking Turtles, that bit's in Jack's mind as he looks for something solid to bang his head against. He hears the bell ring again – the children are now asking how much the two-fingered KitKats cost, and have they got enough for one of them and a dozen Yellow Bellies? There's someone else in the shop for sure. *Jesus!*

He peeks out from behind a display of screwdrivers, which looks like it's been stocked from a Christmas cracker factory, and sighs: it's old Mr Beedley, street gossip extraordinaire. Now he's sunk. Jack's been in the shop with old Mr Beedley dozens of times and he's usually only in for a chat with one of the Banerjees. Nine times out of ten, he'll let Cind or Jack pay for their stuff while he's discussing the daffodils in the front garden of number seven. Usually, this is fine. Cind or he can zip through, say hello (he never seems to want to gas with them much) and make an exit. That won't wash today.

Go ahead, young man, you go through. What's that you've

got? Two point three million pounds? Ruddy marvellous luck! Wait till I tell half the street...

Jack considers his options. He'd never realised Mrs Banerjee was such a gossip. Maybe he'd be better coming back when Mr Banerjee was here. But there's a flaw to that plan that turns him cold: Mr and Mrs Banerjee always seemed to be talking to *each other* whenever they were both in the shop. He can hardly expect them *not* to mention it to each other when they're out back, if they ever go out back together, at least one of them *always* seems to be in the shop. He can imagine them now: *Did you hear that old Mrs Mercer has broken her finger, trapped it in the door last week? And that fellow from across the road, Jack is it? He won two point three million pounds on the lottery. Really? Yes, and I bet you'll never guess what Mr Beedley bought yesterday... Condoms! He must be eighty...*

No, Jack concludes, this isn't a good plan at all. He slides his wallet back into his pocket and heads for the exit. The children are on their way too, bickering about how to share the three Freaky Fish they've bought with the last of their pennies.

He waves at Mrs Banerjee. 'Forgot my wallet.'

'That's okay,' she replies. 'Pay me next time, we know you.'

'No, you're all right; I'll be back later...'

6

THE BROTHER

Jack's brother Richard is outside Jack's front door in full technicolour cycling gear, rolling sweat, chaining his bike to the drainpipe.

'Mornin' bro. You going away?' he asks, nodding at the rucksacks.

'No, I just– ummm... come in.'

Rich tosses his helmet onto the sofa and heads for the fridge. He's two years older than Jack, and without Jack's beard, you'd guess they were brothers. But once you got to know them, you'd soon realise they were stick of chalk and lump of cheese. Whereas Rich is forensic, diligent, careful – Jack is a seat-of-his-pants, fly-by-night kinda guy. While Rich was taking a master's in finance – Jack took a gap year after his English degree. When Rich was investing modestly in ISAs – Jack was getting his fingers burned by online poker. And while Rich has had a string of on-off girlfriends, but never skirted close to marriage – Jack married Cindy at a registry-office cancellation, six weeks after having met her on a beach in Thailand.

Rich works from home, some kind of financial 'consulting' on the back of his accountancy degree, earning enough to allow him not to spend too much time working (he has other interests) – while Jack scrapes by, giving as many English lessons as he can find. Chalk and cheese. Rich sips one of the luridly coloured energy drinks he keeps stocked in Jack's fridge and munches a banana; Jack swigs from a two-litre bottle of Coke and pops nachos from a sack.

'Listen,' Jack begins, as soon as they're settled: Rich lying back on the sofa, stretching out his hamstrings; Jack perched on the edge of a dining-table chair, pulling in his paunch. It's a regular moment they share, Rich stops off from one of his marathon cycles, and if Jack's in, he has a quick breather and a chat; if Jack isn't in, Rich has a key. 'I've got some news...'

'Good or bad?'

'Good news, but serious news. And you gotta promise me, you'll tell no one.'

'Okay, can I have three guesses?'

'What? No, you can't have three bloody guesses, this isn't a game. I told you, it's serious news.'

Rich shrugs a *keep your hair on* shrug. That's the thing about Jack, highly strung. Always has been. Chalk and cheese.

Jack sighs. That's the thing about Rich, flippant. Can't take anything seriously. Chalk and cheese. More like chalk and yogurt, actually. Or maybe it's yoghurt. He's not sure, he'll check later.

'Promise me you'll tell no one'

'Okay.'

'Swear it.'

'What?'

'Swear it. Swear it on Mum and Dad's lives.'

'But – they're dead.'

'It doesn't matter; swear it on *your* life.'

'You know I'm not religious.'

'Oh, just swear it. Swear it on our brotherhood, or whatever...'

'Our *brotherhood...?*'

'Look, do you want to know or not?'

'Course I do. Okay, I swear on our brotherhood or whatever, that I'll never tell anyone what you're about to tell me, unless you release me from this solemn pact. Do you want me to get a sharp knife from the kitchen drawer?'

'You can be such a prick.'

'What is it? You finally won the lottery?'

Jack's face morphs from Dr Jekyll to Lady Di as he feels his muscles go into spasm. 'Did Cindy say that?'

'What? What do you mean, *Did Cindy say that*? Why would Cindy say that?'

'Just tell me, did Cindy tell you that?'

'Course she didn't tell me that. Why the hell would Cindy tell me that? I haven't seen Cindy in months.'

'She suspects I've won.'

'She– look, I'm getting confused here, have you *won* the lottery, or does Cindy *suspect* you've won the lottery?'

'I've *won* the lottery, and I'm not telling Cindy, but she *suspects.*'

'Why are you whispering? Has Cind joined MI5? D'ya think she's bugged the gaff?'

'Oh, Jesus, Rich. Can't you just have a sensible conversation with me? I've won the bloody lottery!'

'You're kidding.'

Jack has his phone ready on the results page, he knew this moment would come, he hands it to Rich.

Rich stares at it, then stares at Jack.

'*That's* why she suspects,' Jack says, relieved to have secured Rich's attention at last. 'She saw my numbers on the telly: April, Eric, Wazza, our birthdays, Maple Road...'

'That's the bloody jackpot!' Rich says.

'I *know!* Christ, I've been doing it long enough. But *nobody* can know!'

'What? Why?'

'Because I don't want *Cindy* to know.'

'Why? Are you going to surprise her?'

'Are you *mad?* No, I'm not going to bloody surprise her. I'm not going to *tell* her!'

'What? *Ever?*'

'Of course *ever!*'

'But – why not?'

'Jesus, Rich, have you been in a coma for the past few months? She's *divorcing* me! If she hears I've won the lottery, she'll want to divvy it up with her bloody family, there are millions of them.'

'Can't you just give her *her* half?'

'*Her half?* She hasn't got a bloody half. She– look, when we got married, Cind tried to get me to drop Wazza.'

'You *what?*'

'She said she wanted a number on my ticket, so she'd feel *part of it.*' He does wiggly air quotes with his fingers and pulls a *Hugh Grant as a pathetic PM* face. 'She wanted me to drop Wazza and use her birthday instead. Where would we be now if I'd said *yes?* We had a massive row about it.'

'What, you and Cind, had a row? Never!'

'Piss off! The point is, *her* bloody birthday hasn't come up, has it? *Wazza* came up, number ten. She always bought her own ticket once I refused to drop Waz, so she's got no right to half the bloody money anyway. It's *my* ticket! She buys her own. I don't see her giving *me* half if *she* wins a mil tomorrow, do you?'

'But, what's the problem with her knowing?'

'Oh, yeah, you can imagine, can't you? Guess what, Cind,

I've won the lottery. You think she'll just congratulate me, gimme a kiss on the cheek? She'll bring up the twenty grand, how her sister shared with us – not that I saw a penny of it – she went out and bought a bloody Golf, then she left me – *in* the bloody Golf! But that ain't the point. Look, don't you remember? Her sister won nearly *quarter-of-a-mil*, and the daft cow split it between her sisters, her parents, her mad aunts, the local koala bears' home. She ended up with less than thirty grand herself. What's Cind gonna do if she hears that I've won a couple of mil?'

'A couple of mil? Is that how much you've won?'

'Two point three.'

'Bloody–'

'Yeah, but look, can't you see what she'll want to do? She'll want to divvy it out to all her pals. Payback time. Not with *my* money she ain't. Once I've got this divorce over and done, I'll be free and easy.'

'Christ, do you think you can keep it a secret?'

'I can if you keep your gob shut. You're the *only* person I'm telling. The only one. It has to stay that way.'

'Right, mum's the word. I'll tip the wink to Beano, but I won't tell him how much.'

'What?! You won't tip the wink to bloody Beano. You won't say a word to *anybody*.'

'Okay! I was joking you. Keep your pants on.'

'Cindy can't get a sniff that I've won, she was round here within seconds of the draw last night. Trying to wheedle her way into my wallet.'

'What did you say?'

'I said I'd stopped doing it, cash flow, that sorta thing.'

'Did she believe you?'

'I think so. What could she say? As long as she never knows, never gets even a *hint*, I'm in the clear.'

'But she's bound to hear sometime, once you're driving around in that Beemer you've always wanted.'

'Yeah, but by then we'll be divorced. I can say anything I like then: got a tasty new job, rich great uncle twice removed died and left me a bit. It won't be anything to do with her. She'll be none the wiser.'

Rich sits back on the sofa, eyes wide. 'Blimey, Jack, you're a *millionaire*. We should celebrate!'

'Are you *listening*? Secret, remember! We can't go out and get plastered and expect to keep mum when someone asks us what's the occasion. You gotta promise me, Rich. You breathe a word, and it'll all be gone. You understand...?'

Rich nods.

'I went to collect it, but changed my mind, didn't want the Banerjees to know in case they told the street.'

Rich looks confused, then smiles. 'You went to collect it? Just now? Is that what the bags were for?'

'Yeah. I didn't want to say anything in the street. In case someone was listening at a window.'

'You went to the corner shop, to collect *two point three million quid?*'

Jack watches as Rich's face does incredulity squared – then it does incredulity times two point three million...

'Did you really think Mr and Mrs Banerjee would have two point three million quid under the sofa, waiting for all the lottery winners to pile in?'

'Course not,' Jack says, hesitantly.

'So, what's with the bags?'

'Well – I wanted to see if they'd be big enough, for when they get the cash.'

'The bloody Banerjees aren't gonna give you two point three million quid, you arsehole!'

'Why not? They've always paid me before.'

'What's the most you've ever won?'

'Thirty quid. Remember I got three numbers?'

'Right, so they'll give you thirty quid out of the till, but they ain't gonna give you two point three million if you show up with a couple of rucksacks and a big smile. They're a corner shop, not Fort bloody Knox. What were you *thinking?*'

'So, how will I get the money?'

'How do *I* know? Phone the lottery *Wongaline*, or whatever it's called, they're bound to have one, they'll tell you what to do.'

'But I don't want them to *know...*'

'Who? The *lottery people?*'

'Anybody.'

'But – look, Jack, you're gonna have to tell the lottery people! How can they give you the bloody money if you don't tell them you've won?'

'I'll do it anonymously.'

'You – look, Jesus! Google the procedures for collecting a big win. You can demand anonymity; they won't splash you in the press unless you ask them to.'

'But they can track your searches on the internet...'

'Who?'

'I don't know, maybe the press. They did that thing with mobile phones, remember? Hacking.'

'That was celebrities, Jack. They're hardly going to have some journo checking out your WhatsApps in case you scoop the jackpot, are they?'

'You sure?'

'Absolutely. Blimey. Whatcha gonna do with it? The Beemer?'

Jack shrugs. 'Don't know really. Haven't had time to process it yet. I'll give you a wad, or you can charge me big time for some financial advice, imagine you'll know how to set it all off against tax.'

'You don't have to give me any. And I think it's tax free.'

'Is it? Even better. But, that's why I don't want Cind getting her kangaroo paws, or claws, or whatever they have, on it. And yeah, the Beemer, of course. Can you believe it? I'm gonna drive a bloody Beemer.'

'Which one will you get?'

'I don't know. I might have to test drive them all.' They sit in silence for a moment: Jack, picturing himself in the front seat of a Z4 – Rich, his mind elsewhere, but going just as fast.

'I've been doing those numbers for years,' Jack says, sipping his drink and staring at the wall.

'Yeah, credit to you. I was all, *It's a waste of money, fourteen million to one shot, put your money in ISAs.* And you've nabbed the jackpot. Credit to ya.'

'It really hasn't sunk in yet. I sort of think I should feel different, but I don't.'

'I think you will. Look, I gotta dash. But great news, bro. And mum's the word. I swear!'

'Yeah, especially not to Cind, okay?'

7

THE SECRET

Rᴜᴄʜ ᴄʏᴄʟᴇs ꜰᴀsᴛ. *Holy shit!* Two point three million quid? He can't believe it. The lucky bugger. But not telling *Cindy?* What sort of a headache is *that* going to cause? He chains his bike and slots his key in the door. He's spent more time than he planned at Jack's, double bugger! He lets himself in and shouts towards the bedroom, 'Are you naked?'

'Course I'm bloody naked! Where have you *been?*' a muffled voice replies. 'You said *twelve!*'

'I know, soz. Got held up. We've still got half an hour, or I can go...'

'No! You get yourself in here *pronto!*'

He sheds clothes as he stumbles down the hallway. By the time he enters the bedroom he's naked as a baby. Lying on the bed, in a similar state of undress, Cindy beckons him forward...

8
___

THE POSH FLAT

It's TURNING out to be the hottest summer since... well, last summer. It's impossible to walk into a newsagent's without seeing words like *SCORCHER* or *SIZZLING* emblazoned on at least three front pages, often in red type and surrounded by zigzaggy 'explosions' and pictures of small children licking ice creams, or much bigger 'children' leaping into fountains in their underwear. There are reports of tarmac melting, cars overheating, shops running out of portable air-conditioning units – and businessmen going to work without their ties.

Why? Jack thinks. Not, *Why is it so hot?* Nobody on the planet doubts that climate change has announced its early arrival. No, Jack wants to know why the newspapers are headlining, day after sweltering day, with the one thing that practically $E - V - E - R - Y - B - O - D - Y$ knows? You'd hardly pick up your paper, read the headline and step outside thinking, *Is it really...?*

He's free the rest of the day so he hops on his bike and heads up Cricklewood Broadway, feeling good. He views the world with new eyes. A rich man's eyes. He can look at things he's never looked at before, because now they're within his reach.

He listens to his bike, clanking and wheezing, the one gear that still engages useless for the flat or a hill.

On the flat, his legs whirl like windmill sails in a hurricane, while giving him just enough speed to keep up with the toddlers-on-reins. On any hill, however, his legs almost can't go fast enough to provide enough forward motion to keep him upright. His eye catches the shiny window of CycloMania, Rich's second home. Jack dismounts and ponders the sleek frames with their stacks of silvery gears and price tags in excess of a thousand pounds. He tries to subtract a thousand pounds from two point three million and concludes it's not worth worrying about.

Back on his boneshaker, he studies the cars that overtake him. There's the tinny rattle of battered old hatchbacks, all boxy corners and rust: Novas, Polos, *Fiestas,* like his own. Then, there's the purr of the big saloons, with their smooth corners and bug-eyed headlamps: Audis, Mercs, and *Beemers*, like he'd love to own.

He remembers the hours he spent as a kid, playing with his uncle's collection of old Corgi and Dinky cars, driving them around the living-room carpet, which had the perfect design for motoring. It was a mud-coloured grid of squares, separated from each other by six-inch lanes, around which Jack would steer Pontiac Firebirds, Chevrolet Impalas, and Roger Moore's white Volvo P1800 (sadly, the *'Saint'* sticker had long since peeled off).

But those weren't his favourite cars. He had two favourites in particular. The first was a pale-blue, Austin A60, deluxe saloon, *motor school car*. It was the motor school car feature that won it for Jack. On top of the car was a red circular blob, as if the driver were carrying a red tyre, lying flat on the roof. When you twisted the blob, the front wheels turned, enabling Jack to have the *reverse-around-the-corner* manoeuvre perfected by the age of eight. But his top car of all was a BMW 3-Series convertible, with the roof down. This was in a dark turquoise-blue, and it stole his heart. He always regretted that Uncle Jezza's carpet didn't have any curving clifftop roads, but beggars couldn't be choosers in Cricklewood.

He's halfway up Shoot-Up Hill now, his schoolboy route to Maida Vale on the sixteen bus for many a year. He's passing some of the courts and mansions that he used to enjoy trying to see inside from the top deck of the bus. These aren't *blocks of flats*. No, these are much more exclusive, the sort of places where *The Saint* or *The Avengers* lived or solved crimes. He knew this because his uncle also had a collection of dusty old VHS tapes that Jack used to watch. *The Man from Uncle* also hung out in this type of place. Most of the buildings are three or four storeys tall, with front gardens or driveways, steps leading to imposing-looking double doors, windows with small balconies. In the driveways, the cars are always Audis, Mercs – or Beemers.

There's a sign out front of Hillcrest Court on the corner of Mill Lane, *For Sale*, with the agent's number. He heaves his bike onto the pavement. He remembers, as a child, cutting through the front driveway, sometimes getting shouted at by posh-sounding people dragging posh-looking poodles. They clearly got fed up with kids doing this, as they've bricked up the Shoot-Up Hill entrance. Bastards.

On a whim, the kind of whim only rich people would ever dare to indulge, he pulls his phone out of his pocket and pings the number in.

'Hello, Saville and Hornby Estates, how may I help you?' The voice is intimidating, condescending, a public schoolboy who's failed his A levels and is temping while waiting to resit. But Jack's not going to be intimidated by class – he has *money!*

'Hello there,' he says, trying to sound as much like Simon

Templar as he can remember. 'I'm passing Hillcrest Court, and I see you've got a flat for sale there. Could you give me the outline details please?' *Outline details?* That sounds good. He's no idea whether it's correct or not, but he'll assume the schoolboy doesn't know either.

'Oh, yes sir, that's a particularly popular property, in a very popular area, good transport connections. Let me pull up the details... Here we go, yes, top floor facing Shoot-up Hill, so great views and afternoon sun, three bedrooms, two bath, over nine hundred square feet, lots of storage space, very nicely decorated. It hasn't been on the market very long; we do expect it to be *very* popular. Oh, and Kilburn Station on the Jubilee line is a five-minute walk.'

He looks up at his flat. *His* flat! Wasn't that easy? How much would a flat like that cost? He has no idea. More than a million? Maybe. But that would be less than half of his pot. And no more rent to pay. 'And the guide price?' he adds. *Guide price?* Very good, Simon.

'They're asking seven fifty, but we know they're negotiable.'

Seven fifty? What's that? Seven hundred and fifty thousand? Or seven point five million? He's really not sure, all the flats he's ever been interested in have been pcm and never went in for decimals. However, he doesn't want to appear unsophisticated, so doesn't ask.

'You said you were passing, sir? If you meant that literally, I'm only in West End Lane, I could be with you in five minutes, tops. The property is empty, and with the sunshine, it would be a wonderful time to see it. It really is spectacular inside...'

Jack looks up again; yep, the sun is around the front of the building, it's going to be bright inside.

'Right. Okay. Yes, I'm outside now.'

'Then I'll be with you in five. See you then.'

Jack stares at the block. Bloody hell. That simple? I want to see inside this posh flat. Yes, I'm ridiculously rich. He looks for somewhere out of view to chain his bike then walks up to the front door. It really looks impressive: some deep-brown varnished wood with a toughened-glass window. Inside, the hall is the size of his sitting room, and a staircase sweeps up and away like something out of *Gatsby*. Now they've blocked one of the entrances to the drive, he wouldn't be bothered by bloody kids, scooting through on bikes and skateboards. Little sods.

He looks out towards Shoot-Up Hill. It's a different view from here, he feels very proprietorial all of a sudden. Never guessed as a kid on the top deck of a number sixteen, that one day he'd stand here. An Englishman in his castle.

Steady on now. He's still not sure how much this costs; if it's seven hundred and fifty thousand, he's in the game, less than a third of what he's got; if it turns out to be seven point five mil, it's a red card. Seven hundred and fifty thousand suddenly sounds very cheap, maybe he's got it wrong. Seven point five million? It could be. He has no clue. No clue what the flat is worth, and no clue, really, how much money he has.

What can he buy with two point three mil? He tries to think of the largest single amount of money he's ever spent. His flat's rented, he got his car off his dad, he can't think. The holiday in Thailand where he met Cindy was nearly four-hundred quid. Is that it? Is that the most he's ever spent on one thing? It doesn't really count as he put half of it on his credit card. He's down to two hundred.

He tries to peer in through a downstairs window, but the heavy net curtains fulfil their sole purpose admirably. He wanders around the side where he finds a kitchen window that isn't netted. Inside, it looks like a TV set, all ready for Nigella or Jamie to flounce in and knock up a soufflé; it's not the sort of kitchen designed with *Perky Pizza* loyalty-club members in mind. There's a central block in the middle, what are they called? And the sink has one of those extendable tap thingies, with the curly sort of chrome spring, like you could use it as a zip wire if you needed to get out in a hurry. Apart from looking flash, he's not really sure what the spring is for.

A car pulls into the drive, little silver Audi A1, very nice. Jack scuttles back around the front. Out clambers a lanky ill-fitting suit, with a fresh-faced schoolboy inside.

9

THE NEW NEIGHBOUR

'Hello there, sir. You here for the viewing?'

'That's right,' Jack says, wondering if he shouldn't have called on a whim, not while he's wearing a raggy pair of jeans and a grubby *Castlemaine XXXX* T-shirt. But, he realises, he doesn't have to worry about any of that – he has *money!*

'My name's Tom.' The suit offers his hand, barely noticing Jack's get-up – barely.

'I'm Jack.' He resists the temptation to ask Tom to call him *The Saint*. 'As I said, I was passing and saw the sign.'

'No time like the present,' Tom says, opening the front door and ushering Jack inside.

They go up in the lift that's tucked beside the stairs, Tom describing how lucky Jack'll be to have a lift, and how it's always working in this building, he's noticed, over the years. Jack wonders how Tom could've got out of school to play in the lift, cos he surely hasn't left school more than a couple of months.

They exit onto a smart landing area, with a polished tile floor and a very healthy-looking pot plant on a stand. The doors are all the same creamy colour and look like they were given a fresh lick only the day before. The door handles are shiny gold, possibly solid. He's seen landings like this in films, always Hollywood films, probably starring Richard Gere in a thousand-dollar suit, or Julia Roberts wearing polka dots. While Tom jangles keys, looking for the right one to open the door, Jack imagines Diana Rigg – sorry, *Emma Peel* – inside, waiting to greet them with Martinis. He's never had a Martini. As Tom tries more keys, the door across the landing opens, and a little face peeks out. Jack might have mistaken it for a Pekinese – had it been a little lower down.

'Allo? I can help you?' she barks. She's half Jack's height, if that, and twice his age – a boomer, without much boom left. Her accent and manner suggest she's probably East European, but maybe last lived there long before the wall came down. She looks like she might even have escaped over it. Tom takes command.

'Oh, hello, Mrs Weiss!' he shouts, like he knows she's a bit hard of hearing. 'It's Tom from the agency, another viewing.'

She steps out, shuts her door and locks it. 'And you are?' she says, looking up at Jack like a suspicious schoolteacher might look down on a naughty child.

'I'm Jack, come to look at the flat.' He offers his hand, but she looks at it like he's trying to sell it to her. She shakes her head, snaps her hands behind her back and leans backwards – not a full Michael Jackson, just a little *Don't even think about it* sway. She looks like a small stumpy tree that's growing on a windy clifftop; her moss-green jacket-and-skirt two-piece, deep-brown tights, and shiny brown brogues add to a *forest grove* ambience. The musty smell that's also recently arrived feels like it might be an expensively crafted cinematic special effect – although Jack has a suspicion the explanation is more prosaic.

'How much are they asking for it? They were very noisy,

you know? I'm glad they've gone. Two small children always running around on the floors and screaming.' Jack wonders if she'd have been happier if the children had been running on the walls, or the ceiling... 'I bought mine forty years ago, cost me ten thousand pounds!' She says this as if it's the largest sum of money any of them could possibly imagine. Jack's certainly impressed. Then he notices that she's waiting for an answer, *I've shown you mine...*

'It's on the market for seven hundred and fifty thousand pounds,' Tom says, speaking as if to a child who can't count beyond twenty – *and* is severely hard of hearing. There are four doors on the landing, Jack wonders if they'll soon be joined by all his prospective neighbours, or are Emma, Richard and Julia going to pass on the chance to say *Hi*.

Mrs Weiss stiffens like Tom has dropped his trousers. Her eyes widen; her jaw falls a couple of centimetres, popping her small mouth open. 'Seven hundred and fif– that's what Labour governments do to you. I've never voted Labour since Harold Wilson devalued the pound. That's why we had Brexit, you know? That Boris Johnson? He's as bad. Him and Wilson, thick and thieves.' Jack wonders if she means thick *as* thieves, decides she probably doesn't. 'Come on then, open it up, show him around. Are you going to be very noisy? You don't play the drums, do you?'

She's beside Jack, like they're considering moving in together, once they've arranged the wedding. Tom throws Jack a worried *Do you want me to get rid of her?* glance. Jack replies with an *I think she's harmless* shrug and shake of the head.

Tom finally breaks in and leads them through a large hall with *bags of storage space*, then straight into a *spacious* living room, which is larger than Jack's whole flat. He only just manages to stop himself from whistling. The sun is cutting across the dark parquet flooring and spreading over the walls. There's a painting, not a poster, a real paint painting the size of a wardrobe hanging to his right. The colours are brighter than he would have thought possible: shiny red splashes that could be fresh from a murder, enough shades of green to satisfy anyone with an Irish passport, cobalty blues, Disney pinks; he suddenly realises they're enormous flowers.

'Very modern,' Mrs Weiss mutters, grumpily, as if her small framed poster of *The Hay Wain*, or *The Berlin Wall* before... you know... might be a tadge musty in comparison.

Jack is still busy being stunned by the size of the living room. His eyes hoover an enormous corner sofa, bigger than his car, dominating the far wall, with a couple of comfy-looking armchairs keeping it company. There are floor-to-ceiling bookshelves; a near-cinema-sized plasma TV; a massive bay window; and enough space to set up a table tennis table if you had a few friends around. Jack wanders over to the window, while Mrs Weiss quizzes Tom about why the sofa goes around a corner.

There's a sixteen bus passing outside, heading for Kilburn, Jack's old school run. It's one of the modern ones, without the open deck at the back, which he remembers from when he used to jump off at the lights without paying the fare – donating that to the sweet or chip shop. He thinks there was a health 'n' safety argument behind getting rid of the open rear decks on London's buses: a tooth-decay epidemic, maybe; or rising obesity rates; possibly even the occasional sprained ankle? Or was it really all down to London Transport's profit and loss account...?

There's a child on the top deck, staring out. Jack waves, the child smiles and waves back. He can't remember anyone ever waving to him. Then it hits him, Mrs Weiss would've been living here when he used to pass the building on his way to school. Maybe not looking out of this flat, hers faces the other way, but she was here. Not that she seems the type to have waved anyway. He feels as if he's staring out at another era, through somebody else's eyes, from inside some sort of Tardis. He *would* be someone else if he lived here. The space. The comfort. The view. The envy and wonder of the children on the sixteen bus.

'Shall we do the tour?' Tom shouts over Mrs Weiss's latest enquiry about why the television is so big but so thin. She's trying to peer around the back of it as if she's searching for a hidden safe. He's sounding increasingly like the party guest who's been collared by the stamp collector.

'Lead the way,' Jack says. I have *money*.

'Bathroom,' Tom explains, in case the bath isn't enough of a clue. It's bigger than Jack's kitchen – the bathroom, that is, not the bath, although that is quite a sight in itself. It's one of those free-standers, with feet shaped like a lion's claws and painted gold. The sort of bath people get murdered in, in horror films. Hopefully *only* in horror films. There's no sign of stale blood between the chessboard floor tiles, Jack notices.

'Kitchen,' Tom says. He's really earning his money. While Mrs Weiss pokes around the microwave and mutters *dangerous things,* Jack marvels at the size of the room. He could probably park his car in the fridge, which is one of those silver double-door jobs that Harrison Ford always has in his Jack Ryan films.

'Master bedroom.'

It's straight from one of those catalogues posh people leave on their coffee tables, Jack thinks, not that he's ever seen one there. Or anywhere else. But it is. The bed is enormous. He used to think beds came in two sizes: single and double. Then he learned about queens and kings. This bed must be an emperor, or maybe it's a Supreme Chancellor of the Galactic Republic. It's bloody huge. How did they get it in? Did they build the flat around it? You could fit six adults in it easily. Room for a well-behaved Labrador and pups.

It's also piled high with enough fancy silk cushions and pillows to satisfy a very fussy film star. There must be a dozen of them. What do you do with them all when you come in from the pub at night, slightly worse for wear, and you've got a dozen cushions to battle with before you can get your head down? And then, the next morning, it would take an hour finding and collecting them all again.

The wardrobes take up one whole wall. Floor to ceiling. He'd love to open them up and see what sort of clobber the people who live here wear. But they're probably full of more bloody cushions.

'Shower room.'

'We're not blind, young man. We didn't think it was a phone box.'

Jack smiles, well done, Mrs Weiss! Tom and Jack exchange glances as Mrs Weiss lifts the lid of the toilet. What does she expect to find in there?

Three bedrooms, two bathrooms, parquet flooring, real 'art', cupboards you could party in, beds you could sleep the family in, he feels like he's on a film set. He envisions, any moment, Hitchcock, well, preferably not him, Richard Curtis maybe, will step out of a cupboard and shout 'Cut!' But the most shocking thing is – he could buy this. He could say 'yes' to Tom and do it. Here and now. Live here, on the parquet flooring, in the jumbo-sized bed, with the view of the sixteen bus route, with Mrs Weiss as his neighbour. With change. Although he'd probably have to negotiate a bit extra for the funky painting of the flowers.

He tells Tom that he needs time to think, says he's *only just come into his money,* and this is the first place he's looked at. Tom says he has more like this, much better for only a little more, one on Fordwych Road, and others up nearer the Heath...

Jack promises to be in touch, says goodbye to Mrs Weiss who has Tom in the grip of a conversation that an anaconda would envy. She wants to know what's the point of double glazing. Jack, meanwhile, has much to ponder, and Hillcrest Court has certainly widened his horizons.

10

THE BANK

AFTER LUNCH, Jack winds up his battered old Fiesta and heads across town. That's *battered* as in dented, as opposed to a fish supper, he always thinks, whenever somebody describes it thus. His Fiesta is ancient to the point of being antique. He got it third-hand off his dad, Syd, who bought it second-hand in 1980 when it was three years old, and it's piddled along quite nicely ever since. It's got no mod cons. None. No electric windows, no satnav, no airbags; it probably doesn't have any horsepower – Syd always said it had one donkeypower.

He'd kept it garaged and didn't like taking it out in the rain, scouring it regularly for the slightest hint of rust. When he found some, he'd scour it again, but this time with wire wool and emery paper until he could see the metal shine. Then he'd hit it with a variety of rust treatments and preventers before slapping on the primer and paint.

Syd worked for Ford, way back when everyone in the UK thought it was a British carmaker, and he taught Jack a fair amount of tinkering when what Jack most wanted was to be inside watching *Football Focus* to see if Eric or Keano had passed late fitness tests. Syd's best piece of advice to Jack had

55

been, *Never buy a new car*. He had two reasons: one, new cars lost half their value as soon as you signed the deal; and two, new cars were being stuffed full of so many computers and electronic shitshat that it was getting impossible even to change a lightbulb. And he wasn't kidding about the lightbulbs.

Their neighbour at the time had bought a spanking new car: electric windows, heated seats, cruise control, Teasmade, all mod cons including some horsepower. Loved showing it off to Syd by washing it while he was tinkering, and Jack and Rich were sighing. Then, one morning, it was United v Arsenal, Jack remembered, because they were able to sneak inside and catch *Football Focus* to find out that Van Nistelrooy was doubtful.

That morning, the neighbour approached Syd rather sheepishly. The neighbour had been trying, and failing, for nearly an hour, to change a lightbulb in his new chariot. Syd, ever the teacher, agreed to help. It was half-time at Old Trafford before Syd came into the house effing and blinding about how they'd squeezed so much stuff under the bonnet that it was practically impossible to get anywhere near the lightbulb assembly, without either removing half the engine first or voluntarily dislocating both wrists.

Never buy a new car, he'd said. So, Jack had taken ownership of the Fiesta, and kept it going with a set of screwdrivers, a universal wrench, and a few choice swear words. Good old Dad, God rest his cancerous lungs.

He parks up when he spots a bank that's well out of his usual zone. He's beginning to realise some of the little precautions that he'll need to take if he's to keep his changed financial situation away from Cindy's eagle eyes, bloodhound nose and kangaroo paws or claws or whatever. When he and Cindy got married, he'd added her onto his bank account to make it a joint. Then, when they broke up, she agreed she'd get her own account, and he could have his back for himself.

Simple, adult solution. Only problem is, they never went through the process of taking Cindy's name off Jack's account. And he's pretty sure he won't be able to do it without her agreeing to the change in triplicate. And he can't ask her to approve it, not now, because then – she'd know...

It's not that he uses his bank account much. He's usually paid cash in hand, and there's never really enough in his wallet to make putting it in a bank necessary. By the time he puts it in, he's taking it all back out again. So, Cindy has access, she can look and see what's going in and out – at the moment, nothing – but it's not going to stay like that for long. Clearly, he needs a new bank account, one that Cindy knows nothing about. He's on a secret mission.

He checks the street one last time before entering. Can't be too careful, doesn't want one of Cindy's aerobics mates or jogging partners to pass by on the other side of the road and see him going into a bank. Tongues would wag, and he can't have that.

He slips through the door, James Bond couldn't have done it smoother, and takes his place in the line. There's only one counter open, and only one person in front of him. He's got all the documents he needs (he's been on the internet) and twenty quid to open the proceedings.

The woman in front moves away and Jack steps forward.

'Hello, I'd like to open a bank account, please.'

The lad behind the screen is wearing a jacket that looks two sizes too big; his shirt is gaping at his Adam's apple; his tie looks like it's been knotted by a four-year-old; and his hair is slicked with enough grease to get him Bogart's role in a *Casablanca* remake.

'Current account?' Humphrey's double asks.

'Yes please.'

'Fill out this form and I'm sure the manager's free to go

through the details with you when you're ready. I'll give you a call if you wait over there.' He points at a small circular table surrounded by what look like three large toadstools.

Jack bridles at this, his plan was to make his presence in the bank as low-key as possible. He doesn't really want a chinwag with the manager.

'Can't you do it? I've got my ID and proof of address; it can't be that difficult.'

'There are a few other details to be sorted out, like whether you want a credit or debit card, and there's an offer on for free travel insurance and airport VIP lounge vouchers. They're brill, you get free booze and newspapers. I was in the Heathrow one once and I saw Piers Morgan.'

Jack can think of a dozen people he'd prefer to meet in an airport VIP lounge; he could probably think of a hundred, but he skulks off to perch on a toadstool when two more customers come into the bank and stare over his shoulder.

He's halfway through the form when a door at the back opens and another youth comes out. He barely looks old enough to be running a school tuck shop, but he introduces himself as Ollie, the manager, and invites Jack through to his office. He's also wearing an oversized suit; have their mums bought them all like that on purpose, planning that they'll *grow into them*?

Ollie's tie should have a warning label for anyone suffering from epilepsy, and he has a hanky sticking out of his top pocket. Trouble is, the hanky isn't folded *à la James Bond*, with two or three crisp little triangles left visible. No, it's stuffed *à la I've got a streaming cold and I need quick access,* so it looks like the arse of a small polar bear who's digging for fish through some filthy ice.

'Right, good morning,' the mannequin from *Man at C&A* begins, as he settles himself into a squeaky leather swivel.

'Hi, I want to open a current account.'

'Okay, lovely. You got your ID and proof of address with you?'

Jack hands over his driver's licence and a couple of utility bills.

'Lovely,' Ollie says again, standing to put them on the photocopier. 'You're lucky to be opening one this month,' he says, as he slaps a couple of buttons and the machine gurgles and whirs. 'You can have free travel insurance and some airport VIP lounge vouchers. Gary out the front once saw Piers Morgan at Heathrow.'

Jack wonders if the sighting of Piers Morgan in the Heathrow airport VIP lounge is the most exciting thing that's ever happened in this branch. He considers that they're probably due a robbery, just to give them all some variation in their customer small talk.

'Great,' Jack says, while scribbling his signature at the bottom of the form.

'All done?' Ollie says as he sits back down. 'Lovely. Now, any idea how much money you'll be keeping in this account?'

Jack's jaw slackens. He's never considered the bank would ask him this. What's it got to do with them? Is there an upper limit, or something? He's never thought of that either. Could there be an upper limit on this account? *Jesus!*

'Ummm, I'm not really sure. Are there limits?'

'It's just that if you're going to put large amounts in, then we have accounts with higher interest rates. You wouldn't want a whole loada wonga sloshing around earning no interest, would you?'

'No.' Jack smiles weakly. He hates being 'sold' stuff. He hates the feeling that he's being subjected to a salesman's 'patter'. What he hates most of all is when he feels unable to do anything except agree with each statement they make, or each question they ask – especially when they start with *You*

TOM ALAN

wouldn't want... 'What do you mean by *large amounts?*' he asks, a little hesitantly, beginning to realise that at some point he's going to have to tell Ollie how much he's got.

'Anything between a hundred thou and a mil would be better off in our *Highflyer* account, there's unlimited access to European VIP lounges with that one, and there's additional security: you wouldn't want to leave your debit card in a Barcelona Starbucks and have some sharp bugger empty your account, would you?'

Jack shakes his head reluctantly. He's worried now. That account was for up to a mil. Is there an even better account for more than a mil? He has to ask.

'What about more than that?' he says, as casually as he can.

'More than a million?' Ollie squeaks back into his impressive swivel and suddenly looks at Jack like he thinks he's spotted a gun tucked into his waistband.

'In theory,' Jack says, shrugging, wondering if Ollie's thinking that he's taking the piss. He really should've ditched the *Castlemaine XXXX* T-shirt at lunchtime.

'We've got what we call the *Astronaut* account. It's really called *Sky High*, but everybody calls it the *Astronaut*. That's got a million pounds minimum balance but there's no upper limit, free travel and health insurance, unlimited worldwide VIP lounge access, worldwide car breakdown and recovery, and a complimentary bank-branded fountain pen and retractable pencil set in a presentation box. That's really neat, look. All the managers get one.'

He hunts in his top drawer and pulls out a plastic box, which he opens for Jack to view. Jack nods as if it's chock-full of diamonds, rather than the cheapo-looking pen and pencil set you'd give to your niece or nephew for passing at least a couple of GCSEs. 'I think Piers Morgan comes into the branch to present it to you, you wouldn't want to miss *that*, would you?' – *A heartbeat* – 'No, I'm only kidding. Don't listen to me.'

Jack smiles feebly. He hasn't expected the simple act of opening a bank account to turn into a Special Branch interrogation. He ponders how to proceed. It would've been far better if this geezer had been sixty and balding. The chance of Cindy, or any of her mates, knowing him then would've been non-existent. Hardly any of Cindy's chums are capable of a sensible conversation with anyone more than ten years their senior, they simply don't speak the same language. But this guy's around Jack's age, yet another millennial: who knows which Pilates clubs or Zumba classes he might frequent? Cindy gives classes over half of London; she could bump into him in any of them.

He winces as he imagines the water-cooler chatter: *You'll never believe this guy who opened an account last week. Real ordinary fella, nothing special about him at all, bit scruffy really. Then yesterday – you'll never guess – two point three million pounds appears in his account. Now, what was his name again? Oh yes...*

Jack takes a breath. 'How's about if I open the bog-standard one, then if I need a bit more capacity, I upgrade it as and when...?'

'Excellent idea. Lovely. Give me two seconds on the magic lantern here and I'll sort you out...'

———

By the time Jack's out on the street again, he's hatched another plan. He'll go into a different bank and open another account. If the person there is an octogenarian, then that's where he'll drop his money. If it's another schoolchild in an ill-fitting suit and a tie to die from, he'll try again at yet another bank. He's already learned from a quick bit of googling that he has six months to claim his prize, so no rush. And, thinking about it, mightn't be a bad idea to spread the money around half a dozen different banks: that way, if Cindy ever got wind, she wouldn't know the full story. Brilliant!

He's pleased with himself and sets off in search of a coffee shop to celebrate with a cappuccino and a pastry, he's deserved it. But two shops down the road, his pace slows – Beemer showroom...

11

THE NEWS

'LISTEN, got something important to tell you,' Cindy whispers, as she passes Rich their post-coital fag.

Here we go, Rich thinks, flumping up his pillow. On the cycle over he's thought about what Jack told him, so he's not completely unprepared for this. He's already decided, pretty much, how he's going to play it. He props himself up on his elbow and feigns polite interest.

'What?'

'Jack's won the lottery.'

Rich stops mid-drag and stares at her, with what he thinks is a suitably *shocked* expression. He lets the smoke bleed out of his mouth like he's lost concentration on the cigarette.

'*What?*' he gasps, letting his eyes widen slowly, his mouth open slightly more.

'I'm pretty sure he has.'

'What makes you think that?' Rich says, expertly morphing his look of shock into one of confusion by narrowing his eyes. He leaves the cigarette dangling in his hand like he's forgotten it's there.

'His bloody numbers came up last night!' she snaps, sitting

up and grabbing the cigarette. He'd normally fight her for the last few puffs, but decides it'll look all the better if he continues his 'Dazed and Confused' matinee performance. 'April, Eric, Rooney, 22, 24 and Maple Road? The whole song and dance. He's won the bloody jackpot! But here's the thing, listen – I went round there immediately after to congratulate him, you know, like anyone would. And d'you know what he said?'

'The jackpot?' Rich gasps, pretending to cough on the dregs of the smoke. 'You're joking.'

'No. The bloody jackpot. But guess what he said when I went round there last night?'

'How much is that?'

'What?'

'The jackpot. How much has he won?'

'It's over two million. Two point three, I think they said.'

'Two point three bloody million? Jesus!'

'Yes. But guess what he said when I went round there last night?'

'You went round there last night?' He's beginning to enjoy himself, but knows he mustn't push it too far…

'I bloody told you; don't you listen? I went round there last night. To congratulate him. And guess what he frigging said?'

Rich shrugs, but a bemused kinda shrug. Not like he simply doesn't know, but like he doesn't understand the question. A sorta *What are you talking about?* shrug, complete with a rapid shake of the head; his Equity card is in the bag.

'He said he stopped doing the lottery!' Cindy finishes the fag and grinds it out in the ashtray on the bedside table, like she's found a mid-sized spider in there. 'Can you imagine? Jack just stopped doing the lottery? It's as likely he'd make a girl smile.'

Rich nods thoughtfully. He's never keen to hear Cind dissing Jack like this, he can't help but think, *But you married him!* But he doesn't say anything – doesn't actually get the chance.

'So, I went over to Banerjees to say hello, you know, I don't see them now I've moved out. And guess what Mr Banerjee told me?'

Rich wonders if it'll look odd if he can guess, or if it'll look odder if he can't. He ends up simply looking gormless.

'Jack's doing his lottery as regular as a Swiss cuckoo. The lying bastard.'

Rich whistles a relatively non-committal whistle, and lets his eyes widen again to show his 'surprise'.

'Did you pop in to his for your mid-ride tucker and coldies this morning?' she asks.

Ah! She's caught him on the hop with that one. God knows what she might be planning to do over the next couple of days, so lying's not a good bet.

'Yeah, the usual five minutes.'

'And he said nothing to you?'

'About the lottery?'

'No, about his bleeding haemorrhoids, what d'ya think?'

'No, nothing.'

'Bloody bastard.'

'What do you mean?'

'Can't you *see*? He's cutting *you* out as well.'

Rich makes an *I'm not sure what you mean* face, and Cindy sighs one of her monumental sighs. She's got a lot of good characteristics, Cindy – but her sighing like you're a moron isn't one of them.

'We're going to have to plan this very carefully, Rich. Jack can be pretty shonky, you know?'

Rich wonders how the 'we' has suddenly found itself embedded in Cindy's 'plan'. He also wonders what *shonky* means, but thinks he can work it out.

'Anyway, gotta go, got a class. You can let yourself out?'

He suppresses a sigh of his own, her high-rising terminals are beginning to get on his nerves, especially now Jack has told him what they're called. He nods, she kisses him full on the lips. 'Early one tomorrow, Richaroo? I got back-to-back classes starting at ten...'

He nods again, but his mind is elsewhere.

12

THE BEEMER

JACK HAS a good ten minutes unmolested in the showroom, which he appreciates. He hates hard-sell merchants; hates being followed around shops and told stuff he doesn't want to know, or things he can read on tickets or has already sussed on the internet. Then, an even nicer touch: the saleswoman wanders past him, nudges his arm lightly, smiles and says, *Let me know if you want to test-drive anything.* Then she wanders away, leaves him alone.

She returns to her chrome-and-glass desk, tippy-tapping with rose-pink fingernails on a sleek laptop, taking the occasional sip from a fancy-looking half-litre bottle of water. Jack wonders what he has to lose. Test drive in a Beemer? Maybe his luck is changing. Then he remembers that he's just won the lottery, and he laughs out loud.

The saleswoman looks up at him, smiling again, her rose-pink lipstick matching her jacket-and-skirt two-piece. She looks a natural blonde, although, if he's honest, he'd be hard pushed to spot false eyelashes or a full set of dentures.

He regrets (again) having failed to dress for the occasion, but he figures maybe he'll be able to adopt a sort of casually dressed but, underneath it all, ruggedly handsome in an understated, unflashy sort of way... Brad Pitt can pull it off, why can't he? He knows there's probably a very obvious answer to that – but decides not to pursue it. Instead, he straightens his back, pushes his shoulders out of their usual slouch, pulls in his tum, and moseys casually over and sits down at her desk.

'Hi, need some help?' she asks, leaving her keyboard mid-rattle, and giving him a smile that sends his natural tendency to be a little nervous with women into shock. His pulse starts to piddle, his sweat pores take a little stretch...

'Yeah, I was looking at the 2-Series convertible in the window. Maybe take it out for a spin? Like you suggested...' He manages to end the sentence there without gulping.

She nods like he's made a particularly wise choice and leads him over to take another look, her tall (rose-pink) high heels ticking on the polished tiles like a precision watch. She opens the driver's door for him, and he sits inside and wiggles the steering wheel, trying desperately not to giggle like a small child with a big ice cream. He waits for her to burst the illusion of *'his kind of saleswoman'*, by telling him everything he's read on the ticket. But, rather surprisingly, she surprises him.

'Can I be honest with you, em...?'

'Jack,' he replies to her eyes, which are enquiring so elegantly.

'Shelly,' she responds, before walking around the other side and slipping smoothly into the passenger seat. Jack tries to stay calm, concentrating on the dashboard and wondering what this car can do that his geriatric Fiesta can't. He knows it's got a lot more horsepower, the wheels are bigger, he could probably fit his winnings inside the enormous boot even if he took them in used fivers, and it's got a top speed he can only experience if he takes it back to Germany – but, in essence, it's got four seats, four wheels, and it'll go forward, backwards and round corners. Despite all that, there's something about it that makes his fingers twitch.

'Course,' he says, nervously turning to face her, *Come on then, sell it to me...*

She closes her door, nods at his, which he pulls shut. The deep, comforting, *kerschlunk* noise the doors make when you close them must be worth five grand on its own, he thinks. He now feels like he's in some sort of superspy sound-proofed booth, ready to be debriefed – well, maybe that's not the best word – he finds his mind blanking suddenly, as he tries to rid it of the image.

'Don't tell my boss I told you,' she half whispers, sliding closer to him so he'd have trouble releasing the handbrake without risking a slap around the face. She's so close he can smell her perfume; it's light and flowery, he's no clue what sort of language people use for perfume, it's all *tones* and *notes* and stuff. He's not much cop with wine, either. This perfume's nice, he likes it, doesn't scratch at the back of your throat like the stuff Cindy sometimes splashed all over.

'But I'm not working on commission, see? I don't care whether you buy a 2-Series or an M4 or you go around the corner and buy an Audi. I'll still get paid my salary. So, two things to let you know before we go anywhere. First, I've driven these, and I'm not a hundred per cent impressed. You like a stiff ride, I imagine...?'

Jack's eyes widen, as they might do, were someone to shove a live cattle prod into his anus. He feels the muscles in his jaw stiffen. He wonders if she's flirting with him, cos he's not sure what a stiff ride is if she's *not* flirting with him. 'Yeah,' he manages to gasp, as all the moisture in his mouth evaporates. 'Moderately...'

'Yeah, me too, and I have to say, in my opinion, the ride on these is a bit spongy, compared to the last model. I drive the last model, and I think it's much stiffer, cornering feels like you're locked to the road. These new ones feel a bit like you're sloshing around on a waterbed – if my boss isn't listening...' She turns her head to check no one's eavesdropping, her hair flicks Jack's face as she does so. 'You're swaying all over the place, I thought I was going to be seasick going around a roundabout.'

'Right,' Jack says, breathing a sigh of relief that she's giving him anything but the hard sell, and also at the fact that he gave her the benefit of the doubt on her 'stiff-ride' enquiry. 'So, you'd recommend the previous model?'

She puts her hand on his arm; it's all he can do to stop himself from squeaking in surprise. 'Not only is it a better car, Jack – but, and this is the second thing – I've got one hidden out the back, exactly the same as mine except it's a cool black. It's less than two years old, twelve thousand on the clock, full-service history, and half the price of this. No skin off my nose, Jack. Your money, your car, but as a driver myself, I'm not trading mine in for one of these.'

'That's interesting,' Jack says, ordering his eyes not to look at her hand, which is still resting on his forearm. He's flummoxed. He can't tell if Shelly's seriously coming on to him, or if she's just one of those touchy-feely people who paws everybody who comes into the showroom.

He tries to concentrate on what she's saying about the car. He's got the money to buy every car in the bloody shop – well, he soon will have. What's thirty thousand or fifteen thousand for a decent car? He's only ever driven crap, and he's adored Beemers since he was driving his uncle's old Corgis and Dinkies around the living-room carpet.

But – why toss it away? Shelly certainly isn't trying to take every penny he's got out of his pocket, she seems to know what she's talking about, seems to care that he doesn't end up with a car he might not like.

'I had a feeling you'd see my point,' she says, nodding sagely. 'So, do you want to have a roll around on the waterbed, or shall we nip out back and go for a spin in a right little goer...?'

Jack wonders if he's ever had such an inviting invitation...

13
_____

THE RIGHT LITTLE GOER

JACK HITS THE GAS. '*BLOOD-Y HELL!*' he gasps, as they accelerate onto the dual carriageway.

'You see what I mean?' Shelly replies, the breeze through her open window blowing her hair back.

'It'll burn off my old car, that's for sure.' Jack keeps his eye on the speedo as they accelerate like he imagines a Saturn V off the Kennedy launch pad might. 'You say you've got one of these?'

'Yeah,' she says, 'red one. Wouldn't swap it for a Ferrari.'

'Wow!' Jack smiles, pushing himself back into the leather and scanning the dashboard, which looks equipped to take them to the moon. Beside him, Shelly looks dreamily out of the window, like she hasn't a care in the world. She's shed her jacket, and is looking cool and serene in a satiny white blouse. Jack's also slightly more relaxed now that her gaze has shifted from his eyes.

'You can always tell a decent driver,' she says, almost to herself, as they tear down the lane at 68mph. 'Takes about thirty seconds, especially when you get onto the dual carriageway, to know who you can trust, and who might drive you into a ditch.'

'And you feel you can trust me?' Jack asks, genuinely wanting to know.

'You're fine, I saw you checking the speedo. The kamikazes never do that. You've got your head screwed on. You'd be amazed how many dummies take me out on a test drive and try to hit the roundabout at eighty-five. They seem to think I like being knocked against the door pillar or strangled by the seatbelt. I'm always relieved when I get a proper driver, I can enjoy an hour out of the showroom and a nice natter, rather than worry about a mountain of insurance paperwork.'

She kicks her heels off into the footwell, and folds her bare feet underneath herself, like a rather contented cat settling in on the front seat. He feels her turning to smile at him, so he eases back slightly on the accelerator, and checks his mirrors again.

'You like the ride? Pretty stiff, isn't it?'

'Really good,' he replies, not detecting any hint of innuendo in her voice, but still hedging his bets, just in case. It's the sort of car that might have a hidden webcam recording everything for some YouTube *Candid Camera* channel.

He's finding it ever so hard to read her. In the showroom she was textbook professionalism: her clothes, pristine and fashionable, with a flash of style and colour bursting from the two-piece formality; her desk, neat, ordered, executive, everything in its place, no clutter; her assured approach, exuding calm, confidence, expertise – all in all a Bryan Ferry 'Slave to Love' kinda vibe.

But now, she's thrown her jacket over onto the back seat, kicked her shoes into the footwell, curled up on the front seat, and taken a leading role in The Boss's 'Jungleland', swirling sax-solo included. Jack steals an admiring glance at her as she stares idly out of her window; he wonders if there might possibly be romance in the air...

'You wanna take the roof down?' she asks, as they come to a halt at a red light.

His face gives her enough of an answer: *Do you want a flake in that, and chocolate sprinkles?*

'There's the button.' She points.

Jack hits it, then gapes as new horizons open. He can't help himself, he's grinning like the strawberry juice is slowly being poured. He finally manages to get his own window wound down, but only after Shelly short-circuits his search for a handle by pointing out another button. He leans his elbow on the sill and steers one-handed, second on the left has to be 'Thunder Road' – if there is a 'Thunder Road' in Burnt Oak.

'I often take mine up to Norfolk, my mum lives there, take her out for a spin along the coast road. When the sun's out, you'd almost think you were in Italy. She loves it. You've really gotta get out of town to enjoy a car like this.'

'I know Norfolk, my uncle used to teach up there,' Jack replies, happy to find a common interest, but imagining himself cruising down the Amalfi coast with the roof down, and María – or maybe now Shelly – sitting beside him.

'Where exactly?'

'He was in Dereham, but I've been up to the coast, Sheringham, Hunstanton. Lovely area.'

He checks his mirror, takes a racing line through a two-laned roundabout, but nice and smooth, Shelly barely moves in her seat, does she nod ever so slightly? He accelerates gently out of it, feels the hint of a pull back into his seat – much more Simon Templar than Neil Armstrong, not that he expects Shelly ever to have heard of *The Saint*.

'Driven anything like this before?' she asks.

He shakes his head. 'An old hatchback, nothing in this league.'

'It's a completely different experience, but you're clearly a bit of a natural.' He feels her smiling at him, but daren't take his eyes off the road. He nods instead. Sees himself from above, looking down from the helicopter he could now probably afford to buy. How quickly his life could change, depending on what he does with the money. He hasn't even collected it, and yet here he is in a flash car with a cool woman.

As he drives back towards the showroom, Shelly directs him through what she calls a shortcut to dodge the traffic, and he's enjoying himself so much that he doesn't realise he's turning into Cindy's street until it's too late.

'Shit!' he snaps, hitting the brakes sharply, to the annoyance of a driver who has followed him into the turn and is now stuck behind him, hand on horn, in the narrow one-way street.

'Problem?' Shelly quizzes.

'Someone I don't wanna see. She lives in this street.'

'We're a bit too far in to turn round, why don't you zip through as fast as you can? You're just drawing attention to us.'

'Right,' Jack says, nodding furiously. 'Good thinking.' He steps on the accelerator. It's an L-shaped street, and Cindy's flat is on the corner, facing them. As they approach, the door opens.

'Oh Christ,' Jack bleats, slipping lower and lower into his seat.

'Woah, Jack! Watch where you're going!' Shelly grabs the wheel. 'Look, keep the speed steady, and I'll steer for you.' It's clear he has no sight of the road as he's almost lying flat with his arms reaching up like a toddler waiting to be lifted. She guides them around the corner and tells him to slow for the next junction.

Once they're out on the main road, Jack reappears, blinking like a mole emerging through a lawn. 'Sorry about that,' he says moleishly, 'that was my wife's flat. We're getting divorced. I don't really want her to know I'm upgrading the car.'

'You don't have to explain.' Shelly laughs. 'I enjoyed the

excitement. It made a change from the usual handbrake turns and Formula One take-offs at the lights. We made quite a good team. I haven't had such fun on a test drive in ages. And actually, it was a bloke came out of the flat, jumped onto a bike, we nearly knocked him off! He had a bit of a wobble.' She giggles helplessly.

He parks up behind the showroom, and Shelly says, 'So, do you want to drive it home this evening?'

'I'd love to, but I couldn't organise it that quickly, I'm waiting for some money to come in. But can you put my name on it? I'll definitely come back in a couple of weeks and buy it.'

Shelly's smile fades. 'I can't do that, Jack. We've got two extremely interesteds coming back tomorrow, and my manager said he wants this sold and gone by the end of their visits. I've got his permission to knock up to two grand off the price to get it shifted. I'll give you all of that. But, if you want it, and really, it's the sale of the century, it has to be today.'

'Have you got others?'

'We had four at the beginning of last week, this is the last one left. We've got more of the waterbeds coming in tomorrow – please, don't ever tell my boss I call them that – and we simply need the space. That's why it's so cheap.'

'Bugger! Is there nothing we can do?'

'There is one thing. We could do a short-term lease agreement, say six months? Then at the end of that, you have the option to buy. In effect, you'll be hiring it for six months, so it'll add to the cost, but it'll mean it's yours this evening. I could have the paperwork done in half an hour...?'

'Would you give me anything in part exchange?' he asks. He's not sure why he does, he could easily leave his car where he's parked it and let it crumble to dust – nobody would steal it. Or he could simply ask a passer-by to help him lift it into the nearest bin. It's hard to believe how small 'small' cars used to be.

'Depends what you got,' Shelly replies enthusiastically.

'Ford Fiesta, it's parked right over the road.'

'Nice,' she says. 'Let's go take a butcher's...'

Jack immediately regrets having mentioned it. 'It's pretty old,' he shouts belatedly, but she's ticking across the yard towards the front, slipping her jacket on as she goes, shaking her hair out over the collar like a movie star; Jack stumbles behind like a teenage fan begging an autograph or a selfie. She stops at the gate, says nothing.

He creeps up behind her. It's clear there's only one Ford Fiesta in sight. Shelly's obviously a car girl, so she doesn't need clarification. It looks like she might need a sit down though; her shoulders are shaking.

'What d'you reckon?' Jack says, as Shelly starts to double over and make muffled, but audible, noises.

'I'm sorry,' she manages to gasp, as tears of mirth start to hit the concrete like rain. 'I've just never – seen – a...'

'Car that old?' Jack finishes her sentence, when it's clear it's medically impossible for her to do it without the aid of an oxygen cylinder, and maybe a shot of adrenalin. He smiles and laughs too. He's not offended; he's more afraid that Shelly will *think* that he's offended.

She straightens up, her face looking like Rudy Giuliani having been asked to model a knock-off, allegedly 'smudge-proof' mascara – in a sauna.

'I'm so sorry,' she gasps again, wiping mascara ineffectually, but she can see Jack's smile and she smiles herself. 'If I twist the manager's arm, he might give you twenty quid for it, but don't suggest driving it onto the front, yeah?'

14

THE DILEMMA

RICH CYCLES HOME SLOWLY. He loves cycling – except when he gets cut up by the loons in the fancy cars. He's sure the crazy blonde driving the Beemer that nearly hit him was sitting in the passenger seat. Some bloody people! Unless it was a left-hand drive – of course. German car, so maybe. He does a lot of thinking on his bike. He has a lot to think about – all of it concerning Cindy.

Cindy's great, he'd never deny it; she and Jack were completely unsuited. That had been obvious from the moment they showed up in Cricklewood, fresh from Thailand, smelling of saltwater and coconuts, searching for a registry office. Jack was caught up in some sort of holiday romance that had got way out of hand, and was powerless to hit the brakes, let alone reverse. Sure, he liked her, but a month shagging in a beach hut on Phuket, while high on wacky baccy and Malibu, was hardly a textbook dry run for a honeymoon in a damp flat in Cricklewood eating Pot Noodles and drinking plonk-in-a-box.

Rich had tried to warn Jack, a bit of friendly 'older brother' advice. That hadn't ended well. Trouble was, he'd once dated one of Jack's ex-girlfriends when they were teenagers. Double trouble was, Jack's view had been that she wasn't quite an 'ex'. Jack had come home one night ranting that they were finished, then the next day, claimed that he hadn't meant it literally. Accused Rich of stealing his girl. Complete misunderstanding that Jack continues to misunderstand to this day, Rich muses grimly.

It wasn't his fault that he found women to be easily attracted to him – and that Jack emitted nerdy warning vibes that he was a bit obsessive and lacked confidence and conversation. Not really many women's idea of a 'good catch', or even a 'make do'. Rich had toyed with the notion that maybe all the sun, wacky baccy and Malibu on a Phuket beach had turned Jack into a free chatting, relaxed Adonis. More likely it had simply addled Cindy's brain or given her double vision.

Rich had half hoped Cindy might come to her senses eventually – but the cancellation at the registry office meant that 'eventually' didn't get a chance to arrive quickly enough. He'd predicted the marriage wouldn't last, and he'd been proved right. The fact that his 'thing' with Cindy started before she asked Jack for a divorce had nothing to do with their breakup. That had been on the cards since the day they met. Anybody would be able to see that. Anybody except Jack, that is.

15

THE PARKING SPOT

Jack pulls the Beemer out of the showroom car park and gives Shelly a wave. He hits the button, and the roof folds back again. She waves like a five-year-old seeing off a favourite auntie after a particularly exciting weekend visit that's included iced lemonade and Black Forest gateau in the local tea shop.

Apart from the *stiff ride* moment, which he's now absolutely certain he got wrong, he's really enjoyed her company. She'd said she trusted his driving, and she really did seem to relax in the car – apart from when she had to steer, because he'd dropped down below the level of the windscreen. But they had been going slow, and she said she'd enjoyed that bit too.

She'd giggled that infectious giggle of hers all afternoon. In fact, if it had been a 'date', an official one, he'd have been pretty sure she would've agreed to see him again. Well, quite sure – which was about as sure as Jack was ever going to feel about his chances with any given potential girlfriend.

She even said they'd made a great team, and that was when he'd started to hope that she might have suggested they go for a drive together sometime, or maybe a coffee, or just asked for his phone number. There was no way he would have asked for hers.

God, no! And risk the embarrassment of her face turning to shock at the very idea that *that* was what he had been thinking about all the time, when she'd simply been enjoying a stiff ride with a skilled driver? He's decided he should learn a few more of these 'motoring phrases' that driving aficionados like Shelly must use all the time. No doubt he could find some on the internet.

He consoles himself with the fact that she has his phone number on the leasing agreement. It's his outside bet for a date with Shelly. It's a long shot – probably another fourteen million to one. Not the best odds, but he's done it once. Does that make it coming up again more or less likely? You'd think it'd be more likely – his luck's obviously in. But that maybe isn't the best logic. He got lucky once, hugely lucky, so the chances of it happening again? The next day?

There's nothing he can do – well, nothing he's *going* to do about it now. She can call him if she ever does decide that she'd quite fancy a spin out to the coast with him, with the roof off. He's rescued his Springsteen tapes from the Fiesta, but the Beemer won't talk to them. Now that he looks at it, he can't even see a slot for the CDs he has back home. It's probably got a USB port hidden under a flap somewhere, or maybe it's something to do with that Bluetooth thingy that he's never worked out. He punches the radio on and searches some equally appropriate music to take him back to his lonely flat.

He finds that Bobby someone, 'Don't Worry Be Happy'. Hmmm, hardly what he'd call 'driving music'. He searches again: Christ! It's 'Barbie Girl' by he's no idea who (or even *whom*) that he turns right down before anyone in the street notices it's blaring from his car. Another search brings him 'Mull of Kintyre'. Mother of God! A summer shower starts to spit at him, and he's stuck in heavy traffic, so he closes the roof and vows to get some Bluetooth Boss sorted out for his next stiff ride.

———

Jack pulls into his street and cruises for a parking space. He's remembered to retrieve his permit from the windscreen of the Fiesta, before handing the keys over to Shelly; he'll deal with the paperwork for that tomorrow, having already sorted the insurance at the showroom. It's never too difficult to find a spot in his street, especially at this time of day, when the school run releases a handful of spaces for an hour or so: their previous occupants all now stuck in the traffic jam he's just escaped from.

Right on cue, a red Corsa shedding rust pulls out of a space in front of his door. Perfect! His luck really is in. He pulls past, hits reverse, and watches the little screen that shows what's happening behind him, complete with a bleeping sound. His dad might not have approved, but he's pretty chuffed with it. He's halfway in when his heart sinks.

On screen he sees the door to the flat next door open. Out steps Lavinia. He watches her like she's a character in a soap opera on TV. She unfurls her umbrella; it's got blue, yellow and red stripes. She's their Romanian neighbour who works in the town hall; the colours are the national flag (she's told them).

They're on nodding terms, he's on nodding terms with half the street: the problem is – she does an aerobics class with Cindy. They *talk* to each other, gossip and chat, lots of goss, sometimes in each other's kitchens (when Cindy lived here), sometimes in coffee shops (even when Cindy was living here). He's no idea whether they're still meeting for coffee, but he suspects they probably are. They got on well, snippets of gossip about X and Y, nuggets of juicy scam about who knows what:

you'll never guess who...? and *I couldn't believe my ears,* or *I see Jack's got a fancy new car...*

He slips the Beemer into first and presses the accelerator, pulling almost soundlessly down the street and round the corner – smooth as Bond. He realises he's got a problem. A much bigger problem than Lavinia, although she's a potential shitstorm of epic proportions on her own. Not her, *personally*, of course...

The street is almost exclusively two-storey Victorians – or are they Georgian, or even prehistoric – many with loft conversions, and nearly all split into flats. Some of them are reasonably sized, but the majority, like Jack's, are pretty small one-bedrooms or bedsits. The residents are almost all renters: loads of singles, one-parent families, one-child families: as pretty much anyone with more than one child will be parking their family saloons, people carriers and Hummers somewhere else. Not in this street. What the people in this street drive – and park here – (if they have cars at all) are small old cars: battered Novas (the 'boxy' ones), rusty Minis (the ones that really were 'mini'), Metros on bricks – and forty-year-old Fiestas that so amuse car-showroom staff if you offer them in part exchange. Beemer convertible? You'd as likely find a Lunar Roving Vehicle.

The problem that all this causes Jack, which he's realising as he drives further away, is twofold: the curtain twitchers, and the children. The curtain twitchers will be on red alert 24/7 the longer his car remains in the street. The longer it stays there, the more likely it's owned by a resident. So, whose is it? The street spooks will be on it like a team of Harry's finest. The children will want to look at it, maybe stroke it, hear him start it, the cheekier buggers might even beg a spin round the block with the roof down. All of this will travel by the bush telegraph, which doesn't really ever have much 'breaking news', and make its way to the Banerjees; Mr Beedley, street gossip extraordinaire; Lavinia; and by any of those routes, back to Cindy.

Conclusion: he can't park there. If he parks in his street, it'll be a more efficient way of showing Cind his new car (and thereby telling her that he's won the lottery) than sending her a photo of him sitting nude on the bonnet via WhatsApp. He might as well park it in front of her flat at three in the morning and stick his hand on the horn.

But where *can* he park? Most of the streets have a residential zone parking system so he's hemmed in to his own zone, or he has to find some free parking somewhere else. He doesn't really want to spend too much time cruising his own zone, in case Cindy or any of her friends spot him driving his sleek black Beemer convertible; he's already noticed how it turns heads. He'd loved the sensation – for all of about twenty minutes. Now he wishes he'd stuck with the Fiesta. What was he *thinking?* How could he not see *this* coming? What's *wrong* with him? He drives out of his zone.

On a small quiet shopping street he finds some free parking. It'll take him fifteen minutes to jog back to the flat, but what can he do? It's a chippy, bookie and mini-mart zone: all the essentials of modern life. He spots a large free space and reverses into it. He's getting to love his little screen showing what's happening behind him. He can see that there's another car reversing in at the same time, but the space is easily big enough for both of them.

He pulls on the handbrake. The little screen shows the other car still reversing in; he hopes they've seen him. What he doesn't know, is that he's tuned to the horror channel...

TONK!

It's not a hard bump, but it rocks him forward. He feels it as much as hears it. It's not a big noisy tonk, it's quite a quiet one, more of a *crump* than a tonk. But it's the force of the crumpy tonk that worries him. The Beemer's still rocking on its notoriously *stiff* suspension, like a child on one of those springy things that look so dangerous in a playground.

He sighs. He's barely owned the car an hour. Fucking *idiot!* Why weren't they looking where they were going? He could see it was a small, pretty old model, it'd better not be a bloody Fiesta. They obviously haven't got the TV rear viewer gizmo. Why aren't they standard, like seatbelts? Like *seats?*

He steps out of the car; a huge raindrop hits him on the head like a well-aimed water bomb. The other driver is getting out too, tugging on a coat. Jack takes a breath, ready to let rip. He knows he'd stopped; he'd even put the bloody handbrake on. If they're going to argue it, he's going to give them both barrels...

'I'm so sorry, I'm so sorry. I didn't see you pull in. I thought the space was–'

She starts to cry, can't say any more for a moment. He notices she's driving a Fiat Panda. It looks a twentieth century vintage, certainly an extinct model, all boxy corners and massive black bumpers. It's a sort of pink colour, but he's sure it was once bright red, he saw enough of them around, when he was about seven.

Her tears are now a torrent, it's a ridiculous amount of liquid, he's never seen such a wet face in such a short period of time outside of a swimming pool or an Icelandic waterfall. It makes her look pathetically vulnerable; she's around his age, millennials taking over the world, he thinks she's wearing a nurse's uniform under her coat.

His dad warned him once, font of all motoring knowledge: 'If you ever get into a smash, even if it's your fault, in fact *especially* if it's your fault, never admit it, their insurers will take you to the cleaners...'

'I'm so sorry,' she whispers again; you'd think she'd knocked him off a motorbike in a head-on, the way she's reacting. 'I came in a bit quick to get out of the traffic, and my back window's a bit dirty. It was my fault. I'm so sorry...'

Jack walks around to the back of the Beemer, praying there's no damage. Praying he can turn her catastrophe into a closing-time anecdote, maybe put a bit of a smile on her face – at least get her to stop crying for a while.

So, there is a bit of damage after all. It's quite a shocking amount of damage actually, given the speed she was going at, and the lack of any sort of 'collision' noise that would've attracted the rubberneckers and the ghouls. Truth be told, there's nobody stopping to gawp, hardly anyone's giving them a second glance as they scuttle by in the rain, which is getting heavier, right on fucking cue... Jack looks at the damage. It's hard to believe she's done it with a Fiat Panda that looks ready to fall to pieces if you drove it over cobbles.

She's hit him dead centre with the corner of her Panda bumper. He's never noticed before, but the old Panda bumpers look pretty sturdy. They wrap all the way around the car like they were originally designed to be used as dodgems, until the cabriolet lozenges won that contract, and all the Pandas were dumped into the showrooms as Fiat's Hail-Mary option. Her bumper looks undamaged. It's almost funny, the rest of her bodywork has more ponks and dinks than the lunar surface, but the bumper looks fresh out of the packet. He wonders if it's made of concrete. His Beemer bumper, on the other hand, has seen better days.

Well, it's seen better minutes – not three minutes ago, in fact, it was looking pretty smooth. Now? It wouldn't be over-egging it to say it's been destroyed. It's like someone's fired an RPG from up the road and has blown his bumper to smithereens. It's caved in completely, like she's driven into it really slowly, but kept on driving while the bumper has collapsed like a warm soufflé and split in the middle making repair an impossibility.

For good measure, both corners have popped off their mountings and are now flying free from the rest of the bodywork, as if the whole thing might start flapping and take off into the gloom like some bored rook at a wet funeral. His number plate is ground zero, the corner of her bumper has detonated on it. Wouldn't be so bad if it was just a bog standard, but this Beemer number plate has a fancy chrome (or maybe it's sterling silver) surround, and a light, so the wires and gubbins are hanging out like a particularly amateurish appendectomy. No wonder she's bloody crying – he feels like bursting a few tear ducts himself.

16

THE DEAL... WITH BENEFITS

'I'LL PAY FOR EVERYTHING,' the Panda driver sniffles behind him. 'I am insured, but if there was any way we could keep this off the insurance, I'd – it's just, I couldn't afford to insure mine if I lost my no-claims. But I'd promise to pay you. Do you think it would be more than a hundred? I could probably pay that off in a couple of months or so – maybe three. Would instalments be okay? I think I might have twenty pounds in my purse now...' There's something pathetic about the way she's twisting her fingers together, like she's trying to loosen a couple in order to offer them as a deposit.

A hundred!? Jack thinks. Then he almost laughs. Now he knows how Shelly felt when she saw his Fiesta parked across the road. A hundred? It's a ludicrous proposition, from so far over the cuckoo's nest it's practically in orbit. A hundred? What is she on? The bulb for the number plate light gizmo thingy is probably gonna be twenty quid on its own, before VAT.

He wonders if the camera for the reversing TV is sited there as well: that'll cost an extremely-good-looking penny. And as for the bumper, its life as a bumper is over. Once ground to shards and mixed with some glue it might reappear as some kind of children's soft-play surface in an East European country, but its life in the fast lane of a western motorway is over. Kaput.

A new Beemer bumper? For the cabriolet, sir? He can't imagine coming home with change from five hundred. He could be wrong – it's probably more. Then fitting: two, three hundred more? And, oh boy, he's just noticed, there's a bit of a dent on the boot. If he squats down, as surreptitiously as he can, he can see it's actually bent the whole thing all the way up to the window. New boot? Three hundred? Four? How would he know? But if he's wrong, he knows he'll be under. Way under. When has anyone come home from a car repair and said, *Wow, it was so much cheaper than I feared?* He wonders if she's even managed to warp the chassis. They'll be into four figures if that's the case. He couldn't have done more damage if he'd attacked it for half an hour with a gang of mates swinging sledgehammers. A hundred? A *hundred?* Thank God Shelly's not here to start giggling.

He straightens up, turns to face this woman. She's a terrible sight. Way worse than his bumper's looking. She looks destroyed. She reminds him of some film he's seen: POWs with no hope left. The rain batters her head, drips off her nose. She's pulled her coat across her uniform. If she were smart, savvy, calculating, she'd have left her coat open, nurse's uniform on the RTA catwalk to win the sympathy vote. But she hasn't. She's just standing in the rain in front of him, head bowed, wringing her hands, waiting for the sentence, waiting for execution. Jack still hasn't 'let rip'.

He feels like crying. But he also feels like hugging her, saying it's all right, don't worry about it. But he knows he can't. It'll look like he's offering her some sort of 'deal' – with 'benefits'. Worse, that's what *she'll* think. He shudders at the thought; realises he hasn't spoken since he got out of his car. He takes a long breath, wonders what the hell he's going to say. She seems to wince, like a trembling fawn in the cross hairs.

He sighs. The problem is, he knows how she's feeling, crying over a bit of buckled plastic. He understands the financial pressure she's obviously under. Well, he did – before yesterday. If someone ever cancelled a lesson at short notice, he never thought, *that's an extra hour's telly*; it was always, *how am I going to pay the electricity bill?* He's lived that life, until yesterday. Now? New Beemer bumper? He could buy a whole new car and not notice it financially. But it's not really that, it's the thought that he knows that he's the cause of her pain, if in a roundabout sort of way.

His heart melts as she does her best, but fails, to compose herself. Her shuddering breaths sear into his consciousness like there are no other sounds in the city. More tears plip onto her coat, fallen open again as she wipes the rain, or the tears, it's hard to tell, from her face. Her uniform accuses him of being some sort of tax-dodging, Beemer-driving, city slicker, while her black, scuffed, flat nurses' shoes, are undoubtedly sucking in water from the puddle she seems unable to move from.

He shakes his head. 'Forget it. I have a mate who can knock it out,' he lies. Knock it out? *Knock it out?* She's knocked it so far in, Mike Tyson couldn't knock it out in his prime. A Tyson-Muhammad Ali tag team would have no chance, even if they had the sledgehammers. He thinks BMW probably haven't got a machine in their armoury that could knock this out. He hopes she knows little about car repairs, or she'll see his comment for the crap it is.

Her jaw drops open a fraction, her whole face loses the tension that has been holding it in place. She suddenly looks stunningly beautiful, in an un-made-up, rain-streaked, tired-out-after-a-long-shift, shocked, frightened, defeated, no-claims bonus-less, and thoroughly miserable, end-of-her-tether sort of way. It's not your traditional 'camera-shoot' sort of beauty.

'No. I-I couldn't,' she stammers, pointing, rather ludicrously, at the scene of carnage in the gutter next to them, as if he might not have noticed the small matter of a tank ploughing into the back of his (once 'spanking') new Beemer. 'Look, it's damaged. I can pay for it, as long as I don't lose my no-claims, it's not a problem, you might have to wait a month or two, but I'll pay for it all, I promise...'

Then there's that *I promise...* It's the *I promise* of a four-year-old girl, promising to be good for Santa: completely, absolutely, undoubtedly genuine. She means it as a legal contract; there's no way on earth she'll break that promise, no matter what. Nuclear warfare could destroy the city and he knows, he *knows*, that she'll be back to this spot the next week with a grubby tenner in her hand to meet the next instalment. He wants to be anywhere else on the planet instead of being here, the cause of so much anguish, to a sweet little four-year-old who's in tears because she's dropped his favourite toy and broken it. How could he be so mean? Monster!

As for paying for it, he thinks she'll be paying him until she's drawing her pension, not that he gives a toss about the money. He really doesn't. How could he? Money? He has fifty kilos of the stuff – nearly a hundred litres of it. He has a meaningless amount of money. The only thing he cares about is that she's genuinely sorry, bitterly so. He's threatened – or the situation's threatened – her precarious financial situation and he can feel it, and he can fix it. He almost wishes he could tell her that he's a double millionaire, because now she's looking guilty about accepting charity from a stranger and he's not sure he'll be able to tolerate that for long.

'No, really, you don't have to,' he says. 'It won't be difficult to knock it out...' He suppresses a smile; wishes he could share the joke. 'Look. It's only a bumper. Nobody got hurt (another of his dad's *rules of the road*), that's the only thing that really matters when you have a bump.' A bump? He looks at what's left of the rear end of his new car and has to bite the inside of his lip. A bump? George Bush would've called it *Shock and Awe*. But a minor plus side: she's even more stunning, now that she's looking at him like he's just landed from another planet, the planet where heroes live.

They're parked right outside a small coffee shop. If he had the nerve, or if this were a Richard Curtis film, he'd ask her in for a drink. A chance to get dry, a chance for her to recover from the shock, dry her tears (if she could find them mixed in with the rainwater). But Jack being Jack, he hesitates. What if she thinks he's trying to take advantage of the position she's in? Or maybe it's his usual problem with women that he quite fancies: all the cheery banter that they've been sharing will suddenly dry up when it kind of turns into a sort of 'date'. He'll get tongue-tied (as usual) and spoil the atmosphere that has him painted as a sort of knight in (slightly crumpled) armour.

He feels the silence lengthening, as it always does in these situations – the ones where he isn't full of wacky baccy and Malibu... *Just ask her!* he screams inside his head. Rich would ask her. Rich would get her to buy him a bloody doughnut!

Let's have a coffee together, you must've had a bit of a shock...

That's all he probably has to say...

'Have a nice evening,' he says instead, knowing he'll regret it, bleeping the Beemer and turning towards home.

———

Milly (she hates being called Millicent) goes to say something, but his back is turned, and she's dreadfully flustered. She surveys the scene as he's walking away. Her life has been on a rapid wash cycle for what? Ten minutes? In that time, she's feared a road-rage assault from a Beemer driver; she's lost her no-claims, and probably her car with it; the bus and Tube to work would take her hours and cost her a fortune. Then suddenly, her life's been returned to her, undamaged. Like a gift. As far as she can see, her Panda is okay. The guy, she thought he was going to explode when he got out of his car, bloody *Beemer*, for God's sake. But he didn't explode, he simply looked calmly at the damage. And then, he just brushed it off. Even the rain's stopped, and the sun's starting to come out again.

She'd better park her car properly and hope his bumper doesn't come off completely when she does. Then, she's going to treat herself to a coffee. Try to get herself dried out a little, she's shivering, although she knows that's shock, she's never had an accident before.

———

As she sits with her cappuccino, the warmth invading her insides like some magic potion in a fairy tale for small children, she goes over what's just happened. He must have thought her *such* an idiot: driving like a plonker, crying so much! How did *that* happen? She *never* does that! And then! Suggesting the repair might be a hundred? A *hundred?* He was driving a BMW! The soft-top? A hundred? He must have thought she was a moron. *A hundred!*

And how would she ever have paid for whatever it *was* going to cost, on her salary? She'd have been paying him off for years. And then, he just brushed it off! What was it he said? *Forget it? Nobody got hurt?* What sort of a guy said that? Colin Firth? Hugh Grant, maybe? *Jesus!* Yeah, him as well.

She sips her coffee, can't decide whether the relief she's feeling is real, or if it's still a bit of shock. She's a nurse, knows it's probably shock. She sits, thoughtless, for a moment. Then the familiar, lonely melancholy starts to seep back, like a fog rolling up a slow-flowing river. She's cried a lot this evening, that's *so* not like her. She's surprised to find she has yet another couple of tears in stock as they roll down her cheek. She berates herself softly, and sadly, as she wipes them away.

You stupid cow! she mouths silently, wringing her fingers as she does, whenever she's stressed. She thinks about the stranger. She didn't even ask him his name! She should have asked him his name. What sort of guy did that? So calm. So measured. *It's only a bumper? Nobody got hurt?* So unlike a bloody Beemer driver, or what she thought all bloody Beemer drivers were like. Not that she knows many – *any*. But they're obviously not. Certainly not him. He actually looked more sad than angry, she thinks now. He didn't seem to have an ounce of anger in him. He was actually quite cute, and obviously kind…

Oh, shit! When will you learn? You do it every time. You were even outside a sodding coffee shop…

Why didn't you ask him…?

17

THE NIGHT

JACK CAN'T GET her out of his head; he's barely slept. Bloody, *bloody* idiot! Him, that is, not her.

She's the nurse. The nurse in the summer rainstorm. The drenched nurse. The crying nurse. The beautiful, drenched, crying nurse who can't drive for toffee but who cares about that? She's honest, and fair, and hard-working, and saves people's lives and has no showy mannerisms, or an edgy, snarky, sarky attitude, or a faux accent from an American, well, Australian sitcom, or high-rising *fucking* terminals.

Why – didn't – he – *fucking* – ask – her?

It's been the story of his love life. With one, notable, catastrophic exception – he's always duffed it. Always failed to make the move that any other sensible bloke would've made.

This has been a bit stressful. Shall we get a coffee and sort it out?

That would probably have done it.

But there he goes again. *Probably.* Rich would never have said *probably*.

It's been a long day, and I'm drenched. Let's get a coffee.

That might have clinched it.

Might.

Why can't he...

It's pouring, let's go in here, get a coffee.

Oh, please. I'm soaked, my shoes are leaking.

I'm Jack, by the way.

I can be anybody you like, cos you never asked me my name, you idiot.

No! She'd never say that.

I'm Jane – no, I'm Scarlett.

What a pretty name.

Thanks, let me get the coffees. I insist. I feel such a wally.

It's fine, really.

I'll never be able to repay you.

There's nothing to repay.

You're so kind, I was really afraid you were going to be angry.

What's there to get angry about, it was an accident.

Do you live around here...?

He stares at the ceiling. The beams from the cars in the street outside moving over it like a lighthouse lantern warning ships away. Does he do that? Warn women off? He's not talking about Cindy. Christ, that wasn't him at all. That was madness. But this-this- *opportunity?* Whatever you want to call it. She was so nice, kind, genuine, unshowy. She certainly brings out the adjectives in him. So, why didn't he just *ask* her...?

He's not lamenting the fact that he's not in bed with her right now. Her phone number would've been enough. A vague *I'll call you. Let's have a drink,* would've probably worked.

Yeah – but there he goes again...

Probably...

18

THE OFFER HE CAN'T REFUSE

'I'M GOING TO BLACKMAIL HIM,' Cindy says by way of a *Breaking News* announcement as she drags on their early-morning, post-coital fag.

Rich doesn't move, but his brain has a life of its own, and it's gone for a wander. *Oh shit,* is his first thought. *Where is this going to take us?* Shagging your brother's (soon to be) ex-wife is one thing, getting caught up in some sort of financial civil war is quite another. Rich has his limits. He's not sure where those limits are, but they're out there somewhere.

'I'm not going to divorce him until he's given me a million. He can have the extra point three. You can't say fairer than that.'

Rich takes the cigarette, takes a pull that (he hopes) might keep him out of the conversation for ten or fifteen minutes.

'You see, I've been on the internet...'

Jesus.

'And it says there that assets in a divorce should be shared fifty-fifty, that's the basic assumption in UK law, but I can let him have the extra point three as a sort of goodwill gesture.'

Oh God.

'And I've also discovered, on the lottery website, that he's got six months to claim his prize. After that, he's lost it. We only have to wait six months.'

We? Where's this royal 'we' coming from?

'So, I'm going to go over and see him tomorrow. Have it out like adults. Give him a gobful if I have to. He'll come good. One point three for him, a mil for us. Can't say fairer.'

Us?

'What d'ya think?'

Rich takes another long drag before surrendering the ciggy. What the hell *does* he think?

19

THE GEN Z ITALIANS

JACK'S GOT a nine o'clock with a group of six lively Italian students, his Gen Z gang, all at least ten years younger than himself. They're loud and sassy, arriving like primary kids to their first school disco, taking over his flat with their presence, their movement, their noise, their tinkling phones, their chewing gum, their laughter, their bright clothes, their perfume and aftershave, and irresistible accents. Within seconds, his usually tranquil flat is transformed into a decent mock-up of an (Italian) sixth-form common room, complete with takeaway coffee cups and chocolate-bar wrappers.

They pay him five quid apiece and spend most of the hour flirting with each other or whatsapping on their phones. Their English isn't bad, it's a bit present tense: *I go cinema yestoday; I and Isabella, we make the pizza on the choose-day with the – how you say the ananas?* It's easy money: their parents pay by direct debit, so he gets his thirty quid even if none of them show – and if they're not telling, then neither is he. If any of them fancy doing a bit of 'work', they mostly like to gossip, asking him about pop stars and soap opera celebrities – his *Mastermind* specialist subjects. They're a breath of fresh air compared to some of the first-certificate exam jockeys who bombard him with questions about mixed conditionals or concessive clauses. He's much happier chewing the fat with a gang of breezy Italians than he is trying to remember the difference between compound and complex sentences.

He thinks Marco and Beatrice are an item, but he can't be sure. He's almost certain that Luca and Roberto are a pair, and possibly Isabella and Sofia. But, if he's honest, they're all so touchy feely, forever switching seats and hugging or stroking whoever's in range, they might all be sharing one of those giant six-seater beds he saw yesterday. They make him feel there's a whole new world out there somewhere, and then some. He envies their live-in-the-moment exuberance, wondering if it's anything to do with their Italianness – and does that have one or two 'n's?

Isabella and Sofia are on his case today, while the other four are either chatting in Italian or whatsapping, almost certainly in Italian. They're concerned about his single status, taking his divorce from Cindy as a given. Isabella has her arm around his shoulder, lounging on him like he's some ancient loveable grandfather with not long to live who they're encouraging to buy a dog.

'Where you go for find new girlfren, Jack? You go disco? Where you go?'

Jack tries to shrug off the questions, directs them towards a conversational exercise about buying a train ticket in one of the textbooks they never use.

Sofia closes the book, attacks him from another angle. 'We go West End for dancing, Jack. You come dancing with us. You find beautiful girl dancing.' She waves her arms in the air and wiggles in her seat; Jack feels he would rather have a tooth pulled than let this conversation play out.

Then Isabella explodes with an idea; he imagines Vesuvius

or Etna would be a bit like her. 'Wait one minute, wait one minute,' she commands, snapping her phone to life and pummelling the screen with her thumbs. It fills Jack with awe every time he sees them in action: how these youngsters perform the skills of a professional typist, at about the same speed, if not faster, using only their thumbs on a keyboard the size of a matchbox. 'Look thees, look thees...' Isabella gasps, handing the screen to Jack. He feels a glow of pride that she's still in English while in this state of hyper excitement. He should move to Italy, could be a lot of work there...

It's the Facebook page of a woman called Gabriella. He flicks down the entries. Gabriella seems to be a model for the smallest bikinis in the world, although sometimes, it appears, only the bottom halves. She appears to live on a sunny beach, surrounded by a rolling cast of muscular bronzed guys with teeth a horse would envy.

'Thees Gabriella, you can call to her Gabby. She very nice girl. She feeneesh with boyfriend las week,' Isabella starts, sounding like a matchmaker introducing him to a blind date in a busy pub.

'Oh yes, very good,' Sofia joins in, scrolling to a particularly nice picture of a topless Gabby, staring coyly back at the camera over her shoulder, while an Italian dobbin leers from the background. 'Gabby, she very lonely, she like many boys, she like you very much. She no speak English but maybe she learn quickly, quickly, *quickly* if she you girlfren...'

'You send fren request, Gabby she like very much the Engleesh boys. She say yes!' Isabella suggests. Jack imagines Isabella as a sort of Latina Emma, Jane Austen's matchmaker-in-chief. She'd have spiced up Regency England a bit, sorted Harriet out in a jiffy – whatever *that* might be in Italian.

'I don't actually have a Facebook page,' he mumbles, which is a lie. He probably can't remember his password, but he does have a Facebook page, and five friends: Rich, Cheesie, Beano, Smithy and Cindy. The last time he looked at it, he's pretty sure, was when he added Cindy, about a year ago. He certainly doesn't want pictures of a topless Gabby popping up on his screen – especially if Scarlett, the woman in the Panda, by some miracle gets in touch. But his lie shuts his two Italian matchmakers up for a few seconds. They stare at him like his nose has fallen off onto one of the unopened textbooks lying on the table.

'You no have the *Facebook?*' Isabella manages to gasp.

Jack shrugs, feeling like they've discovered he's forgotten to put his trousers on this morning. Sofia nudges the other four out of their Italian practice, whispers something fast and incomprehensible, except for the word *Facebook*, which is flagged with eyebrows on trampolines.

Six pairs of brown Italian eyes stare at him with a mixture of wonder and pity. He suddenly has their rapt attention; it's probably wrapped or even rapped; he can never remember which. He decides he'll start next week's lesson by telling them he doesn't use Twitter, or Instagram either: that might keep them quiet for a few minutes.

20

THE FACEBOOK TARDIS

Jack resurrects his Facebook page as soon as the Italians have said their chows. He wishes his brain wouldn't do this, but he has no control over it. It takes a delightful little word, *ciao*, full of Italian charm and style, maybe even a dollop of *brio*, and splatters it with an ugly image of some building-site labourer from Kilburn, elbows splayed, chowing down on a steaming plate of steak-and-kidney pud, peas and mash. Isabella's delicately dropped little *ciaos*, or sometimes even prettier *ciao-ciaos*, have gone forever. It must be some disease that all amateur linguists are susceptible to. There's no known treatment. *Ciao* is now forever *chow* in his head.

He barely recognises his Facebook page. He was never much of a Facebooker. Is that a word? If it ever was, he imagines it's now gone out of fashion. He doesn't hear anybody saying it. There must be a record for the shortest-lived words or phrases in history. Betamax, maybe? Floppy disc? Proud Brexiteer? His page looks more cluttered than he remembers, he's not sure what all the buttons are for. Zuckerberg's clearly been tweaking since he last looked. Jack's last post (is that what they're called?) is a year ago. It's from Thailand: him and Cind in their swimming togs, looking happy on a white-sand beach, holding coconuts and sipping something almost certainly alcoholic through straws. Where has that happy couple gone? Oh, yeah! Cricklewood.

But, a surprise! He's got more friends than he thought. He was sure he only had the five, but he's got twelve! He vaguely remembers the other members of Cindy's Aussie gang; he must've friended them. They do a lot of posting, he sees, as he explores their lives from ten-thousand miles away. Mostly it's them in bars or at sports events. But twelve friends.

It's still a bit pathetic, he feels, regretting that he hadn't confessed to the Italians and thereby undoubtedly increasing his tally by a full fifty per cent in a flurry of flashing thumbs. Although, it would've been a bit more than fifty per cent, he muses, remembering the almost-clad Gabriella – and maybe even a few of the muscular dobbins as well. But he consoles himself with the fact that he rarely uses it. Doesn't look like Rich uses it much either. Or Smithy. Cheesie's done a few, mostly snaps of himself and Debs in front of East Asian temples and soft-sand beaches.

And Cindy's more of a user than he knew. Why didn't he know that? Did she keep it a secret? He could hardly think so. He knew she was on Facebook. They were friends, or had been, when they had been. Clearly they still are – in the 'Facebook' sense of the word if not the other sense, the 'real-life' sense.

He tries to remember why he'd signed up in the first place. It had certainly been BC, before Cindy. He has a vague memory of one quiet evening in the pub: him, Rich, Cheesie, Beano, Smithy. No good reason. Nothing to do, so let's do Facebook. It certainly didn't take off for him. What did he have to post? Went to the supermarket, taught the Italians, United lost...? Especially as he'd probably be telling them all about it in the pub later. Maybe not the super. Or the Italians.

And they'd all know about United anyway. No. It hadn't taken off for him.

Although, there had also been the great *English-language-group* fiasco. His toes burrow into the carpet at the very thought of it. In his defence, Facebook, like most modern internet stuff, didn't come with a thick handbook, for any of its (thick, like him) users to consult, in order to understand how it worked. You seemed to have to make it up as you went along or ask someone who was a week-or-so ahead of you in the adventure.

He'd started to wonder if Facebook might help him to drum up some more customers for his English classes. He spotted a group calling itself *English Learners*, and joined it, hoping to befriend some prospective clients. Sadly, all the English Learners seemed to live in China or Japan, and Jack had no idea about the possibilities of teaching English via the internet. He was looking for bums on the seats around his kitchen table. So his interest waned.

Although he did enjoy the little puzzles that popped up, seemingly out of nowhere. *Can you name a word that starts and ends with the letter E?* Of course he could. *Edible, escape, exercise...* He posted twenty-eight in all, feeling pleased with his proficiency. He got into quite a habit of solving a couple of puzzles every morning before breakfast. Then the group administrators messaged him, politely pointing out that they'd seen he was a native English speaker, and a teacher to boot, so could he please stop giving the answers to the puzzles they were setting for their students...

Beano used to post photos of himself and his latest car outside football grounds. He'd got Wembley, Arsenal, Spurs. It was harmless enough, mildly interesting, a bit weird. The most interesting thing, Jack had always thought, was how did he get the pictures? It was never a match day, there was never another soul in sight, and they weren't selfies – unless he had the arms of a chimpanzee. He must've accosted some passing stranger, or hauled someone out of the club offices. Would you come and take a picture of me and my car in front of Stamford Bridge? Definitely a bit weird. Borderline *avoid at all costs*.

It had seemed so pointless. Jack got so fed up seeing a grinning Beano appearing outside QPR or West Ham, and then Beano showing them his snaps in the pub, that he turned off his notifications. That's when he forgot all about it, as did the others, except Beano. Until he went to Thailand and met Cindy. She was all into Facebook and he got caught up in it again for a while. At least he'd made them all jealous with a tsunami of pix of him and Cindy playing volleyball, him and Cindy on the beach, him and Cindy on the beers... But then, when they returned, he was back to the supermarket, and he lost interest again, when Cricklewood replaced Phuket as his status location. But she, evidently, hadn't.

He scrolls through her page, feeling like a burglar alone in her flat, rifling through her underwear drawers – would they be her drawers' drawers? Lots of fit-looking smilers on spinning bikes, on weights machines, in impossible-looking yoga positions. Some snaps of a few London landmarks, the Eye, Big Ben. He has to go back a fair way before he sees himself. A selfie of them he couldn't remember her having taken in a bar somewhere. Him, looking a bit glum. Was this near the end? More selfies in bars, a bit happier, maybe? He reaches their honeymoon: a wet weekend in Brighton, start as you mean to finish? Another bar selfie. They look happy. Ish. As happy as you can look with the windows behind you blurry with the rain that was lashing outside.

And then, their wedding day. He's not sure why it surprises him so. He's not sure he's seen these. He's no memory of the three of them, Rich, best man, sheltering under a tree, it seems, for an 'all done' commemoration selfie. Is that a trace of trepidation in his eyes? Was he, even then, aware that it might not last? Can't have been. But the suspicion is worryingly strong. Cindy and Rich look happy enough...

Deeper in the Facebook Tardis he finds Thailand. Loads of pix. The pair of them playing volleyball, then in the surf, selfies in a bar with palm trees visible out through the glassless windows. No look of trepidation in his eyes there – alcohol poisoning, maybe... There's even a couple of them in bed, looking dishevelled, like they've just finished... You know... He doesn't remember her having taken them. It's like looking at another person, not her, *him*.

He doesn't recognise the person in the bed who looks like him with a tan, can't find any memory of having been that person, living that moment. The memory has gone. If somebody said the snap was actually some deep-fake Photoshop mashup, that he'd never really been there, he'd be more than tempted to believe them. But he knows it's not. But how can you believe Facebook more than your own memory? It was only a year ago. It's like his memory, the real, *working* one, is no longer housed in his head – it's on Cindy's Facebook page, stored at 1 Hacker Way. He's jolted by his loss of control of it.

He flips back some more, to her pre-Thai life, before they met. It's all sports kit and smiling gymsters, beers and barbies back home in Oz. Crowds of tanned twenty-somethings group-hugging each other like a gang of over-friendly octopuses, or octopi: he should look that up. He feels like a voyeur suddenly. Will she know he's been looking at her pictures? He doesn't think so. Why are they still friends? He wonders if he should de- or unfriend her. Wonders if they're real words. Wonders why she hasn't given him the flick, as she'd say, as she *did* – in real life.

He's about to put his phone down, depressed at the Pathé News feel of his past, which someone else owns, when he sees he's got three friend requests. He's no idea who these people are. Why would they want to be friends with him if he doesn't know who they are? It's a bit creepy. Although, one of them is quite good-looking. Lovely smile. Cherry Smalling? He's quite certain he's never been introduced to a Cherry anybody. He'd have remembered. Was Cherry short for something? He can only think of Cherryade. He'd have remembered, surely. The other two are blokes. Again, no clue. Mike Mullins, Terry Hall. Like Cherry, they're about his age, more tanned, fitter looking. Friends of the Aussies? Being friendly with another friend of the Aussies? It's all very confusing, this Facebook malarky. Maybe he should've got into it earlier? Oh well, fifteen is better than twelve, so he clicks to accept. If he comes clean with the Italians next week, he could break twenty.

21

THE 'CHANCE' MEETING

JACK'S GOT some free time, so he decides to take his Beemer back to the garage for an estimate on the repair. He's pleased he took Shelly's advice to bump his insurance to fully comp from the *Only if I kill someone* policy he'd had on the Fiesta. It had made his credit card scream, but he now knows it was the best decision he made yesterday. Then he remembers, again, he's a millionaire, so it doesn't matter.

He's going to tell her he reversed into a tree. Yes, a big one, a redwood; yes, in Cricklewood. Yes, there are a few. And yes, made of concrete. At least it'll make her laugh, he supposes. But he can't think of Shelly the way he was thinking of her the previous afternoon. That's now emotional small beer. Scarlett owns the brewery. Scarlett (or whatever her name is, she can be called Hulk, or Shrekess for all he cares), Scarlett has blown Shelly out of the water. Scarlett has nuked her. Scarlett has taken over his mind and is taunting him. *Why didn't you ask me, you dummy...?*

He strolls towards where he left the wreckage, bemoaning his lack of initiative when it comes to females. Yesterday was a classic. There was Shelly, all bright-eyed and friendly, chit-chatting away to him, asking him if he liked a stiff ride or a roll around on a waterbed, as they cruised around town in an open-topped Beemer, and he bottled it, as usual. Not that he could get that excited about Shelly anymore, not once Scarlett in her faded pink Panda had appeared in his little reversing TV. Jack's pace slows as he relives their encounter in his mind. It's like watching some trashy *will-he-won't-he* romcom for the third time, and he's willing the main character on even though he's a plonker who doesn't make the move.

He spots her from half the street away. She's leaning on his car, fiddling with her phone. His heart lifts, then flutters, then it goes tachycardic. He feels the air leaving his lungs but he can't stop breathing out. The nearer he gets, the faster his heart beats. It pounds like he might soon need a defibrillator. She's really beautiful, in quite an ordinary sort of way. It's an honest, serious, trustworthy, unpretentious, unflashy sort of beauty. She doesn't look like any of the famous 'beauties' – Kardashian? Shakira? Even Johansson? Leaning on *his* car outside the local chippy?

Her clothes make it look like she's dressed hyper carefully this morning – that, or she employs a professional buyer who's really worth the money. Simple, unflashy, white pumps; nicely faded jeans, the ones that look like she's owned them half a dozen years – not those torn rags that were torn in the factory and are meant to be fashionable but simply make you look like a tramp; and a baggy, beige jumper-thingy with an oversized roll-neck. It looks light and soft and fleecy, has to have a label on it somewhere announcing it's made by a firm called *Huggable*, probably based in Dorset or Devon – a gift from a caring, wealthy, fashion-savvy big sister who's a high-powered solicitor in the City and so rich enough to be able to afford it.

Leaning on his shiny, black, Beemer softie, the whole scene looks like an ad for the car (he can't see the back end from where he is), or maybe *Huggable* jumpers, or some dating app for wholesome singletons – probably called *Fanci-a-coffi*, or *SlowTalkers*, nothing remotely suggestive or tawdry. The backing music will be Lighthouse Family or Sade. The soft focus will be flocculent – it's one of his favourite words. He slows to a halt, wonders for a moment if he actually lacks the nerve, considers turning around and coming back when she's gone. Even that might be better than embarrassing himself.

'Hello again,' he manages to say without incident, as he stops in front of her, having struggled to get his legs going again. She jumps like a startled deer, surprised to find itself on a high street, outside a chip shop. She nearly drops her phone, she's blushing, fumbles with it before putting it in the back pocket of her jeans. She rubs the side of his car guiltily with the cuff of her jumper, like she thinks he might search for (yet more) dents. She stares at him, the same look of fear flooding her face that she wore yesterday. She's doing that thing with her fingers where she tries to dislocate them.

'Oh. Hi. Sorry, I was – um, God, look, I had to talk to you about this. I feel awful. It's clearly an expensive car and there's a fair amount of damage. I mean, look at it – no! Don't. There's – there's a lot of damage. So much. I don't really – I mean, I – I really want to pay for it.'

'Have you been here long?' he asks, suddenly wondering how she's just 'happened' to bump into him at ten thirty in the morning. He's amazed he can wonder this, because his heart is hammering so hard, he's sure she'll be able to see the vibrations shuddering his shirt or hear them smashing on the inside of his ribcage, like Max Weinberg's opening up 'Born to Run', his drum kit squeezed in between Jack's lungs.

'A little,' she says, blushing again. 'I couldn't sleep actually, I felt so guilty. This is going to cost you a lot of money or lose you your no-claims. I can see it'll cost more than a hundred. I don't know why I said that yesterday, it was so stupid. I think I lost my head a bit. I was only thinking of myself. It might have been a bit of shock. I'd had such a day at work. I'm so sorry. I wasn't looking properly. It was my fault; I've never had a crash before. I want to fix it...'

His heart slows a fraction, although it would undoubtedly destroy any defibrillator that came within range. It's probably a known medical side effect of the fact that it's melting again.

'Could I at least buy you a coffee? And we can talk about it?' she says suddenly, pointing with a trembling hand at the coffee shop, which sits between a bookies and the chippy.

He smiles, wills himself not to scream, or re-enact a Ronaldo goal celebration, a United one, not that Real Madrid crap. 'Okay,' he says. 'I'd like that.'

22

THE HEADLESS SQUIRREL

'How long have you had it?' Milly asks as she nods towards the window and places two cappuccinos on the table. Jack's surprised some enterprising nine-year-old hasn't already made off with what remains of his bumper. Even they can probably see it's worthless.

'Yesterday,' he says, without thinking. Because he's thinking what a lovely name Milly is.

She stops halfway to sitting down, her face transforming from a gentle, nervy, enquiring, ice-breaking mode to a stunned stare, like he's beheaded a squirrel with his bare hands.

'You're kidding me,' she says, begging him with her eyes to agree, still only halfway to her seat.

'No. I picked it up yesterday, less than an hour before – you know...?'

He shrugs a *shit happens* shrug. She starts to laugh, slaps her hand over her mouth, her eyes pleading with him to end the joke, say no no no, he's had it *years*...

He smiles again. 'You have to laugh at the timing.'

But Milly's stopped laughing. She looks like she's going to start crying again. The colour fades from her cheeks, there are volumes of horror in her eyes, Shelley and Stoker nudging each other for a better view of the blood and gore.

The waitress arrives and deposits two chunks of cake, looks like a coffee-and-walnut, and a lemon drizzle.

'I thought...' Milly starts – but doesn't finish. 'Oh God! This is so much worse.' She flops onto her seat, plonks her elbows onto the table, and dumps her face into her hands.

'It's fine,' he says, desperate to touch her hand: a soft, gentle, unthreatening touch that only says *I mean it*, and nothing else. But his hands are frozen on the ends of his arms, no life to them. 'Really. You've got to remember; I knew all this yesterday. It's not worse at all. What are the cakes?'

'What? Um, oh, coffee-and-walnut, and – um, lemon drizzle,' she says, looking up; her eyes are wet. 'This is horrible. This isn't what I wanted to happen. I wanted to apologise, sort out the money, not discover that you've only just bought it. Yesterday? I wish I'd never come.'

'Please,' he says, looking into her eyes, and begging her to read his mind, because not even Hugh Grant, or Colin Firth, or Rich would dare to say what Jack would *really* like to say. 'I'm so glad you did. I could see you were upset about it. I shouldn't have left you like that. I'm sorry. But trust me about the car. It's okay. Let's just have a coffee – and, thanks for the cake, you didn't have to – and have a chat, and – it's okay. Honestly. This is nice.' He makes a ridiculous little gesture by spreading his hands that says, the coffee, the cake, the tablecloth, maybe even the shop, which is pretty chichi... but most of all, you and me, here, sitting together, talking...

'Which do you like?' she asks, pointing quickly, her hand still trembling slightly.

'I like them both, you choose.'

'No, really, you – oh, *stop* it! Shall we share them?'

'Great idea,' he says, cutting them both in two and shovelling the pieces around.

They sip their coffees, fork small pieces of cake into their mouths. Jack wills himself to wait until he has something sensible to say, rather than blurt some nonsense out about how the weather's better today, or isn't her Panda a sturdy little thing...

'I feel such an idiot...' she whispers at her cake.

'Please don't. Accidents happen. As long as nobody's hurt, it's just bent metal and broken glass.'

'How can you *say* that? I thought you were going to explode yesterday,' she says, staring straight into his eyes, tears balancing on the lower lids of her own, her lips trembling. She wipes her eyes with her *Huggable* sleeve, she's working so hard to keep her composure. There's still a wariness in her, like she's trying to provoke him into the reaction that she feels she 'deserves' but somehow dodged the day before. 'I was really scared. I was shocked as well; I've never had an accident before. I've told you that. But I was really scared you were going to be angry. Really properly angry. Even – violent? Until you got out, that is. You read all this stuff about road rage and Beemer drivers and – oh God, I'm sorry – I didn't mean...'

He smiles, has to stifle a laugh, not at what she's said, he's thought it himself for long enough, but for how she's reacted. She really is on edge.

'I haven't done the Beemer-rage course yet, I think it comes free with the car. I'm still really a Fiesta man. In fact, you should have seen their faces when I asked the Beemer showroom if they'd take my Fiesta in part exchange. I wasn't thinking. When they looked at it, they laughed. Really, they laughed out loud. In the street. Told me not to dare drive it onto their forecourt.'

She's laughing, looks like nobody he's ever seen before.

Nobody famous. Nobody from a magazine or a film. She's quite ordinary, nice, kind, really pretty, a bit on edge – but she's got good reason, he's not going to hold that against her. But her jumpiness really shocks him. She's *so* anxious. It suddenly hits him that she's more nervous than he is. That's a first; it takes the edge off his own simmering tension – well, a sliver of it. There go her hands again, fingers twisting. He longs to put his own hand on hers, wordlessly tell her to calm down. *It's okay. It really is.* He forks another bit of cake instead, wills his mind to stay calm, say nothing stupid, especially as he notices she's not wearing any rings...

'They've probably had it crushed already, so as not to frighten away any customers.'

More coffee, more cake, more wary smiles from her, him staying calm, waiting for something sensible to say.

'I couldn't help noticing yesterday, you're a nurse?'

'Yes, started a couple of months ago. In SCBU.' She pronounces it 'skiboo'.

'Where?' he says, looking and feeling clueless. 'Skiboo? Is that in Latvia?'

She laughs, tries to contain it, but fails. It's a priceless, genuine, spontaneous, primary-schoolgirl splurt. Stand-ups would pay her to sit in the front row for weeks on end with a laugh like that. Specks of cake bounce around the table, she scrambles to brush them away from him, apologising again. 'Special care baby unit, for premature babies, at the Royal Free in Hampstead.'

His brain freezes. Is this the moment when she discovers what a socially clueless geek he is? He'd pay two point three million pounds, just to rewind time by *one* minute. Latvia? For *fuck's fucking* sake.

'Oh, I'm sorry,' she says, covering his hand with hers; she doesn't seem to have noticed that she's done it, but the effect on him is seismic. He tries to stop his body from tensing, in case she notices and takes her hand away, embarrassed. He wants her to keep it there forever. 'I try not to use jargon with non-medicky people. Forgive me,' she continues, removing her hand as thoughtlessly as she'd placed it there. She sips her coffee, she still hasn't registered that she did it, she was simply genuinely appalled at how she'd hit him with *medicky jargon*. He can't think of her ever committing a worse crime. Forgive her? He feels like nominating her for the Nobel Peace Prize.

The conversation's easy, although he's slightly on edge all the way through in case he dries up and it gets awkward. But it doesn't. She's pretty chatty and laughs easily, he's so happy to see her without tears streaming down her face, and the hand wringing; even the apologising for everything she does has abated somewhat. He can't take his eyes off her as she talks, her hands flicking delicate little gestures around the table like sparrows hopping for crumbs. She keeps sweeping her hair away from her face, as if she's got a playful kitten curling back into view every time she takes her eyes off it.

She makes numerous attempts to convince him to let her pay for the damage: *honestly, as long as I can do it in instalments...* But he gently shrugs her off, won't hear of it: *really, it's not a problem...*

She's got a dental appointment, so, 'It's been really lovely, and I'm so sorry again, and I can't thank you enough and – look, would you – I mean – could I – maybe cook dinner for you one evening?' She brushes another stray hair from her eyes, the tremble's returned to her hand all of a sudden, her smile is quivering, eyes flitting all over the place, she's unscrewing fingers. 'To say sorry, and thank you, again. I don't feel a cup of coffee and me rushing away really says what I wanted to say. You didn't turn up to your car as early as I'd hoped...'

'I'd like that,' he says, his heart detonating silently, killing Max Weinberg instantly. Half of it is relief, that he's survived the half hour they've had – no awkward moments, no lengthy silences, and all without wacky baccy, or Malibu. The other half is that *she's* asked *him*. He'd been building up to the moment, his heart had started racing into the Springsteen song 'Badlands' – until...

He *was* going to ask her this time. He really was – probably. And there's a third half – he knows that doesn't add up, but he's an English teacher, not maths. The final half is that he feels, cautiously, because he knows what pride comes before, he feels that they're going to get on. He doesn't think he's even going to get all nervous about it. With a bit of luck...

Probably.

23

THE ULTIMATUM

CINDY'S WAITING for Jack outside his flat when he gets back. She has a key, he's sure. He never changed the locks, but she always rings the bell and waits. She's gassing with Lavinia on the doorstep when he arrives. He didn't bother taking the car into the garage in the end. Another day. He had more important things to think about.

He walked back slowly, the long way, through the park, running over his conversation with Milly again, savouring her smile, the way she'd relaxed in his company. And he hadn't put a foot wrong, he thinks, can't think of an awkward moment. Well, maybe telling her he'd bought the car yesterday, but he'd handled that okay – ish. He thinks. He's always thought the phrase *walking on air* was silly. Not anymore. He realises he's been smiling at strangers, collecting funny looks in return as you might expect in Cricklewood.

He says a *how do* to Lavinia, but Cindy clearly wants to wind it up. She follows him in.

'You wanna drink?' he offers, not sure why he's suddenly got a nervy feeling in his stomach. He doesn't like it. Milly (*please, don't call me Millicent*, like she's expecting him to be using her name a lot in the future) has puffed a magic something into him that has worked like the softest, most pleasant drug you could ever imagine; Cindy's hoovering it out on the *turbo* setting.

'No. Thanks. We need to talk.'

He bustles with the coffee machine, trying to make it eat a bit of time. His next lesson's in twenty minutes; he prays they arrive early and give him an excuse to turf Cindy out.

'The lottery?' she says, vertiginous HRT, ditto her eyebrows, as she sits opposite him at the table they no longer use for cosy candlelit dinners. It's strewn with English books from the Italians this morning, not that they'd opened any of them, again. Plus a few chewing gum wrappers they've discarded. 'I happened to be in the corner shop, chatting with Mr Banerjee? He mentioned, I didn't ask, he just mentioned, he sees you every week for your lottery ticket...?'

Jack's jaw goes to open, but he clamps it shut. *Don't* show surprise. *Stay* cool. Think! Luckily, Cindy isn't finished.

'You said you'd stopped doing it.'

She is now.

'I have,' he says, thinking quickly. 'Now that this has happened. I didn't get one for Wednesday, cos I forgot. But now, I'm not bothering anymore. My numbers are never gonna come up *twice*, are they?' He's pleased with himself. Brilliant. He's not usually this quick a thinker, especially under pressure; he's useless at *University Challenge*, not much cop at *Mastermind* – although he's waiting for someone to choose The Boss as their specialist subject. He's still got a trace of this morning's magic feeling in his brain. He's calm, he's in control, he might have a girlfriend called Milly.

'You're a crap liar, Jack. You're a frigging window. I can see right through you.'

He's grateful for that last comment – the *window* reference hadn't made sense at all. It's clever, very good. She should write.

He likes this calm feeling he has. Milly's boyfriend (possibly) is a calm sorta guy. He mulls his options, feels no fear of the silence crowding in on him; it can sit there, it can wait. Milly's boyfriend (probably) isn't spooked by silences.

'I don't care what you think,' he says, finally. 'I didn't buy a ticket. I didn't win the lottery. Think what you like. You always do.'

'Let's get one thing straight, Jack. I know you won that lottery. I know that half of that money is mine. I'm your legal wife, and I get half of our assets when we divorce. To show you how fair I am, I'm willing to take a million. And we won't be divorcing until you cough up. Now have you got that?'

Jack mulls whether he should point out that that was three or four things, not one? No, best not. Then he wonders whether to remind her that she wanted to drop Wazza, swap him for her birthday, and without Waz there'd be no lottery win. Again, no. Not now.

'Is that it?' he says finally. 'Cos I've got a lesson I need to prepare for...'

'No money, no divorce, Jack. You do know you've only got six months to cash it in, don't you? And I'm gonna be all over you until then and beyond. I'm going to get myself a very good lawyer and tell them what kind of trick you're trying to pull. See you in court, Jack. Enjoy your lesson.'

Jack sits back in his chair and listens to the door slam. How did he ever marry her? Whatever got into him? But he knows the answer – a haze of wacky baccy and a waterfall of Malibu on a soft-sand Thai beach. That's what got into him – and her...

But this morning, he had two cappuccinos and a bit of cake. And look where that's got him.

24

THE SECOND OPINION

THE SMELL IS CABBAGE. Odd, because it's breakfast time. Even for those who 'slept late', 'had a lie in', 'didn't hear the alarm' or 'missed the bus', it's still technically breakfast time. But the smell is cabbage. A sign of things to come, perhaps...

Milly stirs her coffee, watches what few wisps of cloud there are being incinerated by the early morning sun. Looks like another scorcher is brewing – but, then again, the forecast said more rainstorms later. Bit like life, really. She sighs quietly. She's got Jack on her mind. Is he a potential new boyfriend? Or is this simply ridiculous? She can't make up her mind.

The door to the canteen opens and she spots her colleague Vicky coming in. Milly waves, Vicky waves an *I'll grab a coffee* in reply. Is this what she needs? A second opinion? She's only known Vicky a couple of months; they joined the hospital at the same time and met during induction. They'd hit it off fairly quickly, been out together a couple of times. Vicky's fun, recently out of a relationship...

'Hi, Mills. Everything okay?'

'Yeah, I think so. What about you?'

'Yeah, great, but what's this *think so*, that's not like you...?'

'Well.' Deep breath. 'I met a guy...'

Vicky cocks her head and stares like she's just pressed the *record* button on the tape for a big interrogation in *Line of Duty* – and Ted, Steve and Kate are all unconscious in hospital. 'You're going to introduce a new *guy* into the conversation when I've only got a twenty-minute break? How *could* you? We're going to need at least a night in with a couple of bottles to go over this. So, come on then. How d'you meet him? What's he like? Has he got a brother, cousin, friend? A wandering eye?'

Milly smiles, wonders if this is the best option, but can't think of any others. She scans the cafeteria. It has all the class of a sixties secondary-modern dining room – the furniture looks school cast-off, the windows are bolted closed, and the food, well, whatever the time, cabbage seems to be on the menu.

'He's great, I think. I don't know. Oh, I'm so confused.'

'Bloody hell, Mill, we've got nineteen minutes and all I've got so far is the fact that you need a therapist. Question one, how did you meet? You're not on a dating app, are you?'

'No, no. I – umm, I backed into his car...'

Vicky looks mock shocked. 'Never knew you were that desperate, love. Go on.'

'Oh, it was so stupid. I wasn't looking, couldn't see out the back with the dirt and the rain, reversed straight into his back bumper, tore it to pieces. And then, you're not going to believe this, I started crying. It was ridiculous. The more I think about it, the more ashamed of myself I am. I cried in the street as he inspected the damage. I've never had a crash. I was so pathetic.'

'That's stress, you know? Shock,' Vicky says, suddenly serious, her professional eye surveying the situation and coming to a diagnosis both she and Milly know is on the button.

'Oh, I know. I could see my no-claims going out the window, and I'd probably have to sell the car, I'm running it on fumes as it is.'

'A lot of damage?'

'To mine? Nothing. But I reckon his must have close to a thousand quid's worth.'

'You what? What was he driving, a Roller?'

'Beemer.'

'God.'

'Soft-top.'

'Christ!'

'It gets worse...'

'How can it?'

'He'd owned it less than an hour...'

Vicky stares at her, no expression at all. 'This is a wind-up, yeah?'

Milly sighs. 'I offered him a hundred, worried about my no-claims. I wasn't thinking, I didn't even look properly, couldn't see through the tears and the rain.'

'There was rain? Who is he? Spider-Man?'

Milly forces a *there goes my last train* smile. 'Steady on. It was awful. I kinda collapsed like some – I don't know, some Jane Austen female in a frilly frock and a bonnet.'

'Now, that I'd like to see; Spider-Man meets Elizabeth Bennet, there's a movie I'd queue up for. But how does this turn into *I met a guy*? I've only got fourteen minutes now, and I ain't leaving without the full story. What is it, the police got him on remand for assault?'

'No, no. Nothing like that. He was, I don't know, *ridiculously* nice about it. I think, when I offered him the hundred, he must've concluded I was deranged, or something. He said forget about it.'

It's clear from the expression on Vicky's face that she can't choose which question to ask next.

Milly continues. 'He just said that no one was hurt. Said he's got a mate who could knock it out. Then he walked away.'

'He – hang on, that's not *I met a guy*. That's–'

'Wait, there's more. I couldn't sleep, guilt, so I sort of stalked him.'

'You *what?*'

'No, not like that. I went and waited by his car the next morning; it was my day off. I got there at seven, he showed up at half ten.'

'And...?'

'Well, I thought I'd come to my senses by then. I said I wanted to pay for the damage. I bought him a coffee. That's when he told me he'd only collected the car from the showroom half an hour before I smashed into it. It was a surreal conversation. I wanted to put it right, and it kept getting worse and worse. But I couldn't budge him. He let me pay for the coffees, but nothing else. I felt such a... I don't know. So, I said I'd cook him dinner. Tomorrow.'

'*That's* more like it. So, you like him?'

'He was nice. Really friendly, didn't explode, quite good-looking, very ordinary in fact – for a Beemer owner who seems to have a lot of spare time on a weekday and can brush off damage to his brand-new soft-top without even asking me for my insurance details...'

'Ah!' says Vicky.

'Ah, indeed. *Now* you see my problem...'

'Christ, yes I do. Oh shit, Milly...'

25

THE RAT IN THE LETTERBOX

CINDY'S TRIED HIS FLAT. She's tried The Crown – that was a long shot. She's even tried the bookies – so he's either in The BOGOFF (these Brits and their hilarious names for their pubs – she's sure the second F is 'humour'...) or he's dead, cos she sure as hell's not gonna find Beano in the gym.

'Beano!' she shouts, across into the far corner, where he's nursing the dregs of a half and the racing pages. 'Same again?'

'Er, pint?' he begs, ever hopeful. She gives him the thumbs up and a cheery smile.

'Beano, long time no see!' She places his pint and her G&T on the table and takes him in. He hasn't changed in the couple of months she hasn't seen him; grubby black T-shirt; grubby black beanie hat (hence the nickname); strands of grubby black hair leaking out of all corners.

With his slightly buck teeth and pointy nose, she's never been able to look at him without seeing a rat peeking out through a letterbox. Oh, and a beer scrounger too, always time to go when it's his round. Saves all his money for his fancy cars. Lives in a rat hole so he can drive Audis and Mercs. But the smallest ones in the fleet, always a couple of years old, ex-demo special offers, rent-a-car cast-offs, always on a discount lease deal with third-party insurance begged-in, then he upgrades a couple of years later.

'No, right. Gutted when you pair split up. Bloody gutted.'

'Yeah, me too, but life goes on, eh? How are you? Keeping well?'

'Great,' he says, lifting his pint to her in toast. 'Butcher's dog.'

Cindy shrugs, assumes it means he's fine; why can't these Brits speak frigging English? She rips open the bag of crisps she's bought and sets it in the middle of the table, motioning for him to eat. He doesn't need a written invitation. The only surprise, in her eyes, is that he *doesn't* use two hands to hold them as he nibbles.

'All the old gang okay? Smithy? Cheesie?' She sips her G&T and sits back, away from the bouncing crumbs. 'Don't see them so often now I'm out of the area.'

'Yeah, good. Smithy's birthday last weekend. Big do, completely lathered, the lot of us.'

'Even Jack? He's not a big drinker.'

'Oh, he was here. As a newt. Haven't seen him that lathered since I don't know when. Reckon he might be missing you, is what I think. I ain't *saying* nothing.'

'No, best not,' she replies, half to herself, sadly. She flips the place mat, catches it. Does it again. Pensive, like. Beano stares like she's done a triple salchow on the way back from the bar. 'Does he talk about me? You know, stories? Memories?'

Beano nods. 'Sometimes. Cheers him up, I think. He's been a bit down lately. You know what he's like.'

'Yes, I do.'

'He sometimes retells his old stories about Thailand. Sounds like you two had a hell of a time. Made for each other – uh, we all thought.'

'Me too, Beano. Me too.' Thoughtful again now, melancholy. Then, suddenly brighter. 'He still does the lottery? God, him and his lottery, eh?'

'Course. Bloody clockwork. You could set your watch by him. Fact is, I was with him when he bought last week's ticket. We came out of here after the party, pissed as farts, and he says, *gotta get me ticket*. Banerjees was open, so in we went.'

'Oh yes?'

He nods, sips his pint, licks his finger then delves for the crumbs in the corner of the bag. He'll probably call it lunch, knowing him. She drains her glass, stands.

'Great seeing you again, Beano,' she says. 'Must do this more often.'

'Yeah, right. You sure you won't have another?' he asks warily, almost a whisper, she can see the pulse increasing in his temple.

'No, very kind of you, Beano. Next time, eh?'

'Great, right, next time. Take care, Cind. And, you know, maybe drop in and see Jack? Say hello? Cheer him up? I'm sure he'd like to see you.'

'Yes,' she says, 'I'm sure he would.' She waves at the barman as she heads for the door, touches someone she recognises on the shoulder, smiles back at Beano as she steps outside. But her face turns to stone as she hits the street.

'Gotcha!' she says quietly to herself. 'You lying Pommy bastard!'

26

THE VEGGIE SPAG BOL

MILLY'S CLEARLY MADE AN EFFORT. Not just for dinner, but with the flat in general. It's more of a bedsit; 'pokey' would be an optimistic estate agent's verdict. It's above a kebab shop in Mill Lane, so not a long cycle from his. And Mill Lane's not a bad little area. It's pretty quiet, and close to the Heath.

She's obviously done a job to make it look 'homely'. She's strung some sort of a sheet across the front end, presumably to make a 'bedroom' behind it by the window. She's got a pallet from somewhere, painted it bright yellow, and stood it upright. It kinda separates the kitchen off, if you use your imagination. It's the sort of thing they'd do on one of those TV 'makeover' shows he sometimes watches for a laugh. It'd look good on the telly but would end up just being a bloody great pallet in your kitchen when you're short of space to start with. Still, it's the thought that counts.

The table and chairs fold away, the sort you'd take on a picnic. She's got pictures on the walls, little watercolours, and a couple of small statues on top of a television, which is so small he mistook it for a microwave. So, it's true, he thinks, all they say about nurses being underpaid. He's brought wine and flowers and is trying desperately hard to stay calm, and not try too hard at anything else.

'What do you do, Jack?' Milly 'calls' from the kitchen, after he's come in and given her the wine and the flowers and managed to exchange a peck on the cheek without headbutting her, which he once did with, well, *to* a girl. It wasn't the best start to a relationship that ended soon afterwards, even before her bruising had faded.

She's less than a metre away, but she sort of leans back from the hob and 'calls', like she's surrounded by brick walls and there's half a bright yellow 'door' that's only slightly ajar. He banishes the idea for a new home makeover show which erupts into his brain – *Changing Stables*.

'I teach English,' he replies, resisting the urge to shout back.

'Really?' She stops stirring and faces him over the top of the pallet, bemused, like he's said he's a cat burglar or an astronaut.

'Yeah, but not in a school. I give private lessons, TEFL, or TESL, or TESOL, or whatever they're calling it now.'

'That must pay well,' she says, still quizzical; whatever's in the pot is in danger of welding to the bottom of it if she doesn't start stirring again soon.

'You're joking! I guess, if I could get enough students to give me an eight-hour day, five days a week, I wouldn't do bad, but it's a bit hit and miss. I have a few regulars; most people want weekends or evenings. It'd be nice to have something more secure.'

She's looking at him thoughtfully, although he's more worried about the health of his dinner.

'What?' he says, as she continues to look confused.

She shrugs. 'Nothing really, just the Beemer, I guess. I thought you might be a banker. Or a hedge-fund thingy.'

'Hell, no!' He gasps, realising how strange it must seem to her, pauper of an English teacher driving a Beemer. He's tempted to tell her, doesn't really want to lie to her, but something stops him. Is he afraid suddenly, she'll only want him for his money? Why is being a millionaire, a *double* millionaire, so complicated?

'Right, I see where you are. But as I said yesterday, I traded in a Fiesta for the Beemer. Look, I've got some pics on my phone.'

He swipes through his images and finds a couple of shots of him standing proudly beside his bright-red Fiesta.

'Wow. It's really small, it looks about as old as mine. I thought you meant one of the new ones. I'm sure my Panda used to be that colour. How come yours didn't fade?'

'My dad owned it for years before me, polished it every weekend. Think he might have used factor fifty sunblock. He was really proud of it. The truth is, I've always had a thing about Beemers, ever since I had a Corgi or a Dinky one, racing round the living-room carpet, although that was a disgusting turquoise colour. My first choice was actually the Pontiac Firebird, but would you believe it, Pontiac don't have a showroom in Cricklewood. The Beemer's second-hand, I'm not sure I can afford to drive it much, hence the bike, my usual form of transport.' He nods towards his helmet hanging on the back of the door, remembers her look of surprise when she saw it. 'You could call it my one secret luxury. I don't drink a lot, don't smoke, do drugs, buy expensive clothes or eat in posh restaurants, and I can't get a season ticket at Old Trafford. It's silly, I know, and I'll probably only ever drive it on sunny weekends, but I've always wanted one and it makes me happy.'

'Until I destroyed it...'

'You haven't destroyed it. Metal and glass, remember, you can fix cars.' He looks at her meaningfully, she shrugs a meek acceptance, smiles. He likes that, he's in charge of that issue, he's not going to let her beat herself up, try as she might. It gives him a good feeling that he can act like he won't take any nonsense. He's pretty sure she's 'acting' her role in it as well. He changes the subject, case closed. 'Don't you have one secret luxury?'

She lifts her head, thinking. Luckily, she's also started stirring again. 'You'll laugh,' she says, blushing, shaking her head suddenly.

'I promise I won't. You didn't laugh at my Beemer.'

'I very nearly didn't ask you to dinner because of your Beemer,' she says softly. 'I have a violin.'

He almost asks her what she means, about not asking him to dinner, but he doesn't want to risk where that conversation might end. The violin seems a much safer option. 'Why would I laugh at you having a violin?'

'It's an expensive violin. I'm still paying for it. Probably for as long as you'll be paying for your car,' she says, which he doubts very much. 'And I'm not going to tell you how much it cost.'

'I assume you play it?'

'Yes, I had lessons as a kid.'

'Would you play something for me?'

She looks shocked, blushes again, looks away nervously like he's just asked her to dance; there's some smooth, jazzy sort of music tinkling out of her phone – she doesn't seem to own a 'proper' sort of music system – so it wouldn't be beyond the realms of possibility. She recovers gracefully. 'If you'd like.'

'I would, very much.'

She sighs, a little flustered. 'When we've eaten,' she says, carrying the pot to the table. 'You serious?'

'Course. I'm not at all musical but I'm a good listener. I'll listen to anything, except maybe punk or rap. *Shit!* You don't play punk or rap, do you? Oh, Christ, I hope not, now I've said that. Please tell me you don't...'

She smiles, her beautiful natural smile. She gets more

beautiful every time he sees her, every time she's crying less, looking more relaxed, fingers all in place.

'No, I don't usually play punk or rap. But tell me how you got into teaching...?'

'Oh, that was my Uncle Jezza's fault.'

'Jezza?'

'Yeah, Uncle Jeremy. We always called him Jezza, he hated it.'

She smiles again, mesmerising him. How anyone can be that good-looking, and yet seem completely unaware of it? It's like having dinner with a magician who's absent-mindedly making forks disappear or pulling live rabbits out of your bolognese while you're trying to concentrate on not slopping it all over your shirt. She can't have any female friends, he muses, they'd all hate her.

'He was a teacher, primary, well, *is*. When I was doing my A levels, he invited me into his class up in Norfolk, to help out. I think he secretly thought I might like teaching. It was an eye-opener. He was nothing like any teacher I'd seen before. He had the class eating out of the palm of his hand, sort of...'

'What do you mean?'

'It seemed great, kids getting on with their work, asking him for help – but there was always this feeling that at any moment, it could all collapse into chaos. I don't know if he was that skilful that it never did, or if he was incredibly lucky, but every lesson seemed a bit on the edge, edge of a precipice, that is. Great spag bol, by the way. Really tasty.'

'Thanks. It's veggie.'

He looks at her like she's told him it's made from camels' testicles.

'Serious?'

'Yes, I'm vegetarian.'

'But it tastes like meat. If you hadn't said, I'd never have guessed.' Some real magic along with the good looks. 'So, what vegetable is it?'

She smiles, isn't sure whether he's joking – her eyes pop and she snaps her hand to her mouth when she realises he isn't. 'I'm sorry. It's Quorn.'

'Corn?'

She laughs, the primary-school splurt again, stifles it in an instant, but then wonders. 'Are you laughing at me?'

'No! Seriously, I'm a bit meat and two veg, myself, or sometimes meat-on-a-pizza-base. I...'

She suppresses a smile. 'Quorn, Q-U-O-R-N. It's a sort of edible fungus.'

'Fungus? Like *mushrooms*? You're feeding me *fungus?*'

This time she can see he's joking, she laughs freely.

'The spices are all the same, that's what gives it the taste. The meat, or the Quorn, just makes sure you don't end up hungry.'

'This vegetarian lark isn't as hard as people make out, then?'

'I wouldn't say that, but there are a lot of things you can substitute for meat.'

'Like fungus?'

Her smile is killing him. 'Like fungus. But look, you were telling me about going into your uncle's school...'

'Right, the kids, they were about seven or eight, always bringing stuff in. So, lesson plan out the window and let's have a chat about Grandma's false teeth or Dad's hunting gun. I don't think I could ever teach primary, but it made me think how creative you could be, deciding how you'd construct a lesson. Not that Uncle Jezza seemed to construct many lessons, he seemed to surf them. Some kid would arrive with a semi-conscious hedgehog they'd found in the gutter – and the first 'lesson' would begin.

'There was this one day, one of those book days or

something. All the staff and children dressed up as characters from children's books. I went as Harry Potter. Uncle Jezza decided he'd be the White Rabbit out of *Alice in Wonderland*. So, being richer than me – I felt-tipped a zigzag on my head and stole a pair of Uncle Jezza's glasses – he hired a costume from some theatrical shop in Norwich. Complete fluffy bodysuit with huge rabbit feet, rabbit-paw gloves, and an enormous rabbit head. It looked great and the kids loved it. Then, last lesson before lunch he said to me, *let's go down to reception and say hello to the little kids.'*

'What a nice idea.'

'Yes. Great idea. So Uncle Jezza thought. So I thought. Until he opened the door to reception and bounced in...'

'What happened?'

'Bedlam. Bloody chaos. The teacher had them sitting on the carpet listening to a story. Uncle Bugs hopped in, and the kids went wild. I remember a couple of tots screaming like Freddy Krueger had arrived – they pelted straight out the fire escape. There were kids hiding behind the teacher, crying for their mums. One lad got so upset, he started throwing books at Uncle Jez. A couple of the braver ones tried to pull his paw mittens off; one lad kicked him in the shin.

'In the end, he had to take his head off and shout, *Look, it's me, Mr Dean.* That calmed some of them down. But others just got worse. Some of the ones who'd been crying, started climbing on him, like he was a tree. They started slapping him, in fun like, but they were really belting his legs, I've no idea why. I think by then I'd retreated out into the corridor, to stay safe, and maybe escape any blame. He had to back out in the end, battered and bruised. I'm not sure the reception teacher ever spoke to him again.'

Milly's crying. But they're tears of mirth, so Jack doesn't feel bad.

'Anyway, I did an English degree and a PGCE, but let it all kinda drift. We did a TEFL course as part of the PGCE, and there were a few opportunities to teach English to foreigners, night-school stuff for the local authority, and I got some private lessons and suddenly I was making a bit of a living. All my friends off the course who went into secondary teaching were working like dogs, full-time stress and all that. They were earning more than me, but not enough to justify the workload and the hassle, so I kinda drifted on as I was. I don't know, I might look at going into a school at some time, but not primary. Anything but primary...'

They eat and talk, talk and eat, the food's good and the conversation flows, even though he limits himself to one glass of wine before switching to water, cos he's 'driving'.

They talk favourite films and books, and places they've visited and would like to visit. His film is *A Room with a View*, which surprises (and delights) her, but she doesn't say she thinks it's a 'girly' film, which all his mates (including Cindy) say.

Milly's is *Schindler's List*, which he hasn't seen. His book is *The Martian*, by Andy Weir. She's heard of the film but hasn't seen it. Her top read is any Jane Austen. He's read them all, being an 'English' bod. He lies when they discuss the best places they've visited, not wanting to bring up Thailand on what he's daring to think of as a 'first date' (if only to himself), so he says Valencia. Her top hol so far is Budapest. He wants to go to Istanbul, and she fancies (well, guess what) Thailand, but he ignores that, not particularly wanting to risk her asking who he went with – or who he ended up with. But he *will* tell her, he just doesn't know when. Or how. Or what it might entail. Com – plic – ated...

When they've finished and dropped all the dishes into the sink, he reminds her of her promise, and somewhat reluctantly, extremely bashfully, she brings a case out of a tall cupboard.

27

THE VIOLIN

'You say this is really expensive?' Jack asks, not even daring to stroke the wood, which is polished to a bright sheen. Milly gives him a steely look that says, *Don't ask, seriously*.

'What do you want to hear?' she says, scratching the bow over a few strings and tightening up the thingies on the end of the whatsit.

'Oh, I don't know much classical music.'

'It doesn't have to be classical.'

'Play your favourite tune,' he says, somehow knowing immediately that he probably should have said *piece*, but there's no hint that she's found it funny. In fact, she looks almost offended, like he's suggested a game of cricket using her wildly expensive violin as a makeshift bat.

'It's a bit sad,' she says. 'It's from *Schindler's List*, the film I was telling you about...'

'Okay.'

He sits on one of the small armchairs she has, which had been squeezed behind the bedroom curtain while the table and chairs were out. There's clearly no room for a sofa. She remains standing, looking slightly worried.

'I'm serious,' she says, 'it's really sad. I sometimes cry...'

He shrugs. 'If it's your favourite piece, then I'd like to hear it. Really. What else would I like to hear? Unless you can do 'Born to Run'...?'

She smiles nervously, nods, settles herself. There's a moment when he thinks she's going to try one last time to persuade him to change his mind. But she takes a couple of deep breaths and raises the bow. He's surprised she hasn't got any music out to look at, maybe it's an easy piece...

When she starts, he thinks she's made a mistake with the tuning, or something, it just sounds all wrong, slightly off-key, like a cat in pain, not that he would really know. He hopes she isn't embarrassingly bad, especially if she's spent a lot of money on the violin. There's also a sort of breathy feel to the noise.

He's never been this close to a violin when it's being played, it's almost like someone is singing, badly. He watches her fingers, slender and delicate, as they walk up and down the long bit, he doesn't know what it's called, wiggling and trembling as she moves the bow over the strings.

Then, within a few seconds, there's no other noise in the world, it's as if the whole street has turned off its televisions, the cars outside have pulled up, and they're all listening. He feels the emotion tugging at his chest as she changes key, and the sadness of the piece gets a grip on him. His breathing changes, he feels his lips trembling, it's almost like his heart's slowing.

Milly's completely gone, left the planet; her eyes are closed with concentration and feeling and emotion. She somehow looks even more beautiful than normal; it's hard to believe it's her making this incredible noise. Even he, a musical dunce, can see, and hear, she's a phenomenal player, and the piece is really difficult. It's like she's stroking the in-pain cat, and it's now purring with pleasure, acutely tuned to her touch.

He feels tears rolling down his cheeks. He's never

responded to music like this before, not even 'The River'; it shocks him. Or is it her? She's almost changed into some superhuman being, who can suddenly make him cry with nothing but noise. He's stunned by the power, and the impact. He doesn't know what to do. The notes near the end get higher and higher, it's hard to believe the noise that she's getting it to produce. The final note lasts for ages, he daren't move to wipe the tears away, he doesn't want to spoil the moment for her, or him.

There's a second or two after she's finished, it seems to go on for ever, like the memory of the noise is still haunting the silence. Then she opens her eyes and sees him.

'Oh, I'm so sorry...'

'No. Don't,' he says, wiping the tears away slowly. It's really odd, he doesn't feel at all embarrassed. Maybe she'll think him a wimp, he doubts it, but it's his honest reaction, so he doesn't care. She said it made her cry; he trusts her to understand. 'It was beautiful. Why haven't I been listening to music like this before?'

She kneels down in front of him, takes his hands. 'I tried to warn you.'

He nods. 'I thought you said it was about the Nazis, like a war film?'

'It is.'

'But it's beautiful.'

'Beautifully sad.' She stands and carefully packs the violin away again, then goes to the fridge and retrieves their bottle of wine and two glasses.

There's no way she's letting him cycle home tonight...

28

THE IBIZAN FIDDLE

'You've got a tattoo,' Jack says, stroking the small of Milly's back in the morning sunlight, which is already performing the miracle of making Mill Lane feel like Tuscany, without supplying any of the usually expected features, like endless skies, air conditioning or cheap wine.

'Oh, God! Don't remind me,' she says, trying to roll over.

'No, stay. I want to see it. Is it *your* violin?'

She laughs. 'No! It's some Ibizan fiddle I got at the end of a beery night out with a couple of girlfriends a few summers ago. They didn't have a big selection of decent violins at Nico's Tattoo Lounge, so it was the next best thing. I've regretted it ever since.'

'Why? I like it.'

She shrugs, turns her head so she can look at him. 'Partly because I got it done when I was drunk; partly because if I hadn't been drunk, and I'd wanted a tattoo, I would never have chosen an Ibizan fiddle; and partly because I can't see the bloody thing without booking a session with a chiropractor. It's a disaster from start to finish.'

He smiles. 'I like it. It's very *you.*'

'Hmmm. And where's your *very you* tattoo? I didn't spot it last night.'

'Me? A tattoo? Do I look like a tattoo type of bloke to you?'

She turns over and nestles into his arms, shrugs. 'I don't know. I'm not really a tattoo kinda girl, but I've got one.'

He sighs. 'I remember seeing a guy with a tattoo on his arm when I was about six. I was in a shop with my dad; I'm sure the man was being led away by Dalziel and Pascoe. I asked my dad why he had a drawing on his arm. My dad said he was either a sailor or a convict, I think my view of tattoos was forged then.'

'So, do you think I'm a sailor or a convict?' She smiles.

'Neither,' he says. 'Your tattoo is a tasteful little Ibizan fiddle that anyone who doesn't play wouldn't know from a Stradiwhatsit.'

'You were never tempted?'

'I was too afraid!'

'Of what? The pain?'

'No, think about it. I did my degree at Essex, right? While I was there, I bought a luridly purple T-shirt that told the world that I was a proud University of Essex undergrad. I can promise you now, that T-shirt is not still in my wardrobe, and even if by some freak of nature it was, I don't see me choosing to wear it now. That goes for *all* the clothes I was wearing ten years ago – with the possible exception of a few threadbare pairs of pants and socks.'

She thumps him gently on his arm.

'Which explains exactly why I don't have any tattoos. If I wouldn't dream of wearing any of the quote *fashionable* unquote clothes I was happy with ten years ago, then why would I even consider tattooing my current fashion statements onto my skin, to take with me to the grave? I have a theory that the tattoos of today are the T-shirts of yesteryear. Imagine what you'd be lying next to if I had chosen tattoos to express my pride instead of a purple T-shirt? I could've had Eric Cantona above my right nipple and Wayne Rooney above the left. On my back? Who knows? Bruce Springsteen? Alex Ferguson? You need to remember that if you don't like your Ibizan fiddle, you actually got off largely unscathed...'

He notices a number of small canvasses stacked next to the bed, and looks again at the watercolours on the wall.

'You paint?' he asks, pointing.

'I daub,' she replies, dismissively.

'They're good! I thought they were real. Well, you know – I thought they were by a real artist. No, I mean that you'd bought them. God, can I start my compliment again? It's not going nearly as well as I'd planned...'

'It's fine.' She smiles at his discomfort, which is clearly genuine. 'I know what you meant, so thank you.'

He marvels at how slow she is to take offence at his clumsiness, and him the linguist. 'You ever tried inks?'

She shakes her head, then looks at him. 'Why? Would you trust me to experiment on your back...?'

His mouth opens, no sound comes out, his tongue suddenly wrapped in a tight Windsor knot – until she laughs, squeezes him.

'Maybe a small one – on my arm. Do you think you could do a Fender Esquire...?'

29

THE VOLTE-FACE

It's as he's cycling home that Jack decides to give half the money to Cindy. No, he's going to give a third of it to Cindy and a third of it to Rich. The world looks different. The sun is shining (although a little too much – again). He doesn't want the aggro. Who knows, once Cindy and he are divorced, maybe they can be friends? It was nobody's fault their marriage didn't work... not really, so why not try to make the divorce work?

She was still friends with all his gang, Rich, Smithy, Cheesie, Beano, even though they didn't see each other as much; it would be easier all round if they could handle this like adults. Her threat to wait him out and set her solicitor on him isn't what's done it. He just wants the divorce done. Especially now...

He wishes he'd told Milly about his situation with Cindy before they'd slept together, but there wasn't the right moment. They're seeing each other tonight, a return leg at Jack's flat, where he'll have to cook something vegetarian. He'll tell her then. But first he'll tell Rich and Cindy what he's decided. He feels good. Life has turned a corner, another one, cos he's still practically a millionaire.

He lets himself in and pops the kettle on, takes out his phone. Rich first. His, of course, goes to messages. He's probably out on his bike again; no wonder he's so fit, all that riding. He can't tell him this in a WhatsApp. He'll have to wait. So, should he tell Cindy, or wait until he's caught Rich first?

Strike while the iron is hot, he thinks, knowing full well it's not really that appropriate for the situation, but as usual, he's impatient to sort this all out. She answers second ring.

'Hey, Jack. I hope you're calling because you've come to your senses...'

He takes a breath, wonders again how they ever ended up married.

'I've come to a decision,' he replies, haughtily, doubting whether he should be doing this. But he's made up his mind, get everything sorted out quickly, he'll feel better, that's his way. 'I'm giving a third of my winnings to Rich. I'll give a third of it to you. And I'm keeping a third of it for myself.'

There's a silence on the other end, which is a bit of a first for Cindy, one thing nobody can accuse her of is being in any way hesitant.

'You know, that's not really fair,' she says finally. 'As your wife, I'm entitled to fifty per cent of our joint assets. You should split your half with Rich, if you want to, not give him half of mine.'

Jack's sure she's got her mathematical knickers in a twist, but he hasn't got time to work it out, and what difference does it make?

'I'm not negotiating, Cindy. You want to play silly buggers; I'll give it all to Rich. Then when we get divorced, there'll be nothing in *our* assets to share. I'm sure I can trust Rich to give me back half when the time is right, or simply buy me stuff for the rest of my life. A third is there for you to take, it's nearly eight hundred thousand quid. You wanted a million. Take it or leave it. I'm not restarting the Brexit negotiations.' The idea of giving it all to Rich has only just occurred to him. Stroke of bloody genius. Now he's got her.

'So you *were* lying when you said you'd stopped doing it?'

'Take it or leave it.'

Cindy in silence, he thinks he should record it, might never happen again.

'Okay, thank you. I'm pleased you've seen sense.'

'You're welcome,' he says, wondering if her *thank you* has clogged her throat as much as his *you're welcome* has welded to his.

'What made you change your mind?'

He hasn't expected this, tries to find a way to explain that doesn't include the name Milly. Gives up. 'No reason. Maybe a feeling that it's time to move on.'

'So, how shall we organise this?'

'Well, I haven't been able to get through to Rich yet. Let me tell him, and then maybe we can meet up. I think I have to phone the lottery people for such a big win.'

'Don't go changing your mind now, Jack. My phone automatically records every call, so I've got you by the nuts.'

'Lovely thought,' he says dryly. 'I'll be in touch.'

30

THE PAUPER

'So? How was DINNER?' Vicky asks, placing her coffee down on the table and taking up an *all-ears* pose.

Milly blushes.

'Oh? *That* good? Tell me everything.'

'He's nice. *Really* nice. Quite an ordinary guy. I like him, he's very mellow, very genuine, thoughtful.' She shrugs, fails to hide a *cat's got the cream* smile.

'And did you solve your, ahem, *issue?* Or have you thrown your principles away in the... how shall I phrase this... the heat of the night?'

Milly smiles. 'He's a teacher. Not in a school, he does English classes for foreigners, cash-in-hand sorta gig. The Beemer is his one-and-only luxury. It's second-hand. Says he's always wanted one but can't really afford to use it except at the weekends. Apart from that, he rents a one-bed flat in Cricklewood, and usually gets around town by pushbike.'

Vicky looks shocked. 'Oh. Not a Lord of the Manor after all.'

'Nope.'

'Nor a hedge-funder.'

'God, no.'

'Wow. Bit of a shame that, I was all ready to collect your cast-offs... You seeing him again?'

'Tonight. His place, his turn to cook.'

'He knows you're a veggie?'

'Yes.'

'And he's okay with that? Cooking-wise, I mean?'

'I have a feeling it might be a first for him, we might end up with beans on toast, bit of cheddar cheese, maybe? I might have to educate him. But I'll be happy if he makes me a sandwich. I like him.'

'You're looking happy.'

'I am. I feel like my luck's changed.'

PART 2

LOSING

31

THE LOSS

Jack doubts very much that Cindy records her calls, doesn't really care. He's done it now. He fetches his wallet and opens it up. Better sort out properly what he has to do to claim the money. He stands in the middle of his flat and tries to get his brain to work, while every other part of his body starts to panic: his heart kicks up two gears; a cold sweat breaks out of every pore; his brain accuses him of being an idiot. He always keeps his ticket in his wallet. Where is it? He checks it again, the fifth or sixth time. It's always in with the notes.

He closes the wallet. Begins again. Takes a deep breath as if that might reset the world back to the way it should be. He opens the wallet, opens the notes bit, flicks in between the couple of fivers he has, takes them out, lays them singly on the table having checked both sides of each, searches the (clearly empty) notes section like a lottery ticket might conceivably get scrunched up into the size of a baby ant, or turn itself the colour of the wallet like a very flat, as yet undiscovered, species of chameleon. Nothing.

He empties the cards section, even though he knows he never puts it in there, shakes the wallet upside down over the

151

table like a cartoon Tom or Jerry would, even though he knows the bloody thing is as empty as Santa's sack on Boxing Day.

Has he dropped it? Has he given it to somebody by accident when he was paying for something? He traces back his spending over the last couple of days. He hasn't bought anything today; he bought the wine and the flowers for Milly with his credit card; what was before that? He used his card at the Beemer garage, on the phone to change his insurance, but his card's in a different part of his wallet, he doesn't have to open the notes bit to get to his card. He hasn't taken any cash out of his wallet since he bought the ticket. Milly bought the coffees and cake... Where is it? Has he put it somewhere 'safe'?

He's always doing this. Whenever he goes on holiday, he hides his car keys somewhere 'safe': in the cereal box; in an old sock at the bottom of his sock drawer; in the kitchen bin, under the bin bag... Then he comes back from holiday, and he can't find them. He has to ransack the flat, and even when he locates them (under his pillow or inside the sofa cushion), he often only vaguely remembers having hidden them wherever it is he's found them.

He checks the cereal box, in the sock drawer, under the bin bag. He's no memory of having hidden it *anywhere,* never mind in the bloody bin! He widens the search: every drawer tipped out onto the bed; books off the shelves; cutlery out of the kitchen drawers; places he'd never dream of hiding anything, all the while fighting the panic that is rising in his brain and threatening to shut it down. Then a thought hits him: has he left it in the Fiesta?

He sits on the sofa and tries to think of a moment when, a place where, or a reason why he'd have hidden the ticket in his car. He can't. But neither can he get the thought out of his mind. Where else could it be? He's trashed the flat. He must have put it in the glovebox (it's always empty, he's not a big glove-wearer), or in the side pocket of the door. He fetches his cycle helmet.

———

Jack's heart sinks as he hurtles – well, trundles – towards the showroom, seeing no sign of his Fiesta where he'd parked it. Maybe they've simply moved it a few streets away, or perhaps they've taken the handbrake off and given it a push down the hill.

Shelly smiles and waves at him as he stumbles into the showroom, unbuckling his helmet and breathing heavily. *Christ, I hope she doesn't think I've come to ask her out on a date.* She's in bright yellow today, some frocky sort of thing (he's not good with fashion terminology – like perfume and wine), with enormous buttons the size of saucers and the widest belt he's ever seen. It'd look fine on a Paris catwalk, or in the London Dungeon – maybe not a *yellow* one there... In a car showroom it has more than a hint of a fancy dress charity event.

'Problem with the car? Everything all right?' she asks, pointing at his cycle helmet as he stands panting in front of her *everything-in-its-proper-place* table.

'Oh, yes, great, thanks. It's not about that.' He hasn't got the brainwidth to deal with the Beemer bumper. She looks worryingly expectant suddenly, flattening the pleats in her frock, pushing a wisp of hair out of her eyes. *Jesus!*

'It's about my *old* car, the Fiesta. I think I've left something in it. Is it still here?'

'Yes, it's out the back,' she says, a hint of disappointment clouding her face. 'Kev's giving it the once-over before we decide what we're going to do with it. What have you left behind?'

This stumps him, he hasn't prepared a story. 'Um, keys.

Spare door keys. I think I might have thrown them in the glovebox, or somewhere.'

'Let's go and have a look,' she says as she leads the way out back.

He's surprised to see his car in plain sight, he'd rather expected they might have hidden it behind the bins under a tarpaulin, with Kev beavering away underneath – possibly wearing a balaclava.

'You okay, Kev?' Shelly calls, as they approach. 'This is Jack. He brought the Fiesta in. You didn't find any keys inside, did you?' Kev's got his head under the bonnet but straightens up as they come to a halt.

'Hi there. No, it's clean inside, couple of KitKat wrappers, but no keys.' He shrugs.

'Can I have a quick snoop?' Jack asks, feeling awkward, like he's suggesting Kev needs an eye test.

'Be my guest.'

Jack slots himself into the passenger seat and rifles the glovebox, the side pockets, even under the seats and the foot mats. But it's clearly been hoovered through. He doesn't even find that pair of small green mittens-on-a-string that he used to wear to primary school in the winter months of his childhood – it wouldn't have surprised him. If there *had* been a scrunched-up, winning, two point three million pound lottery ticket anywhere, it'll now be in the stomach of the battered Henry Hoover that's taking a break behind the open boot, smiling malevolently at him.

'Nice little runner, for its age, you know,' Kev says, tinkering away under an open bonnet, as you do. 'Had it long?'

'Umm, about six years, but my dad had it before that since 1980.'

'Wow!' Kev straightens up again, looks at Jack with new eyes, like he's just been told that Jack is, in fact, Lewis Hamilton wearing a pretty impressive disguise. 'Who was the magic mechanic kept this breathing for so long?'

'My dad, really. But he taught me a few basics, stuff you can do with a few screwdrivers and a universal wrench.'

Kev nods. 'Hats off to you. I haven't seen such a tidy little runner, this old, in ages. It's been round the clock, yes?'

'Twice,' Jack says, proudly, knowing that most of the praise is really for his dad.

'But this is the original engine? That's almost a motoring miracle.'

Jack's mind is in fifth gear and racing. Half of it is wondering how he can wangle a peek inside Henry's underpants – the other half is calculating whether keeping this conversation going might be the key. He wishes Shelly would buzz off; at some point he's going to have to confess that the keys are not really what he's looking for. Henry would hardly have swallowed up a set of keys without Kev hearing the clatter. He's already implied Kev is blind; he can't now suggest he's deaf as well.

'We never went very far in it. Up to Norfolk in the summer, maybe, a couple of times to Devon. Dad never went over sixty.'

He can see Shelly beginning to look around the yard, so he presses on.

'He once changed the clutch cable, on his own.'

'You're kidding! How did he know how to do that?'

'A battered old copy of Haynes. Swore by it...'

The clutch-cable adventure seems to do the trick, Shelly makes her excuses and moves back inside. Jack breathes a sigh of relief.

'Listen, Kev, can I ask a favour? As well as my keys, I think there might have been a couple of letters I need, scrunched up in the glovebox, or the side pockets. Would you mind if I checked out Henry's bag? I won't make a mess...'

'Sure, go right ahead,' Kev says, turning back to the engine.

Jack snaps the clips and lifts out the filter. 'Wow, it's pretty full,' he says as he extracts the bag. 'Shall I pop a new one in?'

'I can do that,' Kev yells out from under the bonnet. 'Take that one away with you if it's easier, there's nothing nasty in there, they only use it for hoovering the showroom and inside the cars.'

'Great,' Jack says. 'Look after the old Fiesta, yeah?'

'I sure will, see ya...'

———

Jack wobbles home with Henry's stomach balanced on the handlebars. When he arrives, he opens an old Guardian newspaper over the table and carefully empties half the bag. He spots the KitKat wrappers immediately, right near the top. If the ticket's in there, it should come out first.

There are a couple of possibilities that turn out to be Sainsbury's till receipts. A small spider wanders groggily across his hand. He hopes it hasn't just been born... He empties the bag out completely and sifts through the balls of hair and paperclips but finds nothing but dust and fluff. The total contents of the bag are worth about two point three pence, he muses sadly.

'Bugger!' Now what?

32

THE SHARE

THE REASON RICH didn't answer his phone is cos he was on his daily bike-to-bonk mission, over at Cindy's. He heard it ringing as he was overtaking a bus, but decided he'd check it out when he arrived. Rich uses every cycle ride as a fitness session, although when he's on his way to Cindy's, he eases back a touch, treating it more as a warm-up than a full-throttle ride – that comes after. But, when he arrived, he was in such a state of readiness, that he forgot the call. It's only during their post-coital fag that he hears about Jack's decision, and not from his phone.

'Great news that Jack's caved.'

'What?'

'He's caved in. He's giving us the money.'

Rich still isn't used to Cindy using 'we' and 'us' when talking about them – well, he means him and her. Him *or* her, that is. Their arrangement is obviously secret. And 'loose'. It's not like they're boyfriend and girlfriend – odious terms when you're over sixteen. They agreed *that* right at the beginning. 'The beginning' was technically while Jack and Cind were still 'together' – although it was *after* she had decided to divorce him, or around about the same time, even though she hadn't told him yet – only Rich. This was simply two adults, behaving like adults, to protect Jack's feelings. And possibly Rich's jawbone.

'That's er... great.'

'A third for me, a third for you, and a third for himself. Isn't that thoughtful of him?'

'Really?' Rich gasps, halfway through his turn to drag.

'What? Didn't you know?'

'Well, no. When did he tell you?'

'He phoned a few moments before you arrived. He said he'd tried to ring you. I think he wanted to tell you first.'

'Bugger,' he spits, reaching for his phone. 'Yes, he called me when I was on the way over. No message though...'

'He'd hardly tell you in a text, would he? Here's nearly a million quid, have fun.'

'No, guess not.' Rich goes to steal another drag, but Cindy pulls the cigarette out of his hand. He's no idea what future he and Cind are planning, but their idea was, if they were still 'together' when Cind and Jack divorced, then *that* would be when they would 'get together'. Afterwards. A suitable time afterwards. If they were still 'together', that is.

Now Rich does his sums. If and when they 'get together', they'll have two thirds of Jack's two point three million pounds. Is that a problem? It shouldn't be. Why *would* it be? He tries to reverse the situation in his mind to see how he would feel. He, Rich, wins two point three million quid on the lottery. He's married to Cindy, but they've agreed to divorce. Unbeknown to him, Cindy is bonking Jack. Rich doesn't want to give Cindy any of the money. He tells Jack this. Then, for whatever reason, he decides to give Jack and Cindy a third each, not knowing that they are 'together', hypothetically, in secret. And then they 'get' together, officially, *after* Rich has given them a third of his pot. Each. So now they have two thirds of his pot, and he has one third. What does he feel?

He feels Cindy's hand creeping up the inside of his thigh...

33

THE PREMATURE CELEBRATION

JACK STARTS to tidy up the mess he's created. The flat is
devastated: all his drawers are out and emptied, the socks for the
second time; his books are in dodgy-looking Pisa Towers all over
the place; the shelves are empty except for a few dust balls and a
couple of squashed spider corpses; there's cutlery and pots and
pans covering every surface in the kitchen. All his food is out on
the dining-room table. Every open packet has been searched
twice. Then he's had a think: he got drunk the night he won, not
that he remembers it well, but he's got the evidence of the state
of his sweatshirt and chinos and six empty San Miguel bottles.
So, where might he have hidden the ticket when in a drunken
stupor? You know, not his usual places, but drunken-stupor
places...?

He opens all the unopened packets, in case he's hidden it in
one of them and resealed it, reckoning there was no way Cindy
would be mad enough to open unopened packets in search of
his ticket. He considers checking inside all the tin cans as well,
but he puts that idea to bed with no supper – eventually. Where
else might he have put it when drunk? Has he lifted the carpet
(not a big job), prised open a floorboard and slipped it

underneath? He rolls the carpet back, stamps around on the floorboards, but they all seem firmly in place. How would he ever have prised one up? He hasn't got a huge selection of DIY tools, and none of his spoons look like Uri Geller has been over for tea. He's got a couple of framed photographs on the wall, he takes them down and dismantles them, in case he'd hidden it inside. Why hadn't he simply rented a flat with a wall safe?

Defeated, he sits on the sofa and desperately tries to remember the last time he saw it. He starts with the purchase, which he can barely remember cos it was the night of Smithy's birthday booze-up and he'd had one or two over his usual one. He's pretty sure he went over to Banerjees with Beano, after they'd got the old heave-ho from The BOGOFF pub, although he's a bit shaky on that – could've been with Smithy, could've been with Marcus Rashford for all his memory can really tell him. God, Jack was drunk.

He *must've* put it in his wallet, where else would he have put it? And after that? When he won? Nothing. He doesn't ever get it out to check the numbers when they do the draw, he's no need to, he knows his numbers. But again, he can't remember much of that, he had another unusually 'liquid' night when his numbers came up.

April, Eric, Wazza, 22, 24, Maple Road. He's had the same numbers since who knew when. What does he do now? No point buying the same numbers again. Odds of them coming up are fourteen million to one. Odds of them coming up *twice*? What would that be? Fourteen million times fourteen million to one? Is that what you do? Times them? Or do you add them? He can do that, twenty-eight million to one. Double the odds of anybody else in the country? It's not very good, whichever way you're meant to do the maths. Of course, if he changes, he knows exactly what will happen. Up they'll come, April, fucking Eric, effing Wazza, 22, 24 and shitty Maple Road.

He'd hated Maple Road, it was a bloody freezing pit of a place, with condensation on the insides of all the windows. The wind whistled in through the holes in the rotting wood of the frames in his and Rich's bedroom. Course Rich, being the oldest, got to choose beds, gave Jack the one next to the gale. Why the hell had he ever included Maple Road?

The doorbell rings. He sighs. The last thing he wants is to talk with a human being. For the first time in his life he wishes he had a dog. At least a loyal mutt might have the nous to simply rest its chin on his knee as he collapsed onto the sofa and contemplated the rest of his life *not* being a millionaire. Whoever it is, he doesn't want to speak to them. Doesn't want to listen to them. If it's the god squad, he could end up in jail – but at least it'll be quick.

It's Rich, with a bottle of champagne. It's got that funny wrapper over a fat cork, but probably some cheapo fizzy stuff, knowing Rich.

'What's the occasion?' Jack asks, opening the door with a weary sigh.

Rich's mouth opens, then closes. 'I got your message,' he finally says, somewhat dubiously.

'I didn't send you one.'

'No, right. But I bumped into Cind – in the super. She thought I knew. So she told me; so I know.'

'Oh, right.'

'Thanks, bro, it's very generous.' He gives Jack the sort of wide-armed invitation to a man-hug that neither of them can abide, but Jack turns around and heads back into the flat, leaving Rich looking (and feeling) like a Cup-Final goal-scorer with truly shocking BO.

'Might be wise to pause the bubbly until I find the ticket,' Jack says, scooping stray Cornflakes off the table into the bag, before ramming it back into the box.

'What?'

'Can't find the fucking ticket. Looked everywhere. Not in my wallet, hidden on my bookshelves, sock drawer...'

'Have you tried your cereal box? Remember that time...'

He holds up what is now a packet of Corndust as he heads into the kitchen.

'The bin?'

'Yes. I told you; I've ransacked the place. Can't you *see?*'

Rich scans the flat: yes, it does actually look like Jack's been burgled by a highly trained team who love their work. 'When did you last see it?'

'The night I bought it, when we left the pub after Smithy's piss-up. I went over to Banerjees with Beano or Smithy or someone...'

'You were pissed.'

'I can still buy a lottery ticket when I'm pissed. It's not the sodding *Krypton Factor*.'

'Did you drop it?'

'If I knew the answer to that I wouldn't be standing here listening to you asking me stupid questions, would I? I don't know.'

'Have you looked?'

'What? In the street?'

'Of course, you came straight home after?'

'Well, I did try to get Beano to jump a cab to Heathrow so we could bag a couple of standby seats for a breakfast in NYC... but you know what he's like, he's got no get-up-and-go once it gets past midnight,' he says sardonically.

'Let's go look...'

'It was *days* ago.'

'They hardly sweep with military efficiency, do they? And it hasn't rained, well, only a bit – your ticket might be stuffed under the wheel of a car...'

Rich isn't waiting, he's on his way out. Jack has no option but to follow him.

They crawl along the kerb, Rich on one side of the road, Jack on the other, scrabbling amongst the dead leaves and beer cans, drawing curious looks from passers-by, Jack hoping there's no dog shit lurking in amongst the rubbish. No ticket, but he does have a bit of a win – no dog shit either.

'What were you wearing?' Rich asks as they head back indoors.

'What?'

'What were you wearing?'

'When?'

'When you bought the ticket.'

'How do I know? Suspenders and a codpiece. I don't keep a diary. What does it matter?'

'*Pockets,* you pillock. Did you check your pockets?'

Jack travels back in time. Best cream chinos. He's not much of a fashion monster, but it was Smithy's thirtieth, so he'd pushed the boat out a fraction. And he was still wearing them on Thursday, when he woke up and they were covered in vomit. He'd thrown them in the washing machine...

'Oh shit! Out the back,' he says, like Rich's pulled a sawn-off and demanded to know where the safe is.

They pelt through the kitchen to the small outside landing where Jack has his rusty hanger-thingy screwed uselessly to the north-facing wall. He rips his chinos down and brings them inside.

'I've washed them!' he hisses, pathetically, as he rifles the pockets, and there, front left, is a bodge of paper – there must be a real word for it, but if there is, he doesn't know it – a bodge of paper, soaked through then swirled around with two capfuls of detergent (they were in a dreadful state) and forty degree water on the long wash, then spun out, and left to hang in the humid but sunless air on the line, with his ticket, if this *is* his ticket, finally ending up like this: a bodge of sodding (but no longer sodden) paper. Can he *not* stop playing with fucking words in his mind while he's going insane?

'Is that it?' Rich gasps, looking over Jack's shoulder. 'It's about the right size.'

Jack shrugs. 'I'm not sure. I don't usually put it in my pocket. I keep it in my wallet. Why would it be in my pocket?'

'Can you open it? Is it recognisable?'

Jack looks for an obvious crack in the surface. It's not easy, it's been out there for a couple of days (he empties his line when he needs to use it again, there isn't much cupboard space in the flat). It's pretty solid. He tries round the other side; it starts to break up. He concludes he's more likely to tear it than open it. It's like trying to flatten out a Cadbury's Flake. Not the wrapper – the flake itself.

'Jesus!' he gasps. 'This is hopeless, if this is even it...'

———

Rich sighs. He's not sure how he feels. Bad for Jack, obviously, he's sitting there like his world's caved in. Bad for himself as well, although if he's honest, there's an element of this that he can't take entirely seriously. What with all its links to Cindy and their affair (not that it's an *affair*, Jack and Cind were getting divorced) it had complicated his life horrendously. Maybe it would be better if the whole thing went away. It was bad enough having the aff – the fling – but the fling *and* a lottery win to be divvied up pre-divorce? Messy. Still, it would've been worth seven hundred thousand quid. Ish. Can't sniff at that. Although, he can now – now that it's gone.

'What do you think?' he says, gently. Jack looks close to tears.

'I think I've blown it,' Jack replies, turning the bodge of paper over and over in his fingers, pieces of it flaking off onto the floor, regretting not having paid more attention in chemistry lessons in school, wondering if either of them knows anyone who works in the British Museum, unwrapping mummies, or reading Dead Sea Scrolls...

'It could be worse–' Rich starts.

'Don't.'

'No. Sorry. Do you want me to leave you alone?'

'Yeah, probably best. I've got a lesson in a few minutes, María and Iker. Blimey, I really feel up for that.'

'Try to put it out of your mind. There's not much else you can do. Pretend it never happened.'

'Bloody *clown!*' he whispers, half to himself.

'Yeah, that as well.'

They stand, man-hug, it's not as bad as either of them had imagined. Certainly not as bad as losing a two point three million pound lottery ticket.

Rich goes to leave, stops before he closes the door, pokes his head back in, points at the table. 'Do you want me to leave the bubbly, or...?'

34

THE MOJO

María's her usual self: out of the blocks like a temporary
F1 pit-crew member trying to bag a full-time job. As soon as
she's through the doorway she wants to know all about 'make'
and 'do'. She's clearly got a fixation about 'make' and 'do'. She's a
Spanish speaker, and in Spanish they only have one word for
make and do: *hacer*. Jack knows this from a little time he's spent
in Spain.

So, Spaniards *hacer* their homework; *hacer* noise; *hacer*
sport; *hacer* money; *hacer* a piss or poo – she's particularly
confused why the English use 'make' instead of 'do' for 'making'
the bed in the morning. She feels it would be more sensible to
'do' the bed in the morning and save 'making' it for when you've
lugged a massive box back from IKEA and are now certain
you've got a couple of slipped discs as a free gift. Not that she
says, 'lugged', and she calls it Ee-kay-yah. Jack thinks she's got a
point. Iker's on his phone.

Jack ponders for a moment the difference between making
the bed in the morning, and making a bed you've recently
bought from IKEA. Then he sees it.

'Listen, María. Here's how it's different. When you make

the bed, it's in the morning. But when you make *a* bed, it's one you've just bought from IKEA. You see?' He feels thrilled that he's sussed this linguistic puzzle without having to riffle through any of his David Crystal books. He's getting good at this linguistics malarkey.

She looks at him like he's a semicolon short of a sensible sentence, then she shakes her head. 'Thees no very good. Much better you *do* bed in morning, *make* bed from Ee-kay-yah. Ees more easy.'

He mulls it. She's probably right. He does sympathise with her plight. Any student of English with a forensic brain will soon find the minute idiosyncrasies of the English language a source of endless torment. He wonders more and more how even native English speakers get the hang of half of them. She once came to him, perplexed for an explanation as to why a waiter had smirked when she'd asked him for *two chickens and chips*. The waiter had told her she should ask for *two chicken and chips* – not two *chickens*... Jack had pondered the advice. Somehow, pluralising 'chicken' did seem to bring it (or them) back to life, but he didn't know why. In the end, he was left with the English teacher's least favoured 'explanation': *you just can't say that*.

'I read newspaper,' María starts again, in a quizzical tone, another tangent from somewhere in her never-ending tango (it seems more appropriate than 'tangle' – even though she's not Argentinian) with the English language. Jack's quite happy dealing with her incessant questions and clarifications: he's got nothing else prepared. It's the easiest thirty quid in the world when María's in an inquisitive mood (always) and Iker's on his phone (usually). 'Eet say Lyra have meteoric rise. What eet mean, *meteoric rise?*'

Jack takes a breath. This has the makings of another María 'special' – luckily, Iker's otherwise occupied. Jack's got no clue who or what (a) Lyra is. He could google Lyra, but doubts if it will actually help. So, with nothing else prepared, and Iker on the phone, it might be a better option to lead María by the nose.

Jack knows from experience, always take it back to basics. 'Who, or what, is Lyra?'

'He seenger, Irlandesa.'

María, like a lot of Spaniards, has trouble with *he* and *she*. She often mixes them up or scatters them randomly. Jack's suspicions are raised by the fact that she's described Lyra as Irlandesa. He knows enough of the old español to work out that *Irlandesa* means Irish*woman*. An Irish*man* will probably be an Irlande*so*, he thinks, confidently – but wrongly...

'María. Lyra is man or woman?'

'He woman.'

'Okay. Remember what we know, is it *he* or *she* for a woman?'

'Oh, ees *she*, I no weet, ees she.'

'Right, so Lyra is a singer, *she's* a singer. And is she a *new* singer?'

'Yes, she new seenger, from Irlanda.' She pronounces it *ear-land-ah*, stressing the *land*, for some reason.

'From Ireland?' Jack corrects, stressing the *I*.

'Yes, eye-or-lund.' She tries gamely, but fails miserably, to get her tongue around another English (or Irish) pronunciation.

'When they say she's had a meteoric rise, it means she's become very popular very quickly. She's gone *up* in the charts, yes?'

'Yes, she sell many songs. She very nice.'

'So, she's had a *meteoric rise* means her popularity has gone *up* very quickly, like a meteor.' He smiles, satisfied with an excellent conversation, conducted entirely in English, mostly. Well done, María.

'But meteor, eet mean *meteoro?*'

'I'm pretty sure, let me check...' He consults a handy translator app he has on his phone. 'Yes, *meteoro*. We sometimes call it a shooting star.'

'Yes, I hear this, shooting star. They very lovely. But they no go up. They go *down*. How eet can be meteoric *rise?*'

Jack scratches his head. He doesn't know a lot about space, but María does seem to have a point. Could be a long lesson...

———

Later, María hits him with a left hook, metaphorically...

'You feel een or you feel out?'

'Wha'...? I mean pardon?' She always does this. No preamble. *You feel een or you feel out?* What the hell is she talking about?

'Ees feel *een* or ees feel *out?*'

He wonders for a sec if this is one of Lyra's songs, and María is simply singing the chorus, a sort of Irish-techno 'Da Doo Ron Ron'...? He takes a deep breath. Iker is looking like he's engaged at last. He's probably engaged in a coma, Jack thinks.

'Tell me where you've heard this.'

'Everywhere. When I go bank, or hall of town, they geev you a paper and pen. Then...' She settles herself, like she's about to take his appendix out without anaesthetic. 'Some people they say you must to feel *een* thees paper, other people they say you must to feel *out* thees paper. Which ees? You feel *een*, or you feel *out*...?'

At least the lesson takes his mind off his lack of a winning lottery ticket, although María notices he's not his usual self. Iker probably wouldn't notice if the class was being led by an Egyptian mummy, tightly wrapped in bodged-up lottery tickets, although he does seem to have come out of his coma.

'You lose you mojo, today, Jack?' María says, as they're on

their way out; she even uses the English pronunciation, rather than the Spanish *mo-ho*. It makes him smile. How keen she is. He should give discounts for students as enthusiastic as she is: and fine buggers like Iker who give him nothing to work with.

'Yeah,' he says, shrugging, then without thinking, 'I lost a lottery ticket along with it.'

'You lose *lottery* ticket?' Her brown eyes widen, *child-on-a-first-visit-to-Hamleys* size. 'Eet ween lotta money?'

'A little,' he says, knowing his English understatement will cause havoc with her translating skills.

'You buy an udder. You lucky boy, you buy an udder, and you ween again.'

She squeezes his arm. He smiles, trying to imagine where he might source an udder to bring him some luck. Sainsbury's, perhaps? Thank God he's got Milly. Losing the ticket, having already lost María, might have been more than he could bear.

35

LA PAELLA

As he tidies the flat, in preparation for Milly's arrival, Jack berates himself for having been so hasty that morning. Confessing to Cindy that he had indeed won the lottery, when it turns out he hasn't, has complicated things horrendously. He vows to tell nobody anything in the future, until he's absolutely certain of his facts. He's worried that Cindy might not believe him when he says he's lost the ticket, or destroyed it, or whatever the hell he's done with it. Exactly the sort of thing to make her get *really* arsey about the divorce...

He collects another bottle of wine from Banerjees, checking once again in his wallet for a stray lottery ticket as he gets out his credit card. He also scans the floor as he leaves, but the Banerjees are clearly very active with the broom or the hoover; the floor is spotless. He sticks his nose in the bin outside the shop and scans the gutters again as he heads back to the flat. Nothing.

As he's cooking, he tries to gee himself up a bit, the last thing he wants is to be morose and downbeat on a second date. He's checked his music for something appropriate: that was about as successful as Boris Johnson trying to find a conscience, or a comb. As he said to her, he's not really a music person. Springsteen and the Stones, much as he likes them, don't really promise the atmosphere he (or she) might wish for on a second date, not unless he sits by the player and edits out 'Prove it all Night', 'Hungry Heart', 'Honky Tonk Women', 'Brown Sugar' and a whole lot of others when they explode into the room. He flicks the radio on to *Classic FM* for the first time in his life to save the evening; he's no idea how he knows it exists.

Jack's cooking paella. It's a risk, he's never done it before, but he spent a summer in Valencia with Rich a few years back, and it was pretty much all they could afford to eat when they got tired of *bocadillos*. They found this clapped-out little *chiringuito* on the city beach that made an enormous paella every day and slapped out belly-stretching portions with a San Miguel thrown in (on the side, that is) for five euros a pop. When they were starting to run out of money, they offered to wash up or wait tables and the owner said *Claro, qué sí*, which apparently meant, *Yeah, sure*. Once in the kitchen, Jack was fascinated by the paella process.

The oil in the pan was the first shock. Oil? To cook *rice*? The oil itself was surprise enough, the *amount* was cataclysmic. Jack was convinced the old granny pouring it in just kept going cos she enjoyed seeing his eyes widen to bursting point. Then in went the chicken: all the joints and scrag ends that didn't end up on the *platos combinados* or in the *bocadillos* were thrown into the paella pan. He began to see how paella was the Spanish equivalent of pizza: whatever's left over – in it goes. He and Rich were shocked to learn that they'd been eating rabbits for weeks without gagging on the thought, but in went bits of 'bugs', along with a handful of snails if there were any sliding around.

He spends a few fruitless minutes hunting through the dead leaves and broken flowerpots in his back garden, before remembering that Milly is a veggie and realising that snails would almost certainly count as 'meat'. There'll be no snails for Milly's introduction to *Paella à la Jack* after all. Also, better safe than gastroenteritis in the morning, he reasons...

After the meat had stunk out *abuelita's chiringuito* kitchen, in went the veg: green beans, red peppers, cherry tomatoes, and what looked like butter beans to Jack and Rich but were called *garrofones* by the locals. *Where's the rice?* Jack kept thinking. *Where's the rice?* But not yet, signalled *abuelita* with a wagging finger, cos next came the all-important spices: salt, of course, *pimentón*, twigs of rosemary and a pinch (then another couple) of *azafrán* (saffron), the latter guarded in a box hidden somewhere unseen, as it was the most expensive ingredient in the place. *And the rice?*

No, still not yet. The water next, gallons of it, and only Valencian water *abuelita* insisted – from *el río Turia*, no less – but then the whole thing had to bubble for half an hour, on a fire made of wood from Valencian orange trees, before the rice was finally added. And even then, there was a magic touch to be added: a careful eye had to be kept, once the water had disappeared, until the oil-soaked rice at the bottom started to caramelise, producing the finger-licking, pan-scraping *socarrat* residue that paella aficionados fought over, bending forks and spoons to scrape out the last strands.

As well as the snails, Jack's not bothered sourcing any Turia river water or orange-tree wood, British Gas having to do instead. And 'bugs' has also had a stay of execution, and he'll toss in extra veg to make up for the missing chicken. He's even remembered a couple of lemons to squeeze over their plates when they're ready to go. *Vegetarian* paella? *Arroz de verduras?* It'll be off the cuff, but, yeah, he can do that – *Claro, qué sí!*

Milly's arrival lifts his mood like a Rashford screamer at the Stretford End. How can he let himself get down about money when he has a decent job that he likes, a reasonable flat in an okay area, good mates, and such a nice new girlfriend after the disaster that was, or is, or was, his marriage to Cindy?

Milly kisses him on the lips – not a full Frenchie, it's only seven thirty – but there's meaning to it, it's a girlfriend's kiss. His insides tingle.

'Do you need a parking permit?' he offers. 'We share a spare one in the block, and I've nabbed it for tonight...'

'No, it's all right,' she replies, blushing slightly. 'I thought I'd have a glass or two of wine, so, I um... came on the bus...' Her blush intensifies to fever pitch for a couple of seconds, and he finds himself suddenly colouring like a teenager.

'Nice music,' she says, changing the subject skilfully, after handing him a bottle of wine with an impressive-looking label. 'Pachelbel, 'Canon in D', one of my favourites.'

'I thought you'd like it,' he says, with a show of modest pride – then he catches her eye, smiles, then laughs. 'It's Classic FM actually; you'll find that out as soon as they announce the next piece (*piece*, he's learning). My music collection is a bit limited; I did warn you.'

She flicks through his CDs. 'I'd say you've got niche tastes.' She arches her eyebrows at AC/DC.

'Nice flat,' she says, clearly impressed, wandering around and spooking out the window. 'Really spacious, compared to mine.'

'Thanks. I think Cricklewood's a bit further down the food chain than Mill Lane, you might get more for your money round here. But it's pretty noisy Friday and Saturday nights when the boozers empty.'

'You forget I live over a kebab shop, I know all about Friday and Saturday nights, and Mondays, and Tuesdays... Wow!' she gasps, as he brings the paella in to land. He hasn't got a genuine *paellera*, the large shallow pan used for 'proper' paella, so he's used the biggest frying pan he could source from his neighbours.

Milly looks genuinely shocked, like she was expecting (veggie) sausage and chips, or a (veggie) bacon butty. He hasn't felt this proud since Miss Everett gave him a house point for painting a picture of her when he was about six. 'It's not risotto, is it? No, it's the Spanish one.'

'Paella,' he says, expertly, even managing to say it like there are no Ls in it, just like the Valencians do. He tells her the story of him and Rich working in the *chiringuito* on Playa Malvarrosa, and she listens like he's Michael Palin, or the man who went around the world in eighty days. She's got a sort of star-struck gaze in her eyes, which he feels is totally unwarranted, but he'll take it, after the day he's had. It might not be worth two point three million quid, but it's genuinely priceless to him.

He's been planning to tell her about Cindy, but pretty quickly he knows he's going to bottle it. The atmosphere's too good, he can't wreck it by telling her he's married. Not now. Next time.

'Where does Uncle Jezza work now? Or is he inside for terrorising small children in a rabbit costume?'

Jack shakes his head. 'Oh, he's in Spain. And he's *not* on the run. Been there this last ten years, bit more, maybe. Teaching Spanish primary children in English. It's called immersion. It's a primary school, he's got a class, it's not just a couple of English lessons. He does the whole bit, maths, science, PE, everything, *en inglés!*'

'Blimey. Glutton for punishment?'

'Yes, but he loves it. The Spanish kids are crackers, but in an innocent, enthusiastic sort of way.'

'So, they learn *everything* in English?'

'That's right. Insane. But, according to him, it seems to work. It's a private school, which wouldn't have been his first choice, but he always worked in the state sector here, and he and

Auntie Linda, they wanted to travel, and the immersion gig sounded interesting. For *interesting*, read wacky.'

'Bet he's got some tales to tell.'

'You're not kidding. He told me once, actually it was Auntie Linda, not him, they do this thing called *Show and Tell*. Children bring stuff in and have to talk about it. Sounds a great idea for little Spaniards wanting to practise their English. They get cats and dogs, piddling all over the floor, but the kids love it and are enthusiastic to ask questions. This one girl asked Auntie Linda if she could bring in her horse.'

'A horse? Into school?'

'Yep. A horse. A Spanish horse, at that. Couldn't speak a word of English. Into school for Show and Tell.'

'Did she say yes?'

'She had to clear it with the head, but the head was nuts, she said yes, why not? Why not bring a horse into school?'

'It sounds crazy.'

'Not something I covered on my PGCE.'

'And it was okay?'

'Apparently, although I think my Auntie Linda acquired a few more grey hairs, worrying about whether one of the other kids would walk around the back, and get a kick in the head, or a dollop of horseshit to take home. That would've pleased the parents, I imagine. You can see why I'd never go near primary, not after having been trained by Uncle Jezza. I'd prefer to mix it with a gang of Cricklewood's hardest secondary mobsters than confront Uncle Jezza's little Spaniards with their monolingual horses and Granny's false teeth.'

They're getting along, the conversation's flowing, his nerves are nicely hidden somewhere behind his lungs, so he makes a move on the lottery ticket scandal as he clears the table. Maybe he can win a bit of a sympathy vote if he paints himself as healthily stoical instead of a careless idiot.

'So, quiz question of the night, what would you do if you won the lottery?' he asks, a safe little gambit to accompany the fresh fruit salad he's managed to chop up without shedding any blood.

'I'd give it all away,' she replies without hesitation. 'Save the Children, World Health Organisation, a bunch of local charities for battered women, kids' things. I wouldn't keep a penny.'

'*Really?*' he says, unable to hide his surprise, unable to think of anything else to say, she's shocked him so completely.

'I'm not really into so much glaring inequality on the planet. Children without clean water to drink, while hedge-fund whatsits amass more money than they can ever spend. It sits in their bank accounts achieving nothing, while children and women walk miles to collect water, and we made PPE out of bin bags when coronavirus was doing the rounds. This, in the twenty-first century. Sorry, soapbox, shall we change the subject?'

He feels an idiot. He agrees with her completely, course he does. He's just never put the two things together, poverty and him wanting to win the lottery. He'd have given some of his two point three away, course he would. He was giving over half of it to Rich and Cind. Not that that was the same. No, not at all...

They talk about the paella; they talk about Spain; they talk about his students; they talk about her work; they drink all the wine; they go to bed.

———

He watches the lights from the cars in the street moving across his ceiling. Why do the lights travel in the opposite direction to the cars? When a car goes down the road, the lights sweep across the ceiling in the opposite direction. He's never puzzled it out. Fixating on it, simply giving a damn about it, is a sign he can't sleep.

He's pretty sure he's fallen in love with Milly. He's got a fair idea she's falling – or has fallen – in love with him. They haven't used the words yet, still slightly afraid that this can't be happening, but he feels it. Sees it in her eyes. Senses it in the air around them. There's a sort of excited calmness that he's never felt in anybody else's company.

Cindy had been sex. Sure, she was fun and lively and all the rest of it. But, if he's really honest with himself, it'd been mainly about sex for him. Well, sex while stoned and drunk and on holiday. She'd been pretty keen too.

Milly's different. The sex is great. It's all the rest of it that's really taken his breath away, lit his fire, stoned his crows, emptied his head of any original phrases. All the extra stuff he never felt with Cindy. He could watch Milly all night, he can't put his finger on what it is, but she captivates him. He finds himself staring at her as she makes a point and has to will himself to concentrate on what she's saying, rather than gawp at the beauty of how she's saying it. It's silly things, little inconsequential nothings, like the way she suddenly looks up at him when she asks him something. Like what he might say carries great weight and importance. No one's ever looked up at him like that before. He's almost started to crave it; he feels like a child in class waiting for a word of praise from a favourite teacher in a flowery summer dress.

Apart from the lottery moment, they've agreed on pretty much everything. They like reading, they like films and theatre, they like to travel, to try different foods. They also, the dangerous part, seem to like each other, without having to try too hard, or pretend too much.

Even the music, which he had thought was going to be a barrier between them, ended up, miraculously, bringing them even closer together. In fact, as she named practically every piece (see, it's easy) they played on Classic FM, he'd found he recognised (and quite liked) half of them. There was the helicopter scene from *Apocalypse Now* (that was Wagner, but you say it like it's got a V not a W); and the kiss in the fields from *A Room with a View*, which was opera, Puccini, Italian guy; and even Verdi played a bit on the Nike, *Nothing Beats a Londoner* ad. Actually, he didn't exactly play it for the ad, he's dead, but it was his music, and Jack recognised it!

She seemed impressed that he knew so many of the tracks and enjoyed giving him clues about where he might have heard them. She made him feel less of a musical dunce than he thought he was, the classic gift of a natural teacher, he knows. Then she impressed him by telling him who had written them, and what they meant, and whether she'd ever played them. Yeah, the music had been good, moved the evening along, made it fun, a game they shared, enjoyed playing, so easy.

Why can't he sleep? He needs to tell her about Cind. He needs to tell her about the lottery, although, thinking about it, losing the ticket has kinda solved the little problem of her not liking money very much. That's a kind of silver lining. Losing a winning lottery ticket as a silver lining? It's as daft as Brexit being a success. But she's like that. Full of surprises. Some of them shocking, like the way she hit him with the violin – her playing of it, that is. He can't get enough of her. He's glad he never had to make a choice between two point three million quid and Milly. Jesus! The way he feels, if he honestly had to choose between the money and her, it's the two point three that would be getting the old heave-ho. To his surprise, shock even, he's quite sure he means it.

He's serious. He really is. If he could find the lottery ticket, kicked under the carpet by Iker's big boots, but Jack would have to break up with Milly as the price of finding it? If that was his choice? He turns to look at her sleeping silently next to him. Hair awry, breathing as soft as a breeze you can barely feel... He'd take *her*. He would. He finds it hard to believe it's true, but it is.

But he has to tell her. Sooner or later, he'll have to introduce her to Rich, and probably Cindy, if they end up simply speaking to each other, if not BFF. And they're both gonna give him a bit of a ribbing, the guy who lost the lottery ticket. It hits him suddenly – what if Milly doesn't take his losing the ticket well? What if she thinks he's robbed millions of thirsty kids of water, by being so careless with his washing? Sleep seems further away than ever; his mind spins, his eyes watch the lights, Milly sleeps next to him as silently as a baby. Life should be good.

He gets up quietly, wanders his flat, no longer that lonely place it'd felt since Cindy left. He looks out of the window at the empty street, he's no idea what time it is. The chill starts to grip his shoulders. Before he gets back into bed, he crosses the room, and looks under the carpet by the door. He finds exactly what he was expecting...

Nothing.

36

THE STEAL

'Bɪᴛ ᴏꜰ ʙᴀᴅ ɴᴇᴡꜱ...' Rich says, as he takes a long puff. He's still breathing heavily and is staring at the ceiling, wondering what Cindy's reaction's going to be.

'What's that?'

'He's lost the ticket.'

There's a long silence, during which she takes the cigarette and draws slowly on it. He can almost hear her brain gurgling as her synapses fight with each other to work out a plan.

'He's lying. He's changed his mind. Got cold feet.'

Rich has seen this response coming. Jack as liar and cheat. Always her option number one. If she actually thought anyone would take it seriously, she'd claim that Jack had tricked her into marrying him through a cunning, *Dangerous Liaisons*-style deception. Yeah, sure, and the blond toff-boy's not for turning...?

'I don't think so. I called in on him, he'd trashed the flat looking for it. Everything was out, every drawer, every book off the shelves, he was pretty cut up.'

More gurgling from her synapses. She takes another drag, she *always* does that, before handing the cig to him.

'He's faking it. He's changed his mind and doesn't want to share it anymore. We're not falling for that.'

We're not falling… Here we go again, throwing in a *we* or an *us* like she's not Jack's wife, but is already, in fact, married to Rich. But he *has* fallen for it. Well, no, he hasn't *fallen* for anything. He *knows* Jack's lost the ticket. Jack can't *act!* You'd have more luck asking him to walk a tightrope across Cricklewood Broadway. He was an angel in the nativity when they were infants – until he shouted at Mary to get off his *bloody* foot in the middle of the matinee performance. Wasn't as if she was wearing boots; she was a mite of a thing, Jenny Penn, in her bare feet. Jack smashed the fourth wall good and proper, screaming for his mum and dad in the front row to come up and sort her out. Substitute angel was on duty for the evening show.

'I'm pretty sure it's gone. We found it in his chinos pocket, washed to a pulp, no hope of untangling it, it was mush.'

Silence. What's she thinking? How does she think? Does she have a list of possible actions that Jack might take, in any situation, and go down it in her mind?

'He's setting us up.'

'What?!'

'He's setting us up.'

'Setting us up for *what?*'

'For not giving us any dollarydoos, you dill. He's gonna *pretend* he's lost the ticket so he can cut us out. He's changed his bloody mind.'

'Listen, Cind, I know him. He's my brother. He's in bloody bits about it. He couldn't act this to save his neck. It's as ludicrous as casting Boris Johnson to play Bond. Not the bloody villain, Bond himself.'

She takes the cigarette again. He hasn't even had a puff, but neither has he got the energy to fight for it. The minutes pass.

It's not silence, he can *hear* her scheming. He wonders if he even really *likes* her.

'Okay. Let's believe him. Let's say he's lost it. Or washed it. Or whatever the drongo's done with it. What's he gonna do about it?'

'Nothing. What *can* he do about it? With a bit of luck, he might cry into his beer for a week or two. I'll be happy as long as he doesn't do anything *stupid...*'

She knows what that means; one of life's great euphemisms – blimey, she's beginning to think like Jack.

Cindy shifts in the bed, rolls to face Rich. 'You know, I read an article once, about some dipstick who lost a winning ticket. There was some mechanism you can use, it'll be on the internet, you give the lottery people the details of your numbers, where you bought the ticket, what time and all that. Then, if nobody else comes forward in the time, and the prize is unclaimed, then they give it to you.'

'Really?'

'I think so, it was in a magazine I read in the dentist once. I remember thinking, who in this world could ever be such a complete dill as to lose a jackpot-winning ticket? At least now we know the answer to that little factoid of human behaviour – none other than Jackodillodrongo.'

'Bloody brilliant. I'll send him a text.'

'No! Don't do that!' She sits up in bed suddenly, grabs Rich's hand before he can reach his phone. 'If he's just gonna leave it, that's his lookout. We can do this ourselves! Remember how he was going to cut you out at the beginning? If he's gonna leave it lying around, we can pick up the pieces. He need never know.'

'Are you serious?'

'Serious? Two point three million quid? Course I'm bloody serious.'

'But you can't do that!'

'Why ever the fuck not? He tried it on us!'

Except he didn't, Rich thinks. Not on *us*. But Cindy doesn't know that. And he can't tell her.

'How would we ever hide the fact that we've suddenly got his two point three million quid?'

'We won't tell him.'

'What? So, what, we're not going to spend any of it? No new car? No new house? No fancy hols in the Seychelles? What would be the point of having the money if we can't spend it?'

'We'd tell him *we* won the lottery. With *my* bloody numbers. What could he say?'

Rich's brain is struggling to keep up with Cindy's flow. He's sure she hasn't thought this through; she's making it up on the fly.

'He-he'd suspect,' he stutters, not quite sure that he would. 'What if there was a way for him to check if his ticket was cashed in? What then?'

She shrugs. 'He won't. He hasn't even thought about contacting them to see if there's anything he can do about having lost it, the drongo! He's hardly gonna come to the conclusion that we've used his numbers when we strike lucky, is he? He hasn't got that big a brain.'

'But he might.' Might what? He might think to contact them? Or, he might have that big a brain? Arguing with Cindy is like trying to argue in a language you barely speak.

'Yeah, and he might be Prime Minister one day. Although, actually, you elected that blond clown, didn't you, so maybe *that's* not out of the question.'

Rich doesn't bother to tell her that he never voted for that blond clown, he doesn't know anybody who did. She knows that.

'Right, so this is what we'll do. We'll keep this on the back burner for five and a half months, then if he shows no sign of a brain at all, we'll move in and collect!'

We, we, we… 'I don't like this.' Rich doesn't usually cross her, he's always the one for the easy life, but this doesn't feel right. Jack hiding two point three million quid from Cindy is one thing; he and Cindy hiding it from Jack is quite another. Stealing – no, that's not the right word at all – starting a *liaison* with Cindy, as she and Jack were on the point of divorce? That might cause a bit of a family rift for a week or so, but secretly getting hold of Jack's money, while not telling him that he could have collected it himself, then living a lie with Cindy, for ever and ever, Amen? It would take more than a couple of beers down The BOGOFF to salve those wounds if it ever got out. Which it would. That's the golden rule of family secrets, they always come out in the wash. Just like Jack's ticket. Then everything ends up mushy.

'Let it lie. Let's see what happens. But don't you bloody say a word to him about this! This is *my* plan, remember!' She stares at Rich with a look that threatens damage to his most treasured possessions – his bike, his laptop… other things.

Yeah, he thinks, sullenly. *Great plan.* He's never been keen on the 'farce' format of British comedy; once it gets too far-fetched, he starts to lose interest. He's one of the very few who didn't fall head over heels with *Fawlty Towers*. He's beginning to feel he's getting typecast as Basil: he doesn't have to think too hard to know exactly who Cindy's playing…

37

THE SECRET IN THE PARK

It's one of those days that tourists visiting London pray for, and one of those days that make the residents feel like tourists. The sun is already guaranteeing short sleeves and swishy skirts and provoking a further reduction in the rapidly dwindling number of climate-change deniers. Cricklewood Broadway has the feel of somewhere slightly 'exotic' – and that truly takes some doing. Breakfast tables are on the pavements waiting for anyone who wants to be a continental again, post Brexit; birds are singing; people are smiling, some of them are holding hands; even the buses seem to be emitting slightly less smelly exhaust fumes…

Jack slips out without waking Milly and collects fresh croissants from the bakery; a dozen 'big, ballsy, Valencian oranges' (as the greengrocer's sign dubs them – *or should that be greengrocers'*…?); and some Cafés Balancilla beans, a brand he discovered in the Valencian region, which he sometimes splashes out on as a special treat. He wakes her with the grinder. It fills the flat with a heavy coffee aroma that draws her out of bed faster than any alarm clock. The croissants are already in the oven and are fighting back in the very first gorgeous-smells Olympics. Then he juices the oranges, using the juicer he bought on his return from that Valencian summer – and has hardly ever used since.

They squeeze onto his 'balcony', and watch the early sunlight cut across the rooftops from the east, before it disappears around the front of the building. Neither is working, so why not spend the day together? Slowly, slowly; they're not moving in together or getting engaged. One day. They decide on a picnic. It has to be a London park. So, Regent's or Hampstead Heath? She wants Regent's. It's more touristy, she wants them to play tourists in town. Tourists look at things with fresh eyes; tourists make 'spur-of-the-moment' decisions; tourists hold hands. She wants Regent's – he'd follow her to Central Park or the Amazon jungle if she suggested they go there instead. They make decisions together as easily as two toddlers given a choice between the ice-cream van and the dentist's chair.

They raid the local mini mart like teenage shoplifters, then jump on a sixteen bus to Maida Vale, sitting at the front of the top deck as Jack used to do on his way to school as a kid. He snatches a sneaky glance at Hillcrest Court as they go over the lights at the top of Shoot-Up Hill, but he says nothing. Maybe another time, long into the future, he'll confess his flirtation with a flat for seven fifty.

But now is not that moment. Now, Milly is busy telling him that she's never been to Regent's Park, and how she's heard it's got a lake and a theatre. He basks in her look of awe as he confirms what she's heard, adding the bandstand and the café like he's the author of the London Lonely Planet. Her excitement is hugely infectious. They walk hand in hand up St John's Wood Road, past Lord's, pretending they've recently landed at Heathrow, and *everything* is new. It's not a difficult game to play.

They scoot round the Inner Circle, touring the Japanese and the Rose Gardens, eating overpriced ice creams, cos that's what tourists do, before strolling back to the lake where a band is playing in the bandstand, as he'd promised.

Jack's decided to tell her today, about Cindy, but once again they're having such a great time, he wavers. What if she hates him, for not telling her sooner? What if she doesn't believe in divorce? Maybe she's a raving Catholic?

But he knows these aren't the real reasons for his reticence. There's only one thing that holds him back: the thought that it might change the way she looks at him by the smallest of fractions. That whatever it is shining in her eyes when she gazes at him, dims by the tiniest measurable amount. That the incredible feeling he has when he's in her company starts to bleed out of his pores, as he senses that she no longer shares it as completely and utterly as she used to. It's the fear that he might be a huge ocean liner, mid-ocean, full of happy celebrating people, but holed beneath the waterline...

'I need to tell you something,' he says, facing her on the old car blanket he's brought, and looking serious. His heart is hitting heavily, huge thumping beats he can feel in his throat. 'I hope it's not a big thing. I've tried to find the right moment, I'm sorry I didn't tell you before.'

'You're scaring me,' she says, taking hold of his hands. Is this the last time he'll see that look in her eyes? 'Tell me.'

He takes a shuddering breath, doubts himself again, but he's had enough of not telling her the truth, and he can't back out now with some nonsense, *it was nothing,* or *forget about it,* that he knows won't wash...

'I'm going through a divorce. I've been married to Cindy for just over a year, she moved out and asked me for a divorce about five months ago. I agreed. We were never really suited. It's relatively amicable. I'm sorry I didn't tell you earlier. We were having such a nice time together – well, apart from the very first thirty minutes, maybe. I was always afraid I'd spoil the moment

– actually, any of the time we've shared. I'm sorry. I should have told you sooner.'

She stares at him for too long, and he wonders if she's going to stand up and simply walk away without another word. Are these the last minutes he'll share with her? The last time he'll see her face? Except, maybe, for some teary encounters where he doorsteps her, or accosts her in the street, begging her to reconsider, give him one last chance, as passers-by look at him pityingly, or tall good-looking guys ask her if she needs any help... He knows he should have told her sooner, won't blame her if she's angry.

But it's not an easy one to slip in to a first meeting in a coffee shop, or a first meal together; or even, as he's found, a second. *Hey, guess what? You need to know I'm married.* There's a presumptuousness to it: like, *I know you'll be thinking of marrying me already, so I'd better pull your brakes on before you get too carried away...* It's not his style. But then, what style has it left him with, by not telling her until now? Some smooth-talking, con man predator? At least she hasn't let go of his hands.

'I thought you were going to tell me you were really sick – even dying,' she says quietly, looking down into her lap. 'Cancer, or – you know... *something*.'

'No! I – I just couldn't find the right moment. You don't mind?'

'How could I mind?' She squeezes his hands, looking up at him again. 'I didn't know you before a few days ago. How could I mind what you did with your life before I met you? It's not a crime to get married. Are you okay? Is it going smoothly?'

He's stunned that she's responded in the one way he hasn't predicted – would she be angry, disappointed, would she feel tricked or deceived? He's rolled those permutations around in his mind these last few days, wondering how she'd respond. But no, none of them. She's worried about *him*. How is it affecting *him*? Is *he* okay?

'Relatively. We both agree it was a mistake to get married. It was probably obvious before we actually did. I feel a fool. We rushed into it. It was so stupid.'

'You don't have to explain anything.'

'I'd like to. I want you to know everything. Unless you don't want me to...'

'No, I want to know all about you, but sometimes there's a time and a place.'

'It's been playing on my mind, so I'm going to go for here and now. I hope I don't spoil the day, that's what stopped me last night, and before that. Every moment we've shared seemed too good to spoil. We were having such a happy time, I was afraid I'd ruin it somehow.'

'You won't ruin it. What we did when we were younger doesn't always say much about how we are now. We change, we make mistakes, your intentions were good. I've got an Ibizan fiddle tattooed on my back, remember...'

He smiles, squeezes her hands in return. The relief he feels is like winning the lottery again. But it's different. He's not sure how. But it is. It's something to do with her, her reaction. She's surprised him again, she wasn't angry, she didn't blame him or accuse him. The difference is, she's shown herself to be even better than he'd thought before. Caring about him, not herself.

'Oh, I've changed,' he says. 'Have I learned some home truths! You ready for the full story? You've heard the headline news, the rest is nothing compared to that. But I want to tell you everything.'

'Okay, I'm listening.' She refills their glasses with the wine they've brought and turns and lays back with her head on his lap. The sun bathes her face; she looks serene. He hopes his story doesn't cause it to change.

'Just over a year ago, I went on holiday with a mate, Cheesie. His name's Davie Cheeseman, so everyone calls him Cheesie. We were at a loose end for the summer, so we were in the pub one evening, bemoaning our prospects, when he saw a last-minute holiday deal in the paper. Bed and breakfast in a small Thai pension on Phuket. It was ridiculously cheap, and the photos showed this idyllic beach, and all the trimmings: palm trees, gorgeous sunsets, one or two females in bikinis...'

She pinches his thigh, gently.

'We'd done English together at uni, and we'd both harboured plans to write novels. So, we packed our laptops and our swimming trunks and a few hundred novels on Kindles – well, it didn't turn out quite how we planned.

'The pension was in the town, not on the beach. The ad hadn't shown any pictures of it, just beach scenes. Our room was a pokey cupboard with no air conditioning and a view of the bins behind a hugely popular twenty-four-hour pizza café that ran an air-conditioning unit that was so noisy it drowned out the terrace night club on the roof. The bed was the smallest double imaginable; the mattress was the sort of bit of foam you'd find on a cheap sun lounger in a run-down hotel in Lowestoft. It sagged so spectacularly it was probably marketed as a hammock. And, of course, it was on the 'party' side of town, you know, Ibiza with rocket boosters? The only fiddle in town, however, was the one we'd fallen for.

'We arrived on a Friday night. And, like ridiculously optimistic fools, we thought Friday? Saturday? Okay, maybe Sunday, but it'll ease off during the week. In fact, it kept getting worse and worse. I think we arrived right at the start of the season; the following Tuesday night was twice as bad as the first Friday. It was horrendous; bars and discos, drunk westerners and rivers of vomit. Neither of us are really clubby types, we hadn't planned on this at all.

'Anyway, we finally found a quietish sort of bar-restaurant shack at the far end of the beach, as far away from the high jinks as we could get, that sold enormous sandwiches at half the price of anywhere else in town. So, we fell in with a gang of Aussies, chatting and stuff. They were a sort of fit, beach volleyball, surfing type of gang, smoking a bit of weed but, like us, they were out for a longish stint so didn't really want to blow all their money paying a tenner for a bottle of beer in the clubs. Then Cheesie fell for one of the Aussie women, Debs, and she fell for him, and that was pretty much the last I saw of him, they'd gone.'

Milly sits up at this point and takes his hands again. She's got a sympathetic look on her face, like Jack is suddenly Jacky-no-mates, alone in Thailand.

He smiles ruefully. 'At least with Cheesie gone, I could stretch out in the bed... So, what could I do? It's actually quite a good set-up for a novel, so I tried to write during the days, then headed to the quiet end of the beach in the evenings for some solid grub. I was on bread and cheese from the supermarket the rest of the time, trying to eke my money out until my flight home, everything was wildly more expensive than we'd anticipated.

'The Aussies were there most nights, drinking, not loud or getting drunk, so we got chatting. They told me that Cheesie and Debs had gone on an island tour – thanks for telling me, mate. And I got chatting to Cindy. Seen from this end, it's a match made in hell. We're almost polar opposites: she's loud, brash, hugely sporty, aerobics, Pilates, she gives classes, does massage, all that; and there was me, writing a book and hiding under a tree so I didn't get sunburnt.

'But, for some reason, we kinda got on. If I'm honest, from this perspective, I think I was flattered. I mean, she's an attractive woman, full of energy, I couldn't really believe she'd go for someone like me. That's how it started. And, I don't know, I guess I was a bit lonely, and you know what Aussies are like, they do a lot of that Pommy banter, but they were friendly, and I sort of hung out with them and wrote less and smoked more weed. They taught me to surf, almost, and I was needed to make the volleyball teams even, and rather than walk the full length of the beach back to my hovel every night, I ended up sort of 'living' with Cindy in a beach hut for a month, and by the end of it, I'm still not clear how this happened, she'd changed her ticket and was coming back to the UK with me – to get married.

'It's crazy, I know,' he says, as Milly's face shows a sort of fascinated disbelief, like he's telling her the plot of the shit comedy-novel that he failed to write. 'If we'd left it as a holiday romance it would've been fine, but we got back here and it was cold and my flat was a bit damp, and she found it tough at first to get any work, but we had this 'plan' and I wasn't sure how to stop it. It's crossed my mind, subsequently, that maybe she was using me to get a working visa. I don't know, that might not be fair, she never said anything about ever wanting to work in the UK. There was a last-minute cancellation at the registry office, and before either of us could say *Are you sure?* – we were married, and it went downhill from there.'

Milly shakes her head, sadly, but he shrugs as he thinks back to the break-up. 'We didn't argue much – Cindy was too good at it. I remember one tiff; I rather unwisely accused her of always wanting to have the last word. And that was the last word in *that* conversation. She drained her glass, stood up, walked out of the restaurant, leaving me with two-thirds of a pizza, and the last word. Not that it felt much of a triumph as she proved me wrong, winning the argument with silence and an empty chair.

'It wasn't awful, don't get me wrong, we just had so little in common. She got work doing massages and Pilates classes and the like, and I had my lessons. Then, in the evenings, when I had most of my work, she was either playing netball for teams or was out trying to recreate a Thai-sports-beach culture underneath the Westway in mid-November. When we both had time off, she wanted to hit the town, the West End, theatres, shows, that kinda stuff. Of course she did, she's an Australian, a tourist, but we didn't really have the cash for it, and I was happier staying in with a DVD or reading a novel.

We drifted, rather than broke up. I had a feeling she'd started sleeping with someone else, right at the end. I was never sure, but that hurt the most. I think, for a while, I was in danger of getting a bit down about it all. But I figured I hadn't really done anything wrong, I'd made a mistake, we'd both made a mistake. I guess it was a bit of a relief when she suggested a divorce, I wouldn't have been brave enough to hurt her feelings, especially if I'd been wrong about her sleeping with someone else. As I said, I learned a lot...'

'You poor thing–' Milly starts, but he stops her.

'Oh, no sympathy, please. I was a big boy. It was my own fault. I take full responsibility. She didn't trick me; I don't think so. It doesn't really matter if she did. I was naive, stupid, cowardly, immature. I'm really glad we never had any kids. That would've been irresponsible to boot. At least we only messed each other's lives up, and hopefully, only for a while. When the divorce is done, we might even be friends, well, we might at least keep in touch, if only to reminisce incredulously about how we ever managed to get together. She seems to be more friends with some of *my* friends than I am. So, you see, I'm coming out of that with my eyes wide open. I know I made a massive, stupid, mistake, and I think I need to take things steadily, and make sure my feet are on the ground.'

'Are *we* going too fast...?'

'What? No! God, no, I don't mean that at all. What's happening between us is perfect. I suppose I want the divorce done and dusted, to feel I'm in control of my life again, but meeting you has been wonderful.'

'It's been a bit of a whirlwind though...?'

'Yes, but you've got to remember that my last whirlwind was fuelled by wacky baccy, Malibu, and a Thai beach. What's happening here is just our two lives bumping into each other, I don't feel anything is being rushed, I don't feel under any pressure. With Cindy, if I'm honest, I think I *was* sort of steamrollered. I'm not blaming her, it was all my own fault, I guess I was flattered and weak-willed and all too keen on what was happening...'

'I don't see you like that at all.'

'I hope I've learned from it, changed a bit. I'd like to think so.'

'We all make mistakes.'

'Some of them bigger than others. At least you only ended up with a tattoo you don't like: I ended up with a wife I didn't like, and she ended up with me. If we're going to play *who messed up the worst*, I think my Cindy trumps your fiddle.'

She smiles. 'So, we go slow and steady. That suits me fine. I'm in no hurry. I've got a new job and a new boyfriend in a new city. That's quite enough for me at the moment.'

And it's this that convinces him to save the other 'secret', the little matter of the lottery ticket, for another occasion... not even noticing that she's called him her boyfriend.

38

THE FACEBOOK RULES OF COURTSHIP

'CAN I TAKE A SELFIE OF US?' Milly says, as they're strolling past the lake. Jack's touched by her asking if he minds. Cindy never did that, not that he'd noticed her *not* asking. It's like Milly's from a different era. Maybe it's his?

'Course you can,' he says, easily adopting a carefree smile. She shows it to him, one take. It's like a pro-shot for some upmarket holiday website. *Come to London.* She's so pretty. So genuinely, unselfconsciously pretty. And he looks great. Really great. He's relaxed, he's smiling. Not in a smug, *look at me*, sort of way. Although he feels it. No, he appears kind, sensitive. They look like they're in love and loving London.

'Can I put it on my Facebook page?' she asks, without taking her eyes off her phone.

She can put it on the side of a bus, if she wants. She can take out full-page ads in the *Standard*; fly planes with banners of it over Old Trafford – he actually wonders if he might suggest it...

He shrugs instead. 'Course.'

She veers to a bench and starts tippy-tapping, she's about as fast as the Italians.

'Almost as handsome as you are in real life,' she says, half to herself. Once again, he feels like a five-year-old who's been given a gold star by the prettiest teacher in the school.

'You look beautiful,' he says, gasping as the truth of it squeezes the breath out of him.

She touches his leg in acknowledgement and keeps tippy-tappying with one hand, well, one thumb.

He wonders if he's agreed to something more than just letting her put a photo of him on her Facebook page. He's never got up to speed with the Facebook rules of courtship; he kinda doubts they publish a digital Debrett's for online virgins, like himself. He's picked up a few snippets from the press (and the Italians), about how there is some sort of unwritten code to all things romantic on the internet. Didn't he read somewhere, sometime in ancient history, it might have been a couple of months ago, that there was a sort of unwritten sequence of Facebook 'friending'? Something that all the GenZs had grown up with but some of the millennials, like him, hadn't quite sussed. God help the boomers. Didn't it kinda signify stages of a relationship? Something about friending somebody new, then adding a photo of them, then adding a photo of the two of you 'together', then changing your thingy to *in a relationship,* then all her friends friending you and your friends, then you and your friends friending them all back? Elizabeth Bennet – you had it so easy.

Actually, it really *was* much less complicated before the internet, even as recently as when *he* was only a little bit younger. Your mates used to ask you: *Did you hold her hand? Did you kiss her? Did you put your hand...?*

'Can I add you on Facebook?' she says suddenly, head still down, thumbs going like two squirrels fighting over an acorn.

'Yeah,' he says, cool as you like.

'Are you Jack on here? Or is it John or...?'

'Jack,' he says, almost certain, he remembers little about setting up his profile.

'And what's your surname?'

He takes a breath... 'Potts.' He watches as her thumbs hesitate for a nanosecond. Maybe only half a nanosecond. Then the squirrels are at it again. His admiration for her rises another notch or fifty. It's rare for anyone to respond with such cool. He's used to people double-taking, freezing, or asking him if he's kidding.

The ones who think they're comedians will come up with one of the handful of 'original' responses that he's heard a dozen times at least – 'Good luck with that!' or 'How much?' To be fair, he's always admired Beano, who responded to knowledge of Jack's first and second name combination with a lightning quick, 'At least your parents didn't call you Piss!' before moving on and never mentioning the subject ever again. That was classy, Jack always thought.

The worst responses by far, were people who rubbed the salt in by dredging up every crazy first and second name combinations they'd ever encountered. A neighbour called Joe King. *Yes, really!* A lad in school called Dwayne Pipe. *Honest!* What they never seemed to realise was that they were essentially saying *Jack Potts* was just as daft. Thanks for that. He always vowed he would never speak to those people again, no matter what.

And why didn't Rich ever get similar treatment? Isn't Rich Potts pretty funny? Apparently not, especially when standing next to Jack Potts. Why couldn't his parents have called *him* Paint, or Coffee, or Lobster instead of Rich? He'd never asked his parents what the *hell* they were thinking when they named him Jack. He always suspected that they were clueless to the issue and would have been mortified if he'd ever brought it up. So, he never had. It all makes Milly's response the best he's ever encountered, even nudging Beano into second place. He loves her all the more for it.

'Gotcha,' she says, pushing her hair behind her ear. She's smiling, thumbs busy. Her smile holds as she scans his page, or profile, or whatever people who use Facebook call it. He wishes he had more friends.

'I don't use it much,' he says, worried what she'll think when she sees how many friends he *hasn't* got. Will she think he's a social deadbeat? Is it some sort of social marker that'll ring alarm bells in her head, like her finding a black balaclava mask under his bed? It's a bit like being undressed on a first date. Although, they've actually done that bit. And it was fine. This feels different, worse. Stupid comparison. It's like she's got X-ray vision into his whole life. Only problem is, if what's on Facebook is his whole life, she'll think he died about a year ago.

His phone pings. As she's still engrossed in hers, he checks what's happening. Friend request. Oh yes, of course. Up she pops. The lovely photo of them together. He scrolls down her page, profile, handle, thingy, sees more photos of her with other people. She stands out in all of them, her smile dominating the scene like your favourite celebrity joining you in your living room. She's not one of those people who can say *I never take a nice photo*. She's busy, by the looks of it. Out with friends; a petition against hunger (he should sign some petitions); a poem about friendship; more photos with friends. Smile after smile, none of them forced.

Friends? He's her 528th friend. She's his sixteenth. He hopes again she doesn't notice, but he clocked her scoreboard instantly. Is that because he's got a 'thing' about it? Or is everybody like that? He's already said he doesn't use it much. He can't say that again. Undressing on a first date? Suddenly he knows what it feels like to sit naked in Regent's Park.

39

THE STING

Cɪɴᴅʏ ᴏᴘᴇɴs ʜᴇʀ ʟᴀᴘᴛᴏᴘ, stirs her latte, cracks her knuckles. The Coffee Potty is a favourite little hideaway she frequents when she really does want to be left alone. (Don't the Brits have a way with humorous names for bars and cafés? The Mad Bishop and Bear? The Bishop's Finger! What *is* this thing with *bishops?*) It's got all the usual coffee-shop stuff (including newspapers, free wifi and some top tucker), but Cindy's not here for any of that. Not today. Today she's here because it has one extra, slightly more unusual feature: it has a few *single tables.* These really are only big enough for one, so nobody can 'join' you. If someone were to attempt it, you'd have to move to a bigger table, such a hassle (so, take the hint and piss off). She's got no intention of sharing today; she has work to do. Anything that earns her money is work in Cindy's book. This is big work. Enormous. And secret...

She squeezes her hair back into a tight, businesslike ponytail and fixes it in place with a scrunchie. Then she looks around as she waits for her laptop to liven up. A couple of only-just-not teenagers are having a head-to-head at a tall table, perched on uncomfortable-looking stools, their pushchairs also facing each other below the level of the table, like the tots are also having a good natter. They're getting ready to go, busying over how much each of them needs to pay, whether they're going to leave a tip. They're clearly important calculations. As important as Cindy's – only not quite as big – in the monetary sense.

what – to – do – if – you – lose – lottery – ticket – uk?

Isn't the interweb a modern miracle? She has eight million answers in less than a second. And, as is often the case, the first reply is on the button. Or, on the *money*, as they say. Much more appropriate. There's a form you have to fill in, apparently. That's it. Bingo!

You must complete a separate form for each lost, stolen or la-di-da ticket. Email your form... We must receive your form by 5pm on the thirtieth day after the relevant draw date...

Ah! Not the full six months to wait then? That's unexpected. Probably better to get it rolling, then if Jack does find a brain in his underwear drawer, and contacts the lottery, she can always quietly withdraw her claim. No one need ever know... Least of all Jack. Or Rich. She scans through the form.

Has the ticket been lost, stolen, damaged, destroyed?

Hmmm, the dipstick couldn't even limit himself to just the *one*. He's got three out of four – maybe *lost*, definitely *damaged*, possibly *destroyed*. If she counts the scam she's trying to pull now, he's hit the jackpot again with a potentially *stolen*. She ticks *lost*.

Next bit is name and address, all that bull dust. She knows where he lives...

Name and address of the shop where you bought the ticket?

She can google that.

Does the store have CCTV? Yes, no, unsure...

Hmmm. Interesting one. She sits back and sips her latte for

a moment, calculating. Are the lottery mob really going to lob into Banerjees to have a squiz at their CCTV? For two point three big ones? Maybe they will, otherwise, why would they ask? But are the Banerjees likely to have a month's worth of CCTV recordings safely stored away somewhere? Possibly. But less likely if she hangs on to the form until 4.59 on the thirtieth day, which would give the Banerjees a fighting chance to have wiped the tape a couple of times. Also, she doesn't want to give the lottery snoops too much extra snooping time. Chances are, if they do actually check, they're going to look to see if *someone* bought a ticket there at that time. Surely the machine will tell them that. They're not actually going to ask her to provide a photo of herself to compare with the film of Jack. Hardly.

Does she rock up to Banerjees to check whether they have CCTV, or does she tick the *unsure*? The *no* would be the best option, obv. She decides to scoot over and check, and if they've got a camera, then she'll tick *unsure*. Yeah, bonzer idea.

Date of purchase? Time of purchase?

She might have to buy Beano another amber to nail that down a bit better, no worries.

How was the ticket purchased? Easy one, Jack's always a cash man for his lottery. *Name of the game? Winning draw date and prize amount won? Number of lines? Additional info?*

Additional info? Yeah, he's a complete drongo, but ignore him, give the money to me.

Do you have an image of the ticket and blah blah blah, sign here for two point three million UK quids.

She'll get that printed out and signed up and then lay it low for a while. But not too long. Best not mention the change of date to Rich. Not right now, no. In fact, might be an idea not to mention the plan to him again, hope he forgets all about it. She spooks the cake cabinet; they've got a slice of their double-chocolate sponge with her name on it. She waves at the waitress, points at the cabinet, and dances her eyebrows. A good day's work deserves a little reward – or even a frigging enormous one...

40

THE BGT FINAL

Jack and Milly are hand in hand up Shoot-Up Hill from the bus stop, bumping into each other with the sheer joy of the day they've had. From the park, they'd strolled through Covent Garden to watch the buskers and performance artistes entertain the tourists, while the pickpockets lurked like Joes from a le Carré novel. They hit the river. Metaphorically. More buskers, more performance artistes (noticeably lower class down there) and the pickpockets again, enjoying a change of scenery in a different chapter. He'd asked her if he could take a selfie, then struggled to upload it onto his Facebook page, until she'd helped him, gently, no smirking at the obvious fact that he wasn't a regular. *I should use it more often. Yeah, you really should...*

They'd nabbed a bench, ate the sandwiches they'd bought at an M&S, on a whim, like tourists do. Then they'd strolled up and down the South Bank, he promising to take her to The Globe, she promising him a concert at the Royal Festival Hall. Hopefully when someone is playing the *Schindler* piece. As they turn into Mill Lane, a bike screeches to a halt at the lights.

'Jack!'

'Rich!'

Bugger! Jack's got no real reason he can think of to keep Milly a secret, but there's a feeling tucked somewhere in the back of his brain that were Cindy to find out, she might get awkward, especially if there was an angle in it for her.

Rich hobby-horses his bike onto the pavement and gives Milly a Spanish one-two as Jack makes the introductions. No gentlemanly, English, reserved handshake from Rich. Jack'd expect no less from him. He knows Rich's seen them holding hands, he made his own gentlemanly attempt to help Rich with his bike as an excuse to let go, but it was miles too late. Now, Rich's got his *BGT* judge's cap on, and looks ready to give Milly a bye into the final.

Rich spreads his arms and sings the first line of 'How Long?', the old Ace hit, winking at Milly, making her smile. How does he do that? Instantly hit the stage, deliver a cool line like he's practised all night? Jack knows he'd be panicking if he were in Rich's place: was he sweaty from the bike ride? Did his pits smell? Rich in a panic on first intro to a female? It's as likely as Liz Truss knowing her times tables.

'Oh, a few days.' Milly giggles, looking lovingly at Jack as she flattens the pleats in her dress before grabbing onto his arm.

'Oh, right! I might forgive him for not mentioning you sooner...'

Rich's unconscious, or maybe not so unconscious, 'easy' demeanour that draws applause and adoring looks whenever he meets females, is now in full flow. He seems to relax instantly. Where Jack panics, Rich's tongue loosens, the jokes and winks flow naturally. He's got Milly smiling and laughing in seconds. Jack envies him his easy charm – maybe Jack's reluctance to reveal Milly isn't anything to do with Cindy after all...

They tell him about their day out, the buskers in Covent Garden, the South Bank scene. But Rich wants data of a more personal nature.

'How did you two meet?' he swerves, wheels squealing. Jack can smell the rubber, even if Milly can't.

Milly giggles again, so different from their own first meeting, Jack muses, balefully, when she'd cried non-stop and dislocated all her fingers.

'Oh, I backed into his car,' she splutters.

'Wow, that's a bit forward,' Rich teases, a flirting look in his eye, a soft nudge to her elbow.

Oh, please don't mention the Beemer, Jack begs the god he hasn't believed in since he was a teenager, and he discovered that it was only the 'sinful' things that made life worth living. But, either Milly's psychic, or there is a god after all, as the conversation moves away from automotive subjects.

'A *nurse?*' Rich exclaims, with no less awe or admiration than he'd have produced had she told him she was a brain surgeon, or an astronaut – or a flipper at McDonald's. 'You know, I've got a nagging pain in my lower back, had it for ages, you couldn't have a dekko...? No, only kidding. Nurse, eh? Bedrock of our society. I went out with a nurse once, she worked so hard. Such dedication...'

Jack tries to wind it up, edge Milly away, but Rich isn't finished, not by a long way.

'We should go out for a drink together. I mean, Jack's my baby brother, I need to check you out.' Another playful nudge, this time to her shoulder. 'Gotta make sure you're up to the job...'

'You must come to dinner,' she invites suddenly – innocent as a lamb.

'That'd be great.' Rich beams, clearly delighted.

'Yeah,' Jack croaks, less so, his face draining of blood, his jaw slackening.

'And why not invite Cindy too?' she continues – lamb to the slaughter.

'Yeah.' Rich gulps, suddenly less enthusiastic, his smile weaker.

'Great,' Jack gasps, looking like he's got an invitation to his own funeral.

'Let's do it soon,' she says – mint sauce.

They all wave and smile, but only Milly's smile is genuine.

———

'Was it okay to invite them to dinner? You said it was amicable with Cindy?' Milly asks as they stroll up Mill Lane towards her flat.

'Yeah,' Jack replies, with much too much enthusiasm. His mind is on the rinse and spin cycle: now he *has* to tell Milly about the ticket, there's no way out of that. Half the table talk will be about what a clown he is, losing a lottery fortune. He doesn't really want such a humiliation to be Milly's intro to his friends. He's not sure of the combinations either: Rich flirting with Milly is a given, given Rich. It's not that Jack really thinks Rich would try to steal her, and he certainly trusts Milly, it would just be nice to have solidified his relationship with her before Rich came smarming around. But he doesn't feel good about Milly plus Cindy either: Cindy's a brash Aussie, he's not at all convinced a polite conversation about world poverty or water shortages in Africa is top of Cindy's ice-breakers. He'd be better to kick this dinner into the long grass (and preferably up a lion's bottom) for as long as possible.

'Rich seems ever so nice,' Milly says with a smile...

41

THE INVITATION

Twenty-five minutes later, Rich lights a cigarette.

'Jack's seeing someone,' he says, breathing out smoke and handing the fag to Cindy.

She inhales, thoughtfully, studies the ceiling as if Michelangelo had done the Artex. 'Really? How d'you know?'

'Bumped into them on Mill Lane, holding hands, like young lovers.'

She steals a second drag before handing the smoke back to Rich. 'Did you speak to them?'

'Yeah.'

'What's she like?'

He takes a drag. 'She seems nice. Very pretty, in an English sort of way. Very chatty, she's a nurse.'

Cindy waves for the fag but he ignores her, tries to take another puff, but she pulls it out of his fingers.

'How long've they been seeing each other?' Her voice is even, they could be discussing a new pair of shoes he'd bought, or a sharp haircut. But Rich knows...

'A couple of days.'

Silence. Or what most people would think of as silence. But

Rich knows there's noise inside Cindy's head. Whatever noise synapses make when they're fully occupied is now coming to a crescendo, he can sense it. Like one of those Valencian fireworks he remembers, the *tracas*. They kept getting louder and louder – and then they got louder.

'*That's* why he's changed his mind about the money,' she explodes, jack-knifing up in bed, taking a huge pull on the cigarette. She lets the smoke bleed slowly out of her mouth before continuing. 'His new Sheila's told him he's crook in the head, giving us a fair share of the dollarydoos, and he doesn't want to upset her. *That's* why he's cooked up this cock and bull about losing the ticket! What a slimy, limey bastard.'

'You think?'

'Think? I don't think. I *know*. What else has changed since he said he'd give us a fair share? Nothing. His Sheila's got her nails in his back and her eyes on our money.' She takes another drag, angrily kills the only half-smoked cigarette in the ashtray and slides out of bed. 'I've got an aerobics class in half an hour.'

'They've invited us over for dinner one evening...'

Cindy turns from the wardrobe where a rainbow collection of sports kit swings from hangers like ripe fruit in a jungle clearing.

'*Both* of us?'

'Yeah.'

'You sure?'

'Yeah.'

'Do they *know?*'

'About us?'

'No, the frigging way to San José! Of course about us.' She sighs loudly at the rack and flicks colours aside.

Rich sighs, ever so quietly. 'I don't think so. It was Milly who gave the invite. You know, come for dinner, invite Cindy too. He's obviously told her about you. I'm not sure Jack was too pleased about the dinner invite though.'

Cindy cackles, rattles hangers. 'I'll bet.'

'Yeah. I tend to think like Jack. Might be something we make an excuse for, at least for a month or so.'

She spins, a look of shock distorting her face. 'No! Let's go. It's perfect.' She turns again and pulls some orange leggings off a hanger, drags them on.

'What do you mean?'

'Think about it. He's got a new Sheila, he's clearly moving on, we could start to drop hints about us, get him used to the idea. We could even pretend it started at the dinner, blame him for the whole shebang. Don't you see? It's the perfect opportunity, the perfect time.'

Us? He's uncomfortable with this 'us' that she keeps assuming is in existence. It feels more than he's ready for. A nice low-key *thing* suits him fine, a full-blown 'public property' *relationship*? He hasn't signed up for that, not in his eyes.

'Plus!' she snaps suddenly, yanking on a black sports bra. She jumps onto the bed, kneels in front of him, pulling it to fit. '*Plus!* He'll be much more desperate to get this divorce organised if he's got a new Sheila in tow. It also gives us more leverage when it comes to the money. He wants to marry his Sheila; he'll have to pay up or *this* Sheila ain't gonna give him an easy Tammy Wynette.'

'A *what?*' Rich's heard Jack complain about Cindy's incomprehensible Australianisms. He's not sure she's even speaking English any longer.

'*D-I-V-O-R-C-E,*' she spells out for him, twanging her voice like a steel guitar. 'Keep up, Rich-a-roo.'

'Right.' Rich sighs. 'I'm telling you, Cindy, the money's gone. The ticket's mush. I've seen it.'

'We'll see,' she says, slipping off the bed and hauling on a lime-green sleeveless sweatshirt and a yellow fleece. She tugs on a pair of purple socks and laces up some fluorescent-blue trainers. Rich thinks she looks like she's been dressed by the Liquorice Allsorts man but resists any urge to voice it.

'Fix it up,' she says, then kisses him on the lips, and heads for the door. 'What a night it'll be...'

He nods, says nothing. Ah well, at least it'll be a chance to see the lovely Milly again...

42

THE SCHOOLGIRL

Milly plays Jack her version of Luigi Boccherini's 'Minuet' after dinner; she wants to see him smile this time. He goes through a few agonising *Where have I heard that before* moments, before giving up, and letting the music work its magic. He's captivated by the way she plays with her eyes closed; how does she know where her fingers are? There's that sort of superhuman quality to her he noticed when she played him that other piece; she's quite ordinary normally, in the nicest possible way, no airs and graces, an honest shyness, and then suddenly – this secret superwoman, a superpowered superstar appears and takes his breath away. He could imagine her winning BGT.

In bed, later, he asks her how she learned to play so well, without looking at any music.

'Oh, there aren't many pieces I can play without the music,' she says, turning to him and staring into his eyes, as if she's desperate that he knows the truth, that she doesn't deceive him in any way. 'Only my favourites, the ones I've practised over and over.'

It doesn't dim his awe. 'You must practise a lot.'

'More when I was at school. Music was an escape, something I could do on my own.'

He frowns. She continues.

'My parents always wanted "better" for me. We weren't rich, Dad worked on the railways, Mum did cleaning jobs, we lived in a rented terrace on the noisy side of the tracks.'

'Where did you grow up?' he asks, possibly the one basic bit of personal data he hasn't asked. 'You've got no obvious accent, and I pride myself on being able to locate where people are from by listening to them speak. You're an enigma.'

She smiles, shakes her head. 'Me? Ahm frum 'al-ee-fax!' She drops into the thickest Yorkshire accent he's ever heard, then she laughs at the incredulity creasing his face. He loves her laugh, almost more than anything else about her. She hasn't got one of those 'social' laughs, the ones that most people produce, on demand, at the appropriate moments. No, Milly smiles when one of those laughs is usually required. When she laughs it's a real one. Uncontrollable. She doesn't produce it, it engulfs her, possesses her – it's more like a sneeze. She always takes a few moments to recover when something makes her laugh. Like she's collecting her senses again, rejoining polite society, calming down.

'I don't believe you! *Halifax?* Never!'

'It's true,' she says, blushing, and reverting to the nondescript, unlocatable, non-accent he's used to hearing. 'As I said, my parents wanted "better" for me, and erasing the accent was the first step on the journey. I had private elocution lessons from Miss McCreedy, who worked at a girls' school, from when I was about five. *The rain in Spain*, all that jazz. They sent me to a little girls' prep school, I thought I'd landed on a different planet.

'I guess I saw what Miss McCreedy was doing as a bit of a game, you know, like the Dr Seuss books, sort of fun games with silly noises. Then I went to the prep, and I could hardly understand what the other girls were saying, I thought there was something wrong with them. They were all braying about gymkhanas and jodhpurs in this silly toothy accent. I don't think I'd moved beyond the basics with Miss McCreedy at that stage; I was still practising how to say *bath* and *grass* without opening my mouth too wide.

'God knows where my parents got the money for all this, I guess they didn't spend it on anything else. My dad used to gamble, horses and dogs. Mum put a stop to that once I started going to the prep. Although, that was only after the time they couldn't find the money for the fees, Dad had lost it on a nag, and I was sent home at lunchtime, with a letter in my hand. Mum went upstairs, came down with his best– well, his only suit, his father's gold cufflinks and dress watch, everything he owned that was worth anything. Off we marched to the pawn shop, I'm sure I saw Mum take off her wedding ring. I was back in school with the envelope full of tenners before story time. I'll never forget the look on the headmistress's face as I slid the envelope across her table. I was only about seven, didn't really know what was going on, but she looked at me like she thought I might have gone out and robbed a bank over lunchtime. She always treated me a little warily after that.

'It stopped the gambling. Completely. I think he could see how far Mum would go to make sure I could attend. She was the driving force for all of it. She simply wanted to see me getting a chance to do better than them. When I left the prep school, they moved heaven and earth to get me into the secondary girls' school, I'm pretty sure Miss McCreedy was employed as a string puller.'

'Wow! That must've been great. Enid Blyton, jolly hockey sticks?'

She purses her lips, rolls onto her back, closes her eyes. The lengthening silence starts to scare him. What has he said? He barely breathes again until she finally starts to speak, almost to herself. 'I'll always be grateful to my mum and dad, for what they gave me, what they sacrificed – but I hated it. From the first day to the last, I hated it. They were so different, the girls. They didn't live in terraced houses. There wasn't a girl who lived within three bus rides of me, not that any of them would ever use a bus. Some of them had drivers, they came to school in shiny cars driven by men wearing peaked caps.

'I got invited to a birthday party once. In my eyes, the house was as near to a fairy-tale castle as I was ever going to see. Garden? I thought we were in a park. Swimming pool? In Halifax?! This girl, Philomena, she even had a pony, in a paddock. A paddock? I didn't even know the word. The other girls laughed so hard when it was my turn to ride, and it soon became clear I'd never ridden before. Please don't laugh at me, cos I'm deeply ashamed of this next bit, but I went home and asked Mum and Dad if I could have a pony. I thought we could keep it in the back lane...'

His face is stony, as his heart breaks. She swats a tear off her cheek, takes a deep, shuddering breath, eyes still clamped closed, her voice little more than a whisper. 'Miss McCreedy was the school violin teacher. She knew we couldn't afford to buy a violin, so she lent me one and put me in her class, took me under her wing, gave me lessons during lunchtimes and playtimes, cos I clearly didn't have many friends. I was a misfit, so I played the violin. High school was so bad, how could I invite any of them back to my two-up two-down for a birthday party and to play in the back lane? Of course, if I wasn't going to invite them to my party, I could hardly accept any more invitations to theirs.'

She continues almost without taking a breath. 'The worst part of it was, I couldn't tell my mum and dad how much I hated it. I suppose I should have done, but I knew what they were sacrificing, and I couldn't throw it back at them. If I hadn't had the music, I don't know what I'd have done. I did make a couple of friends through the violin; I wasn't a complete outcast. In fact, once I joined the orchestra in high school, the *poor-little-poor-girl* banter eased off a bit.

'They all appreciated music, so they could see how good I was – I don't want to sound big-headed, but at that age I practised so much I was seriously good – so I kind of gained a bit of geeky kudos. I was first violinist, which meant all the solos, and I was determined not to use the sheet music. It was my one piece of pride. Aside from those moments, school was a social minefield, every day was a battle to avoid some form of humiliation, *they* were ten-a-penny: wearing the wrong colour socks cos my one pair wasn't dry; letting slip an *ey up* in the playground; thinking that Kiri Te Kanawa was a cocktail...

The temptation to laugh, or simply smile, is there, but he locks his facial muscles in place in case she looks over at him.

'I can't tell you the pressure I felt on a daily basis not to stop a glottal or mention that we went to the shops on the bus. In the end, I passed all my exams. Schoolwork was another escape, I got my head down, did all my homework, and passed everything. I think, again, I wanted to show the other girls I was as good as they were, better than they were. And, of course, I wanted to repay my mum and dad, for all that they'd sacrificed. And then, I decided I wanted to be a nurse. Well, that wasn't exactly Mum and Dad's plan for me, especially Mum. I think she wanted me to manage a bank or run ICI or something. One thing they didn't have was a glass ceiling for me. But I wanted to be a nurse. I think, having been so alone at school, I wanted a job where I'd be surrounded by people who wouldn't judge me. And I love it, I really do, but I know they were disappointed. Not so much now, as I've got some promotion and become a bit specialised. You should hear them talking to their friends about me, you'd think I was doing brain transplants.'

She opens her eyes, turns to face him. 'Maybe now you can understand, why I said I'd give a lottery win away? Remember, you asked me? I saw how surprised you were. You see, I never envied what those other girls had, all the money, the big houses, well, maybe the pony, but I never envied them, because I hated them. I hated the way they treated me – and it was all because of money. They had it, we didn't. Simple as that. I never wanted to join them, because I hated their superior attitude, their condescending snobbishness. Their – their *cruelty*. Simple cruelty. That's the word, the smallest one is the most powerful. I learned very early, there's more to life than chasing money. Chasing nice people is much more rewarding.

'To tell you the truth, I almost didn't come out that morning after the crash, to find you. I thought you were probably going to be loaded. Driving a Beemer soft-top? Not working in the middle of a weekday? Not worried about the cost when some crazy girl smashes up your car – your *brand-new* car? Not my type of guy at all. I couldn't have moved in the circles I thought you might be moving in: rich, condescending, snobbish... I thought you were a banker or a stock trader. It was only the fact that you didn't explode at me, you didn't shout at me, insult me.

'You seemed kind, and so I felt guilty. I suppose I wanted to give you a chance, not judge you by your car, as those girls had judged me by my poverty, by the holes in my tights and my lack of a pony. But I could easily have never gone back, written you off, forgotten you. It frightens me that I might have missed you.'

She kisses him softly, looks at him like he's saved her life, pulled her off the tracks in front of a speeding train, caught her when she'd fallen from a tall building... He can feel her love for him pouring out of her like a dam bursting, wonders if he's truly worthy.

He thinks back, why hadn't he exploded at her? Was it because he felt sorry for her? Because she'd apologised so quickly, so naively? Or was it because, at the time, he *was* loaded? Or he thought he was. He starts to say something, he's not sure what, but she's gone back in time again, her internal monologue pouring out of the crack in the dam.

'I suppose, in the end, right at the end, my mum and dad saw that I was happier with my friends in the street. They came to my parties, and they're still my friends. One works in a factory, another is a secretary, none of them are high-flyers, but they've been with me since the start, they know who I am. Even when I went to the *snobby school*, that's what we called it, even I called it that, even when I went to the snobby school, they never turned against me. When I came home, out in the lane, nobody cared what school you went to. If you lived in the lane, you played together, there was never a thought that I'd be left out because I went to a different school.

'I bet you wished you never asked,' she suddenly says, aware of how long she's been talking.

'Not at all. I can understand what it meant to you. It tells me you've got a will of iron. It was a heavy price to pay, but your music is something else. It's hard to believe it's you playing. It's like someone else enters the room. Someone I don't know.'

'Maybe it is someone you don't know. Maybe it's my thirteen- or fourteen-year-old self, in there somewhere, still trying to impress everybody by playing note perfect.' They lie in silence for a few moments, until she asks him – hitting him like a completely unexpected punch to the gut...

'You never said what you would do if you ever won the lottery...?'

43

THE CCTV

CINDY PARKS her shiny black Vee Dub quite a distance from Jack's flat and walks the rest of the way to Banerjees. She knows her personalised plate, *CIN 666*, will alert Jack to the fact that it's her, although the black Vee Dub will be a pretty heavy hint, even for the drongo. She's on her scouting mission, to see if there's CCTV in the shop. She has a vague memory of seeing a camera above the door scanning the counter, but she can't be sure. So she's going to have a squiz. Her fingers are crossed that there's no camera. That way, her path to the money will be that little bit smoother.

She comes into the street from the other end rather than passing Jack's flat, and pretends to tie her shoelaces so that if Jack happens to be in the shop, he'll have a good bit of time to get himself out before she enters. The last thing she really wants is to bump into him. Not that it'll spoil her plan, she can give him any reason for popping into Banerjees, but it's easier to avoid the dill.

There's no movement from the shop for a couple of minutes, so she advances on the door and pretends to read the headlines on the newspapers in the rack, while peering past the stickers on the glass, trying vainly to see if there's anyone inside. Truth is, there could be a whole Aussie-Rules football team scattered around the aisles, and you wouldn't know it until you tried to get to the frozen peas. She pushes the door open and the bell jingles.

'Hello again, Cindy,' Mr Banerjee greets her, looking up with a smile from a newspaper he's perusing.

'Hi, Mr Banerjee,' she replies, picking up a basket. She's relieved it's not Mrs Banerjee, much more chatter from her. A quick peek tells her that Mr Banerjee has returned his gaze to his newspaper, so, as she advances into the shop, she takes a look behind her, above the door. Nothing. She passes the counter and scans up above that as well in case there's a camera looking at the faces of customers at the till. Nothing.

With a distinct spring in her step, she decides to pick up a few things she needs while she's here, content with the news that she's one small step closer to the prize. She picks up a nice bottle of wine and places it into her basket – all ready for a celebration, maybe...

44

THE DISCOVERY

IKER's on his Xbox again: killing everything that moves. He's got a new game, but María can't see the difference between it and any of the other games he already has. This is another *killing people* game. He's got a lot of *killing people* games. The only things that seem to change in all his *killing people* games is who he's killing, where and how.

He's got a game where he kills zombies in a warehouse with guns; one where he kills Martians with lasers, she's sure that one's set on Mars; he kills soldiers on a mountainside somewhere with grenades; this one's set in a forest and he seems to be killing anybody and anything he sees by throwing rocks at them. He's got other *killing people* games, but she's not really interested enough to ask. He has got a car-racing game, which she quite likes, but he says the cars are too slow. She can barely make it around the circuit without crashing. They don't play that one much.

She opens her new book. María loves reading, especially in English. She likes Jane Austen, although Jack's warned her that not many people speak the way Jane Austen wrote. Not anymore. Especially not in Cricklewood. He says the King does,

HITTING THE JACKPOT

the real one, not that footballer that Jack likes – although the King certainly doesn't live in Cricklewood. And that politician he hates, Piece Smugg, or someone: the skinny one with the glasses who Jack says looks like Walter from *The Beano*, not that she knows where *The Beano* is. Somewhere outside London, she thinks. Jack says Piece is a Brexiteer and Jack hates Brexiteers. This one lay down on a bench somewhere, and Jack didn't like that at all. She's not sure why, maybe it wasn't his bench. Or maybe he was someone with no house – what did Jack say they were called? Downy Outs? She's no idea why...

María thinks British politics is very complicated. In fact, the whole country is complicated. Jack says Brexiteers are all little Englanders, although he's warned her about using the word *England*. It's okay for the football, apparently, unless they're playing in the Olympics. Then it has to be *Great Britain*. When it's not the Olympics, and it's not football, you should drop the *Great*, he says. *Britain* is better. Although he says it's safest to use *United Kingdom*, or just *UK*.

She's never known such a complicated country. She's made notes on all this, so she won't forget it. She's keen. But she still forgets it. Jack says that's okay, most British people don't understand the half of it. That's why they voted for Brexit, he says. She's no idea how Scotland, Wales and either of the Irelands (there are two) fit into the picture.

Ireland is even more complicated than England – or Britain, or the UK. Ireland is an island, but there are two Irelands on the island. One of them is in the UK, but it isn't in England, she's not sure which one. Or it might be the other way around – it might be in England, but not in the UK. Who knows? Only Jack.

Jack understands it all, he's quite amazing. She's more worried about saying the words properly. Jack says the two Irelands are pronounced eye-or-lund. He wrote it down like that

for her so she could practise. Then the island that the two eye-
or-lunds are on is called an eye-land. Even though it's spelled
island – with an 's'.

She's told Jack that Spanish is a much easier language to
learn, and she's offered to give him lessons. Anything to spend a
bit more time in his company. Plus, he's interested in this sort of
stuff. As is she. Not many people are. Iker couldn't give a
gorilla's. A gorilla's *what*, she doesn't know. But she can ask Jack.

María loves reading in English, but best of all she loves
reading *about* English. The book she's about to start is about
English. It's about English phrases, especially those strange ones
that English people use all the time – the ones that don't mean
what you think they mean. They make English very hard to
learn. You can say that again.

That's one of the phrases: *You can say that again.* She knows
that one already, she learned it one day in class. She'd told Jack
that she thought the David Crystal book he'd lent her was
fantastic. He'd said, *'You can say that again'*. So, she did. And he
laughed. Not in a nasty way, Jack would never do that. He's too
nice a teacher, all-round Mr Nice Guy. That's another phrase
she's learned, from another English friend she has. She told
them about Jack, and they said he sounded like an all-round Mr
Nice Guy. And that's what she calls him now. Not to his face.
She'd never do that. But to all her other friends. *I've got a great
English teacher, Jack, he's an all-round Mr Nice Guy.* It makes
her feel she's fluent in the language.

She fancies him something rotten. That's another one of the
phrases that doesn't mean what you'd think. *To fancy someone
something rotten.* It doesn't sound nice, it's like a load of fruit
going off in a bucket, but it is nice, apparently. It means you
really like someone. She really likes Jack. But he's already
married to Cindy. He says they're in the middle of divorcing.
María's a good Catholic, so she doesn't really believe in divorce.

She also can't understand how any sane woman would want to divorce Jack.

You can say *that* again!

That's how Jack says you should use it: you say it when you agree with something someone else has said. It doesn't mean you *really* want them to say it again. What would be the point of that? English is hard to understand. Cindy's even harder.

It's one of the few phrases María's confident using. Jack's warned her about trying to use too many of them as they're so complicated. He says it's best simply to learn what they mean, so that you can understand them when other people use them. Actually using them yourself is quite difficult, Jack says, it's really easy to make a mistake. He can say that again.

She made a mistake in the bakery once. She'd read a new phrase in a book and googled it to check that she understood the meaning. It seemed pretty straightforward, so she thought she'd try it in the bakery. The woman there always asked her how she was, so it would be perfect. But she didn't go for a day or two, and by the time she did go, she'd sort of half-forgotten it. But the woman asked her how she was, and she was so excited that she had a go.

She told the woman she was as good as a violin. The woman gave her such a funny look. It took Jack twenty minutes to work out what she had been trying to say: *as fit as a fiddle*. She asked him what a fiddle was, and he said it was like a violin. So why couldn't she say as good as a violin? And how could a violin be *fit*? It couldn't go out running. English? Crazy language. You can say that again.

Now she buys her bread in Tesco.

She opens the book, it's one of Jack's. He lets them take his books whenever they like, you don't even have to ask him. All-round Mr Nice Guy.

What's this stuck between the pages...?

45

THE COINCIDENCE

'Two cappuccinos, please,' Jack says to the waitress. He sighs; he has an awkward little agenda he wants to cover this morning. The lottery ticket saga, and the car, which is obviously going to have to go back at the end of the lease. He's hoping beyond hope that he might be able to retrieve his trusty Fiesta. He and Milly are working this afternoon, so they're having a lazy morning reading the papers in a coffee shop, alongside all the other people pretending to be the leisured classes or continental Europeans.

Jack usually likes coincidences. They're a handy trick in fiction: Mr Collins happens to be clergyman for Darcy's aunt in *Pride and Prejudice*, thereby bringing Elizabeth to Kent and leading to a marriage proposal from Mr Darcy; in *Jane Eyre*, the Rivers, lo and behold, turn out to be Jane's long-lost cousins; in *Oliver Twist*, Charley and Dodger pick Mr Brownlow's pocket, who, as chance would have it, is the oldest friend of, guess who? Oliver's father; in *A Room With a View*, George Emerson moves to Summer Street where, who'd have guessed it, Lucy Honeychurch lives; and in *Hitting the Jackpot...* well, what d'ya know, Rich and Cindy also have the morning off, and also fancy a cup of coffee and a quick squiz at the newspapers.

So, of all the coffee shops in all of Cricklewood, whose do they walk into...?

'Rich!' Jack gasps, as he places his empty cup on the saucer.

'Jack?'

'How ya do– *Cindy?*'

'Jack.'

'What a coincidence!'

It certainly is. Rich, in particular, seems amazed by it.

'Double coincidence,' he shouts, as if he thinks everybody in the coffee shop will want to know.

'What do you mean?' Jack asks, wondering why Rich seems so excited.

'Well, Cindy and I – we just bumped into each other, in the street, just there, just now, haven't seen each other in ages, at all, thought we'd have a coffee, and a catch-up...'

'Yeah!' says Cindy, nodding vigorously, and looking oddly relieved.

Jack's mind explodes: how is he going to keep the conversation off the topic of lottery tickets lost? If his mind wasn't exploding, he might remember that Rich had said he'd bumped into Cindy only a couple of days ago (when she'd told him about Jack's decision to cut the money three ways). But his mind is exploding, so he doesn't remember. He's too busy introducing Milly to Cindy and studying Cindy's face as they shake hands slightly awkwardly. The waitress reappears with her pad and hovers.

'Can we join you?' Rich says, with all the enthusiasm of a condemned man studying a menu.

'Sure,' says Milly.

'No,' says Jack. There's an awkward moment, as Jack's mind

crashes the gears like a sixteen-year-old on an illicit driving lesson. 'I've um – got a little something planned for Milly, which um – she doesn't know about yet, yeah – that we need to get moving for. But it was great to see you. Really great.' He stands, nods at Milly to finish what's left of her drink.

'Yeah, great,' says Rich, suddenly full of overt zeal, and hidden relief.

'Let's set that dinner up,' Cindy says, brightly. 'How about Saturday?'

Jack doesn't wonder how Cindy has heard about the dinner invite so soon, his mind is still a war zone, where the tanks are being driven by sixteen-year-olds who haven't passed their driving tests – a sort of slo-mo military dodgems, with explosions.

'Great,' says Milly.

'Yeah,' says Rich.

'Shall we have it at yours, Jack? It's bigger than mine,' Milly suggests.

'Sure,' says Jack. 'Great. Saturday.'

———

'What's this little something you've got planned, that you didn't have planned when we planned a lazy morning with a coffee and the papers?' Milly asks, squeezing Jack's arm as they walk briskly away down Cricklewood Broadway.

He looks at her and grimaces; he knows he's been rumbled. 'I'm sorry. As I'm sure you've guessed, that was a bit of an excuse. I have got something to tell you; I really didn't want it to come up in conversation with Rich and Cindy.'

'You haven't got *another* wife, have you?'

'What? No, God, no!' He sees that she's smiling. 'Oh, right. No, sorry. No, nothing like that at all, it's something that happened recently. It's not really that big a thing, but I needed the right moment to tell you.'

'Is this the right moment?'

'I've no idea, but I want to get it off my chest. Look, let's go somewhere nice and quiet, where we can talk.'

They wander into Mapesbury Dell, a tiny park hidden behind a triangle of houses just off the Broadway. It has a good selection of clambering stuff for kids, so they seek out a quiet bench as far away from that as they can. He wanted this to be a moment when they were facing each other, so he could see the look in her eyes, and she could see the sincerity in his. He's tired of the deception now, can't believe he's carried it on this long. They find a picnic table and he sits opposite her.

'I won the lottery last week. But I lost the ticket. Destroyed it, actually. It was in my chinos, and I put them in the washing machine, it's now pulp. I wasn't going to tell Cindy, before I lost it that is, but she found out. She wanted half the money because we're still technically married, and I didn't feel like giving it to her because she was divorcing me. Anyway, we'd sorted it. I was going to give her a third and Rich a third. It was then that I discovered I'd destroyed it, and so they won't be entirely pleased with me. I just didn't want to have that conversation until I'd told you.'

Milly's got the same look on her face she had when he'd told her he was married to Cindy. It's a sort of wary expectation, like anything could happen and there's no way she'll be able to guess. 'Is that it?' she says, her eyes cautious.

'What? The thing I wanted to tell you? Yeah. That's it.'

'How much did you win?'

'Two point three million...' No more secrets.

She whistles a little whistle, it's a sort of *wow!* whistle, which Jack wouldn't have expected.

'I tried to tell you the other day, when I asked you what you'd do if you won the lottery...'

'And I said I'd give it all away?'

'Yeah. Did you mean it?'

'Yes.'

'Even now?'

'What, you mean now I know you nearly did win it? Yes, absolutely. But that wasn't my money, I was talking about what I'd do if *I* won the lottery, not that I ever buy tickets, my dad's gambling put me right off. And anyway, I'm pretty happy with my life as it is. I like my job, my friends, you. I'd appreciate a decent pay rise, of course – but I honestly don't feel I need *that* much money to make me happy. I am happy.'

'You don't mind that I washed the ticket?'

'I'd have preferred you to give it to charity, if you were going to get rid of it in some way, but it's a bit academic now. No, I don't mind. My mum used to say, what you never had, you'll never miss.'

'I guess so.'

'You don't sound convinced.'

'No. I am. I'm certainly happier with you and no ticket, than without you and with the ticket. My life was such a mess, I feel better it's gone. What did The Beatles sing about money not being able to buy love?'

She smiles at the implication; he leans over and kisses her to confirm it.

'There's one other thing.'

Her face adopts its wary mask again. He hates these secrets he's always confessing to her; hates the look it puts on her face.

'The Beemer,' he says quickly, hoping to put her out of whatever it is that's making her look so worried. 'That's obviously going to have to go back.'

'Oh, no. Is this because I bumped into it?'

He smiles at her description of it as a *bump*, as opposed to a *smash*, or a *nuclear attack*.

'No! Not at all. I bought it on the strength of the lottery win, there's no way I can run it on my earnings. I'll take it back in and see if they've still got my Fiesta. They only gave me twenty quid for it – I'm hoping they'll sell it back to me for about the same.'

'That's a shame. You haven't had a chance to drive it much, have you?'

'I've driven it from the showroom to our meeting place. Best drive I've ever taken. Now, I'll drive it back again. So, I started with a Fiesta, and I end up with a Fiesta and you. I call that the deal of the century. I'm pretty happy with it.' He laughs, kisses her again. Yes, he's sure life is going to be better without that lottery ticket.

Shakespeare was right, as usual, Jack muses: *All's Well That Ends Well...*

———

'Do you think Rich and Cindy are having a thing?' Milly asks suddenly, as they stroll towards his flat.

'What? A *thing*? Together? Don't be daft. What makes you say that?'

She's not a hundred per cent sure she saw their hands unclasping at great speed as they came through the doorway of the coffee shop, but the blush on Rich's face was unmistakable, and it took Cindy a good few seconds to relax in their company, once Rich had taken half of *War and Peace* to explain that they'd only just met, just now, not before...

'No reason,' she says, shrugging. 'Intuition?'

'No chance,' he says, dismissively. 'They're not remotely suited.'

'Opposites sometimes attract,' she teases.

'Yeah, Cindy and I attracted for about six months. Then look what happened.'

46

THE RETURN

JACK ROLLS the Beemer onto the forecourt, sees Shelly waving through the window. She's in lime today: lime skirt, lime top, lime shoes. He knew a teacher once, way down with the mini muppets, she used to wear the same colour to school every day for a week: shirts, skirts, trousers, wigs, hats, shoes, nail varnish, rings, everything. He always wondered if she had matching underwear, could never ask her. Forever a mystery.

Then, the next week, she changed colour. It went on for months. The children certainly knew their colours when they left her class. Her wardrobe must've had a pot of gold in the back corner. Probably a whole mine. Shelly totters to the door and comes down the steps, looking like a rather well-dressed lime.

'Hey, Jack. Everything okay?' She plants kisses on his cheeks like she speaks fluent Spanish. She has a red rose in a glass vase on her desk. Does red go with lime green? Who knows? Least of all – Jack.

'Not exactly. Come round the back.' He leads her to see where he's secured what's left of his bumper in place with a few dozen strips of gaffer tape.

'Oh my God!' she gasps as she clocks the damage, grabbing his forearm like she's afraid she might topple off her heels. 'What hit you? A Hummer?'

He smiles, trying to picture Milly behind the wheel of a Hummer.

'No idea. Just found it like that, no note, nothing. Some people are bastards.' He's ditched the idea of saying he reversed into a tree, made him look too much of a plonker.

Shelly shakes her head. 'Ah well, I bet you're happy you took out the fully comp, yeah?'

She'd suggested this. He'd balked, forgetting he was a double millionaire, and she'd insisted.

'Yes, I guess so. Thanks, you've saved my bacon. Can you fix it up?'

'Sure, no problem, park it round the back next to yours. It's up on blocks at the mo, Kev's checking out the brakes, but he says it's in tip-top shape. He's given the engine a bit of a tweak, but he said it didn't really need anything doing.'

'Right,' says Jack. Now comes the difficult bit. 'Actually, I was going to ask you about the Fiesta. You see, the money I was expecting to come through, it isn't happening. So, I'm going to keep the Beemer until the end of the lease, as we agreed, but I'm not going to be able to buy it at the end of it. Without the money I was expecting, I won't be able to run it. I was wondering...?'

'You want to buy your Fiesta back?'

'Yes.'

'Not a problem. Actually, I could help you out with the finance of the lease, if you want. One of our interesteds, the one you jumped in front of, he was gutted when this one disappeared. He's asked me to source another asap. If you want to cut the lease short, you can save yourself a few months' worth of payments, and I can get this one fixed up and pass it on to him.'

'Really?'

'Everybody's happy. You get your Fiesta back, save a few quid on the lease, he gets his Beemer, and I'm a heroine. Drop it round the back and then pop in, we can start the paperwork. I can call you when the Fiesta's ready for you to pick up. It won't be long.'

'Thanks. I'll be sorry to see the Beemer go, but without this money coming in, I can't afford to run it.'

'It's a shame,' she says, smiling at him, touching his arm lightly, 'it's very *you*.'

He looks at the car, shakes his head sadly, wonders if that's really true. Then he wonders if he's just had his last ever spin in a Beemer...

47

DA MISS ANT DA PIS

JACK'S PREPPING for his least favourite lesson of the week. Madam Radwańska (he has to call her *Madam* as that was how she introduced herself) is a sexagenarian Pole. He finds the juxtaposition of the word sexagenarian (it means *in her sixties*, as Jack would have explained to María) next to her *Madam*, a delicious irony that always makes him smile, even though he's well aware of what it really means.

He has no idea how Madam Radwańska ever found him. Whoever put her on to him is probably in hiding. Afraid ever to face him again. He suspects it might have been Cindy, but how would Cindy, how would *any* of his 'friends', have come into contact with Madam Radwańska? She doesn't ride a bike, doesn't do Zumba, she doesn't drink coffee in coffee shops, she doesn't seem to do much else except torture Jack once a week.

He's given up trying to use his usual stock of 'openers': *How are you today? How was your week? Have you cheered up a bit since last week's rant...?* She never seems to want to talk about herself, replying to such polite enquiries with a grumpy shrug, as if she'd prefer to be anywhere else, but she never is. What she does want to talk about – *rant* about – is everything that upsets her. Which is pretty much everything.

Her pet rant – get this – is immigrants. Jack spends hours trying to twist the 'conversation' away from any topic that might conceivably lead to an issue that might result in a comment about immigrants. The first time she 'vented' was a warning, and the end of that particular 'lesson' as far as Jack's vocal cords were concerned, although his ears went into intensive care for a couple of days afterwards. He feels he should kick her off his books, but he's afraid she might stalk him.

Madam Radwańska seems to get no joy out of learning English. He doubts whether she's ever known joy. She's the sourest old puss he's ever had the misfortune to work with. If she wasn't paying twenty quid a time, he'd again be tempted to tell her to sling 'er 'ook. Although, he probably wouldn't phrase it like that: it'd almost certainly be the one English phrase she *doesn't* know, so he'll be forced, he really means *forced*, to spend another twenty minutes explaining it to her.

Madam Radwańska has lived in London for over fifty years, so her knowledge of English is right up there – way higher than the majority of Brits who've lived in London for over fifty years. If he tells the truth, and he tells this to nobody except himself, Madam Radwańska's knowledge of English grammar is undoubtedly better than his own. It's just that her knowledge of English is knowledge of an English that was last spoken by Jane Austen, or Charles Dickens, and only when they were putting words into the mouths of the poshest characters in their novels, *Lady Catherine de Bourgh*, or *Samuel Pickwick Esq.* It's an ossified language, heaven help Jack if he ever splits an infinitive or leaves a preposition dangling at the end of a sentence. The way she screws up her face every time he speaks, she clearly thinks Jack is the *Artful Dodger* in disguise.

So why does she insist on torturing Jack by demanding an

English lesson every week? The answer is simple: it's hard to understand how anyone who has lived in London for over fifty years could have retained such a strong accent from their native tongue. It's a mystery that David Attenborough really should pay some attention to. But that's the reason. After fifty years surviving quite happily in London, she's decided she wants a cockney accent instead of her Polish one. Well, no, that's over-egging it a bit. She wants to have the edge taken off her Polish accent. Jack's got his work cut out.

Ironically, Jack is quite fond of her Polish accent. Jack's quite fond of any foreign accent when it's speaking English. He remembers, from his schoolboy French studies, how French people speaking English were invariably deemed to sound 'sexy'. He could never understand why his 'cockney' French accent, on the other hand, was always criticised for sounding uneducated, even 'loutish'. If he were ever to do a PhD, he would study foreigners speaking English. And not only the sounds that they make when they're trying to pronounce *through, choir* or *biscuit*, but also the shapes of their mouths.

One of his happy pastimes, when he and Rich were eking out their time in Valencia, was watching the Spanish evening news on the TV with the sound turned down. Having the sound up was a waste of time, as neither of them spoke much Spanish beyond *paella, por favor* or *San Miguel, por favor...* The Spanish newsreaders kept his attention for hours.

It was like watching a new Olympic sport, to go alongside 'breaking' and skateboarding – he called it lip-gymnastics. The women were miles better at it than the men, especially the newsreaders on *la Sexta Noticias* (a weekday evening news programme). Watching their lips stretch and contract at such speed was captivating. He was, at the time, trying to learn a bit of the lingo himself, and he discovered (alone, in front of the bathroom mirror) that it really did seem to help with a

Spanish accent if you let rip with the lip-gymnastics, especially with the 'eee' sound, which is hugely common in Spanish.

Madam Radwańska will never make it onto the Polish lip-gymnastics team, Jack knows this. This would be the conclusion of his PhD. Madam Radwańska's lips barely move, no matter what she's saying. Her mouth rarely opens to a size that would allow a Polo mint to enter, even lying flat – the Polo mint, not her. And even if you managed to slide one in, maybe when she's overexcited, and saying something like *arsehole* or *arsenic*, her teeth would block the way like the portcullis at the Tower of London.

He takes out his phone and watches the time tick steadily towards the appointed hour. How she manages to ring his bell at exactly the moment when his phone flips to two o'clock is a mystery he'll never solve without hanging himself out of the window to see if she actually loiters around outside with one eye on her watch.

Two o'clock: his bell rings.

'Madam Radwańska,' he announces pompously as he opens the door with a flourish.

'Nghh.'

'Come in, come in. How are you, this beautiful cloudy day?' It's the only way he can survive the coming hour of torture: complete disassociation from his usual self, into a cartoon character teacher who is full of the joys of life, and clear-witted enough to avoid the subjects he needs to avoid. He's heard schoolteacher chums of his say that it's a technique they've had to develop at pace, in order to survive the rough and tumble of the secondary classroom. Jack sighs inwardly, at least he's only got the old bat for an hour a week. He dreads the day when she requests a second hour...

'More dog *miss*, *aht*side, on the pave*mint*,' she growls, teeth clamped together more firmly than if she'd had her jaw wired after a Saturday night fist-fight.

'Really?' Jack replies, with the air of a local government dog-*miss* inspector. 'It gets worse every week.'

She turns her back and sheds her heavy fur, which Jack catches expertly, because he always does, except for the first week when, if he'd had a licence to teach English to grumpy old bats, it would have been confiscated by a catatonic old vamp. Underneath the coat, her 'fashion sense' – the best example of an oxymoron he's ever come across – is all *From Russia With Love*'s villain Rosa Klebb, without the service ribbons. At least she doesn't wear a tie – but he steers well clear of her shoes, just in case...

'Tea?' he offers, as he knows he must, with three Rich Tea biscuits on a plate, of which he only ever eats one.

'Vhy dunt you pibble look after your dogs more carefully, ant pick up your dog *miss*? It's disghasting.' No sign of a tongue getting involved in that sentence, certainly not visibly. There's a slight rippling of her jowls, but apart from that, get her some kind of a puppet, and she could be a professional ventriloquist.

Jack wonders how she knows the dog *miss* belongs to one of 'us' pibble? Don't any of her Polish friends have dogs with bums? But he doesn't say any of this, he simply places the tray (he borrows it from a neighbour every week) on the table and sits down opposite the old crone, smiling like a *Sexta* newsreader.

'Shall I be mathur?' she growls, as she always does. The first half-hour of every week could be played on a tape, it's so formulaic, he muses. He often wonders if the English tea ceremony is half the reason she comes.

'Why not?' he replies. 'Why not, indeed?' He also finds himself lapsing into the Major, from *Fawlty Towers*, whenever Madam Radwańska is visiting. It's another form of disassociation.

'An an adder feen,' she continues, clearly warming to what is obviously going to be the theme of the week; she always picks it. 'Somesink dat rilly buthers me. It's not fanny, Mr Jack. I dunt know vhy you English find dis fanny, stepping in dog *miss* evary day.'

Jack raises a hand in apology, maybe he overdid the Major, and it's produced a smile on his face in the middle of her rant preamble.

'De adder feen is da pis. Day lit their dogs pis evarywhere. It's disghasting.' The way she says *pis* intrigues Jack. She clearly spells it with only one 's', unlike *da miss*, which might even have three. While *da miss* slides out of her mouth like a Jack-the-Ripper era pea-souper creeping up the Thames, *da pis* comes shooting out like a single bullet from a small Russian-made pistol. Jack feels strangely tempted to duck.

'I know.' Jack shakes his head, almost *dunks*(!) his biscuit, but stops himself just in time, avoiding a repetition of the worst scolding he can remember suffering this side of the day in infant three, when Miss Everett caught him picking his nose.

'Zo! Today I vont to spik about the English sub-junk-tif. You know vot dis is, Mr Jack.' Unlike Cindy, Madam Radwańska never adorns her statements with any HRT. Jack knows what the English subjunctive is, it's not a question, and he's got fifty minutes ahead of him to prove it. He thinks he'd prefer to stick with da miss ant da pis.

48

THE HOMECOMING

Jack cracks a bottle of Turia Tostada, his favourite Valencian beer, to celebrate surviving the best part of an hour bluffing about the English subjunctive, and vows that he will mug it up before next week. But no sooner has the cap hit the floor than his doorbell rings. Christ! She hasn't forgotten her coat? No, he helped her on with it, as he always does. He has no option – she turns away from him and raises her arms slightly, waiting for him to slip her hands into the sleeves then lift the coat onto her shoulders – like a doorman at the Ritz probably would. He opens the door cautiously.

'Jacko!'

'Cheesie?'

'Man-hug!' And they do, without either of them suffering any ill effects.

'Hey, Jack!'

'Debs! Jesus! *Debs!* Woah, congratulations! Jesus! Come in, sit down, what are you doing here? A million questions all at once...'

Debs waddles in, heavily pregnant, Jack estimates she's about ten months gone.

'Christ, look, drinks. If I had any champagne...'

'One of those will do for me.' Cheesie points at Jack's bottle.

'And I'll have a juice or a water, only a month to go.'

'A month?' Jack's tone of disbelief would be appropriate had she said she'd only just had the positive test.

'About that. It's all a bit hit and miss out there.'

'Blimey, congrats. Long life, good health, and no hangover in the morning.'

They toast. Stare at each other.

'Where have you been? Last PC I had from you was ages ago. Vietnam, I think, it's on the fridge.' He retrieves it. 'Yeah, Nam, ten months ago.'

'Yeah, sorry. It's not been that easy to get to civilization where we've been hanging out,' Cheesie explains with a shrug. 'We did a long tour around the East, Cambodia, Nam, into China. But we headed back to Thailand a while ago, found a little sort of colony, on one of the smallest islands. They do their own farming and stuff, real self-sufficient kick. It's great, you'd love it.'

'Sounds amazing.'

'Yeah. It's just that with little bundle here arriving soon, we thought we needed to boost our backup finances a little if we're really going to try to make a go of it out there. It's all right catching fish and growing a few pineapples, but you still need a little pot of filthy lucre for emergencies.'

'Yeah, and if I happen to drop my load while we're in the UK, well, it might be the safest place to be. I love the Thai beach scene but having a breech birth in the surf is pushing it a bit, no pun intended.' Debs pats her bulge and looks decidedly squeamish.

Jack nods. He had a toothache while he was in Thailand, not an experience he wanted to repeat. He knew there was probably great dental care available, but as a tourist without

243

travel insurance (he'd suggested it to Cheesie, but they'd never bothered in the end), he was limited to the backstreets – an expensive and painful option. He notices Cheesie and Debs's teeth have a kind of a furry-brown colour, and Cheesie's missing a front incisor.

'We're on a bit of a whistle-stop tour,' Cheesie continues. 'My brother has a language school in Manchester, he's promised us a shedload of work for a couple of months so we can fill the tank. We're gonna save hard, but also drop in on people all round the place to catch up, maybe sofa-surf for a while...?'

'Sure, as long as you like.'

'Cheers, mate.'

'Yeah, thanks, Jack,' Debs says, rather sheepishly. 'And look, we're sorry we bailed out a bit sharpish when we were all together at the beginning. It was my fault, not Cheesie's, we got a bit wrapped up in the moment and decided to sort of elope. We should've done that better.'

'No problem,' Jack replies, gallantly.

'But look, you and Cind! Congratulations! Would never have seen that coming. How is she? Sorry we didn't make it for the wedding, we wanted to, but there was no way.'

'No problem, Cindy's fine...'

'Will she be in soon? I can't wait to catch up.'

'The thing is...' Jack takes a breath. 'The thing is – we're not together anymore. She moved out about five months ago; we've agreed to divorce. It's all amicable, we're still talking, and see each other now and again. But it didn't work...'

'Oh Jack, sorry about that...' Debs says, looking shocked.

'Yeah, that's awful...'

'No, it just wasn't to be, a bit too much whirlwind and not enough forward planning. Life in a Thai beach hut turned out to be very different to life in a Cricklewood one-bed. Who'd have guessed?'

'That's terrible news.' Cheesie gives Jack a squeeze on the shoulder.

'Yeah, way things go. You two look set though?' Jack changes the subject.

'Yeah, it's good. As I said, we really need to put together a bit of backup finance and we'll be away again, to the good life,' Cheesie says.

'You're both looking well.'

'You too, work going okay?'

'Yeah. Fine. So, what are your plans? Stay as long as you like.'

'That's kind, thanks. But the thing is, we need to get this job started asap, my brother's desperate for us to get up there to help him out. We're planning on staying at my mum's for a few nights, Debs wants to catch up with Cind, then we'll be hitching up north in a couple of days, doing two or three months of 24/7s, then come back down here for some more liquid socialising, maybe a bit of a send-off do somewhere. So, if we could stay with you then?'

'Just ring the bell, I'm sitting on your bed.'

'You're a pal, Jack. And there'll always be a bed for you on our Thai island. You know the way, don't you? And listen, we want to do the doorbell heart attack on everyone, so not a word to Cindy that we're about, or Debs's condition, okay? As I say, we're gonna try to catch her before we head up north...'

49

THE DECISION

'¿Qué es eso?' Iker asks, appearing over María's shoulder suddenly. He has a habit of doing that – appearing; he moves ever so quietly for such a big guy. He's like a bear in a forest, she thinks, but then wonders if bears are actually that quiet. A blue whale deep underwater comes to mind instead.

'What's that?' she coaxes gently. She likes to practise with him now and again, although she knows he finds it difficult. Iker's actually slightly better at English than he usually lets on to Jack. He doesn't like being put under pressure to learn or perform. Plus, there's the fact that he's convinced Jack fancies María, and the added complication that, despite her denials, he's sure María's got a – what's the phrase – *a soft dot?* for him in return. Still, his company pays for the lessons, and he'd never have met María if he hadn't been going to Jack for classes, so he's got a lot to thank Jack for.

'What's that?' he asks dutifully. He doesn't mind 'performing' for María. In fact, he'll do anything for María. She's the best thing that's happened to him since slicing bread. That's a phrase he's heard, but he won't say out loud in front of

English people, in case he gets it wrong. Although he doesn't ever say much in Jack's lessons, he does usually listen.

'Ees lottery ticket. Jack say he hide eet, and no can find eet. You remind? Ees een thees book, I take eet from hees bookshelf.' María's often confusing words; she gets *remind* and *remember* mixed up, also *lend* and *borrow*, and *hide* and *lose*.

Iker shrugs, takes the ticket. The last twenty minutes of any lesson is never his best listening time. 'Eet ween money?'

'I think yes, Jack he say eet.'

'Maybe we keep eet? Jack, he has lotta money.' Iker slides the ticket behind his back and grins.

María looks horrified, like someone's harpooned the whale. 'No! I geev eet Jack. He unhappy he hide ticket. I geev it heem.' She holds her hand out and gives Iker a stern look.

Iker knows what María's like. She's very *honesta* – a word he doesn't know in English. If she ever finds anything, an old scarf blowing around a park, she'll pick it up, tie it around the gate at the entrance, hoping the owner will see it. Then she'll want to revisit the park over the next few days, to see if the scarf has been claimed. He hasn't the heart to tell her that someone else has probably stolen it off the gate, she's so happy to think she's helped to reunite it with its owner.

'He ween *beeg* money?' Iker asks, still not keen to give up the chance.

'*Lotta* money,' she corrects, Jack's worked hard to teach them things like this.

'Oh, yes? How much lotta money he ween?'

'No. That's what you *say*, *lotta* money, no *beeg* money. Beeg money is like *thees*.' She spreads her arms as if she's holding a ten-pound note that's a metre wide. Iker smiles, tickles under her arms. She bats him off.

'No.' María shakes her head sadly. 'He say he ween little

money. I geev heem back nex week. He happy.' She holds her hand out again, this time looking sad.

Iker shrugs. He knows María would give it back even if it was worth beeg money. That's what she's like. She'd give it back if it was worth a million. Even as much as two. *Dos millones.* He tries to imagine what it would be like to hold *dos millones* in his hands. Difficult, especially as he doesn't do the lottery. He looks longingly at the ticket, then hands it back to María. He remembers another English phrase he thinks he knows, which he doesn't often say out loud: *easy eet come and eet go.*

———

María tucks the ticket into her purse. It'll make Jack smile, she thinks. He hasn't been his usual happy self recently. This will cheer to heem up. She knows that phrase too. He's a great teacher. All-round Mr Nice Guy. Even to ween a little is better than kick up backside. Jack's told her never to use that one with people she doesn't know well, as it's a little bit rude.

She smiles at the thought of seeing the look on Jack's face, when she gives him the ticket...

50

THE RECIPE FOR CHAOS

JACK's mental cookbook of favourite recipes is only a couple of pages long. Once he's done his paella *monumental*, his *MasterChef* CV kinda collapses. He can do spag bol, but Milly's vegetarian, and she's already done the veggie version, which was light years better than his own usual mince and grease speciality; so that's a ditto reject for his chilli con carne. He doesn't own any cookbooks, so he's been on the internet. That was a disaster. It's hard just to 'find' a recipe on the internet.

You actually have to put a recipe in, like *spag bol*, then it gives you a million ways of making *spag bol*, unlikely that there are, but that's the internet for you. If you type in *recipes*, you get billions of ideas, all with ingredients he hasn't got in his fridge or cupboards. Most of them are things he's never heard of, so probably they won't be available in Cricklewood. You'd have to go to Kabul or Tokyo to get them. What is *shirako* anyway? And *agar-agar*? Maybe he should just go down the chippy? Or order in a pizza. If it was Milly on her own, he'd be tempted. But this is Cindy and Rich as well. Christ, he could do without this! What was that TV show he never watched? *Kitchen Nightmares?* Jesus!

Cooking for four is another difficulty. In theory, cooking for four should simply be cooking for two, times two. Simple. Except it's not that easy to multiply the sizes of his pots and pans, and he's certain he only has three knives. He can't remember the last time he cooked for four. Not counting the appearance of Milly on the scene, since Cindy moved out, a plateful of biscuits for Madam Radwańska has been the closest he's got to 'entertaining' in the last six months. Excluding the times when the Italians show up twenty minutes late carrying takeaway breakfasts from McDonald's.

He's worried because Cindy is coming: he's got a new girlfriend, and he's lost the lottery ticket. The last thing he wants is Cindy kicking off on either of those two subjects. He hasn't yet got round to telling her that he's lost the ticket, it's bound to come up, so he must do that before she arrives. He'll call her. Get the ranting over before the dinner. His worst fear is that she won't believe it, and will still be demanding a million pounds off him. It all seems so unreal now, that mad couple of days when he won the lottery, tried to hide it, bought a Beemer, met Milly, decided to share the money, then discovered he'd lost the ticket – or washed it to pieces. It's like he's a different person now. Is he really happier without the money? He's sure he is, especially now Milly's come into his life. She's worth two point three million quid. Easy. All his worries disappear when he thinks about her and not the money. The bell rings.

'Hi Mill.'

'Vegetable curry,' she says, waving an enormous saucepan in one hand, and showing him a jar of Patak's Korma Curry Sauce with the other.

'Really?'

'Simple. Chop up loads of veg, dollop in the sauce, boil the rice. Brilliant idea?'

'Yes! Solves everything. I've got a bit of veg here. Carrots, onions, spuds. You can put spuds in, can't you?'

'Course you can. Have you got a pepper?'

'In the cupboard, next to the salt.'

'No. *A* pepper.'

'Oh, right. No.'

'Okay. I'll go over to the corner shop and get a pepper, some garlic, fresh toms, and whatever else they have. You got a tin of pineapple?'

'For pud?'

'No, silly. For the *Korma!* Gives it a nice sweet tang. You got any sultanas? Almonds?'

Jack shakes his head, feels like a culinary caveman, but she laughs it off.

'Patak's and Banerjees to the rescue then. Back in a mo.'

She dumps the pan and the jar in his arms, kisses him, and heads back out. Milly to the rescue, he thinks, as he savours the memory of her kiss and her smile and the sunshine she's flooded his kitchen with. That's what she does, solves his problems just by being there. The girl's a genius, *plus* – they won't need knives to eat a curry!

51

THE TWO-TONE BIKINI

'Sparkly midnight-blue or sexy black?' Cindy asks, holding up two dresses, which a skilled and imaginative seamstress could, at a push, make into a two-tone bikini to fit Barbie.

Rich considers the options. The blue is dead sophisticated, he's only ever seen her in it once, when they went down the West End for a show to celebrate a month 'together'. But the black looks hellish sexy, he's never seen her wear it. 'Black,' he says, fancying his chances for later on.

'I thought the blue. Don't want to give Milly an inferiority complex from the off, do we?'

He falls for it every time. She gives him two options: red or white wine, *Bourne* or *The Matrix*, upstairs or downstairs – and she always picks the one he hasn't chosen. He should get clever next time...

'You gonna wear a tie?'

'I wasn't planning to. Why? Do you think I should?'

She shrugs. 'Makes you look sexy...'

'Which one do you like...?'

———

'I think we should tell Jack tonight,' Cindy says as they're getting into her Vee Dub.

'Tell him what?' Rich replies, knowing exactly what she means, but hoping a slight delay in her saying it might allow time for a tsunami or a stray meteorite to wipe out their dinner date.

'About us! It's perfect. He's got a new Sheila; you can have one too! We should bring some fizz. Celebrate.'

He's been dreading this conversation coming up again, but he's not entirely sure why. Is it because he's not convinced how committed he is to Cindy? Well, partly. It's been a load of fun, if a bit stressful with the bloody lottery farce, but he's quite happy as it is. Hooking up with Jack and Milly for some kind of regular foursomes at the cinema or whatever was never on his agenda when he and Cindy had started shag– *seeing* each other. He's quite happy carrying on as they are, at least for a while longer.

But it's a bit more than that.

'Won't it look a bit suspicious? If we roll up there tonight and say, *guess what?* Won't he work out that this has been going on for a while?'

'What if he does? We're getting a divorce; he's not contesting it. I never quite understood why we've kept it such a secret for so long. Let's put it out there.'

Rich takes a breath, tries to think of some words that he could usefully add to it when he breathes it out. It emerges as a long sigh.

'What?' Cindy snaps, with a tone that would send *Crocodile Dundee*, maybe even an angry croc, back a pace or two.

'Nothing. I just don't think it's the right time. Who knows how long Jack and Milly are going to last...'

'What does that matter? Once he's made his move for her,

I've got nothing holding me back. I was a free agent once he agreed to the bloody divorce. I don't see your problem.'

Rich searches for a few spare straws, fingers twitching. 'Why don't we *hint* at it tonight? You know, we get along well over din-dins, all flirty flirty, this could be the start of something big. Then we could sort of announce it next week. Like it just happened, when you gave me a lift home, as it were. I don't want Jack thinking I've been going behind his back for months.'

'Even though you have?'

Rich sucks in another deep breath... 'Not really. Like you said, you were divorcing, so there wasn't really anything stopping us from – you know...'

'Having a bit of a naughty.'

'What?'

'Rooting.'

'Do you have to make it sound so crude?'

'Okay, let's do it in genteel English then, fucking, shagging–'

'All right. I get it.'

'You've agreed with me. There was never any reason why we shouldn't be doing the business with who, or whom, we wanted – don't want him correcting our grammar. So, we tell him.'

'I think it might be better to wait, see how the land lies, there's no rush.'

'You were into my bed faster than lightning through a wet dog once I'd hinted that I might be giving Jack the flick.'

Rich usually sees himself as a good arguer. He's got a quick wit and a sharp brain. He can hold his own in debate with just about anyone he knows, except Cindy. Cindy makes him feel like he's punching balloons, chasing floaters in his eyeballs. Whatever he says has no impact as she drifts effortlessly out of range. Plus, there's always the danger that, at any moment, she's liable to pop back in close and knock his block off with a verbal right uppercut. He needs a new tactic. Needs to come up with a new line of attack that she won't see coming; something that'll push her off balance; pierce her defences with the power of its clever logic and unanswerable rationale...

As they step out of the car, he runs around and wraps her in his arms.

'That's because you're irresistible...'

Outside Jack's door, he puts his arm around her shoulders. 'Look. Jack's going through a bit of a time at the moment. He's got a new girlfriend, which is nice. But he's also pretty cut up about losing the lottery ticket. Do you think it might be a good idea to keep off that subject tonight? It's probably something he feels a bit delicate about...'

She turns and looks at him, but he can't read her expression...

'I know you don't believe him, but let's save that for another time. Let's not spoil his big night with Milly...'

52

THE ENORMOUS JAPANESE PENIS

'WHERE WAS THIS TAKEN?' Milly asks, pointing at a photo in a frame above the television. Jack has insisted that, as he's on home ground, he'll do the cooking, as long as Milly does the chopping and tells him which veggies to put in first. Her skill on the chopping board has made him wonder about the toys she played with as a child. She's diced everything within range by the time Jack's poured the oil into the pan. He pokes his head around the corner.

'Oh, Christ.'

'Is it Japan?'

'Yes.'

'You never said you'd been.'

'I haven't. It's one of Uncle Jezza's.'

'Is it a – you know?'

'A willy? Yes, it is.'

'It's bloody big.'

'Two metres, apparently. Solid wood.'

'Why are they carrying it through the streets?'

'It was a fertility festival. Uncle Jezza was in Japan teaching

English. Actually, there's a funny story behind it. That's why I have it on the wall.'

'Go on then.' She's come into the kitchen, perched herself by the fridge, sipping her wine. 'Smells good.'

'Yeah, me and Patak, distant cousins.'

She smiles; he loves the way she seems to appreciate his unsophisticated attempts at humour. She's got no *edge* – unlike Cindy, who'd been nothing but razor blades. She'd have rolled her eyes at such a lame crack, the main reason he'd stopped attempting them. He feels liberated with Milly; she gives him permission to be himself, verrucas and all.

'So? Your story about Uncle Jezza and the enormous Japanese penis. You can do polite dinner table chat anywhere, can't you? I can take you to meet my parents, no bother.'

He smiles roguishly, sips his wine. 'Right, well, Uncle Jezza went to Japan to teach English. Did a bit of touring about while he was there. Stumbled upon this fertility festival. Just for men, it was.'

'But there are women in the picture. Seem to be enjoying themselves immensely...'

'No, that's right. What I mean is, the festival was only for penises. They have a different festival for, you know, the ladies...'

'You *are* pulling my leg now.'

'I'm not. Scout's honour. Google it. Or ask my Uncle Jezza. They have another festival for vag–'

'Yes, okay, I *am* a nurse.'

'Christ, this was the funniest thing. Honest. It was epic. Uncle Jezza was out on a round-the-world ticket with Auntie Linda. He was a bit of an amateur snapper. That's one of his best, that one. Thing was, he was into slides around that time, long before digital. You remember slides? Little cardboard frames this size, with the pic in the middle, you really had to have a projector to see them.'

She nods, sips wine, wonders if he might be making this up on the fly.

'Rather than cart loads of exposed film around the world, what Uncle Jezza used to do was send them off to Kodak or Fuji or whoever, once he'd finished a roll, but he'd get them to post the developed slides back to the UK, to his parents, my grandparents. Then every couple of months, we'd go along as a family, to have a little show at Granny and Granddad's. Uncle Jezza and Auntie Linda at the Taj Mahal, Uncle Jezza and Auntie Linda trekking in the Himalayas. It was great fun, Granddad would enjoy showing off, telling us the Taj Mahal was in India, all that stuff.'

'Oh God!'

'Exactly! It was dreadful. My grandparents used to make a bit of a thing about it whenever a new box of slides arrived. We'd all go round for dinner, then they'd set the projector up in the front room, turn out the lights and break out the sherry and Quality Street.'

'I can't listen to this.'

'You should have *been* there! Although, obviously, we had no clue what was coming. There we were, Mum and Dad, Granny and Granddad, Rich and I. We had a couple of snaps of Mount Fuji, and a Geisha girl, and Granddad tells us Uncle Jezza's made it as far as Japan – and then up pops the fat man.'

'Jack!'

'What? You pick a name for it. The room went utterly quiet. They all could've died for all we knew. I'm surprised Granny didn't. Rich and I couldn't believe what we were seeing. Then Granny said...' Jack sniggers. 'Granny said, "That's a big sausage".'

'Rich fell off his chair. I was biting down as hard as I could

258

on my hand so as not to make a noise. I'm sure Mum and Dad knew exactly what it was, probably Granddad too, but Granny had no idea. She kept asking questions. *Why are they carrying such a big sausage around the streets? Do you think they've cooked it? You must make sure it's cooked through, if it's that big. It's very stiff, do you think they've overdone it...?* Dad kept telling Granddad to move on, but there were dozens of shots. Uncle Jezza wasn't a great photographer, his method was to shoot loads and hope he'd get one good one. He was in his element when he went digital.'

'Did he do it on purpose?'

'What? The eight o'clock screening of *Deep Throat Sausages* at Granny Josie's? No! God. He had no idea we were making it a big family night in. This was pre-mobile phones, remember, pre-Facebook. You went round the world in those days, you really *went*. Nobody heard from you for weeks. Even postcards could be a bit of a lottery. I remember him telling us, the guidebooks used to warn them, in certain countries, that if you gave your postcards in to the hotel to post, they'd often steal the stamps off them. You had to go to the post office, get them franked in front of your eyes.

'Phoning home was a huge occasion, you had to go to a telephone shop and book a time to make your call. Compared to today, it seemed closer to the experience of Livingstone and Stanley. I can tell you what though, we never had another show. That was the end of Uncle Jezza's photo-porno exhibitions. God, how Rich and I survived without ripping our stomach muscles is a medical mystery. It was *the* most embarrassing moment of my life. At least I know it'll never be beaten...'

The doorbell rings.

'Oh Jack,' Milly asks, as he heads to answer it. 'Did you ever get round to telling Cindy you lost the ticket...?'

53

THE SPUR OF THE MOMENT

María is out shopping. It's browsing really, in the clothes section of the supermarket, but she enjoys looking and trying things on, even if she ends up empty-handed in the end. She's got her eye on a cardi. Jack's taught her that's what she should call a cardigan if she wants to sound like a confident English speaker. Which she does. So, whenever she's out browsing, she has a little game she likes to play...

'How much ees the cardi?' she asks a passing assistant.

'Hasn't it got a ticket?'

'Oh, wait one minute, yes, I sorry, I didn't see eet,' she lies. She gets such a thrill in her stomach that the girl has answered her *cardi* question without a blink, confirming once again what an all-round Mr Nice Guy and top teacher Jack is. She loves engineering these little conversations in shops. She spends half her time asking the staff where the *tinned toms* are, or the *chocky bickies*, so she can practise the quirky little English phrases that Jack teaches them – well, her; Iker's not such an expert on *tinned toms* or *chocky bickies* – he usually looks at the pictures. But for María, it's the equivalent of those pictures you see on the front of newspapers on examination-results day. All those toothpaste smiles and clenched fists? That's María's insides when she gets directed to the *chocky bickies*.

The best thing about her supermarket English lessons is that they're all free. Iker often grumbles that thirty quid a week for the lesson with Jack is a bit of a stretch. Not that he uses that phrase, but María knows what it means. She doesn't know what he's complaining about. He's still claiming twenty quid a week from his firm, even though Jack only charges thirty for the two of them. She thinks Iker might want to cancel the lesson but keep claiming the twenty quid. María doesn't like this sort of wheelering dealering (another one of Jack's, she thinks). She'd pay Jack thirty quid on her own for her weekly fix of her all-round Mr Nice Guy. Thinking of him, as she often is...

She looks in her purse as she pays for her new cardi. It's a snip. (That means a real bargain. You can also say *cheep – for half of the price,* but she's not sure why you'd say *cheep*, or who to, and why it might be half of the price. She'll ask Jack.) There's Jack's lottery ticket. She's looking forward to giving it to him, he'll be so happy. He might even give her a *kees* on her cheeks. The thought sends a tremble through her.

Then she has an idea. She's in Cricklewood, Jack's flat is just around the corner. She could pop it round now. (*Pop* means take, for some reason that Jack doesn't know.) It would be more nicer to take it now, she thinks, somewhat guiltily, without Iker. Not that she'd dream of anything 'happening'. But the kees on her cheeks might be that little bit more nicer if Iker wasn't there, looking over her shoulder, like beeg daddy bear – or even more beegger blue whale...

Does she dare? *Claro, qué sí!* Much better for Jack to know she's found his ticket sooner rather than later. Yes, she should make some straw if it isn't raining... That's another one Jack, all-round Mr Nice Guy, top teacher and *chico guapísimo*, has taught her.

54

THE KISS

'WELCOME, WELCOME!' Jack booms as he opens the door. Rich was right: he's a crap actor. Jack's smile is fixed like he's been dead a week; his eyes betray panic and dread; he bows like he's auditioning for a job as a doorman at the Ritz.

Rich responds as if he's practising for the role of a pompous guest at *Fawlty Towers.*

'Thank you, thank you,' he shouts theatrically. There must be an *Acting for Dummies* book somewhere, which stipulates that repeating every line twice is the key to Hollywood.

Rich hands Milly a bunch of flowers, identical to the garage brand Jack gave her a week earlier; Cindy presents Jack with a bottle of warm Yellow Tail Chardonnay, the price sticker mostly gone.

'Wow! Aussie wine!' Jack blabs, like they never drank Aussie wine when they were living together. Cindy gives him an easy-to-read *I'm so glad I'm divorcing you* smile. The evening is off to a crawl.

With Jack desperately trying to initiate conversations that don't include any obvious (or even not-so-obvious) links to lottery tickets, money, good fortune, luck or cars, and Rich equally gamely attempting to steer clear from talk of girlfriends, boyfriends, fresh starts, marriage or divorce, the conversation ends up being led by the women. Well, by Cindy.

'So, how lucky you are, Jack, to find such a beautiful new girlfriend so quickly.'

Jack smiles a tight smile while swallowing his tongue.

'Yeah, really fort– um, I mean, great, yes, very– um, good,' he finally stutters.

'How did you meet?' Cindy enquires breezily.

While Milly takes a breath, Jack blurts, 'We bumped into each other while we were parking, nothing serious, just a little knock.'

'Yes, then we clicked straight away, we went for a coffee and we just clicked,' Milly offers, sensing that Jack doesn't want the shiny black Beemer convertible meets pink Panda dodgem affair to nudge its way into the conversation.

'Yeah,' Jack agrees, wiping his forehead, 'we just clicked.'

'Smells good,' Rich says, looking around towards the kitchen. Having spent the last few moments trying unsuccessfully to link whatever's cooking to a conversation about new boy or girlfriends, he feels safe to offer it as an opener.

'Vegetable curry, Milly's idea but we cooked it together. She cut everything up – you should see her with a knife – and I poured the sauce over it. Should be done.'

'I love curry,' Cindy says, covering Rich's hand with her own. 'How about you, Rich?'

Rich feels a jolt of nerve malfunction travel instantly to every part of his body, especially his brain, which suffers a mild seizure. He and Cindy never finished their *shall we – shan't we* conversation, so he guesses (as far as his brain will allow him to think) that this is either her attempt to 'break the news', or maybe she's accepted his idea that they should make a display of 'getting along well' tonight, as a prelude to a more formal 'getting together' sometime in the future. He really has no idea.

'Love it!' he says, sounding slightly coarse and vulgar.

'Great,' says Jack. 'I'll open the wine, let it breathe.'

'It's a white,' Cindy says, acidly.

'My favourite,' Jack replies, oblivious. 'Everyone for white?'

'Only once it's stopped breathing,' Cindy mutters.

While Jack busies himself filling four assorted tumblers and petrol-station glasses with wine, Milly serves the curry. Jack and Rich immediately fill their mouths with enormous forkfuls to stave off conversation, then half empty their glasses to cool their burning tongues.

The conversation swirls wildly, from Australian slang (when Cindy asks if there's any more tucker), to favourite film scores (when Jack lets on that Milly is a wiz – his word – on the violin). At times, they veer dangerously close to forbidden topics, Jack and Rich yanking the invisible steering wheel whenever they sense their route is threatening to take them into peril.

Rich is sure that Cindy has adopted his idea of a 'getting along well' display tonight, although as a bottle of Pinot Grigio is opened, her idea of 'getting along well' moves much closer to soft porn than the subtle hints of a blossoming friendship that he had been envisioning. She nudges him playfully whenever he makes a clever remark; laughs uproariously at anything he says that might conceivably be deemed amusing, or merely wry; she leans her head on his shoulder, rests her hand on his neck, ruffles his hair – he begins to wonder if he's got it wrong. She's actually simply telling Jack they're having sex but using some obscure international sign language pioneered by the *Playboy* magazine.

———

Both Jack and Rich seem to hit on the idea of getting Cindy to talk about all things Antipodean as the best way of keeping the conversation away from forbidden topics. They pepper her with questions about life in Sydney, what kangaroos eat, how many deadly spiders and snakes there are – like they're the only two around the table who've never met her before.

The flat's too small for Jack and Milly to exchange words about the mating display playing out on the other side of the table. The only thing that seems to be missing, thinks Jack, is a David Attenborough commentary. However, while they're making coffee, Milly gives him an *Are you seeing what I'm seeing?* flick of her eyes, which is as clear as a ten-minute discussion. Rich and Cindy do seem to be getting along ever so well.

Jack wonders if he minds. Concludes he doesn't. It might chivvy Cindy along to a quicker divorce if she and Rich are 'together', he thinks, although he's still not convinced that they are at all suited. Rich's a bit more sociable than he is, certainly more the brash alpha male than he could ever be. He's also more into fitness, what with all his riding. Maybe it might work. Does he care? Why should he? He's got Milly.

The doorbell rings.

'I got it,' he says.

María stands in the doorway looking like an advert for some Italian – well, probably Spanish, or even Puerto Rican – perfume. Her blood-red jacket has a furry collar-cum-hood thingy, which frames her face beautifully. She's smiling like she's delivering Christmas presents from John Lewis or is about to burst into a carol.

'María,' Jack blurts, as if he thinks she might have forgotten her own name.

'Hello Jack,' she replies, her eyes darting past him to catch the scene inside.

Rich, who she's met on a couple of occasions, gives her a little wave. Cindy nudges him, gives him quizzical eyebrows.

'She's one of his students,' he whispers.

'Come in,' Jack says, chivalry winning over caution. 'Let me introduce you, María, star English student, you've met Rich, my brother...?'

'Yes, we see each other, you usually wear bicycle clothing, yes?'

Rich nods, waves again.

'And Cindy, I think you met once...'

'I think so, yes,' says María.

'I don't remember,' says Cindy.

'And this is Milly,' Jack says, pointing, in case María has failed to spot the only other life form in the room, not counting the small sad-looking cactus on the windowsill, which is actually dead.

'Is it something quick? As you can see, we're having dinner.' María's never cold-called him like this, despite the hundreds of occasions in the past, when his bell has rung, and he's prayed for it to be her.

'Yes, very quick, very quick,' she says, rustling in her purse. With her head down, and her hood still up, she looks like an oversized red squirrel, squirrelling for nuts. Conversation has ceased, all eyes are on María. Jack can't imagine what she wants.

'You remember when you ween lottery? You hide you ticket?'

Jack wonders how life can behave like this. He's got his back to the others so he can't see their faces, but he hears a gasp, he's sure it's Cindy.

Rich might never have been a *Fawlty Towers* fan, but Jack has the boxed set. His favourite episode is *Communication Problems*, where Basil asks the Major to hide his horse-racing winnings from Sybil. But Basil is finally discovered when the

Major tells everyone, *You did give me that money, you won it on that horse...* Suddenly, Jack knows exactly how Basil felt.

'Here ees!' María says, holding up the ticket. 'Was een thees book I take for read. I find eet, I know you hide eet.' Jack really should have noticed before, her ongoing confusion between hide – and *lose*... But his mind's too occupied to realise it now. He thinks the last time he gulped was when he was about seven. He gulps now, takes the ticket from María's fingers. He's alone in the world for a second or two, until María's gorgeous smile joins him, and then, more ominously, Cindy's voice.

'You lying, bastard Pom!'

'No wait...'

'You cheating–'

'Hold on...'

María looks stunned as Cindy screams at Jack. Rich tries to calm her, but she's got a full head of steam up, fuelled by a bottle of Blue Nun they've finished, so she also starts yelling at him. Milly looks as though she's never seen anything like it, certainly not since Johnny went for the waiter in *Dirty Dancing*.

'I told you! Were you in on this little scheme as well? *Lost* the ticket? My arse!' Cindy snarls at Rich, standing suddenly and knocking her chair backwards.

'Woah, hang on...' Rich shrinks further into his own chair, which creaks worryingly.

María's suddenly close to tears, her face breaks, she turns and flees.

'Wait, María, wait!'

Jack catches her in the street, turns her round gently. She's crying openly. 'María, stop. Let me explain.'

'I theenk you happy. I no unnerstan why everybody they shouting.'

'I am happy, María. Thank you. But it's complicated, with the family–'

'Iker, he say maybe we keep ticket, keep money, but I say no. I geev to you ticket back.'

She looks down at her feet, then straight into his face. He's still got his hands resting gently on her shoulders. Suddenly, some primeval sixth sense awakes in him, and he knows for absolute certain that she's going to kiss him. There's a look in her eyes he's never seen before. He tries to stiffen his arms to stop her, but she slips out of his grasp, clasps him in her arms, and kisses him.

He's never been kissed against his will before. Although, *against his will* is a tad disingenuous: the best part of a bottle of Yellow Tail Chardonnay, and a large share of a Pinot Grigio and a Blue Nun ignite the part of Jack's brain that has fancied María something completely rancid for ages – until Milly came on the scene. He tries to get his hands up to push her away, but it's like there's a force field around her he's afraid to touch. There is also a rather drunk part of him that is taking in the moment like it's a dream coming true, while another part of him doesn't want to hurt her feelings, doesn't want to embarrass her, the look in her eyes has told him everything he'd never known before. Why didn't he introduce Milly as his *girlfriend?* He has to stop María, has to tell her, before things get out of control. The kiss seems to go on and on...

He hears a car door slam, an engine start. He recognises the sound of it. María finally breaks away, traces of shock, guilt, pleasure, and even a touch of mild hypoxia fighting for dominance in her features as she steadies herself against the wall.

Behind her head, still surrounded by the perfume-ad halo of fur, Jack spots a pink Fiat Panda rumbling away down the street, bleeding black smoke from the exhaust.

PART 3

WIN SOME, LOSE SOME...

55

THE AFTERMATH

MILLY SLAPS the tears from her cheeks with one hand as she races the Panda away as fast as she dares – not wanting to risk a speeding ticket. More tears replace them. She can barely believe what she saw. Jack kissing María. Jack snogging María. Jack and María getting it on... Whichever phrase leaps into her mind, the effect is the same – an increase in the torrent of brine. She mauls her cheeks, wrestles with the gearstick, and swears under her breath.

'Bloody, bloody... Jack!'

———

'Where's Milly gone?' Jack gasps, as he sprints back into the flat. Rich and Cindy are putting their coats on.

'She went after you, came straight back in for her coat, then stamped out. Never said a word. Bit rude, we thought,' Cindy says coldly. 'Anything the matter?' She smiles a *sweet-as-pie* smile – liver-and-onion pie.

Jack breathes a heavy sigh. As if he needed any confirmation. He's been concocting illusions that maybe Milly had a call from God knows who, emergency at the hospital, maybe, Coronavirus Mk2 outbreak in Hampstead, all nurses on board? And she'd left as a call of duty, angel of mercy with no thought for her own safety, barely noticing the strangers kissing in the darkened street...

But no, she'd followed them out, for whatever reason, and probably watched the whole clinch. Although even he had to concede, that the moonless night, the broken lamp post outside his door, all probably conspired to make it appear, against all notions of reality, that he, maybe, had actually been returning the kiss.

'I only said she was one of your favourite students,' Cindy mumbles, not at all to herself.

'What?' Astronauts must feel like this, when they return from the Moon to find a dog turd on the pavement outside their house.

'*Cindy!*' Rich hisses, not that he's thought to bring a pooper-scooper.

'He said it himself, *star student*.' She makes air quotes with her fingers; her tone is royal piss-take.

Jack breathes in and out slowly, looks at Rich, who stares at his shoes.

'So? What luck. Good old María finds the ticket you *hid*. We back on for the three-way split, Jack? All friends together again?' says Cindy, as she buttons her coat right up to her chin.

He wonders if he ever really loved her, or was he simply drunk and stoned for the whole escapade.

'Piss off, Cindy.'

'Fair dinkum. We'll hold fire on the divorce as well, shall we? Or can we guess from the speed at which Milly bailed out without so much as a kiss goodnight that you're not in that much of a rush anymore?'

'Time to leave,' Jack says, indicating the door that is still open.

'Catch ya later,' Cindy replies as she shimmies through it.

Rich looks like the boy who's been offered a choice between the cane and the slipper. 'We should talk,' he says, hesitantly, although he's not entirely sure what about.

'Yeah,' Jack says, 'we'll catch up.'

56

THE KEBAB SHOP

Jack calls Milly. No reply. He leaves a message on her voicemail, explaining everything. Then he sits and stares at the screen for ten minutes, willing it to wake up with a message: she remembered she'd left her violin case unlocked and had to dash... No. Probably not. So, maybe a reply full of understanding, and forgiveness, not that there's anything to forgive. Not really.

But his phone taunts him with its dull blackness and insolent silence. He knows he won't sleep, he can't face himself staring at the lights moving across the ceiling: lovers dashing to secret trysts, couples on their way to moonlit dinners – well, there's no bloody moon tonight, so tough shit to you! He's going to have to go after her. Explain it face to face.

He hunts for his car keys. Where has he put his *fucking* car keys? Not in his jacket, not on the table, not stuffed down between the cushions on the bloody sofa. Where in God's name– ah! They're in the garage, with his car. Whichever one of the two he's still legally covered to drive. He fetches his cycle helmet out of the cupboard.

It's a warm night for cycling – well, it is if your bike is a good deal less than optimally tuned and you're attempting to break the world land-speed record while ascending a long incline in the wrong gear. He bombs, okay, *trundles* up Shoot-Up Hill, swerving in and out of the buses that block his way with unusual regularity: there's never this many of them when he's perched at a bus stop and in a hurry. He doesn't really cycle like Rich, for fitness. Jack's cycles are for pleasure, thinking, the wind in his beard, to clear his mind. As he grinds his way towards Mill Lane, he rehearses what he's going to say.

Start with María, that'll be the easiest one to explain. *She* kissed *him*. Out of the blue. No reason. Uninvited. A crazy Spaniard. No, she's Puerto Rican, but crazy all the same. (Not that he'd usually stereotype.) He was so shocked he didn't know what to do. He froze. Yeah, for twenty – oh, all right, thirty, maybe forty-five seconds. Minute and a half, tops. He was too stunned to count. Phone her if you like. Ask her...

No. Better not suggest that until he's spoken to María himself. Squared their stories. But what is her story? Has she suddenly turned into a Spanish bunny-boiler? *Puerto Rican* bunny-boiler? He doubts it, but stranger things have happened. Trump won the presidency, more than a dozen people fell for Johnson's *oven ready* slogan. Think about it, winning the lottery is a fourteen million to one shot. And María suddenly getting the hots for him is well within range. Especially now–

The thought hits him like a misplaced lamp post. He pulls his bike onto the pavement to think it through. *Especially now... Especially now she knows I've won the lottery!* Is *that* what she's thinking? She wants him because suddenly he's *rich?* She's never made a move for him before. She's always been a bit flirty, but he'd just assumed that's what she was like. This is getting out of control. He'd never actually wanted to win so much money that it would turn his friends into scavenging lunatics. If he's honest, enough to buy – and maybe even run – the Beemer would've been enough. It wouldn't even have to have been the convertible. Or a new one. A second- or fifth-hand 316i, like the Corgi one he had as a child would've done him fine. Even a turquoise one. That was all he'd ever really wanted. That, and a girlfriend like Milly...

She'd been right when she said there was nothing a whole load of money would do to improve her life. He's rapidly realising that he feels the same. He does now that he's met her. He has a decent job, place to live, nice girlfriend, good mates – well, he *did* have. Enough to buy a small, battered, tenth-hand Beemer would've been enough. It would've avoided all this mess. Cindy wouldn't have turned their divorce into another round of the Brexit trade negotiations; Milly would've been okay with it, she had her violin; and María wouldn't have turned into a *femme fatale*, or was that French?

He remounts his bike and puffs the rest of the way up Shoot-Up Hill before turning into Mill Lane. Another bloody hill, he's sweating freely. There are no lights on in her flat but her car's parked in her space on the pavement out front. He pictures her lying in bed under the front window. Is she crying or fuming? Probably both.

He rings the bell. Nothing. Leaves his finger on it for twenty seconds. Still nothing.

The kebab shop underneath her flat is going strong, the pubs aren't throwing out yet, but there's already an unhealthy queue out into the street. Would he shout up if there wasn't an (almost certainly unsympathetic) audience in attendance? Probably not. If this were a Richard Curtis film, he'd steal a violin off a busker and play a passable version of that *Schindler's List* piece, the kebab shop would send a flood of tears down Mill Lane, and

Milly would appear, teary eyed at the window, to forgive him and understand everything. But the violin busker is having the night off.

'You in the queue, mate?' a deep voice breaks the thought. Jack moves aside, pulls out his phone and calls her. If there wasn't such a racket coming out of the kebab shop, he might be able to hear it ringing in the flat, but all he can hear is beery chat and shouted orders for kebabs and slices of pizza. The call goes to voicemail. Bugger.

He wonders if he dares throw a stone up at her window but decides against. The way his luck is going, it would smash straight through it, the falling glass probably crashing all over her, severing an artery. She'd bleed to death amid kebab fumes, while he was attacked by the crowd from the shop. Even if he managed to hit the window without breaking it, the loose stone would probably bounce down onto some kebab-munching hulk's head, provoking a fist fight that would put Jack in hospital, probably still without waking Milly. And even if all went to plan, the stone didn't break the window, didn't concuss a hungry ape, and Milly appeared, bleary eyed at the window – does he seriously think he could convince her to let him in *before* he'd explained everything? Or would he have to go through it all with the kebab queue listening in and jeering? What – a – mess.

He wonders if there's a way in from the back of her flat. He walks his bike around the block, trying to find an alley or something that would give him access. He could scale a drainpipe (it'd probably detach from the wall, and he'd kill himself in the fall); or maybe she has a fire escape (he'd scare the shit out of her, creeping into her flat in the dark, and she'd stab him with a knife she probably keeps under her pillow – not kept there for him specifically, just for random cat burglars...). But there's nothing.

He remounts his bike, cycles slowly away, trying to think of a Richard Curtis-esque next move. Jack's skills as a scriptwriter are evidently as underdeveloped as his skills as a violin player, stone thrower or cat burglar. He freewheels forlornly towards home, and a guaranteed sleepless night following everybody else's lights across the ceiling.

57

THE TEST

THE TEST SAID pregnant last night. The second one this morning says the same. So, she's pregnant. Now what? Last night's events take on a whole new meaning. She needs to think. She fights back tears, and then stops fighting.

58

THE LAST CHANCE

'Excuse my French, but you look like shit!'

Milly glances up from the swirls of her coffee, stone cold, the cup still practically full.

'Oh, hi Vicky, sorry. Worlds away.'

Vicky pushes a chair with her knee, lands her tray on the table. A full English. Milly looks out of the window at the sun baking the rooftops, a far more appealing sight.

'I don't want to state the obvious, but you don't look yourself...'

Milly attempts a smile, then changes it into a drowner's last gasp for air as she feels her tear ducts start yet another shift. She fights them back. *No more. Enough!*

'I won't ask, but if you want to talk, I'm here for you. Okay?'

Milly nods, still not trusting herself to speak without an accompanying waterfall. She composes herself, twisting at a finger like she's wondering if she can afford some replacements.

'It all went wrong with Jack last night,' she says, addressing her coffee cup.

Vicky slices off a chunk of sausage with quite brutal force, smashes the yolk of one of her sunny side ups with it, and takes it off her fork with her teeth, like she's imagining it's one of Jack's fingers. She nods as she chews. *I'm listening...*

'You know I told you he was married, to Cindy, waiting for the divorce to come through?'

Vicky chews and nods.

'And that he'd destroyed a two million quid lottery ticket in his washing machine?'

Vicky spears the rest of the sausage, raises her eyebrows in a look that says *plonker* as clearly as if she'd said it out loud. Milly threatens a smile, but she fights it off like her life depends on it.

'So, we were having dinner last night, Jack, his brother Rich, and Cindy. A sort of getting-to-know-you thingy. Halfway through, one of Jack's students showed up, María. Spanish woman, I think, stunningly beautiful. She walked in and announced that she'd found his lottery ticket. He'd hidden it in a book.'

'*Hidden* it?'

'That's what she said. She'd borrowed a book; he lets them take whatever they want, and inside was the lottery ticket. Cindy went crazy. Absolutely wild she was, furious. Accused Jack of lying about it, just to cut her out of a half share. She's still his wife, so I guess she's due half his assets when they divorce. He'd already told me he had originally planned not to tell her about it, but then he said he changed his mind. And *then*, so he says, he lost the ticket. Or destroyed it, or whatever. It's so confusing, I don't know what to believe anymore.'

'Do you think he's been lying to *you*, cos you told him you didn't ever want to be wealthy?'

'I don't know. Maybe. But that's not the real problem. The real problem is María. When Cindy kicked off, she really spooked this María. She burst into tears and ran out the door. Jack went after her and we were left sitting there, Cindy, Rich and me. Rich's okay, he's a bit of a flirt, but Cindy, she's a lot steelier. I got the feeling she was sizing me up all evening. Anyway, she said something odd. Something about María being Jack's favourite student. It was the way she said it. Something wasn't right. I went out after them. I was mainly concerned for María; she obviously thought she was doing Jack a favour, so when Cindy started throwing the furniture, María had no idea what she'd done. I got outside, and they, Jack and María, were kissing...'

Vicky puts her knife and fork down, sighs softly. 'Oh Milly...'

'I was dumbstruck. Couldn't believe it...'

'Maybe he was thanking her for finding–'

'No, no, no. This was a full-on lovers' snog. There was a whole load of B-film passion involved. I– I grabbed my coat, got in my car. I felt such a fool...' She puts her head in her hands, rocks it left and right, like the thoughts might sprinkle out of her ears and give her some peace of mind. As she speaks to the table, Vicky watches her fingers grinding into her skull.

'He's been bombarding me with WhatsApps, emails, phone calls. I've been deleting them; I'm probably going to have to block him if he goes on.'

'Why don't you give him a chance to explain?'

Milly looks up suddenly, a shocked expression contorting her face. 'Explain *what?* That he's got two girlfriends?'

A couple of heads turn their way and Milly shrinks down, hides her head back in her hands like she's expecting incoming boiled eggs and whole plum tomatoes to come raining down from the scandalised consultants. The staff canteen doesn't usually provide this type of floor show with brekka.

'There might be an explanation,' Vicky whispers.

'Like what?' Milly hisses from behind a curtain of hair.

'I don't know. Maybe they used to be together, and she was trying to relight the flame...?'

Milly looks up, slowly this time, eyes reddened. 'This was a forest fire of a kiss, Vicky. A fucking conflagration. I felt so small, so insignificant.'

Vicky stiffens. It's the first time she's heard Milly swear, she's sure of it. She's had to modify her own profanity propensity since getting to know Milly. Not that Milly's ever said anything about her potty mouth, it was just that she'd started to notice it herself, like you do when you're the only one in a group who's drinking. You start to stick out more and more as time goes on and you slide off your chair into a pool of vomit or clamber unsteadily onto the table and start stripping.

They sit in silence for a moment: Milly, drowning in self-pity; Vicky, trying to throw her the lifeline of sympathy that's knotting up her thoughts.

'*Talk* to him, before you lock the door, Milly.'

Milly stares at her hands. They're trembling. 'Maybe I'll text him. I don't want to see him. I might send him a text to tell him to stop trying to contact me. That we're finished.'

There's another silence. Vicky covers Milly's hands with her own.

'I'm going to give you some advice. It's just what I think. If you don't want advice, then say so...'

The silence on their table drowns out the chatter from their nearby neighbours. It's all either of them can hear. Vicky takes a slow breath, *last chance, Milly.*

'Go see him. He's obviously got something to say to you if he's sending you messages. You don't want to have this discussion by WhatsApp. You need to be able to see the look in his eyes, hear the tone of his voice. Doing it by WhatsApp would be meaningless. Go *talk* to him. Give him that one last chance, face to face. Listen to what he says, look at the way he says it, and if it doesn't satisfy you, tell him to his face that it's over. That's all I'm going to say. Now you're going to make your own decision, and I'm going to back you whatever it is.'

Milly continues to stare at the table, but she turns her hands and clasps Vicky's. Then she nods silently, as a fresh tear plips into her cold, now decidedly salty coffee.

59

THE VIEWPOINTS

APART FROM HIS LESSONS, he has three, Jack spends the day on his phone. He bombards Milly with texts and voice messages. Some of them are long and rambling, explaining everything (again): María got over-emotional, he could hardly push her away, could he? *Couldn't* he? Of course he could. Gently, but firmly, he could have said *no*. He should have said *no*. Christ, what a tosser he is!

And the ticket. He *did* hide the ticket. But *then*, because he was drunk, he *forgot* where he'd hidden it. He still can't really remember actually hiding it in the first place, although if he'd been sober, which he had been when he hid it, that's one of the first places he'd have chosen. So, he *did* hide it, but *then* he lost it. It's easy to understand, he thinks. Actually, he has enough trouble working out what *he* thinks, he has little idea what Milly and Cindy and Rich might be thinking.

Milly must think he's having an affair with María. What else would she think if she saw them kissing, which she must have done. Well, he can scotch that one straight away. He can ask María to tell Milly that she's going out with Iker. That'll sort it. Won't it? But if she's going out with Iker, why did she kiss him? And kiss him like that! He knows the answer – he doesn't need Pamela Stephenson to write him a *Guardian* column to explain it...

And the ticket? Tell Milly the truth: he told her he hadn't wanted to share it with Cindy, so that's why he hid it – although he hadn't remembered hiding it. Does Milly think he's hidden it from *her*? Because he knew she didn't want to have loads of money? She can't think that! That would be ridiculous. Wouldn't it?

Cindy suspected he'd been hiding it from her all along. But wait a minute. Does she think he's *changed his mind* about sharing it? Oh shit! Of course she does. She thinks he's changed his mind about sharing it – because he's met *Milly!* Bloody hell, that's it! Cindy thinks he's cooked this up with Milly, to keep the money for themselves! No, it's worse than that. She thinks Milly has *persuaded him* to keep the money for themselves. Jesus!

And what's Rich's take on this? Does he think the same as Cindy? Does he think Jack's changed his mind about giving him a third, because he now wants to keep it for himself and Milly? Because *Milly* wants to keep it for himself and Milly?

And what was that performance between Rich and Cindy last night? Are they starting something? They were pretty much all over each other, dogs on heat would've blushed at that performance. David Attenborough might have demanded substantial edits before putting his voice to the action. Although, actually, Cindy was all over Rich. Not that Rich seemed averse to the attention in any way. Was Milly right? Are they already at it? No. No, that really doesn't make any sense. They're *so* unsuited to each other. Even more unsuited than he and Cindy were in the first place...

His phone rings, he snatches it up. It's María. Christ, he can't talk to her now. He buzzes it off.

His mind swirls again: what the hell was María playing at? Bloody hell *that* came out of nowhere. He couldn't understand her attraction to Iker, the great uncommunicative lump, but he was sure it was genuine. So where did that little outburst come from? She *can't* simply be after the money. María? Surely not. But he does need to speak to her, because he needs her to speak to Milly. Put her straight. And soon. But not now.

He tries Milly's phone again. Nothing.

60

THE GIGOLO?

Milly parks down the road from Jack's flat, cuts the engine and sits for a moment, trying to compose herself. Her hands are shaking. Her fingernails would shame a nervous GCSE student sitting their final exam. That serious. She listens to the Panda cooling down after the journey. It ticks and creaks as the metal contracts and the battered plastic settles back into place; she wishes her brain would do something similar. She's always loved her car, her Pinky (used to be red) Panda. Loved it all the more for bringing her and Jack together. Butting his Beemer like that. She'd almost got to the point when she could find it funny, something she might be able to laugh about with Jack one day. Now she's not so sure. Has her Panda tricked her? Or has it been tricked?

Vicky'd been right. Milly owes Jack the chance to explain. Like when they'd first met, and she'd given him a chance to be more than just a rich Beemer driver, now she owes him that chance again. And face to face is best, she wants to see the look in his eyes, because she saw what she saw. To call it a 'shock' debases the language. She'd gone out after them because she was concerned about María. She'd obviously thought she was

288

helping by bringing Jack the ticket, and then Cindy kicked off. She could see that María was completely stunned by the reaction. But what Milly saw when she got to the street... She still can't believe it now. How long has *that* been going on? She suddenly remembers Rich singing the line from the old pop song when Jack had introduced her that first time in Mill Lane. Does *Rich* know he's running the pair of them? Has she been taken for a complete mug?

She hasn't listened to any of Jack's calls or read his texts or emails, but they were coming through at such a rate she's had to block him. She wants to do this face to face, but she wanted to compose herself first. She doesn't want to face him while her anger and disappointment are still so raw. Not that she's calmed down that much...

She gets out of her car and takes a couple of breaths, the morning air is cool, such a relief, the summer they're having. But hold on, her knees are trembling, she can't stand straight. She gets back inside and tries to calm herself down. This is ridiculous. She's only known him a *week*. Just go and *talk* to him. Let him give his side. But she can't talk to him in this state. She's not thinking straight, she can't even stand straight. Breathe in and out, she learned that on a course somewhere. Calm down, think it through logically.

What in God's name was he doing?!

She breathes. She's been through it a hundred times. Why did she *really* follow them out? Was it what Cindy had said? Something about María being his favourite student? Or was it the way she'd said it. A nudge, a wink. Favourite student? Nudge, wink. Milly wishes she hadn't moved. Or does she? Isn't it better to know *now?* Before they go any further? Is this what happened between Cindy and Jack? Has he lied to her about what happened between *them?* Was it not as amicable as Jack said? Was *he* unfaithful to *her?* Is *that* why they're divorcing?

Oh, stop it! Stop it! *Talk* to him. Let him have his say. She steps out of the car again.

As she moves to cross the street a sleek red sports car turns into the road and sweeps past her face, inches from her. It jolts her as she stops just in time, the air ruffling her hair and flapping her clothes. Another step and she'd have walked into it. It's a flash soft-top with the roof down, driven by a striking blonde, her hair flowing in the wind. It's like an advert, although in the advert she probably wouldn't be driving along a side street in Cricklewood, she'd be on the Amalfi Coast, or the Pacific Coast Highway in California, 'Ode to Joy' blasting out of the radio. She double parks right outside Jack's flat and puts her hand on the horn. Within seconds, Jack appears from his front door, waves, then jumps in beside the blonde. Milly ducks down behind her car as the Beemer, yes, it's a Beemer, exactly like Jack's but red, screams away.

Milly straightens up and feels her heart pounding, her world spinning. What's going on? She tries not to come to conclusions that will make her cry again, but it's not easy. Is he in some high-class Beemer *sex* club? Where has *that* thought come from? Get a grip. Has she been reading too many trashy novels? There has to be some innocent explanation.

She wonders how well she really knows Jack. She's known him such a short time, and every time she turns her head, he confesses a new secret; he could be anyone. Some philandering womaniser? A serial bigamist? A-a- a *gigolo*? She's not sure she knows exactly what a gigolo is. She thinks about the females in his orbit: María's a beautiful woman (the cow!); Cindy's attractive in a lithe, fit, tanned, sporty, outdoorsy sort of way; and now this blonde bimbo in the *fuck-me* car.

Oh, stop it, Mills. Stop it! Stop turning it into a novel. There's an innocent explanation. There has to be. An innocent explanation that reveals Jack to be who she truly believes he is: a genuine, honest, uncomplicated *nice* guy. She wants him to be nice. She doesn't want Brad Pitt, or Poldark – she really doesn't. She just wants Jack to be who she really, deep down, thinks he is: someone kind, thoughtful, honest. Most of all, honest. Is that so high a bar?

Suddenly, she slides down behind her car again, her heart finding another gear. It's the woman from last night, María? The kisser. She's coming up the road, wearing that same red jacket she had on the night before, flapping open in the breeze. She's ever so pretty; Milly feels like walking over and slapping her. She hates herself for the genuine, evil pleasure the thought gives her. Her body tenses as she imagines swinging the flat of her palm into María's cheek. Her fists clench and she wonders if she could even punch her. Then she hates herself all the more for the very thought, and hates Jack for having put it into her head.

María rings Jack's bell. Christ! Is he some kind of male prostitute? Do they really exist? Is that what a gigolo is? Milly knows he's not in, he's off with the blonde flooz in the red car. María rings again. Nothing. If she's got a key, Milly's going to cry. But María runs across the street to the corner shop.

Milly has to creep around her car into the gutter on her hands and knees to stay out of sight. She feels ridiculous. What's she going to do if a pedestrian wanders by and sees her crouched between the parked cars? What if someone gets into the other car and drives it away? Or reverses and crushes her into the Panda bumper? She knows it's pretty bloody sturdy.

A moment or two later, María comes out, clutching something in her hand. Milly edges around her car as María rushes over to Jack's flat. Peering through the Panda's windows, she makes out that María has some kind of a notebook. She scribbles something on a page, rips it off and posts it through the door. Then she hurries up the street, red coat-tails flying in her wake like a fashion shoot.

Milly stands up, takes a deep breath, tries to clear her head of the feelings of hate and betrayal. How can she feel like this when she's known him such a short period of time? She's never fallen so far, so fast before. But the overriding emotion she's left with isn't hate, the hate she feels for Jack, and María, and the blonde job she's never even met.

And it's not betrayal, although she does feel that heavily. No, she knows what it is that outweighs all the other emotions, she can feel it grumbling in the pit of her stomach and in every tear that falls. It's shame. Shame at how she may have been duped; shame at how easily she fell for it; and, worst of all, shame for what she's thinking she might do about it.

She reaches into her pocket, and fingers the key to his door – which Jack had cut for her a day or so earlier...

61

THE HOSPITAL

'Thanks for calling, and the lift,' Jack says, stepping out of the car as Shelly closes the roof. 'Would've taken me an age on the bus, and I've got another class in an hour.'

'No probs, all the paperwork's done,' she replies, in quite a brave purple today. She's even got a purple Alice band in her hair, exactly the same shade as her trouser suit and shoes. Does she buy these get-ups in kits? She can't go out shopping with the trouser suit on, comparing Alice bands and shoes to find a matching colour. That would be mad. They *must* sell them in kits, like they do for Barbie in the toyshops.

'I've got your keys in my desk. Kev was wondering whether to buy it himself, for his daughter, she'll be learning to drive soon, but I told him you wanted it back.'

'Thanks. How's the Beemer doing?'

'Oh, it's fine. Kev's given it the once-over, there's nothing major wrong. Needs the whole bumper assembly replacing and a new boot. Couple of hours' work.'

'That's a relief.'

She collects his Fiesta keys and leads him out back where his BMW is sitting with its knickers off.

'Looks worse than it is,' Shelly says, smiling, as Jack gasps in horror.

He nods, strokes his fingers down the paintwork, recognising how difficult his situation is. Not only does he have to explain the kiss to Milly, but how will she deal with him being rich? Quite ridiculously rich. Almost certainly richer than any man she might want to spend time with. He could buy a Z4 now that María's found the bloody ticket. But he still takes the Fiesta, not really knowing why, his mind going into a fast spin. *Shit! Shit! Shit!*

———

He knows Milly's working today, so he shoots straight up to Hampstead in the Fiesta. It's the car he could step into straight away, without having to sign documents, or make decisions. He's never been to the Royal Free before, takes him an age to park, and another one to find his way inside. There are signs pointing in all directions and everyone else seems to know where they're going. It's like trying to walk across a packed nightclub dance floor balancing four pints on a tray while The Pointer Sisters are getting excited.

He can't remember where she works, it has a funny name, but he knows it's with very young, very sick children. Sounds like some place in Latvia. Well, he'd thought so. It's taken him so long just to get inside, he knows he's fast running out of time. He's got a long jog back to the car and then the traffic home, he's going to have to cut and run unless he finds her in the next five minutes or so.

He follows signs for *Information*, wonders if he'll ever find his way back to where he started, and then from there to his car, which he's parked half a continent away in a car park that has his credit card number and is sucking money off it at an eye-watering rate. He finally arrives at the information desk: it's closed. He searches the information board high up behind it for inspiration, time is against him. He suddenly thinks he recognises *SCBU*, wasn't that where she worked? He stops a nurse in uniform.

'Excuse me, what's S – C – B – U?'

'Special care baby unit,' she says, barely slowing down.

'Great!' he shouts after her. 'Thanks!' He sets off at a trot, following the signs to Latvia.

62

THE NOTE

MILLY PRESSES THE BELL. Unless he's got a secret fire escape, she knows he's not in, but she doesn't really want to run into Rich or Cindy. She waits a few seconds, takes a breath, then slides the key into the lock, hates herself for doing it.

It sticks. Why didn't she test it when he'd given it to her? New keys always stick. She gives it a jiggle, rattles the door, and she's in. If she ever gets fed up with the nursing, she can always be a spook, nervelessly picking locks and planting lies – instead of snooping on her boyfriend. Her conscience tries to hold her back, where has she got this overwhelming sense of playing fair, being honest and trustworthy? But she wants to know, needs to know. Who is he? What's he up to? So, not quite overwhelming...

The door pushes the sheet of paper backwards as she opens it. The note's not in an envelope or anything, it's folded in half on the floor. She bites what's left of a nail, knows she shouldn't. It's not at all like her to even consider such a thing, it's such a betrayal of trust. But there's so much going on that she doesn't understand: María and Jack kissing? The blonde in the red car? The truth about his divorce? Who *is* this guy?

She hesitates, wanting to believe that he is exactly who she thought he was, until the previous night, then that morning, when her doubts had suddenly multiplied like a coronavirus on the tube when everyone's mainlining the conspiracy theories. The flat is so quiet it seems like a strange place she's never entered before. She doesn't recognise it; it's usually full of laughter, and passion. Now, all she can see is María's beautiful face...

Milly lifts the sheet and opens it out as silently as she can, her hands shaking...

Jack,
I pregnunt.
We must to talk.
María.

x

Milly gasps, drops the note, steps outside and closes the door behind her.

63

THE GOSS

SCBU HAS AN ENTRYPHONE SYSTEM. He buzzes the buzzer.

'Hello. Can I help you?'

'Can I speak to nurse Milly Patterson, please?'

'Who are you please, sir? Are you a relative of a patient?'

'No. I'm Milly's boyfriend, Jack.'

'She's not on duty today, I'm sorry.'

He knows she is; she told him yesterday. He's tempted to tell whoever this is that he knows she's there, but he's sure that'll be a dead end. Either she's told all her mates that she doesn't want to see him if he happens to bowl up looking for her – or she's really not there. Either way, an argument is going to get him nowhere. His mind spins all his options, hunting for three cherries.

'Can you tell her next time you see her that I need to talk to her. There's been a dreadful misunderstanding, and I just need to explain it. That's all.'

'I can do that. No problem.'

'Thank you. And sorry to have bothered you.'

'It's no bother.'

That's the best he can do. With a bit of luck, she might tell

Milly that he sounded distraught and genuine. With a lottery jackpot bit of luck, Milly might be inside, listening, heart breaking, tears popping. He waits for the security door to open and for Milly to fly out, calling his name...

———

Jack's in a rush to get back for his class. As usual, when he's in a hurry, the traffic snarls up in front of him. Not in the other lane, going the other way, no, that's about as busy as Santa's grotto on a sunny August afternoon. In front of him is a bus, so he can't even see what's holding him up. Is it roadworks? An accident? Jesus!

It's a crappy drive back to Cricklewood, he has to cross the Finchley Road. More lights, more traffic, delivery lorries blocking the way, every zebra crossing full of mums and toddlers or zombies staring at phones. Why aren't all these people at work, or at home watching daytime telly? He's stuck at lights now, so he picks up his phone. Is he allowed to use it if he's not moving? He doesn't know. He looks around for plod, last thing he wants is to get arrested for sitting in traffic with a phone. He pings Milly's number. The usual nothing.

As always, when he's in a hurry, as well as the traffic snarling up in front of him, the nearest parking spot in his zone is four streets away. He jogs to his flat, his student, Julieta, is waiting at the door.

'Sorry, Julieta,' he gasps, struggling to find his keys. It's a name he likes very much, a name that allows him to show off his knowledge of Spanish pronunciation by saying it properly. *Hoo-lee-et-ah*, stressing the 'et' bit for all he's worth.

'Ees no problem,' Julieta replies, switching off her phone and giving him a dazzling smile.

Jack pushes the door open, scrunching María's note back against the wall, and ushers Julieta in ahead of him.

Julieta's been in the UK for a couple of years. Originally from Peru, she works as a dental assistant in Kilburn. María put her on to Jack as a *fantastic* English teacher (and *all-round Mr Nice Guy*) a few months ago, and Julieta's been coming every fortnight ever since. She doesn't want a load of grammatical exercises, or irregular verb conjugations: Julieta just wants to chat. Her English is pretty good already, so what she wants Jack to do is chat to her as he would to his close friends, using all the slang that he usually censors from his speech when teaching anyone but the most advanced learners. She's told him – *as a confidential, ees correct, no?* – that she wants to find a nice English boyfriend and she doesn't want to sound like she's learned her English out of a fifty-year-old textbook. It's not as easy a task as Jack first thought.

She stops him whenever he says something she doesn't understand, it's a clue to Jack that he's speaking at the level that she wants. If the conversation flows for more than a couple of minutes without Julieta interrupting, Jack begins to panic. He starts hunting for slightly more esoteric phrases Julieta might not know, always trying not to go too far by saying something that's so weird she's never likely to hear it again.

Whenever he's reading, he keeps a lookout for odd words and phrases that might suit Julieta. He doesn't really want to give her all the *stitch in time saves nine* kinda crap. Julieta probably wouldn't know the difference, but Jack wants her to have some proper 'edgy' street talk. Problem is, his circle of friends isn't that edgy – well, maybe except Cind, but then, she's an Australian, so all her edgy chat is laced with Antipodean slang.

People might complain that Americanisms are invading the English language, but Jack's sure that Australianisms are running them a close second. In fact, a lot of the things he thought were American, turn out to be Australian.

When he and Cindy first met, he'd had trouble understanding what she was on about half the time. He knew what *tinnies* and *chunder* were, but once she started talking about *bingles* and *bludgers*, he was lost. He's given Julieta a couple of the most common Australianisms and Americanisms, but he'd prefer to showcase the good old British *lingo* (a word which, he's read, probably comes from Portuguese). And there's the problem: dig under the skin of what you think is Brit slang, and more often than not it isn't English at all. Swimming *togs*? Australian – so the Aussies claim: *lippy?* Australian; *mozzie?* Strine. He wants her to have some street cred, not a script from *Neighbours*. There's a good 'un: *street cred*. Better check it's not another import.

'Jack, how are things?' He taught her that right at the start, and she's got the hang of it, if only he could get her to blend the three words into one mushy sound (*Howathins*) rather than emphasising each one as if she thinks he's slightly hard of hearing.

'Great, sorry to keep you,' he says, hoping Julieta doesn't know this one, but she obviously does. 'How was your week?' he continues. He often starts with something like this, or a variation: *Had a good week? Keeping well? Keeping fit?* It might not be cockney rhyming slang, but it's the sort of thing she wants.

'Yes, very good. I have the coffee weeth María this morning.'

'Right,' he says warily. He's not sure how close Julieta and María are, what sort of gossip they might share. He decides to investigate. 'Is she well?'

'Oh yes, she very well. She very, *very* happy. She say you best English teacher in London.'

Jack blushes. 'Do you two often have a natter?' he asks, trying to mine deeper into the content of their conversations.

'What ees *natter*?' Julieta asks, looking perplexed but thrilled at the same time, and opening her notebook with a flurry of brightly painted fingernails.

'Oh, sorry. Yes, it's a conversation. We also call it a chat. Or–' He suddenly sees a way to penetrate María and Julieta's natter even further. 'We sometimes call it a *gossip*...'

'Oh, I know thees,' Julieta replies excitedly. 'Ees *cotilleo?*'

'I'll check,' Jack says, reaching for his phone to check on the app. 'Yes, *cotilleo*, gossip. It's another of those words that's a noun and a verb. You can gossip with María, then you can tell someone else all the gossip that you heard. Actually, we sometimes say *goss*, tell me all the *goss*...' He leaves it hanging there, hoping she might tell him all the *goss*, but she's too busy scribbling in her notebook, pristine teeth biting her bottom lip.

She's quite like María in terms of her laser concentration and an inquisitiveness that borders on the obsessive, but her dress sense is from a different era – a different catalogue. While María is usually dressed as if ready for a triathlon, Julieta looks like she's on her way to a chinwag with one of Jane Austen's female leads at a genteel little tea shoppe in Bath. She often wears those long lacy gloves with buttons at the wrist, long dresses which were probably last in fashion when Jane was scribbling *Persuasion,* and she carries a dainty little handbag in the crook of her elbow. Her black, vegan, lace-up DMs, which peep out from under the frilly hem of her dress whenever she walks, have always intrigued Jack. He's never understood fashion, so he's never felt able to ask for an explanation (after she'd proudly told him they were vegan), fearing he might cause offence or, much more likely, he wouldn't understand.

'Thees very good word. I like eet, *goss*, very much. I have very good *gosses* weeth María.'

Jack's not sure you can actually turn goss into a plural, it doesn't sound right to him. He thinks it might be one of those nouns that don't have a plural, like *butter*, or *homework*, but he's not certain. This often happens with Julieta; they stray so far off the beaten linguistic track that Jack finds he has few signposts to guide him when it all gets a bit muddy. He decides to backtrack to the path rather than plough into the swamp.

'What were you *gossing* about? Tell me all the *goss*,' he invites, pretending he's using his standard teacher's trick of repeating the word they're trying to practise. Jack's mind, however, is anywhere but on language development.

'Oh, we goss about everytheen. María, she like talking, talking, talking. Always talking.'

'How's Iker? Everything okay with Iker?'

'I theenk so. Iker, he no like the goss. He like play video games.'

'Is there any special goss that María told you?'

She shrugs a Latin@ shrug. She's taught him how all the hip young Spanish speakers have started to use the @ symbol as a unisex suffix, instead of having to choose between an *o* or an *a* in words like *Latino* and *Latina, loco* and *loca*. She says you pronounce it to rhyme with 'cow': so latin-ow and lo-cow. It's the only time he's ever wished English had grammatical gender, so he could be one of the first to utter such a cool freshly-fangled usage, and annoy all the pedants.

'I theenk no. No special goss. But she veeerrry happy. More happy than ever before. I theenk she have special theeng happen. She no say yet, she want be sure, but she tell to me soon...'

64

THE END

'You busy?' Milly asks, her eyes telling Vicky that if they're really friends, there's only one answer.

'Not if you're going to suggest we try that new wine bar. Let me get my bag...'

It's a steel and glass affair inside (the wine bar, not Vicky's bag); outside, they're clearly trying to establish a vineyard vibe. There are upturned wooden barrels if you want to prop yourself against one as you sip your Robert Mondavi after a hard day in the fields. If your back is broken, there are some roughly hewn wooden chairs with soft cushions to slump onto. There's clearly been a lot of hewing going on to set the place up, because if the sun is baking the ground (which, mercifully, it isn't) there's a wooden structure supporting an actual grapevine, which is potted in a giant terracotta urn. Only the red buses on West End Lane, and the sky, plump with a sagging mattress of dark summer thunderclouds, bring you back from a Tuscan vineyard to a London rush hour.

'It's over,' Milly says as she takes a first sip of her wine.

'You and Jack?'

She nods, takes a deep breath, lets it out slowly. If she'd

been a smoker, now would've been the time to light up. But she isn't. So Vicky does – a sort of sisterly support ciggy.

'Did you go and see him?' she asks, as she pours a cloud up and away in the direction of the top deck of a bus that's stopped at the roadside, and is chugging like an Italian tractor might, at least in the minds of those who are too sloshed to ask for *another bottle of Feudi di San Gregorio Cutizzi Greco di Tufo – please.*

Milly nods, sips more wine. It's nice wine. Nicely chilled. Nice. She's no idea what it is. Cares less. She feels calm at last. She's let it go. She's let *him* go.

'What did he say?'

'I didn't get to speak to him. I went to his flat, I was about to go to his door when this blonde woman showed up in an expensive car. She tooted her horn, and he came running out and jumped in next to her. Off they went together like an ad for cheap aftershave.'

Vicky takes a breath to say something, but Milly cuts her off.

'And then María, the Spanish one, remember? Another good-looker. The one he was kissing like a porn star? She showed up next and popped a note through his door.'

'A note?'

'A note. I thought she might be booking an appointment.'

Vicky looks at Milly, but Milly won't return her stare; she concentrates on her wine, checking it's safely stored in the glass. She looks evasive. Guilty. As if...

'And – do you happen to know what the note said?'

Milly looks across the street, her eyes lock onto a young woman pushing a pram, staring into a shop window. Milly watches her, chews her lower lip, like she's looking for a way to confess a secret, or an indiscretion...

'It said she's pregnant. And she needs to speak to him.'

Vicky's mouth opens.

'It's over. I'm done with it. Done with *him*. He's all yours if you want him. Seriously, Vicky. Be my guest. I have no feelings towards him anymore. Plus, of course, he's now a multi-bloody-millionaire. I can give you his number; you can probably set a date up over WhatsApp, if he has a spare slot, he's probably got us all on a spreadsheet, he seems quite busy.'

'But you didn't *speak* to him...?'

'There were too many other women in the *fucking* line in front of me!' Milly explodes, rocking her glass as her hand shudders, wine slipping and slopping onto the not-too-roughly hewn wooden table. Vicky hates herself for noticing how Milly still manages to drop her voice for only her second ever *fucking*, not that there's anyone within range to hear it if she screamed. 'He left with the blonde in the car, out for a spin, or whatever – what do they call it? Doggy, or something? Then María's obviously next in line, to talk about the baby. What am I meant to do? Call his secretary for an appointment? He's probably shagging her as well.'

Vicky takes Milly's hand. 'Is he still calling you? Messaging you?'

'I've blocked him. It's over.'

Vicky squeezes Milly's hand, grabs the other, stares into her face, forces her to look at her. 'But you still love him...'

Milly looks down at their hands, entwined into a ball. She takes a breath – but lets it out again, soundlessly.

65

THE SURPRISE

Four missed calls from María. Bloody hell. What's her *special theeng* that's happened? She can't be thinking that she and he have something 'going on', can she? That can't be her *special theeng...*

Jack had sprinted back indoors as soon as he'd seen Milly's Panda rumbling away the previous night, he'd barely given María a second thought at the time. What did she think? That they were 'on', and that he'd just got all shy and run inside? He *has* to talk to her. Tell her there's nothing between them. Tell her he loves Milly.

It's the first time he's voiced this thought to himself. It was so easy to do. The truth always is easy. Why hasn't he told her? He has to tell Milly. Why won't she answer her bloody phone? His Emails? WhatsApps? He tries yet again, nothing. Wonders if she's blocked his number.

Then he remembers Facebook. He's sure you can send messages on that. Unless she's...

He prods at his screen with a shaking forefinger and Milly's digital life opens in the palm of his hand. There they are together in Regent's Park. The *Visit London* poster boy and girl.

Anybody could see how much in love they are. Not just him. Her too. He can see it in her smile. It dazzles in every photo, but in this one, there's an extra dazzle. It's so obvious. Why hasn't he told her?

He roots around and finds the *See More About Milly Patterson* button. Under *Relationship*, it tells him she's single. His heart feels like it's dropped onto the top of his stomach. It's a physical, dragging sensation. He wonders if she had changed it to *in a relationship*, and now she's changed it back? Or maybe she never changed it to *in a relationship*? Was that because she didn't think she was in one? Or was it because she hadn't had time? How do you read these electronic tea leaves? He feels he needs a spook to help him make sense of what all the gizmos and apps are telling – or not telling him. Although, on second thoughts, a twelve-year-old could probably make a good stab at it.

He's learned nothing, but he feels worse. His heart is clearly taking it all to heart. He clicks and scrolls for clues, the sight of her smile making him sadder, which it's never done before. He sends her yet another message, but he knows she won't answer it. He'll have to go round to hers. It's the only way. Face to face. In a panic, he fetches his car keys.

———

He's halfway to Milly's when he changes his mind. He's got to sort the ticket first. Got to sort it with Cindy and Rich that they're going to split it – a third for Cindy, a third for Rich... and then a thought hits him, like a massive roundhouse punch, and he makes a decision, a big one: he's giving his third to charity. Yes. He'll let Milly choose the charities. Whichever ones she wants. All of it. He doesn't want a penny, he wants her. He can see it clearly now that he's got the ticket back and he's lost Milly.

He'd said it before, how she was more important than the money. But that was when he had her and not the money. Now it's the other way around he knows it's true.

He chucks a quick spewie (an Australianism he learned from Cindy) and roars at his Fiesta to at least attempt a bit of speed towards her flat. He'll go to hers first, it's nearer than Rich's. He'll text Rich the news if he has to, what does it matter? Rich won't give a shit. He gets more and more excited as he drives, as he sees more clearly what's been happening. The ticket hasn't made him happy; it's just given him headaches. Milly has made him happy, happier than he's ever imagined he could be with anyone. They haven't needed money. Well, not a lottery jackpot, not a hell of a lot more than what they already have. A picnic in a park, breakfast on his balcony. They don't need a yacht to be happy. And now he's stuck with the bloody ticket again, and no Milly. Well, he just has to reverse that. Simple. Give away two thirds of it to Rich and Cind, then explain things to Milly and let her donate the rest to charity. As he's ringing Cindy's doorbell, he notices Rich's bike chained to the drainpipe...

'Oh, Jack! Struth! Hi.' She's in her dressing gown, nearly, still struggling with a stuck bare shoulder that's preventing her from securing the belt one-handed. Late for Cindy to still be in bed. She's also pretty breathless, as if she's just been...

'Jesus!'

'What?'

'Is Rich here?' he says, suddenly looking at the bike and putting two and two together without the aid of a calculator.

'Well...' It's not often Cindy is lost for words or caught looking flustered. 'What if he is?'

'Are you two *shagging?*'

She shrugs a very un-Cindy-like shrug, void of confidence and her usual chutzpah. 'What if we are?'

'Bloody hell!' He takes half a step backwards, looks Cindy up and down. This is an odd moment: her waiting for him to say something. He wonders if this changes anything. Decides it doesn't. What does he care what Cindy does? What does he care what Rich does? What's it got to do with him?

'Okay, third shares of the win: you, me and Rich, and we divorce asap. Deal?'

She shrugs again, another defensive *If you say so* submission, finally manages to knot the belt, and give her hair a bit of a flattening. She looks like a cartoon character who's just pulled her finger out of the mains. 'Great. Deal.' Shrug.

'That okay with you, Rich?' Jack shouts in through the doorway. 'The lottery? Thirds each, you me and Cindy?'

The silence is breathtaking. Cindy says nothing, which she certainly *wouldn't* be doing if the flat had been empty. Jack's almost enjoying it. It's a surreal moment: he'll tease them about it on some beery evening, Milly sitting next to him, Rich and Cindy across the table, sometime in the future.

'Rich?' he yells, louder. 'The money? Thirds each? Okay?'

'Yeah, great,' comes a distant and hesitant reply. It sounds like he's locked in a cupboard, or trapped down quite a deep coal mine.

'You know, I don't even have to do this, Cind?' Jack says, shaking his head sadly.

'What do you mean?'

'*This* – I mean, you and Rich shagging – that's adultery. I don't need to negotiate this; I probably don't need to give you *any* money.'

'Don't tell me you're not having a bit of a naughty with Milly?'

'You *know* that?'

Cindy shrugs again, tugs her flimsy robe tighter; a passing

couple are staring at her, but she's certainly not going to invite Jack in to argue it out.

'You'd be mad not to,' she says quietly, her voice suddenly full of meaning, no edge, no hidden agenda, no HRTs – the way she used to talk to him. 'She's actually really nice. Perfect for you. Much more so than I ever was. Seriously. Forget the money for a moment. Don't let her slip away, Jack...'

He remembers, suddenly, the woman he met on that Thai beach. He did love her; he wasn't always high or drunk. He remembers her carefree smile, exhausting enthusiasm: so what if it was only a holiday romance – there was romance. 'I'm sorry it didn't work out for us,' he says.

'It did. But not for long enough. I think I might be happier with Rich, and you'll certainly be happier with Milly.'

'Look.' He takes his wallet out of his pocket. 'Good faith, yeah? Here's the ticket. You organise the divorce and the money. I've got more important things to do.' He shouts in through the doorway again, 'Cindy's got the ticket, Rich. Have a good one.'

She watches him as he dashes down the path and gets into his creaking Fiesta, giving her a little wave as it putters into life and rumbles away. He deserves some luck in love, she thinks, somewhat wistfully.

Inside the car, Jack's quiet, his mind working overtime on what he's discovered. His eyes follow the road, but his concentration is elsewhere. After a while, he remembers Rich singing the old Ace hit 'How Long?' when he'd first met Milly, and Jack smiles, starts humming...

66

THE CAR CHASE

JACK FEELS RELEASED: released from Cindy, released from the money. He really doesn't want it. He'll take his third, let Milly choose the charities, and he'll ask her to marry him. He feels happy. Happier than he's felt since he doesn't know when. He remembers the night he won; he had a few seconds of happiness then, but as soon as Cindy called he was tense. He was happy when he met Milly, but there was always the shadow of his marriage playing on his mind. Then there was the money, especially once he learned what her attitude to being a millionaire would be. This solves everything. He urges the Fiesta towards Mill Lane as fast as it will go. He overtakes a mother pushing a pram up the hill like she's standing still.

He spots the Panda outside Milly's flat as he passes the Alliance pub. His dad used to drink in there, when it was an ordinary pub. It's now a 'gastro pub', whatever that means. So, she's in, that's good. And the kebab shop isn't busy; he'll lob bricks at her window until she answers him. He'll shin up the drainpipe. He's going to explain it to her and, and... she'll have to believe him. He should've squared María, he knows that, but there isn't time. He can't wait. He wants to tell Milly the truth–

But wait a minute, the Panda suddenly bumps down off the pavement and is away. Another car has to brake a bit sharpish to avoid running into it. It blasts its horn, but the Panda's off, lights coming on belatedly, heading for West End Lane. Shit! Where's she going, and why's she driving like that?

He steps on the gas, but it's like stepping on an overripe strawberry. His foot hits the floor and the push of acceleration works like a mild summer breeze behind a stationary juggernaut with its brakes on. Whatever, the Panda's still bleeding smoke, she'll have to get that seen to, so it's not like he's following a Ferrari. She pootles down Mill Lane, and he trundles after her. It's like a James Bond car chase, but with shit cars, and run in slo-mo. The *Benny Hill* 'chase' music would be inappropriately fast as a backing track.

First thing, María. He'll explain it all. It was just a kiss. She kissed him. *That's* the thing. She means nothing to him. He was shocked, paralysed. Then the ticket. He'll tell Milly he's keeping his promise to Rich and Cind, but that she can pick charities to give their share to. Anywhere she wants – as long as she'll marry him.

The Panda turns left up Fortune Green Road, it's going at a fair old clip; he didn't know she could be a bit of a girl racer. Where's she going in such a hurry? But the hill starts to slow her. He's catching, sluggishly. He kicks down a gear and the Fiesta responds, like it's remembering what life used to be like when it had a six-pack and a bit more tread. Then everything happens very quickly.

They're coming up to West Hampstead Police Station on the left, a police car swerves out in front of the Panda with blue lights flashing. The Panda brakes, hard. Jack brakes, hard, his wheels lock, he skids.

'*Shit...!*'

It's a bit more than a *tonk* this time. Considerably more than the one she'd given him, when he was a double-millionaire, driving an almost-new Beemer soft-top, and she was introducing herself by backing her rusty Panda into it. It now seems an impossible quirk of luck or fate that everything should have aligned so: the lottery win, the new car, the decision not to park it in front of his flat, the rain that spoiled her view, the fact that a cheap 1970s crap car wouldn't have a reversing camera.

If his Fiesta'd had an airbag, it would've inflated. But the fanciest features the Fiesta possesses are its wind-up windows and a cassette player. He closes his eyes on impact, feels the seat belt sawing into his chest, glass showering his face as he senses the back wheels leaving the ground. They land again with a couple of shuddering bounces, after what feels like a half turn in the air.

It's quiet all of a sudden, except for a hissing noise. When he opens his eyes, his bonnet has flipped up and is obscuring his view through a windscreen that suddenly resembles a spider's web in need of serious restoration. Shards of glass are drizzling into his lap; the steering wheel seems much too close. He's hit his head on something, but he doesn't know what. There's steam bleeding from somewhere in front of him.

Don't let her be hurt! Don't let her be hurt! It's his only thought.

The door resists him opening it, until he puts his shoulder to it. It cronks ajar, so he gives it another shove, then it swings and suddenly drops, hanging on one hinge. The side window has shattered, and more glass tinkles at his feet. He hauls himself up and out, it seems more difficult than normal, like he's lower down than usual. He sways for a second, but doesn't think he's got anything broken, although he aches all over. He suddenly notices that his Fiesta is on the wrong side of the road, turned ninety degrees so that it's facing the back wheel of the Panda. The state of the Panda stuns him.

The back of it is even worse than his Beemer was, way worse. It's totally stoved in, back window in a thousand shards, indestructible bumper folded like warm chocolate, the back hatch is an origami flower. There's a river of liquid pouring out from under her car, he hopes it's the radiator, but, as far as he can see, the front of her car is undamaged. She'll be fine, as long as she was wearing her seat belt. The memory of the Panda bumping recklessly off the kerb suddenly floods his mind like it's the most important fact in the world, its lights off as if in a great hurry, driving carelessly, dangerously, forcing the other driver to brake...

Please, let her be wearing her seat belt. She must've put her seatbelt on...

His legs, back, neck and shoulders ache as he walks up and opens the driver's door. What he sees paralyses him...

67

THE PROBLEM

'BLOODY HELL!' Rich gasps, as Cindy sheds her robe and slides back under the warm covers. 'What the hell was that all about?'

'It was Jack coming to his senses. I've got the ticket!' She flashes it in front of Rich's face, kisses him on the lips. 'Thirds each, we're rich! *Rich's* rich!'

'Yeah, but he knows about us?'

'He guessed. He saw your bike when I opened the door looking less than my usual serene self.'

'Jesus.'

'It'll be fine. Chill out. We're divorcing, he's got the hots for Milly, happy families. Happy *rich* families!'

Rich sighs, lights a cigarette. 'You sure? He wasn't angry?'

'Well, he was *surprised*, put it that way, but he didn't come in and lump you one, did he?'

'No. Suppose not. What did you say?'

'Thanks. What else could I say?'

'No, I mean about *us*?'

'I didn't say anything about us.'

'But, what did *he* say? About us?'

'He asked if we were shagging?'

316

'Just like that?'

'I don't know, he might have said *fucking*, I don't remember.'

'But how did he say it? Was he like, disappointed? Did he seem annoyed?'

'He didn't really seem to give a damn, now that I think about it. He told you to have a good one, didn't he? Doesn't sound like he's suicidal.'

'No. Guess not. Bloody hell. Close one.'

'So, we're in the money...'

'Christ!' He takes the ticket out of her fingers, holds it in two hands, kisses it. 'Two point three mill – well, one point five mill for us, thereabouts...' His brow furrows, suddenly. His eyes narrow, like he should be wearing reading glasses. 'Hey, wait a minute...'

68

THE PROPOSAL

'WHO THE FUCK ARE YOU?' Jack yells.

'Piss off!' Whoever the fuck it is unbuckles his seatbelt and hauls himself out of the Panda. He's a big guy, mean-looking, ugly too. Doesn't seem like he might be one of Milly's doctor or nurse pals. Then, whoever the fuck it is pushes Jack out of the way and runs back down Fortune Green Road.

'Wait a minute!' Jack yells, with all the conviction of a late passenger watching their plane leave the runway and soar into the sky.

A couple of plods are jogging out of the station, attracted by the noise, no doubt, or a call from the blues 'n' twos that didn't stop. They're buckling on radios and lightsabres.

'He's run off,' Jack says, pointing down the road before either plod can say one *Hello*, let alone three.

'Who?'

'Whoever was driving Milly's car.'

'Could you start at the beginning, sir?' Plod One asks, happy that his toys are all in their correct places. Jack half expects him to pull out a notepad and lick the end of a stubby pencil. 'Who are you?'

'I'm Jack Potts. This is my girlfriend's car, Milly Patterson. I thought I was following her. He stopped suddenly and I crashed into the back of him. Then he ran off. I think he might've stolen Milly's car.'

The two Plods freeze for a moment. Then Plod Two gathers his wits.

'This car has been reported stolen, minutes ago, out of Mill Lane,' he says to his colleague. 'I heard the call come in, pink Panda, this has to be it.'

'Right. You take care of Mr Potts here, and the scene, I'm going to see if I can catch Sonny Jim. Quick description, sir?'

'Um, yeah. He was white, taller than me, thickset, stubble, nose ring, dark clothes, dark baseball cap.'

'Okay. Thanks.'

———

Jack's taken into the station where they check him over. He's a bit shaken up, but essentially relatively uninjured. Other officers bustle out in high-vis jackets, to deal with the wreckage and the traffic snarl-up. They sound like they're encased in bubble wrap, their radios in contact with Mission Control in Houston. The desk sergeant gets Jack a tea from a machine and sits him down for a bit. Then, after a while, he gives him some forms to fill in (or maybe fill out, he doesn't specify): details of the crash; description of the driver; what he said. He's busying himself with them when Milly crashes through the doorway into reception like a greyhound out of the traps.

'Jack! You're alive!' She starts crying instantly, huge great gulping sobs, a shower of tears splattering the floor.

'Milly! Of course I'm alive. What are you thinking?' He gets up and puts his arms around her.

'I've just seen your car. I thought you were dead! What were you doing?' She sobs into his shoulder.

'I was following you, well, I thought it was you. I wanted to explain everything, *talk* to you, I went up to the hospital, I've called you, texted you. But why are you here?' He pushes her away gently, so he can see her face. It's their first meeting all over again, except, this time, he's smashed into her car, and this time, he's got her in his arms. He realises he might love her more when she's crying.

'Someone stole my car. I heard it start and drive away. I reported it, not even ten minutes ago. Then the police called me and said they had it here. So, I ran up. When I arrived, I saw *your* car, I never thought you'd have got out of it, it's been totalled – totally. You walked away from *that...?*' She points towards the door, shying away from it at the same time, like there's something out there she doesn't want to see, doesn't want to think about.

'I didn't notice,' he says, 'I just wanted to see if you were okay. Look – none of that matters. I just – will you marry me?'

'*What?!*'

'I love you. Will you marry me? It doesn't have to be soon, I know we said we'd take it slowly, and I've got to get the divorce done, but at least I want you to know how I really feel...'

'But – Jack, the *baby?*'

'The– What baby?'

'María's baby. She's pregnant, she's having your baby.'

He wonders for a second if he might have a bit of mild concussion after all. Maybe a brain haemorrhage? He could be in a coma, of course, lying in a bed surrounded by miles of life-saving wires and tubes, unconscious, dreaming this conversation... 'María's having *my* baby?'

'Yes.'

'Who told you that?'

'I – I read a note she put through your door. I'm sorry, I didn't mean to read it, well, I did mean to – I was in bits, Jack. I saw you kissing her, and then you drove off with that blonde piece in the fancy car...'

'What? What are you talking about? Tell me about María, what did she say?'

'I told you what she said. She's pregnant, you have to talk to her.'

'And it's *my* baby?'

'Well, I'm not sure exactly – she said she was pregnant and had to talk to *you*...'

'But I've never had *sex* with María. She kissed me once. Outside my flat. *Once*. You saw it. I was so shocked; I didn't know what was happening. But I've never had *sex* with her. Jesus, Milly. This is *crazy!*'

'Getting along okay with those forms, sir?' the desk sergeant interjects, a faint, wry smile bleeding across his lips, as if he's thinking, *Here's a lovely one to keep the canteen amused with, later on.*

Jack's phone rings. 'It's María,' he says, pinging it on, putting it straight to speaker phone. He's hiding nothing from Milly ever again. María's voice crackles over the line.

'Oh, Jack! *Dios mío! Dios mío!* I sorry. I sorry. I no know what happen. I sorry, sorry, sorry. I go crazy. I go crazy.'

'Slow down, María. Don't worry. It's not a problem.'

'I no want you theenk I love you, Jack. I only want have one leetol kees. Just one leetol kees, before I marry weeth Iker. I have Iker baby. I marry weeth Iker. He say I marry weeth heem before hees mathah, she keel heem. I no can have kees when I marry weeth Iker, so I theenk I have one leetol kees before. But it become beeg kees, I sorry. I theenk I have the whores moaning. I no want you theenk I want marry you. I sorry.'

'It's fine, María. It's not a problem. And it's *hormones*,

probably, not whores moaning.' His last comment arrests Milly's jaw on its way to the floor. He's beginning to tune in to all these Spanish speakers mangling English. Might be a useful skill to acquire.

'I sorry Jack, you no theenk I want marry you?'

'No, it's fine, María. I've asked *Milly* to marry me, so I can't marry you too.'

'You marry weeth Meely? Oh, ees wonderful news. I so happy. I so happy.'

'Well, she hasn't said yes, yet. So, hold your horses.'

'You buy *horses?*'

'No. María, forget the horses. Look, congratulations on the baby, and the wedding.'

'Yes, thank you, maybe we have double wedding, like the *Pride and the Preja-gee-gees?* And you say Meely, she marry you, or she stoopid cow. Okay? You say her thees. Okay?'

'Okay. I'll tell her that,' he says, smiling at Milly. 'I'll see you.'

He cuts the call.

'Any luck with that form, sir...?' the desk sergeant says, wiping his eyes.

69

THE LATE SUBSTITUTION

As they leave the station, Jack's car is being hauled onto a low loader. Milly's misled him by describing it as being totalled, even totally. He slows to a halt as he takes in the scene of devastation which is, or was, his Fiesta. The front is squashed flat, the engine must be somewhere inside the car, possibly sitting on the passenger seat. They haven't been able to close the driver's door properly, so they've tied it back in place. Both front tyres are flat. Every window is shattered or gone; the hatch also seems to have sprung open and won't close properly, so they've tied that down as well. It's weeping oil and water. They won't need to take it to the crusher, he thinks. It's already been done. He can't work out how he got out of it in less than a dozen pieces.

'I can't believe you walked away from that.' Milly shudders. It seems an impossibility, the sort of trick David Blaine would perform live in a stadium. She pulls him aside; in case it topples off the truck in a *Carrie*-style finale.

As she walks him home, he tells her the whole story of the ticket, and what he's done with it, and what he's planning.

'You don't have to do this for me,' she pleads, when he tells her he wants her to choose charities for his share.

'I'm not,' he says, stopping and facing her. 'I'm doing it for me, it's brought me nothing but trouble, I want to be free of it. I want the money to go to people who need it a lot more than me. I said I'd give a third to Rich and Cindy, and I'm going to keep my promise, but my third – *our* third – is going to charity. You see, you've changed me more than you think, more than I expected. This is what I want, you and me. That's what makes me happy. Besides, if I'm ever sleeping on the streets, I'll expect you to teach me how to play your Ibizan fiddle, and Cindy and Rich to toss a tenner in my hat. I know Cindy will share their cut with her extensive family, so she and Rich aren't going to end up living in Beverley Hills.'

Milly squeezes his arm, lays her head against it. They walk on, slowly.

'I'm sorry I doubted you,' she says, suddenly, not looking at him. 'I feel such a teenager. I did come round earlier to give you a chance to explain, but then the girl with the car...?'

'Shelly? She works at the Beemer showroom. She came to pick me up, so I could collect the Fiesta.'

'Oh God. I can't tell you what went through my mind...'

'What do you mean?'

'Nothing. Really. Anyway, she turned up and I didn't know what to think. And then María, I'll never forgive myself for snooping on her note. It serves me right. I've never done anything so underhand, I'm so ashamed. I'm so sorry.'

'Forget it,' he says. 'I'd have done exactly the same, and I'd probably have come to the same conclusion. I imagine María's been in bits, I've avoided all her calls, and all she wanted to do was apologise. I was so shocked when she kissed me, it would've cleared it all up if I'd answered her calls and put her out of her own agony. I've been a bit of a teenager too, now that I think about it.'

As they're passing The BOGOFF, Jack suggests a quick one. His neck is beginning to ache more than the rest of him, which Milly says could be a bit of whiplash. He fancies a brandy; Milly orders a white wine for herself. He's barely had his first sip when the lounge door swings open.

'There he is! You limey bastard. What's this?' Cindy crosses the room like a boxer eager to land the first punch, with Rich in distant tow. She slams the lottery ticket down on the table.

'Hi Cindy,' Jack says. 'You've met Milly, haven't you?'

'Yeah, right, hi all. Now what's *this?*'

'It looks like my lottery ticket. Why?'

'And your numbers?'

'What about my numbers? They're on the ticket.'

'Not all of them.'

'What?'

'Where's frigging Wazza?'

'What do you mean? Where's frigg–' He grabs the ticket, stares at it. 'Fuck!'

'What's going on?' Milly whispers to him.

'Wazza's gone.'

'What do you mean?'

'Wayne Rooney. Number ten. It's not here. It's number one instead. I don't understand.'

'Do you know how much we win with five numbers?'

Jack shrugs. 'No, I've no idea. A million?'

'A *million?* Dream on. One thousand, seven hundred and fifty pounds.'

'Don't be daft!'

'Look it up, one thousand, seven hundred and fifty pounds. Divide that by three and let's pop a bottle of Krug. It'll probably cost more than the winnings.'

'You're kidding?'

'Can you see a smile?'

They're staring at each other when the lounge door opens again. Beano slopes in, bringing the only smile into the room. He's halfway to the bar when he spots them, looking at him. He stops mid-stride, clocks the lottery ticket that's the centre of everyone's attention. His smile fades, a look of confusion crosses his face...

Jack sees the confusion on Beano's face, his own mind doing somersaults back in time, to that night, when he, or rather Beano had bought the ticket...

'Hold on...' Cindy says, half to herself, remembering a conversation from a few days before. Then she yells. '*Beano!*' Alex Ferguson never silenced a changing room so efficiently. 'Mine's a G&T, Beano. Rich'll have a pint. Jack needs a double brandy and Milly will have – is that a sweet or a dry, Milly?'

'Oh, a dry one, please.'

'A large dry white wine. And get one for yourself, Beano, we're going to have a chat...'

———

Beano carries the tray to the table, looking like he's heading for the gallows, but doesn't know the charges. He passes the drinks as graciously as he can manage. He's never paid over thirty quid for a round of drinks. He feels slightly faint; he's had to use his debit card. He picks up his own glass last (tap water, please). Cindy points at a stool, vacant for him. *Switch the recorder on please, Sergeant...*

'Good to see you again, Beans. And so soon. You told me half a story the other day. About you and Jack buying his lottery ticket after Smithy's party. I don't think you ever finished the tale. Time to finish it now.'

'Right,' Beano says, still nonplussed, and looking less than pleased with his seat of honour and the audience he's got.

'So?' Cindy prods.

'What about it?' Beano replies, nervously.

'Where's Wazza?' Cindy snaps, slapping the ticket down on the table.

Beano leans forward, stares at the ticket, goes to pick it up but changes his mind, like he thinks somebody might be fingerprinting it later. His expression scrolls through bewilderment, yet more confusion, then what looks like a dawning realisation as a fragment of memory burrows from his subconscious... 'Oh fuck.'

'Fuck what?' Cindy coaxes, a schoolteacher encouraging a child to confess to blocking the sink with loo-roll then deliberately flooding the floor of the toilets.

'We were drunk,' he says.

'Meaning?' Cindy snarls.

'Well, *you* were drunk too. You remember, Jack?'

'Vaguely.'

'Yeah, you were plastered, it was Smithy's birthday. We went into Banerjees to get your ticket. You weren't feeling good. You gave me the money and went back outside...'

'Did I?'

'Yeah. I think you were having a little *empty,* in the gutter...'

'Oh.'

'And?' Cindy again.

'Oh, Jesus,' Jack says quietly.

'And, I was pretty drunk too, like I said. Not responsible for my actions. Had a skinful. Smithy's big do. I thought it would be a laugh.'

'What?' says Jack, trepidation in his voice.

Beano shrugs. 'It was a bit of fun. A lark.'

'What was a bit of fun, Beano? This *lark*?' Cindy says menacingly.

'Jesus! You subbed Wazza, didn't you?' Rich gasps, putting his pint down.

'It was a *joke!*'

'I don't understand,' Milly says. 'What does it mean?'

'It means he left Wayne Rooney, number ten, out of Jack's team, and put on a substitute,' says Rich, mouth agape, eyes popping. 'How *could* you?'

'It was a *joke!* A bit of a laugh. Imagine if we'd won? I'd have been a hero.'

'But we *did* win! We did frigging win. But with Rooney, you pillock. Who did you sub Rooney for? Who's number one?' Cindy's got her head in her hands.

'It's Jordan bleedin' Pickford, isn't it? Beano's a bloody Toffee,' Rich growls, his head dropping backwards onto the back of his chair with an audible *clunk*.

'England's number one,' Beano murmurs at his water.

'Jesus, Beano. Do you have any clue how much England's number one has cost us? Have you any clue?' Cindy screams at the table.

Beano shrugs. 'A bit.'

'A bit? A frigging *bit?*' she yells, straightening up. 'Two point two nine whatever frigging million frigging bits. That's how much England's frigging number one has cost us. Does anyone fancy another drink? I think it's Beano's shout. I think it's Beano's shout for the rest of his miserable life, which I don't think is going to be very long once I get him outside in the car park. What the hell got into you?'

'About eight cans of Special Brew and a couple of chasers.' Rich sighs, remembering the night – well, some of it.

'It's still a million if you get the bonus ball,' Beano whimpers, still looking at his drink.

'What?!' Cindy again, apoplectic.

'Five and the bonus ball is a million quid,' he says, looking up sheepishly.

'A *million*? You sure?'

Beano shrugs again. 'Everyone knows that...'

There's a long silence around the table – then Cindy wrenches her phone out of her pocket, hammers the screen with her thumbs like she's trying to destroy it. 'Come on, bonus ball, number one! Bonus ball, number one! Bonus ball number...' Her whole body freezes. She stares at the screen with a look that no one can interpret. Jack thinks it's horror; Milly thinks it's amazement; Rich thinks she's arrested; Beano thinks his life is in the hands of England's number one.

'Well?' Jack says. He's surprisingly calm, he notices. He doesn't really care what they've won. He's got an odd sense of relief that it's not two point three million quid. He sort of feels he'll never order, or buy, two point three anything of anything ever again. His most pressing feeling is that he's disappointed that Milly's chosen charities won't be getting seven or eight hundred grand, whatever it was. He hopes she's not too upset. But a third of a million would be some consolation...

Cindy still hasn't moved. She looks straight at Jack. 'Do you remember I once asked you to put my birthday on the ticket, instead of Rooney?'

Jack nods.

'And do you remember what you said?'

'I said no. Imagine if this had happened? Which it has. We wouldn't have won with your birthday.'

'Do you remember when my birthday is?'

'Sure,' he says. 'Thirteenth. Unlucky for some... Oh shit. It's not thirteen, is it? The bonus ball isn't thirteen. It can't be!'

Slowly, she turns her phone around and shows the table. *Bonus ball: 13.*

'Oh Christ!' Jack gasps, but his heart's not in it, it really isn't, he knows he's on the verge of laughing – the look on Cindy's face.

'If you'd been less of an absolute *arsehole*, Jack, we'd have won a million pounds. A cool million!'

He shrugs. *So, it's all my fault.*

Rich lets out a long sigh.

Beano wonders if this makes his plight any better, or a whole lot worse...

70

LA BODA

A PENSIVE SILENCE has fallen over the group in the corner. There's an occasional sigh, furtive glances around the table. Nobody seems to be talking to anybody else. You'd think they might have come straight from a funeral.

Or be planning one.

The door opens again, a coolish breeze blows in, and with it comes María in her blood-red jacket, Iker behind her in a green shirt. They look like the most gorgeous Santa you've ever imagined, and an enormous elf.

'*María!*' Milly shrieks, standing. 'Congratulations!' She rushes over to hug her like they've been friends for years. The news of María's pregnancy provokes more hugs and kisses, and some manly slaps on Iker's back, the like of which he's missed since he moved to the UK.

'Beano!' Cindy screams, 'Champagne for María and Iker. Champagne for *everybody*. We'll probably need a couple of bottles...'

Jack has to smile at María's confidence with the old lingo as she commands the table with their news.

'And after we marry, Iker, he say we speak English all the

times, cos he no like speak Spanish, he want speak Catalan, but I no want learn Catalan, English hard enough. So, we speaking English together, we make better more quickly for lesson with Jack, best teacher in London.'

As the drinks arrive and the toasts subside, María manoeuvres Jack away from the table.

'I so sorree,' she starts, looking at her shoes.

'You don't have to apologise, María. Really, it's fine.' He lowers his voice to a whisper. 'It was a nice kiss...'

She blushes so much she almost merges with her coat. 'I so worried.'

'Well, stop. You and Iker are having a baby, Milly and I are together. I couldn't be happier.'

'Meely, she very nice girl.'

'I know. She's extraordinary.'

'I no like thees werd.'

'Extraordinary?'

'Yes. Ees same *en español*, we say *extraordinario*. I no like eet.'

'Why ever not?'

'I theenk about thees werd when I see eet een English. What ees? You say Meely, she ordinary? That no ees nice. Then, what mean *extra*ordinary? Eet mean *very* ordinary. Extraordinary ees very ordinary. I no like thees. Meely, she no very ordinary. She very *special*. Extra special. No extra *ordinary*.'

Jack mulls over the idea that he's being introduced to his own language by a Puerto Rican who looks like she's auditioning for the role of Mary Christmas. Yeah, he can live with that.

'Okay, she's not extraordinary, she's extra special.'

'Thees, very good. Now you say thees Meely, before she find other boy who say thees first, and you feeneesh life eating pizza and watch TV.'

71
THE RUNNY POO

As THE NIGHT morphs into *the night*, the door opens one last time.

'*Debs!* What the *hell* are you doing here?' Cindy screams. 'You said you were going to Manchester. And what the hell is *that...?*'

'Hi Cind,' calls Cheesie, squeezing out from behind Debs, holding a well-wrapped, but very small baby in his arms. Milly is one of the first out of her seat to fuss.

'Christ, this *is* a little one,' she gasps.

'Popped out this morning,' Debs says proudly.

'Yeah,' says Cheesie.

'You are joking!' Milly gasps. 'This morning? And they let you out?'

'What? From M&S? Course they did,' says Debs, looking away guiltily.

'From–'

'Marks and Spencer,' Cheesie replies, grinning.

'What...?'

'Yeah, we're serious. We were in Marks this morning, bit of last-minute shopping before we headed north. Roaming around

333

the ladies' lingerie when Debs started moaning. I thought she wanted me to buy her something, so I was ignoring her. Next thing I know, she's rolling on the floor in a pool of water, screaming.'

Debs butts into her own story. 'It was so quick. I just knew it was coming. I'd had a few gurgles in the night but thought it was too early. But this was the real deal.'

'I called an ambulance,' Cheesie adds, 'but the assistants put a call over the tannoy, *Is there a doctor or a midwife in the store?* We got one of each within minutes. Monty popped out before they got a chance to get her into soft furnishings. Lucky she was wearing a skirt, I thought.'

'The staff were brilliant,' Debs continues. 'They yanked loads of baby stuff off the shelves, threw them in a bag and gave them to us. Bloody good clobber too. None of those T-shirts you'd swear were reconditioned tea cloths you see some littlies wearing.'

'The ambulance arrived just too late to do anything except whisk us off to hospital for a check-up. They're both as right as rain.' Cheesie looks at them proudly.

'They think we had the dates wrong by a couple of weeks, he's perfect. He came out easy as a runny poo...' says Debs, equally proudly.

There's a moment while Debs remembers that she's in England. She covers herself well. 'But I'm bustin' for an amber...'

'A what?' says Milly.

'A beer.'

'Aren't you breastfeeding?'

Debs looks horrified.

'More drinks!' Cindy yells.

Beano sighs. 'I got 'em.'

72

THE PLANE NOW LEAVING...

CINDY STANDS, raps the table with her knuckles, steadies herself with her other hand. 'Announcement, guys, bit of hush, please.'

The bar quietens, even those not in the corner group seem to be following the twists. 'Debs and Cheesie told us their plans yesterday, their little Thai hideaway commune. They gave us an invite to come and visit them, any time. You said that, yeah? You're not backing out?'

'No way,' Cheesie gasps. 'Why?'

'Rich and I have had a think, and as soon as I've completed a little administrative business...' meaningful look and a wink towards Jack, '...we'll be joining them, for six months in the first instance, and after that? Who knows...?'

There is a moment of silence before the cheers go up. Jack looks particularly shocked by the news, but he raises his glass, makes his way over to Cindy.

'Thanks,' he says, quietly, edging her slightly away from the group. 'I hope we can still be friends.'

'Course we can, ya daft Pom, we're expecting you and Mill to come out for a squiz sometime.'

'Course we will.' He looks into her eyes; she returns his stare. 'Look, I meant what I said earlier, I'm really sorry we didn't work out as planned...'

'No worries, mate. It was fun before we got married, let's make it fun again once we're divorced. Deal?'

'It's a deal,' he says, hugging her.

Rich pulls him aside. 'Promise you're okay with all this, the last thing I want is for you to feel I've stolen another of your girlfriends...'

Jack smiles. 'I'm surprised, I'll admit that; I would never have put you two together. But I'm a hundred per cent okay with it. I hope you make a better go of being together than Cindy and I managed. Really, I'm pleased for the two of you. You sure you can handle the beach-bum lifestyle...?'

Rich raises his eyebrows. 'Cheesie assures me there's decent wifi on the island, so as long as I pack my laptop, I should be able to do a little bit of financial wizardry between breakfast and lunch. If it doesn't work out, there's always Cricklewood. That's going nowhere. But what about you? What are your plans...?'

73

THE OTHER BEEMER

THE BAR DOOR opens one last time. Yes, I know I said it was the last time the *last* time, but how else was I going to squeeze this in – *and* make it a surprise...?

All heads turn, Jack and Milly; Cindy and Rich; María and Iker; Cheesie and Debs – oh, and Beano. It's a female, she's wearing a deep-blue jacket-and-skirt two-piece, matching high heels, straight out of a posh fashion catalogue. She's looking around, as if she's expecting to see someone. Then she clocks Jack, a look of pleasant surprise lighting up her face – a look of shock, maybe a hint of dread, darkening his...

'Shelly!' he shouts, a little half-heartedly, wondering if his world is about to collapse. He's never seen her in this pub before in all the years he's been coming. She can't be looking for him, to ask him for a date? Mother of God, no...

'Jack? Oh, hi.' She walks over to their table. María looks admiringly at her jacket; Milly looks warily at her smile. 'What a bloody disaster,' Shelly says. 'Just my luck. I had a hot date here from my dating app, but I'm an hour late. We had a last-minute sale at the showroom. Looks like he's gone.'

'Let me get you a chair,' Beano offers, pulling another stool next to him. 'Can I get you a drink...?'

Jack stares at Beano, wonders if it's the first time he's ever heard those words coming out of Beano's mouth in that order.

The night continues, it's turning into one that they might one day call *that night*. Cindy seems to be finally processing the fact that the money, well, the vast *frigging* bulk of it, has gone: down the dunny, as she would say. Does say. Frequently. Especially with an accompanying glare at Beano. But she's clearly trying to come to terms with it. Although she's stopped ordering Beano to buy drinks, when she gets a round in herself, she excludes him. But he's rescued later on by Shelly, who's taken her blue jacket off (she's wearing matching blue underneath), has settled in, and buys him one in return for the one he bought her.

María has shuffled in next to Milly. They seem to have hit it off like long-lost sisters: they're laughing incessantly. Milly keeps touching the engagement ring, squeezing María's hand, they radiate happiness like two kids who've prised open the biscuit tin while their parents are 'busy' upstairs.

Rich has found himself stuck next to Iker. Rich is no English teacher, he's clueless about how you talk to a foreigner who has minimal English. He doesn't know that you have to slow down, give your partner time to process a sentence before starting another; ask yes/no questions; use the present tense for everything; use your hands like you're bringing a helicopter in to land on a rocky outcrop on a stormy night. Instead, he shouts. At least they've discovered that they both like video games, so they end up naming games to each other, then swapping their highest scores. Iker hasn't really mastered English numbers beyond twenty, so there's a lot more than two fingers involved in their 'conversation'.

As Shelly delivers the drinks for her and Beano, she

squeezes in next to Jack, and puts her hand on his arm. Milly's antennae swing round, although she continues giggling and joshing with María like it's late on New Year's Eve.

'Great evening, Jack. Thanks so much for taking me under your wing, I was on my way home for dinner on my lap in front of a DVD if you hadn't rescued me. Beano's a nice chap, isn't he?'

Jack sighs silent relief. 'Beano's a great lad,' he gushes. 'Tell you what, he drives a pretty decent car, I think he's got a little Merc, or an Audi, always leases them, but he trades up every couple of years. You should take him for a spin round your showroom, you might be able to interest him in a 1-Series. Especially if it's a bit of a bargain.'

'Really?'

'Really. He likes a good car, it's about the only thing he'll spend his money on.'

'I wouldn't say that; he seems to be buying everyone drinks...'

'Anyway,' Jack says quickly, 'get him into your showroom, I think he had a Beemer once, he loved it.'

'A man after my own heart. Now, Jack, got a little something you might be interested in.'

'Oh yeah?'

'Yeah. Look, if you think I'm insulting you, tell me. It's only an idea, right?'

'Go on, I'm not easy to insult.'

'Right. Well, the thing is, we have a very valued customer, been with us nearly forty years. She's got a two-door, 3-Series Beemer that she's had since the mid-1980s. 92,000 genuine mileage, and we know it's genuine because we've done the service every year, the fullest service history anyone in the showroom's ever seen. We're thinking of trying to get it into the *Guinness Book of Records*. One lady driver, garaged off-street, the car, not her. She's rarely driven it anywhere further than Brent Cross. It's an absolute gem, Jack. I've had a drive and it's lovely, it's like a little bomb on wheels. Stiffer ride than a – let's keep it civil in mixed company, yeah? I'm thinking it's the sort of car you'd be able to tinker with. You'd need to remember though, there's no computer, the windows are all manual, the radio is a bit shit, but it has got a cassette player...'

'*Cassettes?*'

'Yeah, is that a deal breaker?'

'Not at all. I kept my Boss tapes from the Fiesta. It's not a soft-top, is it?'

'Well, it is, but it hasn't got the automatic gizmo; you have to fold it away yourself, and then yank it back out again like you're putting up a tent. But it's in really good nick, mainly because she's never been able to fold it down and put it back up again. She tried it once, it's showroom folklore apparently, long before my time, she had to come into the garage to get us to put it back up again. Don't think she's bothered since.'

'That's okay,' he says brightly. 'Why's she selling?'

Shelly smiles. 'That's a story. She's a funny old duck, she's lived in her flat for forty-odd years, top end of Cricklewood, just realised it's worth three quarters of a million. Told us all about it. I think it's turned her head a bit. Her husband never talked money with her when he was alive, so she'd no clue. She's decided she wants to downgrade the flat and upgrade her car. Said she fancies one of the new ones with automatic windows and roof. She was so excited when she saw how easy it was to put it down and then back up again. It was like showing it to a child. Anyway, the guy who I had lined up for *your* car? He'd backed out, bought an Audi. So, this old dear is buying yours.'

'She's not called Mrs Weiss, is she?' There's a hint of suspicion in Jack's voice.

'Yes. Silvie Weiss.'

'Mrs Weiss! Bossy little thing? East European? Looks like a Pekingese?'

'That's her. You know her?'

'Not really. When I thought I was in the money, I viewed the flat across the landing from her. She ended up inviting herself to join in the viewing. Neither the agent nor I felt we could kick her out.'

Shelly laughs. 'That sounds like her. Blimey, you were looking at the flat across the way from her? You really were expecting a bit of money, weren't you?'

He nods, wistfully. 'I thought I had a two point three million quid lottery jackpot. Beano and I bought the ticket when we were drunk. I gave him the money while I was throwing up in the gutter. He decided, in his drunken state, that it would be hilarious to switch one of my numbers.'

'My God. Beano? Don't you hate him?'

'No. It's the sort of thing I'd have done to him. Besides, I met Milly because I thought I'd won the lottery. Tell you a secret, she smashed into the Beemer. I couldn't bring myself to bankrupt her no-claims bonus. That's how we met.' He picks up Milly's hand, kisses it. 'So, go on, how much do you want for Mrs Weiss's old Beemer?'

'We don't really like doing second-hands, my boss would be pretty chuffed if I rolled it in and out within the week, he still hasn't forgiven me for your Fiesta, you know? We gave her fifteen hundred for it, and the ticket says two grand, but we'd take a cheeky offer, well, I would – from you.'

Jack rubs his chin. 'How about seventeen fifty?'

'Really? Yeah, we'd take that.'

Jack smiles. 'Cindy,' he shouts down the table. 'Throw us up that ticket. I wanna show it to Shelly.'

Cindy's somehow got herself dragged into conversation with Iker: *a Catalan who doesn't speak much English, with an*

341

Australian who doesn't speak much English, they're getting on surprisingly well, Jack thinks. Cindy passes the ticket up without breaking off from her conversation.

'Here you go. Five numbers, but no bonus ball, one thousand, seven hundred and fifty quid.'

'You serious? Is this *the* ticket?'

'That's it. I'll come in and do the paperwork tomorrow?'

'Great. Oh, one other thing. I was going to tell you the other day, but I got distracted, then I forgot. Sorry. But when you were on your phone, switching your insurance back to the Fiesta, I'm pretty sure you didn't change it back to third party only. I think you might have a fully comp on the Fiesta. You might want to remember that when you get your new Beemer...?'

Jack looks at her. 'You're right, I didn't tell them to change it. Christ! That means I'll get something for the Fiesta. It's my lucky day!'

'What's your lucky day?' Cindy shouts across the table.

'Bought a new car,' he replies. 'A Beemer.'

'Wow! That'll cost ya!' All heads are turning.

'What's this?' Milly says, squeezing Jack's hand.

'Just bought myself a Beemer,' he says, smiling.

'How much is that costing you?' she asks, looking a little surprised, worried even. All other conversations have stopped.

'It's all right, I've got it covered. One thousand, seven hundred and fifty quid. A real bargain. Soft-top and all.'

Cindy frowns. 'Hold on. That's the same – wait a sec, where's that ticket? Send that ticket back down here...'

Rich catches Jack's eye, he starts to smile.

'Can't, I've given it to Shelly for the car. Real stroke of luck it's the same amount, don't ya think?'

Milly's smiling, Rich is laughing.

'Where is it?' Cindy starts again. 'You said a third of that ticket was mine.'

'No,' Jack says, looking thoughtful. 'I said I'd give you seven hundred thousand quid. Rich as well. Can I owe you guys?'

Cindy takes a breath, looks at Rich. 'What the hell are *you* laughing at?'

Rich shrugs, raises his hands in surrender. The laughter spreads around the table. Even Cindy starts to smile.

'You bloody Poms,' is all she can say as Rich wraps her in a hug.

Shelly touches Jack's arm. 'Look, I forgot to say. I meant to; you can change your mind if you want...'

'What?'

'The colour.'

'What about it?'

'It's a bit – odd...'

'Odd?'

'Well, it's not a colour I have in my wardrobe, not sure I'd ever have it...' She flinches, like it's a hippy-rainbow respray.

'Go on...'

'It's a strange sort of bluey thing, I don't know, it's kinda turquoisey...? I think...'

Jack smiles, then laughs.

'Perfect!' he says, hugging her. 'Absolutely bloody perfect.'

74

LA VACA ESTÚPIDA

ANOTHER CUSTOMER, fed up with the racket coming out of the group in the corner, feeds the jukebox. Jack's ears twitch – it's 'Thunder Road', one of his favourites. *I never knew they had The Boss on the jukebox in here...* He zones out from all the other noise around him. He feels content. He had, although it turns out he never really did have, and now certainly hasn't got, two point three million pounds. How does that feel? It feels surprisingly all right. He's got Milly, he's got a Beemer. What else could he want?

Milly nestles up next to him. 'Hey, Jack. You know, my violin cost almost as much as your new car?'

He gives her wide, shocked eyes, then smiles. 'That means we both got a bargain.'

'You getting itchy feet, seeing those four heading off on their travels?'

'A little, I suppose. I'd like to go and see them out there. But only for a holiday. Would you fancy it?'

'As a holiday, absolutely. I told you I'd love to visit Thailand.'

'Okay, we'll do that. Definitely. We'll have to save up.'

Milly nods. 'I guess so. Does that mean you're heartbroken that the money's gone? Well, the vast bulk of it...'

He shrugs. 'No. I'm disappointed that your charities aren't going to get what we thought they were going to get. But no, life is good.' He takes hold of her hand.

She nods, squeezes his. 'It was a nice thought. We can still give what we can. But listen, I've been chatting to María a lot tonight. She's a case, isn't she?'

'Yeah? Such a keen student, isn't her English good?'

'It's wonderful, although she has an odd turn of phrase sometimes...'

'What do you mean?'

'We were talking about her and Iker, and she told me I'd be a *stoopid cow* if I didn't agree to marry you.'

'She said that to your *face?*'

'She said that to my face.'

'Bloody hell, she *is* a case. I'll have to do a little lesson on polite-company conversation, yeah? You're not annoyed?'

'No, she's great, a breath of fresh air, I love her. But I didn't want you to get any ideas, so I want to tell you something now.'

'What?' he says, when it becomes clear she's not going to go on until he responds.

'I just wanted you to know – I'm not a stoopid cow.'

'But I never thought you were,' he protests, suddenly looking worried. 'I'd never think that!'

'No, you're not listening, Jack. Listen to me, I'm telling you, I'm *not* a stoopid cow.'

'But I don't–'

María suddenly screams, throws her arms around Milly. 'Oh, Meely, *enhorabuena!* Jack, my all-round Mr Nice Guy, congratulations. Everybody, Jack and Meely, they go to be marry. Thees you lucky day, Jack.'

There's a cheer, he takes kisses, a huge squeeze on the upper arm from Iker, Jack looks utterly bemused, until...

'Hey, wait a minute–'

75

THE TICKET

THE CROWD in the corner are quite boisterous, there's a real party atmosphere. Something is being celebrated, maybe more than one thing, it's clear to all the other customers. One of the group breaks away from the table and stands in front of the jukebox, looking pensive. She's dressed like she's been for a run, a multicoloured collection of tight-fitting Lycra. She's the most colourfully dressed in the bar by a street. She slots a coin and makes her selection before hightailing it back to the table.

'Right, listen up, all you limey bastards! I wanna hear you sing...'

There's a roar of approval in response. Yes, it really has finally turned into *remember that night...*

The Beatles explode out of the jukebox: 'Can't Buy Me Love'.

Amid the cacophony, Jack pulls Beano aside, slips him a two-pound coin.

'Here, no hard feelings. Go get yourself a ticket, mate. This one's on me...'

THE END

ACKNOWLEDGEMENTS

Hitting the Jackpot is my debut work of fiction. Many people have helped to bring it to publication, I owe them all an enormous debt of gratitude. Betsy Reavley at Bloodhound Books wrote the magic words, *'...I would like to offer you a contract...'* That email will never be deleted. Betsy also suggested I adopt the pseudonym *Tom Alan*, adding immensely to the whole adventure. Tara Lyons and Abbie Rutherford (editorial and production) answered my many questions patiently and guided me through the whole process. I am also grateful to Hannah Deuce and Kate Holmes (marketing and PR) for helping me to establish a presence on social media, and for assuring me that I wouldn't have to dance on TikTok. I was asked to give my ideas regarding a cover for the book. I did, but confessed that I wasn't much of a designer and wouldn't be at all offended if they ignored my ideas. I would like to sincerely thank the designers at Better Book Design for doing exactly that, their cover design rocks.

I cannot thank my editor, Morgen Bailey, enough. Her forensic eye and detailed suggestions have changed my style of writing (and speaking) forever, and improved *Jackpot* hugely. Working with her has been a pleasure and an education. I ~~just~~ want to say thank you. Thanks also to Ian Skewis for mopping up the blood after Morgen's editing and for producing bloodless proofs.

Away from Bloodhound, many thanks to my dedicated team of beta readers who spotted typos and offered praise and encouragement: Laura, Beth, Abbi, Jude, Gail, Peter, Shaz, John, Grace and Pete. I would also like to thank all the Spanish junior children who passed through my class at the British School of Vila-Real between 2006 and 2020. Many of their intriguing (and sometimes unanswerable) questions about the English language (as well as their boundless enthusiasm) made their way into the character of María.

Finally, thanks to my wife Jill, who has read *Jackpot* in all its various forms since I started writing it in March 2020, when Spain locked down for Covid. At that time, we could only leave home to visit the supermarket, the chemist or the health centre. Jill aborted one trip to *Mercadona* when she saw how busy it was inside. On the way home she was stopped by a Guardia Civil (national police) patrol car. The (armed) officers wanted to know what she was doing. She told them (in excellent Spanish) she'd been to the supermarket, so they asked her where her shopping was... I was pleased she didn't end up in the back of the car, as I had another draft ready for her to read.

A NOTE FROM THE AUTHOR

If you are interested in the writing process through the eyes of a debut novelist, then the blog on my website https://tomalanauthor.wixsite.com/tom-alan has a number of posts describing the journey of *Jackpot* from inspiration to the book you're holding in your hands. If you enjoyed Jack's linguistic tussles while trying to teach English to foreign students, then (also on the website) you might want to check out my two volumes of memoirs. These catalogue my time in Spain teaching the entire primary curriculum to a class of lively seven-year-old Spaniards – in English.

A NOTE FROM THE PUBLISHER

Thank you for reading this book. If you enjoyed it please do consider leaving a review on Amazon to help others find it too.

We hate typos. All of our books have been rigorously edited and proofread, but sometimes mistakes do slip through. If you have spotted a typo, please do let us know and we can get it amended within hours.

info@bloodhoundbooks.com

Printed in Great Britain
by Amazon